Sign of the Rat
By Indigo Jones

Sign of the Rat is an adventure novel, featuring a teenage archaeologist. His nickname is "Trouble."

Go with Trouble on his dangerous travels. His journey begins in a curio shop in Manhattan and takes him to Paris. His final destination is a secret laboratory lost in the jungles of Vietnam. Exploring fabulous Halong Bay, he discovers the source of a frightening puzzle, the sudden appearance of prehistoric species. On this risky expedition, it isn't easy to know who's on his side. A rich junkyard king, the daughter of a jewel thief and a movie addict bring help and harm. Some of them are enemies, waiting for Trouble to solve the puzzle.

As always, proceeds from sales of our books are donated to charity. Specifically, we've contributed to Doctors Without Borders, the American Red Cross and Second Harvest Food Banks (now called Feeding America).

See more about our books at

www.SiliconValleyNovel.com

Cover monster and Curio Shop rat were derived with slight changes from illustrations © Andreas Meyer, a dazzlingly talented artist.
In all other cases, artwork for this book was created by combining, enhancing, altering and then sketching photographs. We can't travel the world and collect all the images needed to illustrate our stories. So we license the work of talented photographers, then modify and combine their work to fit the storyline of this novel. As a result, our sketches are derivative works. They are based on copyrighted images licensed from agencies representing visual artists listed at the end of this book.

This book's story and characters are fictitious. Some well known public agencies, locations and establishments are discussed, but only in a fictional way. The characters in this novel are entirely imaginary.

ISBN-13: 978-0-9824024-1-2
ISBN-10: 0-9824024-1-4

Published in the United States of America by Un-Tied Artists

Sign of the Rat

By Indigo Jones

Hidden in dark shadows, Trouble waited, listening to traffic boom along New York City's Seaport Street. A freight truck hit a pot hole, tires thumping, tailgate rattling. A pair of motorcyclists wove through slower autos, bike engines screaming in high revs. The car noise masked his crunching track shoes when he raced across Seaport Street, dodging taxis. A carnival of horns blared around him. A tourist bus farted diesel fumes in his face.

At the curb, he exhaled in relief, feeling safe for a moment, but it wouldn't last. Trouble stared at a weird car. Shiny green paint coated a stretch limo version of a small van. It was certainly a bizarre shape. From the front, the auto looked like Darth Vader's mask in *Star Wars*. The car had a bad feeling to it.

Then he noticed the front door of his parents' curio shop was open. Someone used acid to dissolve the door locks, turning them into melted lumps. The old granite stoop was littered with glass bottles. Chemical formulas cluttered the labels. Vapor steamed from acid residue left in the bottles. A smell like rotten eggs clung around the doorway, indicating burglars used concentrated sulfuric acid. Clearly, this wasn't a normal break-in.

Noises floated along the hallway and through the open door. It sounded like their shopkeeper, Bleerio, was grunting to move a heavy table. Maybe the thieves were gone and Bleerio was cleaning up the mess. Trouble decided to go inside. He walked across a squeaking plank and shed his backpack. His nose itched from musty dust coating a thousand antiques.

A crystal ball rested on the floor, blocking his path. Trouble squatted to retrieve the Gypsy crystal and replace it on a holder. He grabbed the cold sphere, heavy as a full garbage can. The curved glass showed a distorted image of the main showroom.

For a moment, Trouble thought the crystal ball had mystical powers. Staring into the globe, he could see around the corner. Then he realized the image was a reflection, giving a fisheye view of antiques and his parents' desks. The view also included a pair of thugs, dressed as ninjas. Instead of wearing black cloth for stealth, these two were clothed in lime green, like the car parked outside the shop.

A ninja spoke. "Where is the crate?"

Startled, Trouble gave an honest answer. "I don't know what you want. I've been gone for two weeks." Jet lagged by a twenty hour flight, he was in no shape to face a crime scene. Trouble craved a hot shower, some food and a warm bed, not a home invasion.

"We want the crate. The one delivered yesterday." The raspy voice was followed by a metallic twang. A knife blade vibrated like a guitar string when the weapon struck deep into wood. The *hira-shuriken* lodged only inches from Trouble's head.

A second ninja reached under his robes and pulled out a thick club. He flicked a trigger and curved prongs shot from the club's end. Lightning sparked between the prongs. "This," the second ninja announced, "is a cattle prod. It's used on livestock with tough leather hides. They feel pain and move out of the way. Imagine how it's gonna burn your skin."

Trouble stalled. "We've got crates in the basement, full of stuff. You can have all of them."

Together they hissed, "That's not what we want."

"Talk," the first ninja demanded.

"Or we'll use this," the second ninja leered. He waved the cattle prod like a spear and charged.

Trouble had to try something. He grabbed a sword hanging on a dusty suit of armor. The cold handle felt like a five pound ice cube in his palm. He licked anxious, dry lips and tugged. But the weapon was a showpiece with only a stub of blade. Trouble looked at the useless sword in disgust, yet he threw the blunt knife anyway. Heavy Crusader's steel arced across the display room. The metal lump missed the ninja and collided with an antique mirror, shattering glass in a hideous crash. A thick oak frame swung off the wall and thudded on the floor.

The ninjas raced through a maze of antiques, toppling a stack of tapestry chairs and a Chinese gong. Green streaks zigzagged toward their victim.

Trouble pulled a boomerang off the wall. He savored its heavy wood, relieved to have a weapon. The vee-shaped wing was inscribed with dream symbols from Aboriginal tribal lore. His father would kill him for using this prize in a real fight. Yet Trouble had to defend himself. He whipped his arm and the Aborigine weapon twirled in a high arc, making a sharp whistling sound. With a loud thunk, the wooden vee punched a ninja, causing a yelp of pain.

The other green blur flew at Trouble. He yanked a flintlock pistol off a wall, cocked the weapon and pointed at the blur.

The ninja made a juke step like a break-dancer, vanishing behind a huge mahogany bureau. A green head popped up. Trouble jerked the trigger. Nothing happened.

The ninja stood erect and walked toward his enemy, gloating. He flashed a long knife. "I will cut you like an Eskimo carves a totem pole, boy."

Trouble felt his palms grow cold and moist with fear. Fighting was hopeless. He had to run. Sprinting along the hall, Trouble knocked over a Chinese dragon vase and a 1920s French bistro table. He hoped obstacles would slow the ninjas chasing him.

Then a green blazer appeared in the door. Maybe it was another ninja from the car. Trouble was caught and couldn't get away. He turned to see ninjas making their way through hallway debris. One flashed his knife and the other flaunted a wire hoop, called a garrote. Trouble knew the garrote was going to be looped over his head and pulled tight, strangling him. His heart banged like a washing machine out of balance, wobbling around Trouble's chest.

There was still hope. He could escape through an old tunnel, leading from the shop's hallway to a river. In the 1920s, smugglers used the passage to move illegal goods. Trouble was so frightened he couldn't remember how to open the trap door. He tried yanking on a candleholder, hoping it was the trap door lever. The brittle metal snapped out of the wall. He threw candles and heavy brass holders at the ninjas. They laughed, not even slowing down.

The ninjas got closer. In desperation, he twisted an African voodoo mask. Tense red eyes in the ebony face stared at him, but no trap door opened. Backwards he walked, licking dry lips. The cattle prod appeared, snapping lightning off its tips. Electricity sparked again and left a burnt odor in the air.

Suddenly, Trouble remembered a suit of armor in a little alcove. He'd always been frightened by that metal man. When he was small, Trouble had nightmares about a black knight coming alive after dark. That's because his mother once pivoted the arm on that suit of armor and the floor vanished by magic. She thought it would amuse Trouble, but it scared him instead. Now the black knight would be his salvation.

Black Knight To The Rescue – But Is He Friend or Foe?

Gliding backwards, he sensed

daylight around him. Trouble was almost in the door. He reached for the medieval knight and didn't make it. Trouble collided with another person and twisted, fighting to grasp the suit of armor. But the person behind Trouble pulled the lever. Rusty metal creaked and a huge section of floor dropped out of sight.

The ninjas shrieked in rage, vanishing down a slope. The trap door swung closed, healing the floor. Trouble relaxed until a smarmy voice caused him to bristle. He turned around and saw his worst "frenemy," a friend who sometimes flips sides and becomes an enemy.

"Your customers play rough." Flix laughed. His perfect blonde hair lay sculpted to his head, a TV news anchor look. On his way home from Warwick Academy, Flix wore a green school blazer. He adjusted his gold silk tie. Flix resembled a model in a catalog ad, crisply dressed without a smudge on his light khaki trousers.

Bleerio stumbled out of a closet, where he'd been hiding. The shopkeeper squinted at bright sunlight radiating around the open door. Bleerio used a hand to shield his eyes from the glare. "Flix," he shouted. "Thank goodness. You came just in time to save us."

Trouble gave Bleerio a killing look, angry at getting no credit for defending the shop. Disgusted, he pushed around Flix and moved into the doorway.

Bleerio rushed to Flix. "Never mind Trouble. He's had a long trip. I'm delighted you're here. Come in."

"The delivery arrived?" Flix seemed excited.

"Any minute. A note said they'd try again this morning. Sorry about missing them yesterday. I had to go out for groceries. I'll make tea while we wait for the delivery company. Join me."

Flix trailed Bleerio out of the showroom, fading along the hallway and into the kitchen.

Trouble stayed at the open door and stared at an empty curb outside his home. A trail of water led to the spot where an exotic green car used to be parked. It looked like soaked ninjas ran to the car after getting dumped in the East River. They made a fast exit, leaving no clues behind. Why they broke into an old curio shop puzzled Trouble. He didn't have long to reflect on their motives. The ninja car's spot was claimed by a delivery truck, rumbling to a halt.

2

A brown-clad driver jumped from the delivery van and waved at Trouble. "Got something for you. Must be important. Your box came a long way."

"Where'd the shipment come from?" Trouble asked.

"Vietnam. Know anyone there?"

"My dad has an agent in Vietnam. We got a few collectibles from him. Haven't heard from Dr. Cam in years, though."

"You heard from him now." The driver opened the truck's cargo door and hopped inside. He grunted, shoving a wooden crate to the van's tailgate. "Give me a hand."

Trouble grabbed one end and they lowered the crate on a hand-truck. "Mind running the crate inside?"

"Naw. I'm ahead of schedule. Just sign here."

Trouble grabbed a plastic stylus from the electronic tablet and scrawled his name. Then his instincts urged Trouble to yank the address label off the crate. He didn't trust Flix. The less Flix knew, the safer Trouble felt. He folded the dirty label and put it in his pocket. Trouble went ahead and cleared a path for the hand-cart. They dropped the crate in the main showroom, near an Inquisition chair. The driver left.

Puzzled, Trouble studied the crate. It was an expensive box, with thick hardwood planks fitted together, smooth as a dining table. Metal corners reinforced the crate. A dozen screws held the top in place. Trouble assumed something important must be inside, to deserve such an expensive shipping container. He found a toolbox and pulled out a screwdriver.

A few minutes later, Trouble used a pry bar to force the lid off.

Crate From Vietnam Is Delivered
To The Old Curio Shop

Inside, wads of bubble pack cushioned a large metal box. Jungle rot blotched the olive green surface. Faded stencils on the box read "U.S. Army .50 caliber ammunition." New labels were plastered around the ammo canister. The bright yellow stickers warned in a dozen languages that the contents were hazardous. The lid should be opened with great care.

Annoyed at receiving something dangerous, Trouble grunted the faded green box out of the crate and dropped it on a desktop. A foul odor leaked from air holes drilled in the box. Trouble bent over, placing an ear near the holes. Was something moving inside? He couldn't tell for sure, but it sounded like a creature stirred, perhaps waking from sleep.

Bleerio wove through antiques, giddy with excitement. His Adam's apple bobbed in eager swallows, floating like a wine cork in a river. A silly bowtie twisted at a screwy angle below his long neck. "Oh, there's the delivery I promised Flix." The shopkeeper examined the crate's lid, looking disappointed. "Where's the shipping label?"

"Fell off. Blew away," Trouble lied.

Bleerio shrugged. "Still, this must be that shipment I mentioned, Flix. You know, the one from Vietnam."

"You mean Colorado, don't you?" Trouble winked at his friend, hoping the shopkeeper would understand.

"No. I mean Vietnam." Bleerio looked grouchy. "Didn't you see the label before it blew away?"

"Uh, not really."

Flix gave a sarcastic laugh. He dipped his long fingers into a blazer pocket and pulled out a gold-plated pen knife. A manicured fingernail pressed against a small diamond and Trouble heard a click. An Xacto-like blade appeared. Flix used his blade to scrape the lid, peeling off a thin curl. He held the scrap to his nose and inhaled a pine-like scent. "I can tell from its odor that the planks came from an evergreen tree. So Bleerio's right. The box was shipped from Vietnam, probably from the country's highlands. There's lots of cypress groves in that area. Vietnam is famous for golden cypresses. Those trees are evergreens." Flix held the curl of wood in his open palm, offering it to Trouble.

"They teach you about Vietnamese golden cypresses at Warwick Academy, Flix?"

"Yes, and more. You ought to go back to school, Trouble. I know PS 126 won't make you a Warwick man, but you would learn something useful." Flix dropped the cypress scrap and toyed with latches on the ammo box.

"I learn a lot of useful things in my travels. For instance, I can read the labels on that box, in Vietnamese, French and English. They all say the same thing – watch out."

"For what?" Flix gave Trouble a condescending stare. He released a latch holding down the lid.

Trouble warned Flix again. "That ammo canister holds something dangerous. I'd leave it alone, if I were you."

Bleerio stepped around Flix and put his palms on the cold steel lid. Oxidized paint flaked off and fell on the desk. "Aren't you curious? I am."

"Curiosity killed the cat, Bleerio." Trouble gave the shopkeeper a stern look.

"And satisfaction brought the cat back to life." Flix talked in a smug tone. "I'm quoting Eugene O'Neill, a playwright. But you wouldn't know about literature, Trouble."

"I know we aren't in a stage play. This is for real. Let's wait, Flix. Let's think before we open the case."

"Wait as long as you like." Flix turned to leave.

"No, don't go," Bleerio pleaded. "I'm sure there's something valuable inside. You might want to buy it."

Flix shrugged. "I might indeed. Tell you what. I'm in a hurry, so I'll take this problem off your hands, sight-unseen." He opened a tooled leather wallet and pulled out a crisp hundred dollar bill. Flix talked in rich, smooth tones. "Get some food for that empty kitchen of yours. Don't worry about the ammo box. I'll find a way to safely open it, after I get home."

"Yeah, right," Trouble snorted. "Come back tomorrow. We'll have the box open. See how much you're willing to pay, then."

"All right. I'll be generous. Two hundred." Flix offered Bleerio a second bill carrying the image of Benjamin Franklin.

Bleerio looked starved, like he hadn't eaten in days. He pleaded, "Trouble …"

"I'll think about it. Come by tomorrow." Trouble closed the open latch.

Flix hesitated, trying to look like it didn't matter. He edged toward the hallway.

Bleerio cracked. "I can't take this." He lunged at the ammo box and flipped both latches. The lid sprang up.

The three of them recoiled in shock. An awful stench bubbled from the canister, stinking like an overflowing toilet. It smelled like a well-used public restroom on a hot, crowded day. Bleerio gagged. Flix pulled a silk handkerchief from his blazer pocket and covered his nose, turning away. Only Trouble looked inside the box, locking his eyes on a demented vision, an enormous sewer rat.

Only it wasn't a normal rat. A spiky tail made the animal look part dinosaur. A T-Rex jaw held rows of teeth curved like fishhooks. Milky, psychopathic eyes sat at the end of a twitching nose. Rancid turds clogged black fur thick as a chimney sweep's broom. Trapped inside the box, the creature was forced to sleep in its own toilet droppings. Now, the animal was determined to get free. The rat placed his front paws on the edge of the box, flashing talons sharp as a doctor's scalpel. The creature poised itself to spring out.

Trouble jumped at the lid, slamming it down. Bleerio overcame his revulsion to help, fighting to get the ammo box shut. Even Flix joined in the battle.

Fighting back, the rat punched fists at the lid like a boxer, then slammed its spiked tail into the thick metal. Dents appeared in the lid. A last blow opened the lid enough so the rat could wedge its mouth in the gap. Terrible jaws snapped viciously. "Pepper spray," Trouble shouted. "Bleerio, hit it with pepper spray."

"Uh, yeah." The shopkeeper ran to find cayenne pepper spray, the type used on muggers.

Trouble jumped atop the desk and pressed on the lid with all his weight. Flix tried to snap a latch and almost paid for it with a finger. He pulled away in time to avoid the fishhook teeth, but they ripped his shirt cuff. Amazed, Flix blurted, "How can that thing be so strong?"

Struggling with the lid, Trouble could only grunt a response. "A chimpanzee is the size of child, but eight times stronger than a grown man."

"This rodent must be part chimp." Flix gave the rat a look of admiration.

Bleerio flew in the room, skidding to a halt. He pointed at the rat and blasted the creature with a full dose. It must have burned like torches were shoved in the eye sockets. Yet the rat fought even harder, furious after being attacked. The shopkeeper ran out of the room again, yelling, "I know."

"Get back here," Trouble screamed. "We can't hold it."

"I'm coming. Wait a minute. I know where they dropped it."

"Who dropped what?" Trouble demanded.

"The ninjas. Ah, got it." Bleerio returned with the cattle prod. "This will solve the problem." Ignorant how metal conducts electricity, Bleerio rammed the prod against the lid, pulling the trigger. Lightning jolted the rat, Trouble and Flix. Shocked, they recoiled. Bleerio slammed the lid and closed its latches.

Trouble and Flix were knocked on the floor. Dazed, they stared at Bleerio.

"Well, er. It's a deal. Two hundred for the rat. We'll throw in the old ammo box. Probably worth two hundred dollars itself, a genuine war relic." Bleerio looked sheepish.

Trouble cracked a smile. It was impossible to hate Bleerio.

Flix got to his feet, brushing dirt off his khaki trousers. "You should pay me to take this horrible thing. But all right. I said I'd pay and I will. To prove I'm your friend, here's the money." He offered the bills to Trouble.

"Five hundred," Trouble countered. "For the ammo box. Another thousand for the rat. That thing's gotta be rare. At least, I hope it is. You can sell the creature to a museum."

Flix didn't say anything. But he didn't leave either.

Trouble lifted the box and turned toward the hallway. "You don't want it, so I'm throwing this thing in the river. That's where it belongs, in my opinion."

"OK." Flix talked softly. "As an apology. It was mean what I said, about Warwick Academy being superior to your school. Here's a thousand." He shoveled bills on the desk. Bleerio snapped up the money and wrote a quick receipt. He signed and gave the chit to Flix.

Trouble felt queasy. There was something weird about this deal, but he needed money. He didn't want to push for more and lose the sale. Trouble handed over the ammo box. "What are you going to do with the rat?"

"Find a zoo or museum that wants the creature." Flix laughed. "Or sell it to Hollywood. This rat belongs in one of those sci-fi films I love." Flix walked out of the room and vanished.

Trouble heard a car stop at the curb and a door slam. He sprinted to the hallway, convinced he'd see a lime-green exotic driving away, packed with smirking ninjas and Flix. But a golden Porsche Panamera pulled from the curb instead. Flix sat on the back seat, dialing his cell phone. The chauffeur must have put the ammo box in the trunk. Everything looked normal. Yet Trouble felt suspicious.

3

Trouble walked inside the curio shop, winding through a narrow entry. The knight in armor stood watch over tapestry chairs, stacked in a heap like a wobbly staircase. The sad old furniture was a reminder of how many forgotten antiques lived here. Sales were rare. The curio shop smelled of ancient dust and mildew, spiced by fresh rat turds from the delivery crate.

In the shadows, Trouble discovered Bleerio counting money, licking fingertips to separate crisp bills. The shopkeeper's eyes were dreamy. He imagined all the things he could buy with a thousand dollars. Trouble cringed, knowing he needed half the money. "Er, Bleerio …"

The shopkeeper looked up, smiling. "Flix is a great customer, isn't he?"

"I suppose."

Bleerio went right on, as if Trouble agreed. "Yes, and he's the only customer who says nice things to me. Usually, I have to flatter them." He frowned. "Even with my compliments, they seldom buy anything."

Trouble was concerned about this growing friendship between Flix and Bleerio. He decided to probe a bit. "Flix says nice things to you. Like what?"

"Nothing big. We just talk." Bleerio looked puzzled.

"OK. What do you guys talk about?" Trouble shoved a table lamp in position and righted its shade, waiting for the shopkeeper to respond.

Bleerio's egg-like face held a peculiar smile. His paisley shirt, shrunken too many times in a dryer, ran down short arms to narrow wrists. He wore corduroy trousers ending in flared bell bottoms, exposing his crepe-soled loafers. The pants were several inches short, riding high above white crew socks. The shopkeeper's clothes made him look like he'd fallen in a glacier in 1970 and thawed forty years later, coming back to life. Finally, the shopkeeper broke the silence. "Flix knows about the 1970s, just like me."

Trouble was surprised. "He's researched the 1970s? I thought Flix got his nickname because he's a film buff, a walking encyclopedia of movies."

"Sure." The shopkeeper nodded several times. Bleerio's eyes ran around the shop, checking to make sure they were alone. "Would you like to know a secret?"

Trouble hesitated. "I suppose. But then it won't be a secret, will it?"

"Just promise you won't tell anyone." Bleerio acted like he was dying to reveal his secret.

"Definitely. No one."

"Good. I'll show you." The shopkeeper ran up the lid on a rolltop desk. Inside, the store's laptop computer displayed an Internet screen. A *Wikipedia* entry showed villains in James Bond films. Beaming in pride, Bleerio pointed at an image taken from a 1971 movie called *Diamonds are Forever*. "Flix says I look just like Mr. Kidd."

Leaning over the rolltop desk, Trouble peered at a small picture labeled "Mr. Wint and Mr. Kidd." He stared at Mr. Kidd, then shook his head in agreement. "Yeah, there's a resemblance."

"Sure is," Bleerio announced. "It's flattering, you know."

"I guess. What'd this guy do in the film?"

"Shoved an old school teacher in a river, blew up a helicopter – and best of all …" Bleerio paused for dramatic effect. "Mr. Kidd dropped a scorpion down a man's shirt. Whaddya think of that, Trouble?" The timid shopkeeper glowed in excitement.

"I guess everyone has their dark side. Looks like you've found yours."

"What's that mean?" Bleerio shoved his hands on his hips, glowering at Trouble.

"No insult, meant. I hope you draw on the villain side of yourself next time we negotiate price. We'd get more out of a sale."

"I got a thousand for that rat – and you were going to throw it in the river." Bleerio sulked.

"I was bluffing, my friend. You know, testing to see how much Flix wanted the rat. Maybe next time you could be less eager. We might have gotten the full $1500 price."

"A thousand was good enough. You might be well fed, Trouble. I'm starving. Haven't had anything to eat but sardines all week. I'm sick of them."

"You still have some fish?"

"Yeah, in the kitchen cupboard. Three cans. And you can have them all." Bleerio eyed the money. "Um, how much is mine?"

Trouble sucked in a long breath. "I wish it could be more, but I can only give you four hundred."

"Not even half?" The shopkeeper looked faint.

"I'm really sorry. I've got some expenses coming up. They're urgent, can't wait."

"Like what?" Bleerio demanded.

This wasn't going the way Trouble wanted. He debated what to do. "I'll show you. Then you'll feel better about sharing the money, OK? Wait here."

"This better be good." Bleerio closed the Internet and shut down the computer.

A moment later, Trouble returned, cradling a penguin. The arctic bird was large, about the size of a two year old child. The injured penguin had flecks of blood in his fur and his eyes crinkled in pain. "He needs surgery. I have to pay a vet to fix his flipper. It was torn in a fight."

The shopkeeper let his disgust show. "Where'd you get that thing?"

"I brought him home from Everest, in my backpack."

"A penguin's more important than me?" Bleerio sulked.

"Albert's been in the family a long time. And he got hurt defending my friends, Nuru and Tattoo." Now it was Trouble who felt upset. "The sardines are for Albert, not me. I'll give him some fish and put him in my bed. Then I'll come back to help you clean up. OK?"

"Albert," Bleerio muttered. "A penguin who's been in the family. Like I haven't been in the family."

"It's a long story. I haven't got time for it. Just calm down, will you?"

The shopkeeper didn't answer, but he did look a bit less angry. Still, Trouble knew it was prudent to take $600 off the desk and put the money in his pocket. He didn't want to go around the shop looking for it. Bleerio played that trick on him once, when Trouble was a little kid. The shopkeeper found Trouble's allowance and decided to hide the money in an empty fish tank, letting Trouble search everywhere. Only when he broke down crying did Bleerio produce the allowance.

When Trouble picked up the money, the shopkeeper glowered. "It could have been me, hurt by the ninjas. I suppose you'd still give Mr. Albert priority. He's a member of the family," Bleerio huffed.

"No. That's not true. I'd be sad about Albert. But I would've called the paramedics and made sure you got helped first." Trouble felt calm saying it. His words spoke the truth.

Bleerio coughed, looking shy. "Well, that's good to know. Uh, you learn any news about your lost parents? Like where Indigo and Julia went?"

"No." Trouble reached in a pocket and felt the ridged edges of coins. His fingers drummed the cold metal in a steady beat.

The shopkeeper seemed uncomfortable and tried to shift the conversation to another subject. "You discover anything on your trip? Maybe you found an old artifact we could sell. I'd call Flix. He said he'd look at anything new I had to offer."

Puckering his lips in disgust, Trouble shook his head. "No. Nothing." He didn't trust Bleerio. The backpack held an ancient scroll. It was a priceless relic, but it might also be key to finding his parents. After all, the scroll predicted he'd encounter a rat and warned him to beware.

"All that money and you came back empty handed. No jewel encrusted cups, rare tablets, nothing?" Bleerio sagged into an antique armchair.

Trouble gave a sad laugh. "Well, I did explore the inside of Mount Everest."

"Huh?" The shopkeeper didn't understand.

"Yeah," Trouble continued. "Turns out the world's highest mountain is hollow. There's a lost civilization hidden inside."

"Oh, great. Wonderful. You can publish an article in some journal. They'll send us a copy and we'll spread cheese on the pages, turn the magazine into a sandwich."

"OK, I get the message. Be patient. Things are gonna improve."

"Heard that before." Bleerio sank deeper into the chair. The sagging ginger moustache over his lip gave him the sad look of a walrus.

"I mean they're going to get better today." Trouble gave his friend a mischievous grin.

Bleerio ignored the grin and stared with dull eyes at the disheveled room. "Like how are things going to get better?"

"Like this. I'm taking you to the café for dinner. My treat." Trouble knew Bleerio loved eating at the café down the block. It was the shopkeeper's favorite. Hunted outlaws Butch Cassidy and the Sundance Kid ate there, on a visit to New York City. Then they left to rob a bank. A 1970s movie about those famous gunfighters was Bleerio's most watched DVD.

For the first time since Flix left, Bleerio looked happy. "I'll call to reserve Butch and Sundance's table."

"Great. Be right back, soon as I feed Albert and put him in bed for a nap."

"Sardines are in the cupboard on your right. Don't take too long, OK? I'm starved."

"I'll be fast." Trouble hustled off. Ten minutes later he returned. Bleerio had done an amazing job on the display room. It looked almost normal. The ram's head chandelier hung straight from its ceiling chain. Bronze vases appeared clean instead of smothered in gray dust. Wooden Swiss clocks now showed the correct time, their arrow-shaped hands set with precision. Their inner springs ticked like egg timers, wound after a long sleep. Pewter ale tankards stood in an even row, ready for a medieval tavern. The shopkeeper even polished away the tarnish from a silver teapot.

"Great job. Thanks. Looks ready for the next customer. Except for that crate." Trouble pinched his nose. The rat's odor clung to the shipping container, even after the smelly creature left.

Eager to get a restaurant meal, Bleerio offered to help lug the crate outside and toss it in a dumpster. Grunting, they hoisted the wooden crate and took it down the block. Swinging the heavy shipping container over the debris box, they dropped the weight. It fell with a clang, spilling its remaining contents. They began walking toward the café and Trouble felt better.

It didn't matter that he lived in a grunge building on a block forgotten by the rest of New York City. His scrap of Manhattan was built after the Civil War ended, in the 1870s. Five story brick structures squatted wall-to-wall along the block. Each building sprouted a battered tin awning like the bill of a tattered baseball cap. Plumbing ran along outside walls, proving the buildings came from an era before indoor toilets. The pipes formed varicose veins bulging on the elderly brick skin. Metal fire escapes zigged along façades, convenient scaffolding for graffiti artists tattooing bricks with elaborate lettering.

Yet the blight was isolated. The far end of Trouble's block transformed into a shining tourist Mecca. Glittering stores attracted a million visitors to the Fulton Fish Market each year. Trendy boutiques tempted people with the latest clothing styles. Street performers entertained tourists, who came in busloads to walk safe, well-lit streets. Trouble yearned to live in that neighborhood, where every building was restored. But he was grateful an economic downturn stalled renovation in his section. His parents needed cheap rent or they couldn't display hundreds of antiques, hoping people would buy them.

Rich customers were turned off by the appearance of his block, however. A junker car loitered against the curb, its windshield covered in parking tickets and threats for tow away. Dust coated the dented car's roof and fenders. Its front bumper had fallen off and rested on pavement. Sitting there, the bumper looked like a prize fighter's tooth guard, spat out when he lost the match.

Fish odor clung to sidewalks. The stench remained long after shopkeepers quit hawking cod and salmon from ground floor stalls. Graffiti-splattered metal shades barricaded those shops. Trouble had never seen the merchants open for business. Suddenly, an idea hit him and he stopped walking.

"What is it?" Bleerio snapped.

"Did you see anything strange tumble out of that crate?"

"No. Let's eat." The shopkeeper walked toward the café in brisk strides.

"Go on. You can even order for me. You know what I like." Trouble spun around, heading for the dumpster.

"OK. But you are paying?" Bleerio shouted.

"Definitely. Be right there." Trouble broke into a run.

The shopkeeper hesitated. His growling stomach won over curiosity.

Trouble went the other way, heading for the debris box. Contractors were renovating the insides of a building. A long chute ran from a window to the dumpster. Wallboard chunks and their white dust now coated Dr. Cam's shipping container. His box from Vietnam was covered in rotting produce and egg shells, coffee grounds and Kleenex.

Someone had poached use of the debris box and slopped household garbage inside. The smell was gross. There was also a danger of being hit by debris from the construction chute.

None of that stopped Trouble from hopping inside and shoveling filthy items. On the bottom sat his goal, a bulky satellite phone coated in slimy bacon grease. It had tumbled out of the shipping crate. He used an old rag from the dumpster to wipe down the item and found a letter taped to the phone. The chute rumbled, indicating heavy trash was flying toward his head. Trouble rolled from the dumpster and thudded on the ground, careful to shield his finds. Bruised yet excited, he took the phone inside and concealed it in his room.

Trouble cleaned himself in a bathroom and headed for the café, to join Bleerio for dinner. Once the shopkeeper went to sleep, Trouble would examine the letter and satellite phone. He might have found an important clue.

4

Around midnight, Trouble checked his repair job on the front door, making certain the portal was secure again. Satisfied, he gave a pat of gratitude to the knight who saved him from ninjas. His tap caused a harsh rattling of old metal. After that mistake, Trouble was careful to make little noise, avoiding squeaky floorboards, treading softly on old stairs when he ascended. Hesitating on a landing, he listened for Bleerio's snoring. Trouble wanted to make certain the ever curious shopkeeper was asleep and wasn't likely to walk into Trouble's room unannounced. Bleerio was always polite to clients, but he never knocked on a door and instead rushed into a private room.

His parents' bedroom had a strong lock, but Trouble didn't feel comfortable going inside their sanctuary. It brought him too much heartache. He kept walking upstairs to a door that should open on the building's flat roof, but didn't. Beyond the door was a rooftop storage area he'd customized for himself. He adopted the small hideaway as a bedroom in the first grade. Julia amazed Trouble by understanding his choice and helped him insulate the walls against winter cold and summer heat. Indigo showed Trouble an abandoned fire station, where they took apart a bunk bed and toted the pieces home. He slept in the upper bunk and used plywood in the lower slot for a desk.

Trouble slid a bolt in place to keep the door closed and surveyed his clubhouse. Light filtered through a milky plastic dome on the roof, capturing dust motes floating in moonbeams. Trouble expected he'd feel nostalgia for his secret retreat and was surprised when he didn't. Nothing seemed familiar. He was a stranger in his own room. Maybe his mood came from the weird lighting. Trouble flicked on a desk lamp. Neon blubs under the mattress blinked to life, revealing a wall like a scrapbook. Ads for toys he admired were torn from magazines and thumbtacked on the wall. The clutter of pages resembled a pile of Autumn leaves.

Only one page always remained on top. The *National Geographic* article featured his parents in a major archeological discovery. A photo showed them in front of a Siberian burial mound. A caption explained the picture was taken at two in the morning. Above the Arctic Circle, the summer days have no end. The sun only dips toward the horizon, instead of sinking out of sight, bringing on the dark of night.

A haze of buzzing insects blurred the photo as the creatures made the most of their brief lifespan. Repellant smeared over skin and clothing kept bugs away from Indigo and Julia, so their features were clear. A watch cap covered most of Julia's short blond hair. Her mood radiated satisfaction at making a rare find, a tomb that hadn't been robbed of all its historical artifacts. Trouble's mother held the remains of a Bronze-Age chariot, hidden inside the burial chamber. A Scythian ruler wanted to ride off once he'd crossed to the spirit world.

For his mom and dad, this was a moment like finding the lost tomb of Pharaoh Tutankhamen in Egypt's Valley of the Kings. Indigo's static image in the Siberian photograph hummed with excitement, but then Trouble's dad was always hyperactive. Long curly hair, mustache, tight pants made Indigo seem a gypsy artist, rather than a scientist. With a jolt, Trouble realized the picture showed his father holding a satellite phone.

That same phone lay hidden under his desk. Trouble hesitated to examine the instrument, afraid he'd be disappointed. He couldn't bear to hit another dead end where a clue vanished into a blank wall. Still, he must try. With the deliberate care of a pickpocket, Trouble groped for the slimy container he'd plucked from a dumpster. The phone's pouch had a Velcro flap and it made a ripping sound when he peeled up the fabric. Tension at what he'd find inside unleashed a torrent of questions. Issues flew around his mind like dry brush in a cyclone.

At last, the Velcro parted and he removed a clunky cell phone with an antenna like the handle on a golf club. He tried powering up the phone and got no response. Frustrated, he removed a battery charger and plugged-in the device. The phone remained dead. It seemed he'd be unable to check his father's call list – or better yet, hear a voicemail from a colleague. Trouble sagged in his chair, staring at the phone in disgust. Wait a minute – there was a note inside a baggy. Maybe the scrap of paper held key information.

Trembling fingertips fought to unzip the baggy's seal and he quit trying to be nice. Trouble yanked the plastic, ripping open the pouch. He tugged out the paper, expecting it to be an unpaid phone bill or something equally useless. Excitement shot through him when Trouble unfolded the note and recognized his father's handwriting. He blinked in amazement, too excited for careful reading.

"Close your eyes … take deep breaths … calm down," he told himself. Trouble dared a look at the note –

"Julia – At last, after all our searches, I've discovered an active FOY. Couldn't call you. My phone is useless, damaged from a strong field generated by the FOY. Sent the phone home in case you can have it repaired. I also sent you e-mails. Can't tell if you got them. Government censors are now blocking communication between Tran Van Cam's lab and the outside world. I asked Dr. Cam to include proof of the FOY in the package. Hope he did and it arrived OK. Come at once. Miss you terribly. Oh, don't bring Trouble. It's too dangerous for him.

– Love, Indigo

Trouble's face burned in anger. They could go around the world on risky expeditions, but it was "too dangerous for him." What about the Khumbu ice falls and the snow leopards, huh? Mount Everest isn't a picnic in Central Park. He snorted and the penguin stirred, opening an eye. "Go back to sleep, Albert. It's nothing." The tuxedo bird gave him a sleepy gaze and twitched his yellowed beak. Trouble was relieved when the bird rolled on his side and went back to dreaming. "Tomorrow," he promised in a whisper, "I'll take you to a veterinarian and they'll finish repairing your flipper. Everything will go fine. You'll be like new again."

But tonight, Trouble had to find a way to Vietnam. Indigo's note sounded urgent and Julia had disappeared. There was no time to wait. For the trip, he needed money and his passport. He'd looked everywhere in the building and couldn't find where his parents shoved the document. The search was maddening. He'd always been able to discover birthday presents and peek at what he was getting. Never once had they fooled him. But the most important item he'd ever searched for eluded him. The trip to Mount Everest was awful. He'd been forced to have Bleerio ship him air cargo, packing Trouble in a crate and taking him to the Seaport Company across the street. Nuru and Tattoo sent Trouble home the same way.

Now Frank, the security guard, would tell the police if he found Trouble inside the Seaport Company's property. Trouble had to find that passport so he could ride as a normal passenger in a jet. But he also needed money to buy the plane ticket. Indigo once said the most expensive item in the shop was inside their office safe – the beautiful Scythian Sapphire. Maybe his passport was also in the vault. It was time to crack that safe. Fortunately, the best safecracker in the world lived behind his shop – well, a reformed safecracker. Chiaro's father hadn't touched a job since he got out of prison. That didn't matter, though. This job wasn't stealing, was it?

Trouble had to visit Chiaro tonight, before she went to sleep. Going downstairs didn't feel right. A creaking step might awaken Bleerio. Worse, a kid alone on the street at midnight was vulnerable. His best route to her was via rooftops. He'd done it before, but now Trouble was larger. Could he still pop the skylight and wriggle through? There was only one way to know.

He stood on his chair and unlatched the plastic dome. Soot and leaves slid off when he lifted the skylight. It wasn't hard to un-pin the hinges and set the dome aside. Now came the tricky part, pulling himself through the hole. A first try convinced Trouble he needed to remove his jacket. Despite a blast of cold air, he pulled off the warm coat and rolled it up, tossing it outside. A soft thump indicated the coat awaited him.

He jumped high enough to get his arms outside, but Trouble's chest wedged in the opening. A muffled "ouch" leaked from his throat. Should he drop inside and give up? Pressing with his elbows might wedge him tight. Bleerio would never quit razzing Trouble about the night he called the fire department to free a dumb kid.

Humiliation lost to desperation. Trouble had to reach Vietnam. There was no other way to contact his father. OK, push. Push harder. Grunt. There was a snap as a piece of molding broke off. Suddenly Trouble lurched atop his clubhouse and rolled off, thudding on the soft tar roof. He looked around. A lazy moon sat like a volleyball on the horizon. Streetlights mixed orange glow with moonbeams, turning the roof a bizarre purple color. The weird lighting emphasized splotches of neighborhood graffiti frosting his rooftop dome and nearby access hatches. Angry bursts of paint added violent colors to dull cement and tired brick. Vent pipes cast long shadows, bent over ridges separating the buildings.

Trouble wove through a tangle of TV antennas and satellite dishes, working hard not to get caught in a spaghetti of cabling. Dried puddles warned him of soft spots that might cave-in, sending him into an abandoned apartment. He skirted a deep chasm. So far it was easy. Next came a real challenge. He needed to balance on an old plank bridging a gap between his block and the one behind.

Water Tanks On Buildings In Manhattan

Trouble's luck held and he wobbled to safety. Now where exactly was Chiaro's fire escape? He didn't want to upset an elderly lady by choosing the wrong window, like he'd once done. Trouble narrowly made it back and closed the dome before police knocked on their street door. Bleerio convinced the cops nothing was wrong, but that might not happen this time. He moved along the roofline, peering downward, fighting to remember landmarks. It wasn't working. He couldn't decide which set of rusty stairs was the right one.

Concerned about a mistake, Trouble swung around, hoping to get his bearings. The horizon was dotted with water tanks, giant wooden barrels sitting atop a trestle. The old-fashioned reservoirs seemed out of place in Manhattan, yet they were necessary for everyday activities like brushing your teeth or flushing a toilet. He scanned chimneys and spotted a familiar one. Yeah, this was Chiaro's building. They'd sat against that chimney and talked.

He moved forward and halted in mid-stride. Legs and shoes poked from behind the smokestack. Someone was sitting there. Could it be Chiaro? That was her spot. She liked going on the roof. Chiaro wanted to be a chef and loved the smell of ethnic restaurants, wafting from kitchen vents. She taught him the scent of Polish stuffed pork and Assyrian *shawarma*, though he was clueless how the dishes looked or tasted.

Now, however, the restaurants were closed and the only smell was tobacco from smokers inhaling a last cigarette on a fire escape, before going to bed. Trouble choked back a cough and moved cat-like toward a person he hoped was Chiaro. Finally, she came into view, dressed in a beret and a faded Disneyworld T-shirt from her family's one vacation together. The thin cotton shirt was tucked into military style fatigue pants, ending in thick-soled boots. Chiaro squatted with her back against the chimney, butt resting on her boot heels.

5

Trouble moved to get a better look and realized tears streamed down Chiaro's face. Her bony cheeks were sucked inward, expressing grief. This was definitely not the time to ask for help. He turned to leave and her restless brown eyes popped open, glaring at him.

"What do you want?" Chiaro's voice was hoarse from crying.

"Uh, nothing. Just came to see how you were doing." Trouble scrunched his shoulders, trying to seem innocent.

"Well, you can see how I'm doing." She wiped damp cheeks with the backs of her hands. "Lousy."

"Want to talk about it?"

"No." The word came out like a sob.

"OK … See you later, then." He stepped back and hit a vent pipe, making a soft thud. Trouble started to leave and Chiaro began talking.

"My dad's busted again."

"Geez, I'm sorry. I thought he'd gone straight."

She nodded. "Me too."

"Er, big or small?"

"There's no small when you've got priors, like him. Besides, he never did small jobs, only huge ones." She gave a sad laugh. "You know what I mean. Crack the biggest safe so you can retire in style."

"Well, you're dad's the top ... at least that's what people say about him. He's the best in the world, I heard."

"Was. Now my dad's behind bars. Twenty years, at least."

"What'd he do?" Trouble was astonished by the length of the prison term.

"Nobody got hurt, if that's what you're thinking." Chiaro put her head between her knees.

"No, of course not. Your dad's always been very nice to me."

Chiaro gave him a suspicious look. "You only met him once."

"Yeah, but he seemed nice."

"Well, he is." She pulled her head up and stared at the moon. "He just picks lousy friends."

"They hurt somebody and he got blamed, huh?"

"No. Not a single person got hurt. Nobody even lost money. That's why it's so unfair."

"Then how can a judge send him to prison for twenty years? I mean, it doesn't make sense."

"Because the judge thinks my dad stole a lot of diamonds and hid them. But he didn't. There weren't any diamonds in the vault. It was a set up, a sting. His gang got conned. Some diamond merchants needed insurance money."

"I don't get it." Trouble was puzzled.

Chiaro explained. "Works like this. The diamond merchants gave my dad secrets he needed to rob the world's toughest vault, in Amsterdam. They made the job so easy it's a slam dunk. But when my dad cracked in, the vault was empty. The merchants took their diamonds out the day before. So they kept the gems and got insurance money. Later, they'll sell the jewels on some black market. They made double money. My dad took the fall."

"Ouch. Sorry. Er, I don't mean to pry …"

"But how'd he get caught?"

"Yeah. Your dad's smart."

"His friends aren't. They didn't listen to my dad. They left evidence in their apartment instead of ditching it."

"Bummer. Big bummer."

"You and your mom are all alone, huh?"

Bitterness frosted every word when Chiaro answered. "My mother quit a while back."

"You going to live with her anyway?"

"No." Chiaro pushed herself upright. Her legs were numb from squatting and she wobbled. Cold went right through her T-shirt and she wrapped her arms around her chest.

"It's dangerous to live on the streets," Trouble warned.

"Yeah, I know." She gave him a cynical look. "Don't worry about me. I'm going into foster care. Tomorrow, I move in with a family that owns a flower stall, about a half mile from here. I'll be all right."

"That's good. You get food, shelter. Go to school."

Chiaro gave a brief laugh. "You should talk."

He blushed. "I'm not a drop out. I'm goin' back. Soon as I find my parents."

"You're two years behind, Trouble."

"I read the books. Did the lessons. They'll let me skip to my real grade ... I hope."

"Yeah, maybe. I stopped by last week and Bleerio said you were in the mountains. You going camping or something?"

"Not exactly. I travelled to Nepal, did some trekking in the Himalayas. I went because I got a letter from my mother, posted in Nepal – so I thought. But the note came from ... someone else. He needs help. That's why I gotta find my father. Indigo's the only one who can help." Trouble's face brightened. "But now I have a real clue. My dad's in Vietnam. I gotta get there. It's not far from Vietnam to Nepal. Kinda like flying from Miami to Manhattan."

"Hot to cold. I see what you mean."

"No, Vietnam is close to Nepal. Check it on Google Earth – or spin a globe. You'll see."

"I believe you. You're the world traveler, not me."

"Just one trip to Mount Everest. That's all." Trouble felt shy.

"Just a short walk to the world's highest mountain." She mocked him. "So calling your dad is cheating. You gotta drop in on him, bop over to Vietnam and say hello. Why send him an e-mail when you can fly halfway around the world?"

"I can't e-mail Indigo – or call him."

"Sure."

"No, really. His letter warned my mother. He said the government turned off the Internet in Dr. Cam's lab. Plus dad sent his phone back 'cause it's busted."

"You read your parents' mail?" Chiaro looked shocked.

He frowned. "My mother isn't here. Maybe she's in Vietnam with him. Besides, I didn't know the letter was for Julia when I opened it."

"Fine, I give back your boy scout honor badge. Quit sulking."

"I'm not angry. I'm … bummed."

"You? Trouble, you've got everything under control. Buy a ticket to Vietnam, take a taxi to Dr. Cam."

"I don't have money for a plane ticket. And I can't find my passport. My parents hid it."

"You brag every year about knowing what they're giving you for Christmas, 'cause you find all their hiding places."

"They put my passport somewhere I can't reach."

Chiaro held her hands up in disgust. "Get a ladder. You quit because it's on a high shelf?"

He cringed. Well, here goes. "My passport's in their safe."

It took a moment for Chiaro to figure everything out. Then she got mad. "You creep. You didn't visit to see how I was doing. You came to get my dad, so he'd break into your safe." She grabbed a piece of shattered brick and threw it at him.

He ducked. "Hey, be careful. I didn't expect to find you on the roof crying. Besides, I didn't bring up safecracking. You did."

That softened her. Chiaro let out a long breath and it fogged in the damp air. "See you around, Trouble."

"Wait. I mean, maybe you could help."

"What's in it for me?" Chiaro shot him a bitter look.

"You got a warm place to spend the night?"

"No," she admitted. "The landlord evicted me. The apartment's rented. They moved in yesterday."

"We got a couch downstairs. Better than sleeping on a roof."

"Just happens to be near your safe, huh?"

"That's a coincidence. I wasn't expecting you to …"

"I'll try anyway. Probably won't work, I warn you. I don't have my dad's skills."

"You don't gotta try. I'll find another way …" Now it was his turn to feel depressed.

Chiaro grabbed his arm and tugged. "Come on. Can't hurt to try the safe, can it?"

"I don't think so." Yet something nagged Trouble. His mother warned him against playing with the combination lock. But he couldn't remember what she said. Well, it didn't matter. They'd find out what happened when you play with the dial, soon enough.

6

Trouble led Chiaro across the roof and gave her a boost atop his clubhouse. She dropped to the floor and he tossed his jacket inside. He made a running jump to reach handholds, pulling himself through the skylight. A minute of work repaired the broken molding and sealed the plastic dome. Weak moonlight filtered through the dome and cast an eerie radiance. The wall photos looked fluorescent, highlighted with a strange blue glow, like the inside of a bubbling aquarium. He put a finger to his lips, asking Chiaro to be silent. They crept past the landing outside the shopkeeper's bedroom, pausing to make certain he was asleep.

At the bottom, Trouble flicked on lights and the showroom came to life. Antique clay pots crowded around bronze winged lions. The metallic beasts were lost in time, their faces caught in a frozen snarl. Shadows from the lion's wings fell across tapestry chairs with pale embroidery. The patterns on the fabric were faded pastels and the seats looked too fragile to support any weight. A tortoise shell umbrella stand flanked the old furniture. Canes and brittle walking sticks sprouted from the umbrella stand, as if forgotten by visitors from centuries ago. Moldy books crowded the shop's tables. The leather volumes were edged in white mildew and the collection of books spilled across dressers and credenzas in chaotic piles. "Well, this stuff is what my parents collect on their travels. It used to sell. Now we don't get many visitors."

"I guess it's nice stuff." Chiaro hefted a black swirl of rocky clay. "What's this?"

"Bird poop." He smiled.

She dropped the heavy object with a thump. "Euww, gross. Why didn't you warn me?" Chiaro wiped her palms on her military style pants.

"Don't worry. You can't get any germs from touching it. That thing's a fossil, about a thousand years old."

"What kind of bird makes such a big mess? Gotta be a giant pigeon." Chiaro bent closer and squinted at the lump.

He read a small plaque to her. "This poop came from a Moa. They lived in New Zealand hundreds of years ago, eating bugs and bushes. Moas looked like wingless giant turkeys. They grew to nine feet tall."

"I can see why your parents brought home dung instead of a bird. Poop fit in their luggage – and a nine-foot bird's too big for carry-on." Chiaro gave the icky swirl a hesitant shove, moving the lump back where she found it. "Where's this safe you want opened?"

"Over there." They walked toward a bizarre display. He pointed at a huge rock, shaped like pliers. A stuffed crocodile lay wedged head-first in the pliers.

Trouble lifted the crocodile from its spot. The dead animal was a tough hide, crammed with cotton wadding. The dark green skin had the gloss of patent leather and bumpy ridges on its back were jet black. Its toothy jaws weighed more than all the rest. He laid the croc on a nearby couch. "This is where you can sleep. Warmer than the roof."

"Thanks, but I'll sleep alone, if you don't mind." She put the stiff crocodile on the floor. Chiaro walked around the dark rock, staring at bulges above the jaws. The bulges looked like snake eyes. She felt them tracking her, circling the display. "What is this thing?"

"Fossil of a snake. Give me a hand moving it, will you?"

"Forget it. I hate snakes."

"This one's dead. Besides, all we got is the head. It used to belong to a *Titanoboa*. They lived in a remote jungle area of Colombia, 'bout sixty million years ago. *Titanoboas* ate crocodiles. That's why my dad stuffed a croc in its mouth."

"This is just the snake's head?"

"Yeah. Whole thing must've been forty feet long. Weighed more than a ton."

"I can see why crocodiles lost the fight." She gave the snake head a respectful look before touching the craggy fossil. Cold and rough, the snake felt like coal left in a wintery basement. "Why do we need to move this thing?"

"Safe's underneath. Careful. It's heavy."

"No kidding." They both grunted, straining to be gentle, but the weight hit the floor with a thud.

Chiaro rubbed her lower back. She examined a large stone box acting as a pedestal for the snake fossil. The stone box was carved with images of javelin throwers. The faces of the spear carriers were worn away. No eyes remained, only bumpy cheeks and pointed ears. "The safe's in here? This box has a creepy feeling."

"Should. It once held a dead Roman senator. Legend says Cassius was buried inside, but there's no proof." He saw a puzzled look on her face. "You know, Cassius and Brutus. The guys who stabbed Julius Caesar to death."

"Oh, yeah. That explains everything." She rolled her eyes.

*Roman Family Cemetery – A Carved
Stone Coffin Is Called A "Sarcophagus."*

"You heard of Cleopatra?"

"Sure. Beautiful, smart. Every woman wants to be a Cleopatra. Live the good life."

"Her life wasn't so good. She met Julius Caesar, fell in love. He goes home to Rome and gets killed. Marc Antony takes over, rubs out Brutus and Cassius. But Marc makes the same mistake Julius did. Antony visits Egypt, falls in love with Cleopatra. Then they both get killed."

"I'll skip that part. I'll stick with the gold and perfume. Cassius fit in this box? Seems too small for a guy's body."

"People were a lot shorter then. Five foot man was a giant. Give me a hand. We gotta lift the lid." He bent over, gripping the stone top. The alabaster was slippery and his fingers curved around the edges of the lid for a better grip.

Chiaro was worried. "It isn't gonna stink, is it?"

"No. Somebody swiped the body two thousand years ago." They lifted the heavy carved lid, sliding off the top and propping it against the stone box.

Inside, an antique iron safe lay on its back. The black enamel surface was scarred with dings and scratches, marks left by frustrated thieves. The enamel plate showed an Indian tepee near a barren tree. Fine gold paint edged the door, a promise of hidden valuables lying inside. Her eyes traced the raised letters of "Diebold Safe & Lock Co., Canton, O." Chiaro studied a worn brass door handle and big dial.

"I've never worked one this old." She knelt down and put an ear against cold black steel. A few slow turns of the dial and Chiaro popped to her feet. "I don't get it. This dial's a phony. There's no tumblers inside.

All I hear are bearings spinning." She pointed at a key hole. "I think it takes a key to unlock the door, not a combination."

"Oh no," he groaned. Trouble sagged into a desk chair. "That's what my mother meant. She told me playing with the dial won't do me any good."

"You know where your parents kept their keys?"

"Sure. In their pockets. Well, thanks for trying." He got up to leave. "We can put the lid and snake back in the morning."

"Wait. You give up too easily." Chiaro went to her messenger bag, left on a table when they entered the room. She drew out a locksmith's kit.

"You know how to pick locks?" Trouble was relieved.

"Simple ones. This lock's old. So it's pretty simple." Chiaro stuck metal probes in the lock and fiddled. A minute later, there was a click. "You wanna open the door?"

Trouble rushed to the safe. A crank of the brass handle freed the heavy door and he tugged it open. Hope sank to despair. His passport was inside the safe, but no sapphire. The brass shelves were empty, except for one carefully folded note. Trouble opened the thin white paper and read his father's handwriting.

"What's the note say?" Chiaro moved alongside and mouthed the words. "Eye Oh You $125,000 or you keep the sapphire." She laughed, then felt sorry for Trouble. "Too bad. Looks like your dad hocked the family jewel. Guess you were counting on it for money, huh?"

"Yeah." He sagged, looking at the paper with numb eyes. "This is a real bummer." Trouble didn't know what to do. There didn't seem to be any way to raise funds for a trip. He let go of the debt note and watched it float into the safe.

"You gonna be all right?" Chiaro felt worried.

"We'll make do … somehow." Trouble looked at the mess he'd created to break into the safe. He didn't have the energy to clean up. "Um, you go to bed. We'll put things back tomorrow."

"I gotta leave early for the flower shop. Probably won't be here when you get up. Why don't we do it now, huh?"

Trouble couldn't look at the mess any longer. "Bleerio will help me. See you 'round." He shuffled out of the room and headed upstairs.

"Yeah … thanks for the couch." Chiaro tried sounding upbeat, hoping to perk up her friend. "Hey, stop worrying. It'll work out."

"Sure." The lonely word fell down the stairs like a broken toy. "Be sure to kill the lights. They're expensive."

"Got it." She hit a switch and the room went dark. Chiaro hunted for the couch, tripping over the crocodile before touching padded leather. Curling up to stay warm, she tried a soft, "Goodnight." But there was no response, only the distant sound of Trouble's door closing.

7

The next morning, Bleerio yawned with exhaustion and stumbled into the showroom. His hair was a mess of tangles clustered around his bald skull. Long fingers scratched itchy sideburns, flaring over his jaw like mutton chops. He pulled off wire-rimmed glasses, rubbing sleepy eyes. He looked around the antique store, shocked at the mess. He'd cleaned up recently, yet the crocodile's bumpy tail peeked from behind the couch, where it shouldn't be hiding. The *Titanoboa* fossil was on the floor, instead of lying atop the Roman sarcophagus. The lid was off the coffin … and worst of all, the safe was open. He ran to the old metal box and peered inside. There was only a slip of paper, no money, no sapphire. Bleerio let out a shriek. "Oh, no. We've been robbed!"

Trouble peered around the rolltop desk. "You got that right."

"How can you be so calm? Those slimy ninjas came back. They broke into the safe and took the sapphire." Freaked-out, Bleerio sputtered. "Call the police. I want them arrested … I want them in prison."

"Calm down, will you? Ninjas didn't take the sapphire."

"Then who did? Someone broke into our safe. I don't know how they found it, but they cracked our safe open." The shopkeeper reached for a phone.

Trouble ran over and took away the phone. "Chiaro opened the safe – at my request."

"You broke into our safe ... why?"

"For the sapphire. I was going to sell it – or take it to a pawnshop. But my dad got there first."

"I don't understand. You agreed we were robbed. What's going on?" Bleerio looked faint. His face was pasty white.

Trouble gave the shopkeeper a disgusted look. "I meant the rat we sold Flix. On that deal, we got robbed."

"Whaddya mean?"

"I'll show you. Come here." Trouble grabbed Bleerio's moist hand and led him to the rolltop desk. "Look at the screen." A news service article reported a record sale on eBay. A very unusual rat had been discovered in Manhattan. It was a throwback to a prehistoric generation of rats. The creature was reported growing at an alarming rate and very dangerous. A private collector bought the rat from Mr. Le Roi Braun, known as the Bronx junk king. A sale price wasn't disclosed, but it was rumored to be $300,000.

The Old Curio Shop's Rolltop Desk & Laptop Computer

Bleerio read the article and went limp. He fainted into the desk chair, fanning himself. "And we don't even have money to pay rent."

"Plus the vet wants $2500 for operating on Albert. And I need to find my parents. But your 'friend' pays a lousy thousand dollars. All the time, Flix knows the rat is worth a lot more."

"That can't be … Flix wouldn't do that to me." Bleerio sat upright. He read the article again and looked smug. "You're wrong, Trouble. The rat was sold by a junkyard owner. It says so in the article. I told you Flix was innocent."

"Was he?"

"Yes, of course he was." The shopkeeper's face clouded in anger. "Flix is a Warwick man, not a junk dealer. And his last name is Ashley.

This revolting junkyard man's name is Braun." Bleerio crossed his arms in satisfaction. "I've proven Flix is innocent."

"You have?"

"Yes, darn it."

"Got bad news for you, my friend. You better sit down again."

Bleerio recoiled, falling into the chair. "What do you mean?"

"I mean that Madison Ashley is Flix's mother."

"Yes. I've seen photos of her in the paper, in the society pages. She always wears beautiful gowns."

"Bought by Flix's rich dad."

"How would I know who buys her clothes? Maybe she has her own money." Bleerio dared a peek at Trouble. He looked so confident the shopkeeper cracked. He talked in a shy voice. "Does Mrs. Ashley have money?"

"Some," Trouble confirmed. "Ms. Ashley came from a family that was rich. But they lost most of their fortune with poor gambles in the stock market. Even so, Ms. Ashley owns a lovely brownstone near the Metropolitan Museum of Art. The maintenance on that home, plus her high society lifestyle, would have bankrupted her a long time ago. Except ..."

Bleerio gritted his teeth so hard Trouble could hear the grinding sound. The shopkeeper hated losing a quarrel.

"All right. Tell me. I can't take it any longer." Bleerio muttered the words with his eyes shut tight.

"OK. Ms. Ashley lives in a brownstone and Flix attends Warwick because she's married to a very wealthy dude. His money comes from … well, you know all about his business." Trouble stopped there.

"I do not!" Bleerio screamed.

"Sure you do. He sold the rat. I'm talking about Mr. Le Roi Braun, the self-declared junk king. Flix uses his mother's name. Warwick likes that name – and they like Mr. Braun's money."

Reluctant to concede, Bleerio tried a last defense. "It doesn't matter. Braun doesn't have anything to do with us."

"I wish." Trouble went to the safe and retrieved an IOU signed by his father. "My dad needed money for an expedition. So he went to a kindred spirit, another man who deals in old items – Le Roi Braun, junk dealer. Dad offered the Scythian Sapphire as collateral for a loan."

Bleerio dared a look at the IOU. "Oh, no."

"Oh, yes. Signed by my dad and countersigned by Le Roi Braun. Gotta be a made up name, by the way. '*Le Roi*' in French means 'the king.' "

"We've been had." Bleerio slumped in the chair. He looked like a rumpled towel, tossed across the seat.

"True. And there's worse."

"I don't want to know." Bleerio clapped hands over his ears.

Gently, Trouble lifted the shopkeeper's fingers to restore his hearing. "You gotta know. It's important."

"What?" Bleerio sulked.

"Those ninjas were no accident. I think Mr. Braun was making sure he got back my father's loan."

The shopkeeper recoiled. "I don't believe Flix had anything to do with those creeps."

"I hope you're right." Trouble shrugged. "Because I'm going to pay Flix a visit this morning, before he limos to Warwick and attends his classes on how to be an obnoxious preppie."

Bleerio stared at Trouble like he'd gone insane. "You don't make any sense. One moment, you're claiming Flix sent bullies to steal a precious shipment. The next second, you're knocking on his door."

"First of all, I said it was Flix's dad who sent the bullies. And second ..."

"Yeah?" Bleerio scrunched his bushy eyebrows into a single caterpillar.

"Second, Flix is the only person I know with a lot of money. I'm in the same predicament my dad was, when he pawned the sapphire. I have to make a deal with the enemy and hope I survive." Trouble started to leave.

"Wait," Bleerio shouted. "What are you going to sell Flix? We don't have anything he wants."

"I'm gambling we do have something he wants, very badly. At least his father wants it."

Bleerio was too confused to speak. He sat there with a puzzled look on his face. Then his eyes lit up. "Of course. More rats."

"And other creatures like them." Trouble pulled the shipping label from his pocket and waved the crumpled paper. "I know where the rat came from – and they don't. Want more rare rodents? Fine. Send money." He gave the shopkeeper a grim smile and headed along the hallway. At the doorway, Trouble paused. "Bleerio – one last thing."

"What?"

"I left Albert at the vet – you know, the penguin I found inside Mount Everest."

Bleerio stuck his head around the wall and stared at Trouble. "So?"

"When the vet calls, tell her I'm getting the money for Albert's operation. I should have it tomorrow."

"OK …" The shopkeeper scratched his head in amazement. "You're going to get money for food, too. Right?"

"And the rent – I hope. Gotta go or I'll blow my subway connections." Trouble glanced at his watch and frowned. He waved goodbye and sprinted out the door.

8

The subway ride was a blur of huge advertisements, viewed through gritty windows. The train roared, trembling along rails at amazing speed. Bright lights in stations alternated with dark tunnels. Trains going the other direction blasted shock waves, rocking Trouble. He was always vigilant, watching for threats. Someone might try to rob a kid alone, wearing a student daypack. Worse, they might kidnap him. He was relieved to hop from the car and sprint up flights of stairs to street level.

He looked around to get oriented. The Metropolitan Museum of Art loomed nearby, draped in banners featuring a visiting exhibit of Egyptian artifacts. Waiting to see King Tut's relics, groups of school kids wore the same color blazers. They crowded the museum steps, anxious for the building to open.

Central Park's green spaces and gorgeous foliage beckoned Trouble to explore, but he ignored their appeal. He focused on tree-lined streets running along "Museum Mile," one of the most expensive neighborhoods in Manhattan. Jogging a few blocks, he turned on one of those streets. Trouble bent his path around delivery trucks and a city maintenance crew. Exhaust fumes from the crew's diesel generator were as obnoxious as its racket.

This Manhattan was so different from his world. In this neighborhood, nannies in starched uniforms loaded babies in strollers. Clothed in pretty outfits from Nieman Marcus, the babies looked like dolls. Through lace curtains, he saw housekeepers fluffing comforters in

Townhomes Near The Metropolitan Museum Of Art

bedrooms decorated by famous designers, like Laura Ashley. Windows were squeaky clean and brick walls gleamed, sandblasted to ensure townhomes looked new, though most were over a hundred years old. There was no gum residue sticking to the power-washed sidewalks. Leafy trees covered the street, arching to intertwine boughs with neighbors across the way.

Trouble checked his notes and halted before white columns bracketing a wide door. He confirmed the street number, etched in a shiny brass plate and his mouth went dry. Trouble knew Flix's parents had money, yet their home was at a level above other rich people in this neighborhood. For one thing, they owned a pair of brownstones, combined into a single mansion. Other wealthy people could afford only one building. Plus the Ashley-Braun mansion was taller than surrounding brownstones, having seven floors instead of the usual five.

He couldn't help questioning his sanity in coming here. Yet there seemed no alternative. Trouble gulped, then reached toward a huge knocker on the dark green door. The brass felt cold and heavy as a ship's anchor. He forced himself to rap three times on a door large enough for a castle. Trouble realized the sound of a door knock was lost inside that cavernous building. He found a doorbell and mashed the button hard. Chiming resonated behind the door, sounding like England's Big Ben Clocktower striking noon. A security camera whirred above his head and he looked into its zoom lens.

A skeptical voice asked, "Are you at the correct address?"

"Yes. I'm here to see Flix Ashley." Trouble reminded himself it was important not to squirm.

"Your name …?"

"Trouble. Don't worry. It's a nickname." He gave the lens an innocent smile, hoping it would help.

"Your real name is … ?"

"Trouble Jones … Um, Flix knows me."

"He does?"

"Yes." Trouble felt more confident. But it didn't last.

"Is Master Flix expecting you?"

Flinching, Trouble admitted the truth. "Well, not exactly."

"Please wait." There was a loud click and the camera lens whirred, returning to its wide-angle view of the street.

Trouble waited … and waited … and waited. Then things got worse. The door swung open, moving in a slow arc. Behind the door lay the brownstone's foyer. It looked like the lobby of a grand hotel, not something found in a private home. An open space rose all seven floors to a stained glass canopy. Elaborate wrought iron balconies crowned each level and climbed stairs like black ivy. Huge ferns draped their leaves across wide landings, breaking the even parade of brick and iron. An elevator box shot upward, racing to the top floor. The lift's cage was covered in a decorative mesh of gleaming brass and gun-metal steel.

But it was the garden atrium that snapped away Trouble's breath. Inside a glass cage, rare black swans floated in a pool. The huge birds lapped up breakfast, scattered on tranquil water by their attendant. Around the pool, a uniformed gardener spread fresh rose petals. The crimson petals matched the bird's scarlet beaks. Their lush black wings resonated with ebony pebbles lining the pool.

Trouble stood there, amazed by the dazzling world hidden behind a plain door. His trance was broken by a security guard looming over him. The man looked like a secret service agent, wearing a dark suit with a bulge where a gun was hidden. Crepe soled running shoes and an ear bud with lapel microphone completed his attire.

The guard's voice boomed. "Come inside."

Trouble moved closer, straining his neck to look at the tall man's face. The guy must be six-eight, Trouble decided, probably an ex-pro basketball player.

The guard raised a fist, making his arm look like a sledgehammer. A thick finger shot from the fist, pointing at a chair. "Sit there and wait. I will be taking Master Flix to Warwick Academy soon. He's willing to spend a moment with you before we leave."

Rare Black Swans In The Atrium Pond Of Flix's Mansion

"OK. Thanks." Trouble nodded and moved toward the chair. He decided not to sit down. It'd make him seem inferior when Flix arrived.

The security guard didn't insist Trouble sit down. He waited, his face expressionless, feet apart. His eyes never left Trouble, but they didn't look threatening, at least not yet.

A soft padding grew louder, announcing Flix before he appeared in person. Butter leather shoes led to pleated trousers. Their beige wool made a nice contrast with a burgundy Warwick blazer, complete with the Academy's feather and dagger crest. A Latin motto bent around the crest, declaring *In Pecuniam Veritas*. A silk ascot filled the open collar of a royal blue shirt. All the hues complimented Flix's tanned face and thick blond hair, swept back to hang against his jacket.

Flix put out his hand and shook with Trouble. "Good to see you again. What's up?"

His suave tone bugged Trouble. This was all so pat. But it went with a guy who'd duped Trouble out of more money than the antique store made in a year. He swallowed rage, forcing himself to speak in a calm voice. "We need to talk."

A quick shrug led to the obvious response. "So, talk."

"It's a private conversation." Trouble's eyes went to the bodyguard.

"Oh. Well, in that case, let's go in the theater. It's quiet in there." Flix turned and the bodyguard tapped his watch, a Geoffrey Roth original, machined from a sold block of stainless steel.

"We leave in four minutes, sir."

"We'll make it short. Won't we?" Flix gave Trouble an inquisitive look.

"Yeah. This won't take long." He walked behind Flix, entering a dim auditorium. Motion sensors triggered runway lights and began raising dimmers to a brighter setting. A dozen plush chairs appeared out of the darkness, arranged in tiered theater seating.

Flix patted a switch and the walls sprang to life in backlit movie posters. *Transformers*, Harry Potter, *National Treasure* and *High School Musical* competed for attention. A life-size cardboard image of Darth Vader threatened actor Ben Stiller, costumed for a *Night at the Museum*. Fortunately, Spiderman was poised to rescue Mr. Stiller. Only one image

Flix's Home Theater

seemed out of place, a printed lobby card showing Tyrone Power and Maureen O'Hara in a 1942 classic.

Trouble stared at the autographed poster in surprise. "I didn't know you liked films that old."

"It's my grandmother's favorite. We show the film on her birthday, every year. ... Er, what did you want, Trouble? Our time is limited, unfortunately." Flix played with a stack of Blu-Ray discs, a fresh batch that arrived in yesterday's mail. He shuffled titles, smiling at some, frowning at others.

Trouble fought to shake free of his intimidating surroundings. Letting himself feel angry helped. "You made a nice killing off my rat, Flix. I let you get the better of me that time. But if you want more, we're going to split the sale, equal halves, fifty percent each."

For a moment Flix appeared surprised. Then his expression vanished. "More prehistoric rats just dilute the price. Find ten of them and the creatures are worthless. The animal was valuable because it's rare, like the black swans in our pond."

"Then I'll get you other creatures." Trouble paused, waiting to see what happened.

"But it takes, what ... ?" Flix batted the topic back at Trouble.

"I need funds for an expedition. The advance gets repaid from my share, after you sell the creatures I find."

"That might be interesting." Flix tossed a movie in a trash can. "I already have a better copy of that film. I'll have to speak with my secretary. She's getting careless." He glanced at Trouble. "How much money do you need – and when do you need it?"

Trouble fought back a gulp. He assumed the same amount his dad borrowed should be enough. "A hundred twenty five thousand. I want it this week."

Flix shook his head and laughed. "That's way outside my allowance. I'll talk to my dad, see if he's interested."

"He should be. He's bound to remember a rat that cost him a thousand dollars and sold for three hundred times that much."

This time, astonishment lingered in Flix's eyes. In a moment, surprise became greed. "You really think you can find more unique creatures, throwbacks like that rat?"

Trouble nodded. "I'm sure of it."

The bodyguard walked inside and waved to Flix. "We gotta leave, sir."

"All right." Flix turned to go. He gave Trouble a knowing look. "I'll call you. I'm sure something can be done to help find your parents."

Trouble played along. "Thanks." Then he added a bit of pressure to the greed he'd thrown at Flix. "The *New York Chronicle* said they'd run a story about the situation. I'm seeing them next. That should turn up people interested in an expedition." It felt nice to give Flix a smug look and be on top for once.

The trick worked. Flix halted mid-stride and stared, looking worried. "Hold off on the *Chronicle*. Give me a twenty-four hour exclusive."

"Why should I?" Trouble acted smug enough that the bodyguard moved between them.

Flix stepped around the giant so he could see Trouble again. "I get an exclusive and you get a better deal. Sixty-forty."

"Seventy-thirty," Trouble countered.

"No. Sixty for you, forty for me – or the paper gets my side of the story."

"Done."

Flix grabbed Trouble's hand and they shook on the deal. The trio walked quickly along the foyer. Construction noise boomed through the mansion's open door. Flix grabbed his briefcase and shouted to be heard over street repairs. "Call you tonight."

Trouble didn't wait for them to leave in a luxury car. He waved and sprinted toward the closest subway entrance. The rat-a-tat-tat of a jackhammer and its cloud of dust didn't bother him. It appeared certain Flix would call with good news in only a few hours. This was a time to relax, celebrate a little – get a large pizza delivered, made with an extra thick crust and dripping in toppings.

Flix waited for his chauffeur-bodyguard to open the limousine's door. Then he slid on a hand-tooled leather seat and dropped his briefcase to the floor. The limo's interior reeked of glove leather accented by his mother's $2,000 an ounce perfume. Flix reclined in the chair, like he was enjoying a feature film in his home theater.

The golden Panamera jiggled a bit when the chauffeur belted himself behind the wheel. A turbocharged 500 horsepower engine started with a throaty roar and dulled to a murmur. There was a rumble of super sticky tires on pavement when the extreme performance limousine glided into traffic. The car's luxury floated on a computer-controlled air suspension, delivering power to all four wheels. At the touch of a button, the Panamera could shift personalities, transforming from insulated cocoon to kidnapper-evading racecar. That's why so many of the ultra rich owned a limousine made by Porsche, a company known for building insanely fast cars.

A thick privacy window separated Flix from the Panamera's front seats. He turned on a microphone so he could talk to the driver. "I need to see my father. Please take me to him."

"Are you sure?" The driver's eyes stared at Flix via a rear view mirror, attached to the windshield.

Flix nodded. "Yes. It's important."

"Your father's business is across the Harlem River. You realize, Master Flix, that area is different from where you live."

Flix gave a cynical laugh. "Oh, yes. As different as my father is from my mother. It's the Bronx versus the Hamptons."

They rolled along in silence, going cross-town. Traffic was thick, making for slow progress. They crept in a start-stop motion, edging forward. At last, they moved on a bridge where the cars flowed toward Yankee Stadium. Beyond its shadows, graffiti splattered across metal doors of rusting warehouses. Glass fragments speckled sidewalks where old cars were parked, with tires drooping over the sidewalk.

They turned on a side street and bumped over potholed asphalt, running into an industrial area. Sets of railroad tracks ran alongside them. After a while, the rails fanned across their path, holding flat cars stacked with freight containers. They came to a high fence and halted, waiting for a gate to slide open. The huge barrier crept at a snail's pace.

The chauffeur coughed discretely to get Flix's attention. "I don't mean to pry, sir. It's been a while since you've seen your father, hasn't it?"

"You mean, have I seen him since he was injured? I know about the brawl with his late partner."

"There's never been any proof they were fighting. The courts ruled his partner's death an accident, not murder." The driver again looked in the mirror, trying to catch Flix's eyes.

He refused to make eye contact. "The surveillance tapes were flawed. Poor quality control – or clever planning."

"Your father was badly injured. As you know, his legs were crushed all the way to his hips. There was no place left for attaching artificial limbs. With all due respect, sir, no one would plan such a fate for himself."

"Yes, I'm sure you're right. That part certainly wasn't planned."

"Well, however you feel about your father, I should warn you his appearance shocks people."

"I promise not to stare."

The chauffeur didn't answer. Instead, he drove inside the

Junkyard Car Crusher

compound, weaving the Porsche Panamera around skip loaders full of recyclable metal. Abandoned cars were stacked high as an office building, waiting to be scavenged for parts. Cranes lifted auto bodies into crushers, chewing fenders, hoods and roofs into fist-sized chunks. Flat bed trucks loaded bales of shredded metal and plastic-wrapped cubes of "fluff," cement-coated debris used in sealing landfills. Industrial smells leaked through car vents. Ugly aromas of old rubber and flaking paint mixed with dust and grease.

They passed another area where the cars were stripped of anything that could be resold on the used auto parts market. Workers removed instrument panels and vinyl seats, unbroken glass windows and batteries. Their drills made high-pitched zipping sounds and added a smoky flavor to the dirty air. Other crews dragged engines off their mounts and pulled transmissions. Each part was labeled, catalogued and sent to a warehouse for storage.

They drove into the warehouse, leaving people behind, joining a small army of robots. The androids raced to their destinations at freeway speeds. The warehouse interior was a dangerous blur of heavy equipment flying up and down, zinging along rows, zipping around corners. Lights popped like camera flashes whenever a

Robotic Warehouse

73

robot dropped its load on a shelf. The brief pulse allowed a photo to be taken, for inventory management. The area was much too vast for normal lighting.

The warehouse ended at a beehive structure, shaped like a football stuck in the ground. Its curves seemed out of place amid a perfect grid of shelves. A luxurious RV sat nearby, with a wheelchair ramp leading to its door. The limo halted and Flix got out, not waiting for the driver. He felt disoriented, confused where to go.

"This way, sir." The tall chauffeur pointed at a revolving door, cut into the beehive.

They spun through the door, walking toward a guard station filled with TV monitors. Flix started to explain and a waving hand cut him off.

"Mr. Braun's expecting you. We notified him of your arrival."

A barrier slid away, revealing the beehive's interior. Flix drifted inside the core and his eyes involuntarily flew upward, scanning a honeycomb filled with order takers, each in their own niche. A pipe ran up the beehive's axis, supporting a robot arm. There was a loud whirring noise and the arm spun downward in a dizzying arc. At the end of its path, the robot came to a soft landing, placing Le Roi Braun in front of his son.

Despite the chauffeur's warning, Flix was stunned by his father's appearance. Thinning hair billowed in wisps around eyes sunken in a mottled face. His flesh was going white from Vitiligo, an illness that bleached singer Michael Jackson's skin of its natural color.

Le Roi Braun

An open tuxedo shirt flowed down his father's torso and flared on a leather disc. He seemed a melted candle, dropped in a holder. There was only a torso – no hips or legs. The lower half of Le Roi's body was gone, diced by a car shredding machine. Gradually, Flix realized a metal brace held his father on the leather pad.

Le Roi's intense eyes seemed to regard Flix with a mixture of amusement and hatred. Flix realized it was the burning gaze of a shattered man, jealous of a healthy boy with a great future. His mouth went dry and he couldn't speak.

Le Roi enjoyed his son's discomfort. When he tired of that game, Le Roi spoke. "I assume you've come for money. Why else would you visit?"

"To see how you're doing." Flix tried to put warmth in his voice, but failed.

"A year ago, I might have believed you." He shook his head and thin strands of hair drifted like spun cotton. "Now, you're too late."

"You told us not to visit until you felt better. Then you quit answering our phone calls."

"OK. I'll cut you slack. You deserve it."

"For what?" Flix was taken aback.

Le Roi toyed with a loose bowtie, hanging around the collar of his dress shirt. "I would've paid ninjas a lot more for that rat. You got the creature for a lousy thousand bucks. You're a clever rascal. You have style, like me."

"The ninjas threatened torture. Is that your style, father?"

Le Roi frowned. "How they get something is their business. My business is buying low and selling high." He laughed. "But you know how it works. There's gold inside junk. I dig it out and sell it, all around the world."

Braun hit control buttons, sending him on a twisting circuit of a honeycomb filled with computer operators. He flew back to earth, landing before Flix.

"Yes, very impressive, father. Er, my business is ... smaller."

"Another rat?" Le Roi's eyes came alive.

Flix resented his father's smug look "I didn't like having that animal stolen from me."

"The rat was mine. I funded the expedition, not you. Besides, I dumped the profit in your trust fund. You get it all when you turn thirty. Why are you complaining?"

"I ... didn't know you gave me the money."

Le Roi shrugged, as much as his brace allowed. "Forget it. So what do you want?"

"Spring break is coming soon. I'd like to travel."

Braun smirked. "With your buddy Trouble? His father hit me for a loan and never repaid the money." Le Roi held up a small jewel case and popped the lid. Light sparkled off the red gem in a fireworks display. "You like this *padparadscha*? You should. The sapphire is more than a hundred carats, at $5,000 a carat. You're looking at a half million dollars."

"It's beautiful … but I thought sapphires were blue."

"Crimson sapphires are rare. That's why they got their own name, *padparadscha*."

"You took the stone as collateral, when you funded the expedition?"

"Yes. I got it in return for a loan, like the one you want – for another expedition. Am I right?"

Flix nodded. He saw there was no point trying to hide his motives.

"I thought so. Greed runs in the family."

"There's more creatures like that rat. You can sell them for a huge profit."

"Yes, I can. There's a lot of wealthy people in the world who'll bid for them. Some want to start a Jurassic Park, filled with dangerous animals. Others are superstitious. They think medicinal powders made from these creatures will cure their illness. I don't care what they do with the animals, so long as they pay on time."

"Exactly." Flix nodded. He looked to the chauffeur for support, but got only a blank stare.

Le Roi ran a bony hand over his chin. "After this mission, the Jones family is out of the loop. I want their source. No middleman. I'm sending pros to escort this boy, Trouble. They'll report to me."

"I will, too." Flix nodded a little too eagerly.

"No. Your mother wants you in Paris, visiting the Louvre Museum."

Flix recoiled in shock. "You don't talk with my mother."

"But I read her e-mails. You go to Paris. That's final."

"Yes, father." Dejected, Flix gave up. "Well, I better go. You look tired."

Le Roi studied his son, considering a sly idea, inspired by his jealousy of the healthy boy. In a quick movement, Braun grabbed the gem box and handed it to Flix. "Give this to your mother. She likes these kind of things."

Flix took the suede box and was surprised by its weight. He'd expected a golf ball light enough to float. Instead, the case felt like a paperweight. He flipped open the box, admiring how the sapphire glowed, brighter than neon. The gem's many angles caught light the way a prism does, splitting beams into the colorful hues of a rainbow. He snapped the lid closed with a loud click and his eyes automatically went to his father.

For the first time, Flix noticed a plastic bag taped to his father's chair. Tubes snaked from Le Roi's shirt, filling the bag with material normally flushed down a toilet. He realized his father could no longer go to the bathroom. Surgeons had arranged another way to drain his wastes.

Flix remembered the bodyguard's warning not to stare at his father's damage. Dragging his eyes from a hideous mess to a box holding a beautiful gem, Flix took a deep breath. He gave a serious nod. "Thank you for the sapphire." To himself, he added another thanks – for giving me enough money to go along with Trouble. In a few hours, Flix could easily sell a gem of that quality – no questions asked.

10

Bleerio spun a nickel on the Formica tabletop, watching it blur like a spinning fan blade. He waited to see how the coin landed. "Heads," the shopkeeper announced. "I win." He took the nickel and dropped it in a chrome Select-O-Matic. The coin flew through the machine and out a reject slot, caught in Bleerio's waiting hand. A light glowed inside the small, round shouldered device, indicating it was ready. The shopkeeper didn't need to flip menu pages inside the Select-O-Matic to discover a favorite tune.

Long ago, Bleerio memorized codes for all the 1970s singles he'd inserted, the top hits of their day. He punched one of the letters A through K, then tapped a number from 1 to 10. A jukebox crammed in the kitchen's

1950s Crosley Select-O-Matic

Jukebox

pantry came to life, selecting a yellow-labeled 45 rpm record. The vinyl disc dropped on a turntable and one more time, Isaac Hayes belted out the theme from *Shaft*.

Trouble groaned. "Again?"

"I've only played it a couple times." Bleerio looked like he believed his lie, which really irritated Trouble.

"A couple hundred, maybe."

"OK. Next time, you pick." The shopkeeper drifted away, enjoying his 1970s time warp, imagining himself a hip private detective.

Needled by his friend's behavior, Trouble complained. "You know, my parents set this kitchen up to be a 1950s diner, not a '70s disco. That's why they put in this booth." He slid a hand across sparkling ruby naugahyde, making a squealing noise, annoying Bleerio.

"Yeah, well you still got that dumb pink neon hamburger, and the Coca-Cola sign. If it was up to me, I would'a taken them down. Long as I'm redecorating, I'd rip out that Bakelite pay phone, too."

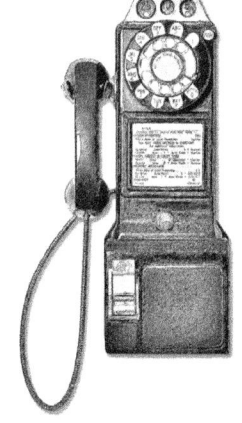

"If it doesn't ring soon, I'll help you tear the phone out of the wall." Trouble ran a finger inside a greasy pizza box, hoping to find a blob of cheese that escaped a dozen previous checks.

"You hungry? Maybe we ought'a order another one." Bleerio poked at the white box.

"Naw. This one's sittin' in my stomach like an icy rock." Trouble slid from the booth. He grabbed the box, heading for a trash bin. His downcast look and slumping posture showed a defeated attitude.

"Hey, don't look so glum. You can always go to the *New York Chronicle*. Tell 'em how the rat was really found. That's sure to turn up a sponsor, somebody wanting more of those nasty animals."

"Telling Flix I'd go to the *Chronicle* was a bluff. I tried them and they weren't interested. They thought I was crazy, a kid making things up to get attention." He grunted and the pizza box folded with a satisfying crunch. It felt good to destroy something, vent his rage. Trouble crumpled the box again, jamming it in a trash bin.

"Oh." Now even Bleerio looked dejected. "Well, it's pretty late. Guess I'll head for bed." He yawned and stretched. The shopkeeper pushed himself out of the quarter-round booth. His legs were stiff from sitting for so long and he moved slowly. Bleerio was alongside the old pay phone when the chrome and charcoal box gave an annoying buzz, then grunted a short chime. "Who'd be calling this time of night? Gotta be a wrong number. Ignore it, Trouble, and go to bed."

"Whoa, I can't ignore that call. Could be for me." Trouble slid across checkerboard tiles, gliding to a halt alongside Bleerio.

The shopkeeper looked at Trouble like he'd gone crazy. "Anyone you know would call on your cell phone."

"Nobody can reach me at that number."

"How come?"

"I stopped paying the bill months ago, when we ran out of cash."

"Didn't know. Sorry." Bleerio saw Trouble's anxiety as he waited for the shopkeeper to move out of the way. But instead of moving, he picked up the bulky handset. "Curio Shop. We're closed. Can you call tomorrow?"

"No. I have to talk now."

Startled, Bleerio moved the receiver away from his ear and stared at Trouble. "It's Flix."

With a quick movement, Trouble snatched away the handset, slipping between Bleerio and the wall-mounted phone box. "Yeah, Flix. It's Trouble. What's up?" He tried to sound calm, but his pulse throbbed in his ear. There was a lot at stake here, like Trouble's whole world.

For a moment, there was no answer. Then Flix spoke. "You need to have a cab take you to JFK airport. My Air France flight to Paris leaves in two hours. There's just enough time for you to make it. So don't mess around. And be sure to bring your passport – or you aren't going anywhere. They won't let you on the plane."

"I've got a passport, but I still need money."

"I'll advance the plane fare. Just get here. I'm already at the airport."

"OK. Next question. Why are you flying with me to Paris, instead of talking about this at home?"

"I'm supposed to tour the Louvre Museum during Spring break. But I'm going with you on this expedition, instead." A distant background voice came through the phone, announcing a flight departure to Rome.

Trouble sagged against the kitchen wall. "I really need to go alone."

"Can't. My father won't fund a trip unless you reveal the source. You get half the profit on any creatures we bring back, less expenses. But after that, you're out of the loop. It's a one time thing. Take it or leave it. Sorry."

"Look, be reasonable. I almost got killed on Everest – several times, in fact. This trip is also dangerous. There aren't going to be chauffeured limousines and five star hotels, Flix. Expeditions aren't your kind of thing. Stay in Paris. Make your mother happy."

"It's either me going with you – or my dad's goons. You do it my way and keep half, less your expenses. Do it his way and … Well, he plays rough."

"Did your father send those ninjas?" Trouble's grip on the handset tightened.

Flix hesitated. "No."

"Then who did?"

"They came on their own. They're bounty hunters, of a sort."

"Oh, so your dad put them on me, huh?"

"Maybe. I didn't send them. Be reasonable. You still get a lot from this trip, possibly a million dollars. Plus finding your parents."

"What about Bleerio? He needs money to live. And I have to pay the shop rent. Plus utilities."

"You can wire him money from Paris. Then we'll hop a plane to Vietnam."

Trouble didn't answer. He stared at the phone with enough rage that Bleerio recoiled and started to leave the kitchen. Trouble covered the mouthpiece. "Wait. Don't go. I'll need your help in a minute."

Puzzled, the shopkeeper halted in the doorway.

Flix's voice came out of the handset. "You there?"

"Yeah, I'm here." Trouble said it with all the disgust he felt at being robbed of his money and freedom.

"Are you in or out?"

"I'm in. See you at the Air France counter, JFK. It'll take about an hour to get there."

"Good." The connection went dead.

Bleerio shrugged, looking confused. "What am I supposed to do?"

The handset dropped in its cradle with a solid thunk. "Call me a taxi. I have to pack."

"Where are you going?"

"To JFK, the Air France terminal. I'm headed to Paris with Flix." Trouble frowned.

"Can I go?" Bleerio stared with pleading eyes. His wire frame glasses made the eyes seem watery and sad. It was like looking at a Cocker Spaniel, begging for a treat.

"Wish you could go with me. But you're the only person smart enough to manage this antique store."

"You really think so?" The shopkeeper's face sparkled in pride. He stood up straight and brushed dandruff off the shoulders of his polyester disco shirt.

"I know so. You're the only one who can run the Curio Shop." Trouble patted the man's back. "Call a taxi, will ya? I gotta pack." He sprinted out of the room.

Bleerio shouted up the stairs. "What about the penguin?"

"The vet said his operation went fine. You should be able to pick up Albert in a couple days. Oh, he eats raw fish. Buy some for him. Fish market's only two blocks away."

"Uh, yeah." Bleerio grumbled, "I house-sit a dumb penguin and you go to Paris." With reluctance, the shopkeeper dialed a taxi dispatcher. A minute later, he yelled, "They said a cab would be here in a few minutes. Told them you'd be outside, waiting. That OK?"

"Well, it's kinda late to hang around outside." Trouble panted, running downstairs. He double-checked to make sure he had his passport. "Flix is going to wire you money from Paris, when we get there."

"Oh. That's good." Bleerio's mood improved.

Trouble heard brakes squeal and ran to the front door, thinking a taxi arrived. He ripped the portal open and stumbled over Chiaro, huddled in the door frame. He stared at her in amazement. "What are you doing here?"

"I need a place to stay. The flower shop thing didn't work out." Too hurt to look at him, Chiaro stared at a taxi parked along the curb.

"What happened?" Trouble felt surprised. She'd talked about foster care with enthusiasm. Now Chiaro looked crushed.

"They don't want me. They want a zombie. Some creature who doesn't mind a trillion rules. No body piercing. No tattoos. I can't dress like me. I have to wear old hand-me-down clothes they provide. I share a bedroom with three other 'orphans.' That's what they call us. I gotta take the subway to the wholesale flower market at four each morning. Forget it. I ain't doin' it." Chiaro spat on the sidewalk to show her disgust.

"Well ... I really don't know if you can stay here." Trouble saw Bleerio shaking his head in a 'no,' pointing his thumbs earthward in disapproval.

Chiaro watched the taxi driver get out of his car. The man seemed humble, annoyed and impatient at the same time. His shaved head reflected the streetlight's glow.

"You the airport fare?" the driver asked.

Trouble nodded.

"You going on a trip?" She wiped tears from her eyes.

Trouble looked at the cab's yellow doors, avoiding her stare. "Looks like it. I gotta find my parents. Plus my dad's needed real bad at Mount Everest."

"I'll go along. I can help." Chiaro pushed herself to her feet.

"Ah, that would be awkward. Flix is paying for my trip and he expects one person, not two."

"Flix is rich. He can afford both of us," Chiaro reasoned. "Besides, you need someone on your side."

Trouble hesitated.

"I can pick locks. You saw that. Got a lot of other skills you don't know about," she pleaded. Chiaro's eyes turned on him like search beams, trying to melt any hesitation.

"Look, I'm sorry. But you have to own a passport and there's no time to get one. It takes weeks."

"You mean one of these things?" She reached in her messenger bag and pulled out a small blue booklet with a U.S. seal embossed on the cover.

"That legit?" Trouble was skeptical.

Chiaro gave a careful answer. "Good as yours."

"Mine's real."

"So's mine," she lied.

He took the passport from her and leafed through pages. It appeared legitimate.

The cab driver became anxious. He tapped a restless finger against the face of his wristwatch. "Look, kid. You going to the airport or not? I got another fare, if you don't want me."

"I'm going." Trouble lifted his pack.

Chiaro begged him. "Please."

He caved. "All right. I can't promise anything. Flix could still veto you."

Ignoring his warning, Chiaro cracked a smile. "Oh, I need my passport back."

"Yeah, sure." Trouble gave her the passport and slid in the cab's back seat, wondering if he'd gone crazy.

The cab's dirty yellow hood dragged to a halt under a bizarre parade of concrete umbrellas. Those funnel-shaped roofs gave visitors to JFK Airport some protection from bad weather. Trouble paid the cabbie his fare and popped the back door open. A blast of cold air laced with foul smells attacked his nostrils. He inhaled a cocktail of auto exhaust, diesel bus engines and kerosene-like jet fuel. Despite the unpleasant odors, he shoved the door wider, pushing it against a mesh of plastic construction fencing.

Chiaro hopped from the other side of the cab, ducking incoming traffic. She bounded alongside Trouble. "Hey, this is Delta. You said we're going on Air France."

"Yes, I know." He shut the car door and the taxi sprinted away, jerking around an airport cop. She wore an orange reflective vest over her leather jacket, padded with body armor.

Chiaro splayed her arms wide in disgust and stared at Trouble. "You knew we were going to the wrong place when you told the cabbie our destination?"

"Yeah, I did." Trouble looked around to make sure it was safe to cross the busy drop-off area. "Come on. I'll explain inside."

In a few steps, the terminal's glass doors slid apart, letting them exchange cold night air for an overheated interior. People smells contaminated the environment. Aftershave, perfume, shampoo, body odor and unwashed diapers made jet fuel seem natural by comparison. Trouble found an empty bench and squatted on it. He patted the worn black leather. "Sit down."

Chiaro plopped on the bench. "OK. Now what?"

"You wait here and I'll talk to Flix."

She looked around, feeling nervous. "I have to wait alone?"

"Yeah. I won't be gone long."

"Um, it's late and this place gives me the creeps. I should come with you."

He shook his head. "No way."

Chiaro shriveled. "You're gonna dump me. That's why you're leaving me here." With a quick motion, she bolted upright. "I don't even have cab fare for going back to Manhattan. You've been real mean to me, Trouble."

"Will you calm down? You're attracting attention." He glanced around. Trouble was anxious an airport cop would see them and wonder why a pair of kids were alone in the terminal at this time of night.

She put out an insistent hand. "Gimme cab fare back."

"OK, you wanna cut out, it's fine with me." He reached in his jeans pocket and pulled out some cash. "This ought to do it."

She took the money. "How come you're not taking me on this trip? I want to know."

He stood up and glowered at her. "Because you won't wait a few minutes. I'm going to see Flix. You're here when I get back, I'll buy you a ticket. Otherwise ..." At a loss for words, Trouble flapped his arms. "Well, anyway, good luck." He grabbed his daypack and headed for the doors.

She yelled after him. "Hey. I'll be in there." Chiaro pointed at the women's toilet.

He spun around and looked where she was pointing. "Well, that's dumb. I can't go in there to find you."

"Dumb, huh. Where else am I supposed to wait? I sit out here and some punk in a hoodie will poke a blade in my neck and tell me to follow him."

"Yeah, well how am I supposed to get you? We could miss the plane."

"Yell, stupid. I'll hear you." Chiaro gave him a smirk and turned around. She walked into the restroom and disappeared, never looking at him.

Muttering to himself, Trouble lunged through the sliding doors and turned the wrong way. Realizing his mistake, he spun around and began trotting, heading down a ramp. Once he got beyond the concrete roof, cool drizzle misted his hair. For a moment, Trouble halted and stared at an enormous Airbus 380, its cream body flooded in light, making the words "Air France" stand out behind the cockpit. He crossed an access road, heading for a porch shielding the long front of Terminal One.

With a swish of doors, he entered the terminal and began jogging, anxious to spot Flix. Soft honking awoke Trouble from his single-minded focus. He moved aside to leave room for a battered electric vehicle, hauling an elderly woman to another gate for a connecting flight. Nearby, an airport employee shagged rented luggage carts, abandoned in the lobby area.

The terminal felt chaotic and stressful. Groups bustled through an endless string of doors, going in and out. Displays flickered and rolled, updating which flights were arriving, departing, connecting, on-time and late. Speakers blared warnings not to leave luggage unattended, but safety messages were often cut off by flight announcements. Then officials made requests for Air France passenger so-and-so to use a white courtesy telephone. The information overload dazed Trouble, leaving him confused.

Airport Crowds

He ran past a kid in a black Hugo Boss suit, wearing a dazzling silver turtleneck. The boy acted self-conscious, like a model on a runway, showcasing expensive designer clothes. Hands in pockets, the boy paced a narrow strip in tight steps, pausing to lift a wrist and check a gold watch. His attitude and posture resembled Flix. But Trouble kept going since the kid had dark hair and Flix was blond.

"Psst, Trouble."

He stopped and pivoted, searching for Flix. Trouble's eyes focused on the smirking kid wearing an expensive silver and black outfit.

Flix lifted his wig and gave a laugh. "Good disguise, huh?"

"Not if you want me to find you."

"I don't want my 'chaperone' to find me. He thinks I'm in a toilet, relieving myself." Flix checked to make sure they weren't being watched. He pulled a thick envelope from a pocket and gave it to Trouble. "Money. Buy a coach ticket on the next flight to Paris. Wire the rest to Bleerio when you get a chance. I'll be sitting in first class. I won't be able to visit you or my bodyguard will get suspicious."

Trouble opened the envelope and stared at a pile of hundred dollar bills. "Coach, huh. Sure. No problem. Keeps my expenses down. And you said my expenses come out of the profits."

Flix nodded. His eyes glowed. "So where in Vietnam are we going?"

"We'll talk about it in Paris."

"Why not tell me? Knowing what part of Vietnam won't let me steal the creatures. After all, you have the contact's name and address. I don't."

Trouble ignored the plea. He didn't feel comfortable giving important data to Flix. The less that rich kid knew, the better. "Our next step – when and where?"

"What do you mean?" Flix went from excitement to irritation.

"I mean, when and where do we meet in Paris?"

"The time and place are on a slip of paper in the envelope. Don't call my cell. They may have it monitored."

Trouble gave him a puzzled look. "Who's *they?*"

"My mother, or my father. Either one might check on me." Flix squirmed a bit, looking anxious. "I gotta go."

"I need to know where you're staying, in case there's a mix-up."

"Look, I'm staying with friends of my mother. They're hosting me for this Spring break gig. You can't call my friends – or we'll never break loose on our own."

"Paris is a long way to travel when I don't know how this is going to work." Trouble watched Flix, trying to catch any sign of an ambush.

Flix snorted. "You should talk. I'm doing all this on trust – and I just handed you a wad of money."

Trouble aimed the envelope at the check-in desk. "I gotta buy a ticket. And you gotta take a poop." He smirked, enjoying Flix's discomfort.

"All right. This time you win. But there's no trip to Vietnam without more trust." Flix yanked off his wig and threw the brown mop in a trash can. He strutted away at a rapid clip, his nubuck loafers gliding along thread-worn carpet.

Trouble let out a slow breath. This trip was "loads of fun," and they were still inside JFK International. He could hardly wait for his next meeting with Flix. Taking Chiaro along was looking better all the time. Maybe she was right. He needed someone on his side. Well, first he had to purchase tickets or neither of them would be going to Paris.

Paris

Jet travel left Trouble and Chiaro feeling woozy. A nine hour flight was followed by stumbling around an unfamiliar airport, deciphering signs written in French. A bored customs clerk with a frizzy blonde moustache yawned over their passports. He stamped the pages with faded ink and pointed a tired finger in the direction of trains for Paris. Connections led them to a station where strangers guided them in broken English. Heading for an unfamiliar neighborhood in an enormous city, they carried a lot of tension. They could only hope they'd taken the correct route. The sleek train zoomed away like a rocket. Outside the windows, the world was a blur of tiles interrupted by brightly colored ads.

Half an hour later, they staggered into the world's largest

Outside Châtelet Les Halles Train Station

underground station. A moment of confusion vanished in recognition they were at the correct destination. Banks of escalators led them to an enormous shopping mall and then to the surface.

Chiaro spun around, taking in her surroundings. Her cheeks inflated in a "wow," but the word never left her lips. She was too much in shock.

"Paris." Trouble opened his guide book. "We're in Les Halles district. The book says this area began as a Medieval open-air food market. Farmers and butchers came every morning at dawn and set up stalls. Rich people sent their servants to buy meals. Changed a bit since then, huh?" He gave a shy smile.

The shock remained frozen on Chiaro's face. "This place has money."

"Don't get used to it." He pointed down Rue Berger. "We're staying across the river. It's a bit of a hike." Trouble headed along the street, trailed by Chiaro.

They walked alongside metal trellises supporting lush vines, climbing over arches. The combination managed to look modern and quaint at the same time. Beyond the vines, fountains gushed water and the bright colors of a merry-go-round spun in a dizzying blur. The street's other side held modern townhomes, designed to blend with

Forum Les Halles

traditional Parisian architecture. Tall windows on each story had a narrow balcony. An apartment dweller could stand outside, watching people strolling with their dogs among sculpted green hedges.

Behind the park, Rue Berger funneled into a narrow lane, filled with restaurants and shops. They walked in a modern area, with trendy cafés flaunting their hip style. Slick yellow chairs seemed hot-buttered. Blood red umbrellas sheltered patrons wearing a Gothic look – jet black hair, pale skin, pierced nose and ears.

Chiaro grabbed Trouble's arm. "They've got a Skechers store." She dragged him to look in a shop window. "Would ya' look at those kicks." Chiaro pressed her nose to the glass and cupped hands around her face to blot out glare. "Oh, they have Krixies. I've always wanted a pair. And they got 'em in purple."

"Uh, Chiaro, come on. We got a ways to go."

She ignored him and bounced to get a better look at the Skechers' inventory. Suddenly, Chiaro pivoted, glancing along the street. "They also got a McDonald's … and a Häagen-Dazs. I'm starved. We could get a burger and then go next door for ice cream."

"OK. I could use a bite. The airplane meal didn't fill me up. Tell you what. I'll go for some McDee. But I'm not eating at the Dazs."

"Don't like ice cream, huh?" Chiaro sprinted for the McDonald's.

Trouble ran to catch up. "I got nothing against Häagen-Dazs. It's just I like this little spot on Île Saint-Louis. For me, the ice cream's better."

She looked at him like he was crazy. "Well. Whatever. You're paying for my hamburger. I can try your ice cream."

In a few minutes, they inhaled enough food to make them queasy. Trouble wolfed a double quarter pounder with cheese and large fries, washed down by a Hi-C Orange Lavaburst. Chiaro binged on a crispy chicken BLT, chocolate chip cookies and baked apple pie smeared with grape jam.

Burping, their journey continued, weaving along one-way lanes just wide enough for small European vehicles, like Smart Cars and Minis. Trouble had to peel Chiaro off the window glass of exclusive shops and yank her from the doorways of outrageous boutiques. They turned a corner and the smell of water came to their noses. Anticipating his ice cream, Trouble speeded up. A block farther, he reached the Seine River, where huge glass-domed tourist boats drifted under ancient bridges. He turned to Chiaro and found her missing. She was a hundred feet away, gaping in shock. Concerned, he walked back to her.

"Is that what I think it is?" she whispered.

He spun, trying to figure out what she meant. "Yeah. It's Notre Dame."

"Like the *Hunchback of Notre Dame*? You know, the Disney film. And the musical."

"And Victor Hugo's book." He shrugged. "Sure, that's it."

She wrinkled her nose, as though she were inhaling the building's grandeur. Her eyes tracked a spire poking through dark clouds and followed layers of slate roofing tiles to walls tall as redwood trees. "Kinda big for a church."

"That's because it's a cathedral."

"Oh."

Notre Dame de Paris

"The ice cream?" He pinched her sleeve and tugged.

"I'm coming." Her shock lifted and Chiaro followed him across a stone bridge, leading to the island where Paris began, starting as a Roman trading post. Their path was crisscrossed in long shadows, cast by arcing buttresses supporting Notre Dame's walls. Chiaro kept feeling the urge to spin around and check if they were being followed. "You feel like someone's watching us?"

"It's the gargoyles, those stone birds atop Notre Dame. They're supposed to ward off evil. But they feel nasty to me." He pointed at a line of statues around the building's roof.

"They do anything useful, besides stare at people?" she complained.

Gargoyles On Notre Dame's Roof

"When it rains, water comes out of their mouths. They act like downspouts."

"I'm glad they're employed." Chiaro looked around. "Where's the ice cream shop?"

"Next island. Gotta cross another bridge. Not far after that." A short arch carried them to a second island, where they trotted past dozens of unique shops and tiny, family-run hotels.

In the middle of a block, Trouble halted in front of a brown wooden façade. An elaborate sign spelled the shop's name in gilt letters. "This is it. You don't gotta eat any. But I'm loading up."

"I'll try some. Maybe it'll be good."

An hour later, they waddled out the door, feeling blimped.

"I'm movin' to Paris," Chiaro announced. "I've never had chocolate like that in my life. And all the flavors..." She rolled her eyes. "We're staying here, right?"

Trouble gave her a sad look. "We can't afford the neighborhood. This is Flix territory. It's a place for people with a lot of money."

"You got money."

"Not as much as you think. Had to send most of it to Bleerio. Also had to pay for your ticket, remember?"

"So get more from Flix."

"Yeah, right." His stomach was too full for an argument. Trouble shuffled away, heading toward their hotel.

Once they got off the island, the neighborhoods descended with each block they walked. The shops offered fewer luxury goods. Expensive restaurants became *Prix Fixes*, implying they served simple dinners for a cheap price. After a half hour walk, Trouble swung into a narrow alley, a one block ghost town in the heart of a bustling city. The path was an opening between neglected industrial buildings. Squatters lived in abandoned factories, screening upper floor windows with plastic bags. On the ground floor, glass was boarded over with sheets of plywood, plastered with handbills and posters. Wind and rain shredded awnings and ruined old business signs, completing the alley's neglected look.

Halfway along the narrow opening, clotheslines blocked their progress. Trouble and Chiaro ducked under bed sheets and underwear. Soon the alley widened to a narrow street, paved with cobblestones. The rough paving was first laid down at a time when oxcarts roamed Parisian streets. In a nearby room, poet Marie de France was busy creating the earliest written version of King Arthur and his knights of the round table.

Factories gave way to homes that were part of the original ancient city. Walls were made from rough hewn timbers glued with coarse mortar. Trouble saw few windows, since homes were built at a time when glass was rare and mostly used in churches. Scarce materials and crude techniques made for small buildings, one room wide but five stories tall. The thin structures leaned against each other, stiffened by a plaster of raw cement, like a cast on a broken leg. Stairways climbed as steep ladders and there was little space on each floor. People living in the cramped one-room flats were forced to hang their bicycles through a window – when they were lucky enough to have a window.

Chiaro and Trouble halted in a small plaza where the lane split in several directions. Odors of rancid grease and burnt meat hung in the air. The cramped square was lined with restaurants flaunting pigs turning on a spit, a steel bar run through the pig from butt to tongue. Fat oozed like sweat off the pigs' skin and spattered on yellowed window sills.

"Um, Trouble, tell me we aren't staying here," Chiaro pleaded. "I don't like this place."

"Paris is expensive. This is all I can afford. Don't worry. I'm sure the hotel is better." He unfolded a map at the back of his tourist guide and checked directions. "It ought to be here." He ran his eyes around the plaza. "There it is." He pointed at a bent sign with faded letters.

"That's it?" She pinched her nose to indicate disgust.

He frowned. "Come on. It's getting late and I don't want to lose our reservation."

"Yeah, like a hoard of people are waiting for the chance to stay here." She looked at him like he was crazy.

He ignored her attitude. "Traveling students are happy to crash here. Come on." Weaving around plastic chairs, he ducked under a patio umbrella. Trouble nudged a door, pushing it open. He tripped on the raised threshold and fell into a small lobby. In the dim interior, his foot kicked a brass pot, sending it under the lobby's one chair. The seat billowed stuffing from its cracked vinyl.

There was a tall window facing the plaza, but its glass was tinted with midnight blue film. Light leaked through bubbles in the plastic. Splits in the bubbles let crosses of sunlight hit a row of plants. The poor ferns never saw enough sun, never tasted enough water to be anything but dusty runts. A slow current of dust spun off the plants and wound upward in a lazy spiral.

The door shut behind Trouble, squeezing light out of the room. He slid toward the front desk and hit a tarnished bell. It gave a dull clink. Trouble hit the bell again and got the same limp clink. "Hello?" he shouted.

A chair squeaked and a closet door opened behind the lobby desk. In the dim light of a greasy bulb, Trouble saw a man eating Cheerios from a scratched plastic bowl. Milk drizzled on his chin. He wiped the chin and flipped open the lid of a battered school desk. The clerk slid his cereal bowl inside the desk, safeguarding his food from a cat lying atop a filing cabinet. The desk, filing cabinet, cat, man, cleaning supplies and a tattered vacuum cleaner were all crammed in the closet.

The clerk slid behind his front desk, really just a carnival booth stuck at the back of the tiny lobby. His thin hair sat glued across pasty skin. His dull-white shirt might get washed once a year, but never ironed. The collar peeled up, one side bent so it licked the man's cheek. His stained black tie ran like a crayon streak around his neck where the shirt collar hadn't been pulled down. The clerk squinted at Trouble through round glasses, then leaned to catch a look at Chiaro. "You have reservations?" he asked.

"Of course." Trouble yanked a folded sheet from a pocket and smoothed the paper on the desk.

The clerk held up the printout for examination. "Internet," he mumbled. There was a delay as he digested information. He squinted at Trouble. "You are too young for travelling alone."

"We need a place to stay until our parents arrive." Trouble said it calmly. After all, it wasn't a lie, even if the statement was misleading.

"Your parents will stay here also, when they arrive?"

Trouble fought against his anger. This was a hold up. The guy wanted a bribe for letting them use his flea bag hotel. Low on funds, Trouble decided to bluff. He yanked the paper off the desk, snatching it from the clerk's sweaty palm. "No, our parents won't be staying here. Look, you're full. We'll go elsewhere." He turned to leave.

The clerk pinched Trouble's jacket sleeve. "No, I have your reservations. Here are your keys." He dangled a pair of room keys, hung from chipped plastic tags. "I just need your passports. I must have them … Interpol, the Surete require I hold your passports."

"We keep our passports. You keep this." Trouble put Euros on the counter.

The clerk wagged a scolding finger. "You will get me arrested."

Trouble dropped more Euros on the check-in desk. "Final offer."

A lump bounced in the clerk's throat as he swallowed hard, staring at the money. "Well, it has been a long time since they audited me ..."

Chiaro snorted a cynical laugh. "Yeah, like never."

The clerk gave her a puzzled look. "*Pardon?*" he asked in French.

"She means you only need to see our passports, not keep them. True?" Trouble leaned on the counter, letting his fingers creep toward the stack of Euro coins.

In a flash, the money vanished in the clerk's pocket. "Yes, you are right. I can explain how I saw your passports. Er, you do have them?"

Chiaro yanked her passport from a messenger bag and popped open the document. She held it far enough away that the man couldn't steal her valuable booklet.

"And you, sir?"

Trouble nodded. "I have mine, yes."

"May I see it?"

"No." The guy ticked him off. Enough was enough. The clerk had his bribe.

There was an awkward pause. The man cleared his throat. "You must pay in advance. Three nights."

"The reservation is for two nights only."

"Ah, yes. A slight mistake. Two nights, up front."

"Sign a receipt, please." Trouble again slid his reservation on the desk. He tapped the paper. "And print your name underneath. Thank you."

There was a moment of hesitation. "All right." A signature flew across the paper. The clerk extended a palm for his money. The hand wilted under Trouble's stare, lifted the pen again and printed the man's name.

The receipt went inside Trouble's daypack and out came the exact amount of money, in an envelope. He waited for the clerk to count bills. A smile, a nod, and the keys went in Trouble's hand. "Top floor."

Chiaro looked around. "Where's the elevator?"

"No room for a lift." The clerk pointed at what appeared to be a ship's ladder, an almost vertical tier of steps. "Everyone takes the stairs." He shrugged an apology. "Even me."

"Fine." Trouble was happy to escape. He scampered upstairs, followed by Chiaro. When they got to the top floor, both of them felt winded. He gave her a key and unlocked his room.

The only furniture was a nightstand and a bed jammed against a small window. He kneeled on the mattress and checked his view. All he could see was a ventilator shaft running between the ground and the roof, where the sun hid behind a thin cloud. A dandruff of peeling paint coated the shaft. Window sills held pigeons and their droppings. The hotel's fire escape consisted of rusty bars bent in a "U" and caterpillaring down the shaft.

Trouble bounced off the bed and went along the brief hall to a shared bathroom. It was filthy. Black scum grew in a tub only midgets could use. Rust inked the porcelain sink. A split carved the toilet tank lid in pieces. Concentric stains darkened the toilet bowl like geological rings in a rock canyon. Short, curly hairs littered a brief shelf behind the battered toilet's seat. There was no paper for wiping.

Chiaro's voice came to him. "I don't believe this place."

He walked to her room and looked inside. She pointed at a waste basket. A wine bottle and soiled Kleenex littered the trash can. A scratched glass on the nightstand held an inch of chardonnay. Lipstick marks walked along the rim. Cigarette smoke clung to walls in a yellow scum, reinforcing the odor of butts left in an ashtray. The bedspread lay on the floor and rumpled linen covered the mattress.

"That rodent didn't clean the room before he rented it to you." Chiaro tried to open the window for fresh air and found it painted shut. She grabbed the wine bottle and prepared to smash the window glass in rage.

Trouble snatched the bottle out of her hand. "It's only two days. We'll swap rooms. Mine was in better shape."

"It's not fair. That disgusting man should clean things."

"And Flix should pay for a decent hotel. But he didn't." Trouble offered her the other key. She took the exchange. He tore dirty sheets from the bed and rammed them in a pillow case. He started out of the room.

"What are you doing?" Anger edged her voice.

"Getting new towels and linen." Trouble spun in the doorway to look at her. "Try to get some sleep. Otherwise, jet lag's gonna hit you like a truck. OK?"

"Yeah." Demoralized, she limped around him, moving to the other room. Her door shut with a soft click. He waited to hear a privacy bolt snick in place before descending. He made up his mind to locate an Internet café and find something for her to do tomorrow. It was going to be a busy day and he couldn't take Chiaro with him. Then an idea hit him. Trouble paused on a landing, snapping his fingers in excitement. "Yeah," he announced to himself. "She'd really like that."

Opéra de Paris

Trouble surfaced from the Opera Metro stop and looked around, getting oriented. He stood on an asphalt island and watched a swirl of traffic blast past. Tour buses blared multilingual descriptions of the ornate Paris Opera House. This building inspired Gaston Leroux's novel about a disfigured phantom. Later, Andrew Lloyd Webber turned the novel into a hit musical. At the moment, Trouble felt stressed as that outcast phantom of the opera.

An argument with Chiaro that morning was followed by a long subway ride. He'd gone to a huge flea market on the outskirts of Paris, yet been unable to find a used sportscoat his size. Trouble settled for a blazer with a school crest on its breast pocket. The coat was a size too large and he'd stuffed crumpled newspaper in the shoulders to keep from looking stupid. The balls of newsprint kept slipping, forcing him to stop and adjust them. During one of those halts, he discovered Chiaro following him. She hadn't gone on the "assignment" he'd given her.

There was no point in confronting her. Chiaro would resume the argument where they'd left off. Her insecurity about getting ditched in Paris was bugging her too much. Trouble was forced to waste precious time losing Chiaro, ducking through businesses, running along snaking alleys. She was good at the game and it took him quite a few twists to evade her. As a result, he was half an hour late for his meeting with Flix.

Chafing with impatience, he waited for lights to change. Finally, he joined a pedestrian mob flowing around the vast traffic circle. To make faster progress, Trouble attempted to jog. But his quick motion drew stares from policemen stationed along the boulevard. He smiled at them and slowed to a brisk walk, normal for Parisians. Dripping with sweat in the muggy air, Trouble squeezed around shoppers. He dodged people clustered outside boutiques, their eyes lingering over rare jewelry and silk scarves in rainbow colors. He kept going toward an enormous plaza. Classical architecture ringed the square, anchored by a bronze column, made from cannons seized by Napoleon Bonaparte in his many victories.

He walked over thick red carpet, fanning into the plaza like a river delta. A quick repair job on his shoulders gave him courage to enter a fancy hotel. A doorman in long coat and white gloves tugged a glass door open for Trouble. Resentment burned through him when he saw how this hotel compared to where he was staying. The plush crimson rug took him past an ornate staircase, where carpet fell downhill in a red waterfall. Gilt molding cradled decorated ceilings. Oil paintings covered silk walls.

Typical Parisian Restaurant Décor

Signs directed him to Olivier's, one of several restaurants inside the hotel. Olivier's had a glossy bar running the length of its reception area. Glass shelves behind the bar held sparkling Venetian crystal. Soft back-lighting along the shelves emphasized the delicate lines of crystal pitchers with pouring spouts wrapped in fine gold wire. Trouble walked along red leather barstools to enter the dining salon. He found his path blocked by the maitre d', definitely a snob.

The man surveyed Trouble and cocked a disdainful eyebrow. He posed a question like an army sentry challenging an intruder. "You are staying in the hotel?"

"No. I'm having lunch with Flix Ashley-Braun." Trouble shrugged and regretted it. The gesture caused his newspaper wadding to slip, letting his blazer droop at the shoulders.

The maitre d' gave Trouble a skeptical look. "You are dining here?"

"Yes, I am." Trouble knew not to flinch. He looked around the maitre d' and spotted Flix, dressed in Madras pants, blue sportscoat and a yellow oxford cloth shirt. Brown loafers without socks exposed his tan ankles. "Ask Flix if he's dining with me. He's over there."

After a brief hesitation, the snob caved. "This way. I will take you to Master Flix."

Trouble followed the maitre d' into a dining salon where elaborate chandeliers glittered like crowns on kings and queens. The walls were lined by shimmering mirrors, flooding the area with reflections of diners, waiters, tables and impressive flower displays. Huge arrangements of delphiniums, roses and tulips shielded customers, making each table a private booth. The table's center held a small lamp with fringed shade. Its soft glow felt like candlelight. A delicate lace tablecloth lay covered in a diamond of starched linen, easy to launder when stained.

A waiter pulled out Trouble's chair so he could sit down. Another waiter unfolded a starched napkin and offered it to Trouble.

He took the linen square and spread it across his lap. "Thanks."

A third waiter handed Trouble a huge menu with tassels dangling off the binding. He didn't bother looking at today's entrées and gave back the stiff gold board. "I'll have a croque-cheval. Would it be possible to get Mornay sauce on the side?"

"Yes, monsieur. And to drink?" He pinched his eyebrows in a questioning look.

"Ginger ale. No ice."

"Very good." The waiter glided away. His assistant appeared, filling Trouble's water glass before vanishing behind a screen.

Flix stared at Trouble in irritation. "You're late."

"Couldn't be helped."

"Really. The Paris Metro isn't that different from Manhattan's subway, is it?" Flix poured sarcasm on his words like syrup on pancakes.

Trouble returned the animosity with a calm smile. "I lost a half hour ditching a tail. Seems you've got a problem with your security, Flix."

"Me ... I haven't ..." Flix's eyes lost their arrogance for a moment. "No one is aware you're in Paris. I haven't told them."

"No one?" Trouble enjoyed keeping Flix on the defensive. The power inversion felt nice for a change, even though it was based on deception. The tail he'd ditched was Chiaro, not someone Flix knew.

A waiter glided toward Flix. "Are you ready for dessert, sir?" He glanced at Trouble. "Or shall I hold dessert until monsieur's sandwich arrives?"

"Go ahead. Enjoy." Trouble nodded.

Flix made a tragic gesture with his arms. "I'm afraid I have to run soon." He looked at the waiter. "So bring the crêpe."

The waiter vanished and Flix stared at Trouble. "I think you're making up this security issue. There wasn't anyone following you."

"Think again. You called me in Manhattan. Your parents pay your cell bill. Maybe they saw my number in your call log."

"Nonsense. My mother trusts me." Flix tried to look calm and failed.

"But your father doesn't trust you. Does he?" Trouble allowed himself a brief smirk.

"That's beside the point. I used an airport phone to call you." It was a lie, but Flix didn't care. He was determined to win the argument.

Trouble reached for the bread basket and lifted a cloth hiding an assortment of rolls. They smelled delicious. He used silver tongs to grab a bun. "They took out all the pay phones in airports. Everyone uses their mobile phone now."

"Only the pay phones in public areas were removed. Airports still have phone booths in executive lounges. That's where I called you."

"Maybe your bodyguard overheard our call. He's with you in Paris, isn't he?"

"Of course. But he's …" Flix hesitated, afraid he'd give away too much.

Trouble bit into a roll. He loved the taste of the *pain au lait*. The fluffy bread's sweet flavor was addictive. Chewing, he mumbled, "Go on … your bodyguard what?"

Flix gritted his teeth. "He's on our side."

"How is that possible? Your parents sign his paycheck."

"I bribed him. I need his assistance in covering for me. While I'm gone from Paris, he'll send e-mails to my mother. He'll use my e-mail account, so she thinks I'm visiting boring museums."

"What about the family you're staying with? They'll be concerned by your absence, even if your bodyguard assures them."

Flix squirmed. "I was going to explain all this. But you got here late."

"OK. I'm sorry. So explain now, while I eat this monster sandwich." Trouble saw waiters carrying Flix's crêpe, stuffed with baked fruit and covered in melted cocoa. Snowflakes of powdered sugar dusted the rich chocolate. Behind the dessert came a beautiful ham and cheese sandwich, topped in a poached egg.

They stopped talking while being served. Flix's waiter positioned the steaming crêpe platter, then spooned dollops of fluffy strawberry whipped cream over the chocolate sauce. Trouble's waiter bowed his curly head over the long sandwich covered in melted gruyere cheese and topped with a wet poached egg. Light danced on the waiter's gold cufflinks as he poured a thick, creamy sauce over a portion of the sandwich. When the staff left, Trouble gestured to Flix. "Go on. I gotta eat. I'm starved."

"My mother's Parisian friends are leaving tonight on a short trip, three or four days. So I reserved two seats on an Air France flight. It leaves at seven thirty tonight. You have to be at the airport two hours earlier." Flix took a delicate bite of thin pastry. A look of delight spread across his face.

Trouble hurried to swallow, even though his food tasted divine. "We're going to what country?"

"Vietnam, of course." Flix looked annoyed.

"Which airport? Vietnam has two airports handling international flights."

"Hanoi, obviously. It's the capital of Vietnam. Hanoi offers a lot of good hotels."

"You're flying first class with me in coach?"

"Sure. You want to keep your costs low, right?" Flix shrugged.

Trouble sliced another piece of his calorie bomb. He poured more creamy cheese sauce over the slice. "Right, keep my costs down." He inhaled a bite and mumbled, "Just one thing."

Annoyed, Flix didn't respond. Instead, he savored more of his dessert. He ate in precise bites, careful not to let melted chocolate drizzle on his perfect clothes.

Trouble cut another piece and had the fork poised at his lips when Flix spoke.

"What's this other 'thing' you want to know?" Irritation simmered in Flix's eyes.

The dripping slice of egg, ham, cheese, bread and sauce went back to a gorgeous china plate. Trouble blotted his lips with a napkin. "What happens if our expedition takes longer than a few days? It's not likely we can make contact, find creatures and capture them in such a brief time."

Flix looked smug. "That's my problem. You introduce me to your contact and I'll do the rest. Then you're free to search for your parents." He pointed his fork and knife at Trouble. "Finding them was your goal, remember?"

"Yes. And you'll send me a check for my share, once it's all done?" Trouble lifted the heavy silver fork and stuffed more food in his mouth.

"Exactly."

After that comment, they ate in silence. Flix consumed his dessert with amazing speed, seeming to race Trouble. Sensing a waiter approaching with the lunch tab, Flix rose from his chair.

Not wanting to be stuck with a huge bill, Trouble ignored a last slice on his plate. He also got to his feet.

The waiter halted at the table, offering the chit to Flix.

"Could we have separate checks, please?" Flix removed a credit card from his wallet.

"I'm afraid not sir." The waiter levitated a golden salver on his white gloved fingertips, floating the bill at Flix.

Not wanting an ugly scene in his restaurant, the maitre d' approached. "Is there a problem?"

Trouble looked at Flix. "Reservation was in your name. They'll insist you pay. Tell you what. Put my share on a tab. Take the meal out of my trip expenses. That's fair, isn't it?"

Flix seethed at not having things turn out the way he'd intended. "Fine." He snapped his credit card on the waiter's tray.

With a quick flip, Trouble lifted his daypack from the inlaid parquet floor. "See you later." He reached to shake Flix's hand, but the gesture was refused. Trouble gave the maitre d' a wink and left Flix standing there, waiting to sign the card receipt.

Knowing he had little time, Trouble jogged to the hotel lobby. He checked to make sure Flix was still in the restaurant. Then Trouble slid through the business center's door. Tense minutes passed as he checked flight schedules via the Internet. Satisfied, he logged off and opened the door a crack. Flix wasn't in sight, so Trouble dared a fast trip to the men's room. He left his used blazer on the door hook of an empty stall and tossed the newspaper wads in a trash bin.

To avoid Flix, Trouble found his way into the kitchen area, where cold air from freezer doors contrasted with oven heat. The odor of sizzling garlic fought against raspberries in cognac. Assistants chopped vegetables at an amazing rate. They diced carrots fast as machine guns fired bullets. Ignoring threats from cooks wielding sharp knives, he sprinted around prep tables to a delivery alley. Outside, he opened his Paris guidebook and got oriented. A few blocks of fast walking brought him to the closest Metro stop.

He disappeared underground and rode the Paris subway. The car slid over rails as he clutched a cold steel pole. Within minutes, Trouble was in a very different type of world. Instead of luxury goods, ground floor shops featured locksmiths and vegetables delivered to your flat. He jogged past a discount big box store. His path bent around a bistro featuring teas from all over the world.

A block away he found Chiaro, hunched in a squat. Leaning against a wall, she looked bored and upset. She kept spinning the dial on her Nano iPod, unsatisfied with every tune. She didn't notice him until he stood in front of her and spoke.

"You didn't go on the tour?" he asked.

Startled, Chiaro jumped to her feet. Her look of relief became annoyance. "What tour? The guard wouldn't let me inside. Your 'assignment' idea was a bad joke, Trouble. Ha ha. Very funny."

"Bet you didn't even talk to him."

"Of course I did," Chiaro huffed.

"Yeah, right." He walked to the guard, dressed in a tweed sportscoat. The man looked more like a teacher than a bouncer. Trouble asked, "Do you speak English?"

"Certainly. English, Italian, German and Chinese – in addition to French, my native tongue." The guard consulted his watch. "I'm sorry. The next tour doesn't start for an hour. Would you like to wait in the cafeteria? It offers food prepared in our classes. Today we feature soufflés and duckling à l'orange. We also have a gift shop with cookbooks and souvenirs. Would you like a visitor's badge?"

"No, that's all right. I've an errand to run. Oh, would you explain to my friend what institute is located here?"

The guard looked shocked. He recoiled in genuine surprise. "But of course. This is the most prestigious cooking institute in the world. A brochure, perhaps?" He offered Trouble a glossy catalog.

"Thanks." Trouble walked to Chiaro and handed her the brochure. "You were so busy tailing me that you missed going on a tour. They give demonstrations on how to cook famous dishes."

Chiaro's face went red in a blush of embarrassment. She couldn't talk. "I ... I ..."

"Yeah." He grabbed her sleeve and pulled her toward a Metro stop.

She yanked free. "Hey wait. That guard says another tour begins in an hour."

"Fine. Stay here." He offered her an envelope with cash.

Chiaro stared at him. "What about you?"

"I'm heading to the airport. There's just enough time for me to catch an Aeroflot flight."

Confused, she pivoted her neck between the cooking school and Trouble. "But the hotel bill. Aren't you gonna pay?"

"I did that already, remember? I paid the tab up front. Plus a bribe."

"Oh, yeah." Chiaro wilted. She glanced longingly at the famous culinary institute. Being a great chef was her dream.

He tapped her shoulder with the envelope. "Here. Take it. Use the money for air fare to Manhattan. Enjoy the school before you leave."

"What about your expedition?"

"I'm going on it." He shrugged the daypack over his shoulder.

"I'm going too." But she didn't say it with conviction.

He stuck the envelope under a flap on her messenger bag. "I gotta leave." He turned towards the Metro stop, marked by an elaborate arch framed in wrought iron. A glass awning fanned like a sea shell above the Art-Deco "Metropolitain" sign.

She grabbed his arm. "I can't stay in Paris. This place is too expensive. There's gotta be money in your expedition. Otherwise, Flix wouldn't waste his time on it." She began walking toward stairs leading to an underground station.

He caught up with her. "There's no way to be sure we'll discover something valuable. Truth is, I'm going there to find my parents."

Entrance To The Paris Metro (Subway)

She ignored his warning. "When we get to the airport, we're meeting Flix?"

"No. I'm not meeting Flix. I'm beating him."

"Uh, oh. You guys had a falling out, huh?" She jogged to keep up with Trouble's pace. They hit the Metro entrance and began skipping downstairs. They entered a world of yellow tile walls and huge billboards advertising Orangina sodas and Casino toothpaste. "This Russian plane, where's it taking us?"

"First Moscow. Then Vietnam." They arrived at a station platform and a train whooshed to a halt, opening its doors. "Last chance. You can still go back and catch the cooking tour." He gestured toward exit stairs.

Chiaro walked past him and boarded the train. "Nope. I've always wanted to see Vietnam. Dreamed of it my whole life." She gave a defiant laugh at her own joke. Before that moment, she'd thought of Vietnam as just a different style of cooking.

He jumped through closing train doors. "You're crazy."

"I'm crazy? You're the one going on an expedition without Flix's money. Now that's crazy."

And they argued like that all the way to Vietnam.

Stepping from an airport bus to a Hanoi street corner felt like going from a refrigerator to a steam bath. Chiaro wilted in tropical humidity like a plant someone forgot to water. Trouble found his lungs inhaling moisture with every breath of air. All they could manage was standing on the curb, hoping their bodies would soon adapt to the climate.

Around them, teens on motorscooters blurred past a woman struggling through a crosswalk. Her traditional cone hat and linen pajamas seemed to come from a time warp. She lugged cloth-wrapped food bundles in a shallow woven basket. Her bulging shoulder tote sprouted carrot tops. Trouble felt sorry for her, dodging scooter riders with no regard for pedestrians or traffic signals. The impatient teens wore T-shirts, baseball caps and the latest cool shades.

Chiaro dropped her messenger bag to the curb with a grunt. "You have any idea where we are?"

"I bought a guidebook in the airport." He pointed at a map. "I think we're here, at the Long Bien bus station."

"How can you tell?" She looked around and all the signs were written in the Vietnamese alphabet.

He extended an arm toward a brick tower in the distance. It looked like a castle on a chessboard. A red flag bearing a large star flapped atop the dark tower. "That's

Hanoi Citadel Tower

gotta be the old citadel, where Vietnam's emperors once lived." Trouble spun around. "Behind us is water. That's probably the Red River."

"OK. So where are we going?" Chiaro hoped it wasn't a long walk.

"The Old Town's not far. Let's get something to drink there."

"Why don't we get something here?" Chiaro didn't feel like walking, even for a cool drink.

Trouble let his gaze drift toward a pair of dark green blurs hovering nearby. He leaned closer to her ear and whispered. "We have company. Flix knows he's been stood up. He called ahead and hired ninjas to find us. They're wearing green outfits. It's the same bunch his dad used to threaten Bleerio at our curio shop."

Chiaro pivoted her neck, scanning for the ninjas. She caught a hint of green color, vanishing into shadows. Darkness couldn't hide their mean intent, though. Afraid, Chiaro shuddered. "Are they waiting to kidnap us?"

"Probably. But not 'til after I make contact with my dad's agent." Trouble saw a break in traffic and moved into the crosswalk.

Chiaro matched him, step for step. She didn't want to fall behind. "Your agent's here, in the city?"

"No." He dodged an aggressive motorcyclist and kept going.

Spinning like a dancer, Chiaro swept around. She caught the ninjas off guard, exposed in the open. Their faces were concealed in green cloth, except for the eyes. They moved together in a pack, sliding through the tide of shoppers. "Two ... three ... no, more. At least four of them." Her ballet moves brought her alongside Trouble. "Guess labor's cheap in Vietnam."

"And Flix has bucks to spend. Thanks for checking them out."

"Sure." As if on cue, they both looked down the street in different directions. It seemed normal, but felt tense. Striped awnings sheltered narrow merchant shops from the overhead sun. People were buying fresh greens and long white radishes, stuffing canvas totes with vegetables. Vendors sat cross-legged on the sidewalk, arguing with customers about the price of bean sprouts and pineapples. Trouble slid around a mountain of ice keeping fish cool. The blank, round buttons of their dead eyes stared passively back at him.

"See any unusual cars?" he asked.

"No. Just bicycles, mopeds, the usual stuff. You?"

"Yeah. Lime green stretch limo, weaving like crazy. People are honking at it in outrage. You hear them?" He accelerated, moving faster.

Chiaro bounced on the far curb, feeling safer just from being outside the traffic swirl. "I hear a lot of bells trilling. Some trumpet horns, those old fashioned hand squeeze things. It's hard to know what's normal for Hanoi traffic – and what's outrage, as you call it."

"Their car isn't normal for Hanoi. It looks a lot like one I saw in Manhattan when I found ninjas inside our shop. They aren't trying to hide anymore. They know we spotted them." He tried jogging. It wasn't easy. The sidewalks were narrow and jammed with poles, signs and people. A barber had set up shop in the street, with a turquoise beach umbrella sheltering a customer in a chair. A line of men waited their turn to be shaved and clipped. Trouble had to maneuver around a cluster of old men sipping beer. He wove past colored banners streaming from windows.

She fell in line with him. There wasn't room to run alongside. "I think the ninjas have changed plans. The car means they'll take us now, force you to reveal your contact."

"I think you're right." Trouble brushed against a man's shoulder and excused himself in English. But the tone of his voice said as much as his words and the man nodded.

Chiaro spun again. "They're closing on us. We have to do something."

"Got any ideas?"

"Yeah." She pointed at a theater in the distance. The building was painted wild colors. Neon signs in Vietnamese, English and French announced "Water Puppets Show."

"That's two blocks away," he complained. "See anything closer?"

"Nope." Chiaro took a risk. She hopped off the curb and sprinted, curving around motorbike riders waiting for a light to change.

Trouble followed, sensing the ninjas close behind. Suddenly, the light changed and loud engines ripped past. Their exhaust fumes polluted his overtaxed lungs, crying for dry air to breathe. A block at that pace left Trouble out of breath. He didn't notice vehicles congealing in front of him at another stoplight. He collided with the back of a micro-delivery van and bounced off.

Chiaro arrived and bent over, retching in the street. "I can't take this," she moaned.

"We have to keep going."

"I can't. Leave me. Run."

"No." The micro-van revved its engine, anticipating the light would change soon. He grabbed her arm. "Come on."

"What?" She tried to move and stumbled.

"Get on." Trouble indicated the tiny van's rear bumper.

"Oh, now you're thinking." She gratefully accepted the ride. Her street boots perched on a narrow metal strip.

The driver felt his van sag and looked in his mirrors. But Trouble and Chiaro were hidden by the van's cargo box. He popped a door to get out and inspect. Traffic surged and he changed his mind. The door slammed and he popped the clutch. Trouble lunged to grab a rack atop the van, barely catching the railing. He pulled himself aboard, grinning.

His satisfaction didn't last. A ninja snatched at his daypack and caught a loose strap. The man held tight, running behind the van, faster and faster. The daypack moved off Trouble's shoulder and he bent an arm, trapping the pack with his elbow. It became a tug of war, with Trouble holding the van's top rack and pulling against the ninja.

The van driver slapped his transmission into a higher gear, jerking forward. His speed increased, going faster than the ninja could run. Still, the martial arts expert refused to let go. He allowed himself to be dragged behind the van. His knees scraped along rough asphalt. It must have been very painful, for the man let out a howl of anguish and released his grip on Trouble's daypack.

A moped thumped over the ninja's green uniform, leaving dirty tire marks. The ninja rolled to his feet just as a hot looking motorcycle roared toward him. A swift leap became a kick, sending the motorcyclist tumbling off his bike. People swerved to avoid the downed rider. Motorcycles bashed into each other, creating a massive pileup. Smirking, the ninja limped away, but not before he shot Trouble and Chiaro a nasty look.

Despite a traffic jam, the lime green limo kept going. It vaulted a sidewalk, pushing away advertising signs, crushing vendor baskets. Tires running through fruits and vegetables sprayed colored juice over the car's panels, turning the vehicle into a work of modern art. The injured ninja hobbled toward the approaching car and almost got squashed. Ignoring their comrade, ninjas inside the car pressed their attack on Trouble and Chiaro.

The delivery van slowed for a turn. "Here's where we get off." Trouble leapt for the curb, followed by Chiaro. They bounced off a storefront and looked for the Water Puppet Theater.

"Behind us," Chiaro sighed.

"No, it can't be." Trouble looked along the street and saw she was right. To make the theater, they had to run toward the ninjas, not away from them. Yet there didn't seem to be anywhere else to hide.

"Might as well try." She put on a burst of speed and Trouble followed, weaving through a dense crowd of stunned onlookers.

Surprised, the limo flew past them and slammed to a halt. A moment of confusion was followed by screeching tires. The stench of burning rubber even reached Trouble's nose.

He couldn't waste time watching the limo snake backwards, its engine screaming in high revs. The car had to be close. Trouble heard its tires thump on the sidewalk and a trash can fly into the street. At the theater, he and Chiaro got a break.

The ticket taker was chatting with a friend and had his back to them when they sprinted past. The friend became agitated and began sputtering about gate crashers. The theater employee turned around to see ninjas exiting the limo, hurtling toward the entrance. Thinking they were the gate crashers, the foolish employee put himself in their way. He demanded payment. A brief exchange ended in a stomach punch, sending the employee sprawling, clutching his abdomen. Ninjas stormed the theater, looking for Trouble and Chiaro.

Inside, a swimming pool held wooden puppets floating in the tank, maneuvered with long rods. Stage lights highlighted the puppets' bright colors. A vivid green dragon with gold scales breathed smoke and slithered after a wealthy mandarin. Tired servant puppets carried the mandarin, lying on a red gurney. Their faces were chalk white with carved black features. An orchestra in silk robes played traditional Vietnamese string instruments and wooden gourds. A high-pitched flute mimicked bird songs. A medley of colored flags wagged through the air like a flight of birds. The eerie music was interrupted by crackling fireworks and flashing blue lights. The ninjas fanned out, spreading themselves along the rows, inspecting the audience.

Behind the ninjas, Trouble and Chiaro hid under velvet theater curtains. The green menace committed their full attention to the audience and Trouble signaled Chiaro it was time to leave. On tiptoe, they slid from the theater into bright sunlight.

Ahead of them, the lime green stretch limo sat abandoned. Collisions with vendor stalls left every fender dented. Spider webs of smashed glass laced its windshield. The hood buckled from a head-on smash up with a pole. A tire was going flat. Worst of all, the car smelled like old fruit rotting in the sun. A vegetable and fruit smoothie blotched the limo's sides as though a giant barfed on the car. Even in that horrible state, the limo was their best chance for a quick escape. Its keys were in

Vietnamese Water Puppets

the ignition. The powerful engine idled in surging rumbles.

"Too bad I don't know how to drive a car," Trouble groaned.

"I do." Chiaro flew to the driver's side and jumped in the seat, slamming her door. "Get in."

He looked at her in amazement. "You're kidding."

"I said I could drive and I mean it." She patted a seat, inviting him.

Down the block, the injured ninja limped toward the damaged limousine. When he spotted Trouble and Chiaro, the wounded ninja let out a howl of anger.

Knowing they were out of time, Trouble hopped in the car. Chiaro revved the engine and ground the transmission into first gear. She released the clutch and the car shot forward like it was fired from a cannon. Motorbikes swerved to dodge a rocketing green menace.

"OK," she admitted. "I'm still learning."

15

Gritting his teeth, Trouble endured Chiaro's manic driving. He was amazed no one was killed yet, especially himself. She floored the limo and its gears screeched in complaint. The green car swerved around a sudden corner and squealed through a row of flower stalls. Dented fenders knocked over metal buckets, spilling a dazzling floral array in the street. Golden sunflowers tumbled over pale blue lilacs. Yellow bells of daffodils tangled with red gladiolas. Vivid bouquets carpeted the busy street in a burst of color. Petals and stalks were crushed under the wheels of impatient scooters and zooming mopeds.

Chiaro's eyes darted to the rear view mirror. "Looks like we ditched 'em." She straightened the wheel and said. "Whaddya say? I heard you mumble something."

"I asked how you learned to drive a car with a stick shift."

"My father taught me."

"I thought he was in jail for a jewel heist."

"Before he went to prison, my dad showed me how to slim-jim a car window to snap open the lock. He let me hot wire the ignition. Then he took me to an empty parking lot and taught me to drive."

"That's illegal. You're lucky you didn't go to jail with him."

"Naw. We put the car back, right where we found it. No dents. Just a little wire hanging under the dashboard. That's all." She turned the limo and ran over a curb, edging close to a shop offering wicker bird cages. They bounced in their seats. "Don't worry. I'll turn wider next time. Still learning, like I said."

"Yeah. Um, Chiaro, like how many times did your dad take you on a driving lesson?"

"Once." Grinning, she took her eyes off the road to look at him. A wall of cars, scooters and peasants on bicycles loomed ahead. Entire families rode a single moped, with kids wedged in the laps of driver and passenger. Chiming bells and shrill horns bashed the air with loud noise. The tide of approaching traffic was getting close. Chiaro slammed on the brakes, squeezing the rubbery pedal to the floor. The abrupt stop pushed Trouble into the dashboard with a bruising grunt.

"Phew. That was close. You OK?"

He rubbed a sore arm. "Yeah. No seatbelts in the car. Guess wearing a seatbelt isn't ninja-like. Too safety oriented." He saw an English street sign and recognized the name. "Turn there. We're close. Gotta ditch this car and walk a few blocks."

"Can't we park closer? My legs are still tired from all that running. And the air-conditioning in this car is kinda nice, you know."

"Chiaro," he lectured her, "this limo stands out. Someone's gonna see it and tell the ninjas. They probably have spies everywhere. They'll search the neighborhood where they find the limo, looking for us."

"All right," she groaned. Chiaro swerved the car, arcing through a wave of oncoming motorbikes. The flurry of motors sounded like they were flying through buzzing hornets.

He yelled over droning engines. "That alley is good."

"Sure." Chiaro turned too wide this time, knocking down a pole. An awning crumpled behind them, setting off angry shouts from street vendors.

The long alley twisted and curved, a narrow spine of asphalt. Garbage cans and old baskets hugged the cramped passageway. Suddenly, their path ended in a wall stenciled with advertisements and cell phone numbers. Scooters and motorbikes sat crammed against the wall like sheep in a stockyard pen. Chiaro mashed the brake pedal and tires squealed. Rubber smoke billowed through open car windows, flooding Trouble's nose with acrid odors. He braced for the worst.

The car slid, turning completely around. The limo jerked to a halt, its rear bumper touching one of the motorbikes. At first, it seemed no damage was done to anything, other than burnt tire rubber. Then, a scooter toppled, setting off a domino effect. More bikes fell in a cascade of noise, loud as a dump truck unloading scrap metal.

Chiaro looked sheepish. "Uh, oh. We better get out of here."

Trouble tried to force his door open and couldn't. Fallen motorcycles prevented the door from swinging outward. Toppled chrome frames and black leather seats were layered on top of more frames and bent kickstands, like a motorbike shop that dumped its inventory in the street for a year-end sale. He squirmed through the door window, his ears assaulted with screams of anguish from bike riders. They looked down, peering at the mess from balconies above the alley.

His shoes hit ground and Trouble ran, fast as he could, to get away from an angry mob. He didn't have to tell Chiaro what to do. She kept pace despite sore muscles and heat fatigue. They ran from the alley and sprinted a long block, until burning lungs forced them to halt. They stood under an awning, panting, gasping for air.

Out of breath, Chiaro struggled to ask a question. "How ... far ... to ... where ... we're going?"

"Not far," he gasped. Trouble straightened from his bent posture. He looked around. In the distance, he spotted a bright yellow tour van, small enough to fit down narrow streets. Red lettering in a dozen languages announced shopping tours in Old Town, a picturesque enclave with buildings dating from the 1400s. His eyes tracked the yellow van until it vanished from sight. "We're going that way."

"Oh, good. You know where to go." Chiaro felt relieved, certain they'd soon be resting in a trendy café, drinking a cool beverage.

They entered Old Town through a wall built around a huge tree. The strangler fig's leafy canopy shaded the wall and several homes. The tree appeared to melt on houses like thick syrup. Over decades, strangler fig roots buckled walls like a squeezing python. Crushed stone blocks were swallowed into the center of the expanding tree. Rings of growth increased the thick trunk. New sprouts helped feed and support branches longer than a big rig tractor-trailer truck. At ground level, the tree became

Old Town Hanoi Residence Damaged By Strangler Fig Tree

an impromptu Buddhist temple. Burning incense sticks jutted from knobs and tiny gift flasks of rice whiskey peppered crevices.

They walked through the tree and found Hanoi's Old Quarter to be a tangle of curving lanes, with few street signs. There was barely enough room to squeeze between tides of people. Vendors hawked rolls of cloth and plastic bags of vivid dyes, displaying more wares in the street than in their narrow shop front. The encroachment was so bad a peasant delivering brooms had to walk her bicycle along the street. She moved like a worm, wriggling through shop displays.

Narrow footpaths wove through a maze of goldsmiths and porcelain merchants. In an alley, craftsmen bent over large curves of

Broom Vendor Walks Her Bicycle Through Old Town Hanoi

buffalo horn. They carved chunks of translucent bone into chopsticks or candle holders. Tourists hunched around the artists to watch their sharp, polished blades shape the next object.

Each lane in Old Town harbored related specialties. Modern boutiques shared a block with silk tailors, crafting traditional Vietnamese and Chinese style garments. A twisting alley held student hostels for backpackers travelling with little money. A street of kites and paper lanterns in hot colors transitioned to somber blacks for grave headstones. That curving lane ran into a wider street. Here, multilevel homes were built in a plantation style. These façades dated from a brief era of French colonial rule in Vietnam. Every street had one thing in common. Shop fronts and homes appeared to be amazingly small, some being only six feet wide.

Trouble halted before a home larger than its neighbors. The three-story building was only wide enough to be a one car garage in an

American suburb. He checked his notes. "I think this is the place."

Chiaro looked at him like he was crazy. "You said this guy was rich."

"He is."

She didn't buy it. "Nobody rich lives in this home. I mean, yeah, the place is three stories. But the front's small as one of those vendor stalls." She pointed at the other side of the street, where striped awnings covered a parade of shops.

Trouble shrugged. "Look, you could be right. But I gotta try. This is the best fit to what I know. Stay out here if you want. I'm goin' inside. OK?"

She looked around, feeling nervous. "I'd rather come with you. I stay out here and a ninja might see me."

"Fine." Trouble walked under a porch and went through a pair of open doors thick enough to guard a fortress. Behind the doors was a reception area with ornate carved wooden chairs, tea tables and Japanese paintings. The décor was heavy with dark, thick wood. Red paper lanterns and banners provided color. Black wood pillars were embroidered with silver lettering in oriental languages Trouble couldn't decipher. Royal blue curtains separated the reception area from other quarters beyond. A pretty woman in a blue sarong matching the curtains rose from her desk to greet them.

She guessed from their clothing they were American and spoke in English. "You've come to visit someone?"

"Um, yes. I'm here to find Dr. Tran Van Cam."

"Your business with him?" Her expression remained pleasant, but her body stiffened.

"We're friends. It's a social visit, not business." Trouble slouched on purpose, hoping to look more casual.

"I see." She waited a moment, thinking about her next question. "You met Dr. Cam on a previous visit to our trading house?" Her eyes flicked to Chiaro, then locked again on Trouble.

"Well, I didn't exactly meet him. I was too young to remember anything. Just a baby. My parents met Dr. Cam. I found your address in their notebooks." He drew a faded snapshot from his daypack and gave it to her. The photo showed his mother pushing a stroller holding Trouble. His father and Dr. Cam had their arms across each other's shoulders in a gesture of friendship. They stood under lanterns with gold symbols and streaming tassels. The lamps in the photograph still hung from the merchant's exposed beam sealing.

She took the snapshot from Trouble and glanced down. A quick smile and her posture thawed. "You were much smaller then."

"You recall the visit?" Trouble felt hopeful.

"I too was smaller. Yes, I remember your parents. They are well, I hope." She handed the photo back to him.

"I don't know. They've been missing for two years. I've reason to believe Dr. Cam saw my parents recently. I was hoping to talk to him. Is he home?"

"My brother no longer lives with us." Her voice turned cautious. She peeked around them to make sure they weren't being followed.

Trouble returned the precious photo to his daypack. "Can I leave a message for Dr. Cam? Maybe he'd be willing to phone me."

"On your cell? No." Her fingers moved toward the desk, touching a hidden button. The gesture wasn't lost on Trouble. He knew she was summoning help, in case it was needed to toss them out.

"Why can't Dr. Cam phone me?" Trouble stiffened, resentful at being thwarted when he seemed close to his goal.

Answering the buzzer, a man appeared in the doorway framed by a blue curtain. He wore loose black clothing and stood with his feet apart, hands flat on his stomach. "I can answer your question. Dr. Cam won't talk on cell phones. Vietnam's wireless network was installed by a Russian company, working with our government's Ministry of Internal Security. In other words, no cell phone conversation in Vietnam should be regarded as private. Others may be listening."

Chiaro moved alongside Trouble. She asked, "Is there another way to contact Dr. Cam, to arrange a meeting, perhaps?"

"That's up to grandfather. It's his choice, not ours. We must respect the judgment of our elders." His answer went to Chiaro and Trouble. But his stern look was directed at the woman in the blue sarong.

She nodded and went back to her desk, busying herself with correspondence.

Chiaro nudged Trouble, urging him to speak.

"Yeah. So could we talk to your grandfather?" he asked.

"Grandfather spends this hour with an old friend. It is a precious time for him. Interrupting them weighs heavily on me."

"We could return later. What hour is best?" Trouble fought to present a friendly smile. It didn't work.

"Try again tomorrow. I will tell grandfather of your visit. If he wishes to see you, I'll bring you inside." The man's face went stony. The conversation was over. They were to leave.

"See you tomorrow morning, then." Trouble waved goodbye. He also waved at the woman, but she didn't look up.

"Ten a.m. OK?" Chiaro asked. But the man had already vanished. The blue curtain was no longer pulled back. It was closed, swaying gently from being released.

They turned to leave. Behind them, a soft whisper floated a pair of words, "Ten minutes."

Chiaro and Trouble looked at each other in amazement. They spun around, staring at the woman behind the writing desk. She didn't look at them. But all five fingers on one hand flashed twice, repeating her message in silent code.

Trouble smiled. It looked like he might get help after all. "Let's get a snack, huh? Walk around a bit."

"Yeah. I'm starved." Chiaro sounded like she meant it.

They walked past the thick outer doors and he whispered, "You really hungry?"

"Definitely. But I don't see any restaurants."

"Maybe in the next block." He gestured along a thread of bare pavement winding between vendor displays. Sidewalks were heaped with clay pots in a variety of sizes, from small rosebuds to large cauldrons.

The pots were stacked in a pink and brown terracotta pyramid. Over the top row of pots hung carved puppets, draped in bright theater silks, looking like colorful laundry. The sizzle of hot oil and fast chopping sounds escaped nearby kitchens. Smells of peanut oil and cilantro leaked into the street.

A brief exploration located a tiny restaurant, with a screen hiding activity inside the kitchen. "Better be fast food. We don't have much time." Chiaro tapped her wristwatch. She looked at a menu printed only in Vietnamese. Chiaro asked a woman behind the counter. "English?"

The waitress nodded.

Chiaro tried a longer question. "English menu?"

The woman nodded again. She reached under the counter and produced an inkjet printout slid inside a plastic sleeve. Struggling to pronounce the words, she announced, "Very … good." Her finger pointed at the most expensive items the restaurant sold.

Trouble looked at them and teased Chiaro. "I'm willing. Are you?"

"Dog meat seasoned with extract of giant water bug? You gotta be kidding." Chiaro rolled her eyes in disgust.

"Well, there's always boiled porcupine with its quills on the side. For toothpicks, I assume."

"Oh, this is unreal. You're bluffing. You won't eat this stuff."

"Maybe if I'm hungry enough. But not today." Trouble handed back the menu. "Thanks. But not for us." He smiled and nodded.

"No?" the woman asked. "Very fresh." Her narrow finger pointed to a wicker basket on the ground. The bodies of pigeons lay heaped in the basket, their skin pimpled with goose bumps where feathers were torn out.

Chiaro wagged her head and yanked Trouble's arm. "Let's get outta here before she offers us samples."

"Fine with me." He smiled politely and stepped outside. From down the street came a delicious odor. A man using a cinderblock for an impromptu hibachi was cooking meat. Fine strips were trapped in a mesh clamp, roasting over a charcoal fire. He'd taken the shield off a desk fan and was using its whirring blades to blow aroma in the street, attracting customers.

His simple menu was translated in a dozen languages. Chiaro and Trouble could eat any food they wanted – as long as it was Bún Chá. The Bún part proved to be rice noodles dipped in a papaya sauce, promising a sweet and sour taste. Chá was pork barbecuing on the hibachi. A picture indicated crunchy greens, hot peppers and pickled garlic could be added.

The flavor combination teased Chiaro's stomach and it rumbled. Shamed by the noise, she blushed. "Sorry."

"No problem. Noise during meals is a compliment in Asian countries." Not wanting to be rude by pointing, Trouble leaned his head in the direction of a gentleman slurping noodles from a bowl.

"Can we really get some?" Chiaro couldn't believe it. Hot food. New flavors. It was too good to be true – and it was.

"Take out?" Trouble asked, hoping the man knew a little tourist English.

"Sure thing." He laid the hot mesh on a cool cinderblock and rose from his squat. A few steps inside the restaurant, he grabbed white cartons sealed with lids. "Phở Bò or Phở Gà?" Sensing their confusion, he explained. "You want your rice noodle soup with beef or chicken?"

"There's no Bún Chá takeout?" Chiaro almost whimpered.

"Sorry. Vietnamese believe in comprehensive eating. We lay out all ingredients at once, so you can have full appreciation from all five senses – sight, smell, touch, sound, taste. Bún Chá is a sit down meal. Half hour, at least."

"We'll settle for takeout. I want beef." He glanced at Chiaro. She looked crushed – so close and yet so far from her goal.

"Chicken." She made the word sound the way sharp gravel felt to bare feet.

"Cold or hot?" The owner pointed at a microwave.

Trouble checked his watch. "How long to heat?"

"Five minutes each. Not long." He smiled.

"Cold," was Trouble's quick reply.

"Cold," she echoed in a sad voice.

The owner took their money, made change and returned to his ritual of fanning smells to attract customers.

Chiaro and Trouble squatted at a table and made a few hesitant slurps. The watery soup had a sour, pickled flavor and the tiny scraps of meat looked a weird gray. The broth smelled like a sweaty t-shirt. When the owner wasn't watching, they threw his cartons in the trash.

He looked up when they went past him. "Good, yes?"

"Great." Chiaro gave the owner a warm smile.

They walked a few steps. "You can go back for the Bún Chá," Trouble offered. "Tonight."

"I'll go back in another lifetime." Chiaro said it with a bitterness forged in a childhood of disappointments.

"Well, let's see what happens next. Maybe we'll get a break. Contacting my dad's agent will be easy."

"I doubt it," Chiaro snapped. "Nothing about this trip's been easy, so far."

16

Trouble and Chiaro stood across the street from the merchant's home, staring at its French Colonial façade. A heavy timber frame supported pale stucco walls. The house resembled a narrow Parisian home, except for red tiles on the pagoda-style roof. A nest of wires ran overhead like a sun shade, casting a mesh of shadows on the home. Trouble glanced at the afternoon sun and double-checked his wristwatch. "She told us to come back in ten minutes. Where is she?"

Mesh Of Power, Phone, & TV Cables Above Old Town Hanoi

"I dunno." Chiaro rubbed her stomach. "I'm too hungry to care."

"We'll eat soon," he promised, gesturing at nearby market stalls.

A vendor approached them, stepping over wooden bowls of eggs and brussel sprouts. She wore wrinkled pajamas, dyed the dark purple color of eggplant. White whiskers sprouted on her upper lip like an old caterpillar. Fine lines covered her cheeks, giving her skin the texture of dry leather, buckled from too much time under a harsh sun. The senior citizen held up a basket of limes, offering them for purchase. "You buy?"

Trouble wagged his head. "No limes. Sorry."

The woman scowled. "No buy, no stay here. You leave. Make room for customers."

As a "parking fee," Trouble offered her a coin for one of the limes.

Hanoi Old Town Marketplace

"Not enough." She plucked a lime from the basket and sniffed it. "Very fresh. Picked today. Best limes in Hanoi."

He doubled the offer and she looked tempted. "You have bag?"

"To carry one lime?" He felt astonished.

The woman spotted his daypack. She took his coins and gestured to his pack.

Trouble unslung the nylon hiking bag and opened the top zipper. He expected the merchant to drop a lime inside. Instead, she dumped the entire basket of fruit. There wasn't enough room and green balls bounced on the ground, rolling away.

The vendor woman pointed at errant limes, scurrying in all directions. "Your fruit. You get. Hurry. Others take."

To appease the woman, Trouble bent over and collected a few limes. But every time he reached for some limes, he lost more from his open pack than he grabbed.

Chiaro started giggling at his predicament.

"OK, what's so funny?" he snapped.

"You." She zipped his pack. "Forget the rest of them."

"Why? I mean, I paid maybe ten cents for a hundred of them. Shouldn't I get my money's worth?" Trouble laughed at himself.

"You did. Got more time on the parking meter." Her eyes flicked to the house across the street. "Looks like we didn't need the time, though."

Trouble followed her gaze, peering through dense shadows cast by a rat's nest of power lines, TV cables and phone lines running over his head. Hands were pulling aside the blue curtain and tying it back. His excitement died when a man stepped through the open curtain. It was the same guy who'd stalled them earlier.

Instinctively, they moved backwards, drifting into shadows. Their feet scattered dropped limes, kicking the small balls in every direction. Trouble and Chiaro watched the guy look around for a moment, then walk toward the Bún Chá restaurant. They waited for him to vanish around a corner.

"You wanna try it?" Chiaro offered, pointing at the open curtain.

Trouble thought for a moment. "Yeah." He stepped toward the merchant's home, ignoring limes splattering under his shoes. Chiaro followed, adding to the mushy green trail.

The vendor woman quit acting like a peasant who knew only tourist English. Angered by their mess, she yelled at them. "Hey, you two. Come back here and clean up this mess. Right now. Or I'll call the police. Have them take your passports."

They were almost to the blue curtain when the street vendor caught Trouble's arm and tugged hard.

"Here." The woman stuck a broom and dustpan in his face. "Clean up now. Or I'll have you arrested for vandalism."

Trouble looked at her in astonishment. "Where'd you learn to speak American like that?"

"Saigon – I mean, Ho Chi Minh City. I grew up there, in an orphanage for war children. They wanted our fathers to visit and take us home with them, to America. So they taught us your language. Now get busy." She gave Trouble another scolding look and yanked on his arm, pulling him backwards.

Trouble was about to grab the broom when Chiaro intervened. "I'm sorry about the mess. Could I pay you to clean for us?" Chiaro poured a mound of coins in the woman's hand.

"You're lucky things are slow. Otherwise …" She gave them an angry frown. But the broom went to work, pushing slimy pulp into a dustpan.

"Come on, before she changes her mind." Trouble slid toward the open blue curtain. He was forced to halt and Chiaro was unable to stop. She collided with his back.

"Why'd you quit?" Chiaro grumbled.

He moved over so she could look. Ahead of them, the receptionist stood with a finger to her lips, requesting silence. When they nodded to show understanding, the receptionist beckoned them inside. She led them into a meeting hall with elegant Japanese décor. Tiers of wooden balconies ran around the large room. Exposed beams crisscrossed the open area, leading to a distant roof.

They walked from the long but narrow meeting room to a courtyard lined with Shiva statues. The bronze Indian figures encircled the area. Every sculpture's forehead was decorated with a third eye. Trouble felt uncomfortable around the statues, as if they could read his thoughts. He cleared his mind and studied patterns of bright tiles. The trail of colors led to intricate lacework panels. Whitewashed walls made the area feel like a miniature Taj Mahal palace, the grandest and most famous building in India.

Shiva Statue

The home's next section formed traditional Vietnamese sleeping quarters, with screened bed areas. Mattresses were thin padding on wooden planks. A short roll served as pillow. The only modern fixture in a "bedroom" was mosquito netting, a deterrent to the ever-present threat of malaria.

They walked through an archway, entering a kitchen that might have come from a Manhattan restaurant. The area was packed with an industrial gas stove, stainless steel counters and refrigerators built into walls. Racks of pots and pans hung overhead. Magnets held an impressive array of knives in suspended animation. In the center, a prep island allowed cooks access to sinks. Fitted under the prep table, a wine cooler kept a collection of expensive vintages safe from tropical heat. Rubber mats covered a floor fitted with drains so everything could be hosed down for easy cleaning after a meal.

Their shocks didn't end with the kitchen, however. The dining area beyond was air-conditioned and cloned from a Paris bistro. A zinc bar claimed one wall. Mirrored shelves supported a world-class array of liquor bottles and cocktail glasses. Industrial strength espresso makers smelled of that morning's brew, though their brass shown as brightly as the bar's mirrors.

The other wall was lined with plush banquettes. Opposing the leather seating were marble tables and wicker chairs. That type of furniture is found in cafés lining Avenue des Champs-Élysées, often called the most expensive strip of real estate in the world. Rent for an exclusive shop on that boulevard reaches $150,000 a square foot.

"You're right," Chiaro hissed.

"About what?" Trouble whispered. He had no idea what she meant.

"This is definitely the home of a wealthy merchant. Maxy bucks he has. The force is with him."

"I told you so. You never believe me." Trouble bumped the edge of a Carrera marble table and it didn't even tremble. But his leg hurt from the encounter. "Ouch," he muttered.

The receptionist hissed at them. "Argue outside, where no one can hear us." She opened thick glass doors and they walked from an ice cube tray into a hot shower. The shocking temperature change vanished from their minds when they saw a stunning view from the merchant's terrace.

It was a scene from a Hollywood movie. Below them, a crazy swirl of cars and motorbikes hummed past, blurring in a surf of traffic. The buzzing necklace of motion became a counterpoint to a vast, tranquil lake beyond. At the near end of that lake, the red trestles of Morning Sunlight Bridge arced to Jade Island. Waving flags and bustling tourists added motion to the bridge's timeless curves. In contrast, the pagoda of Turtle Tower sat in tranquil isolation, appearing to float in the middle of Sword Lake.

For a moment, they stared in reverence at the view, forgetting why they'd come. Then the receptionist sighed and broke the mood. "We have little time," she explained. "You must be gone when my husband returns."

Chiaro felt shocked. "Your husband? I assumed he was your brother. I apologize."

"There is no need to apologize." The receptionist bent her head in a sorrowful look. "Ours was an arranged marriage, a merging of two powerful families. That is what my husband meant when he said we must respect my grandfather's decisions. My husband knows I will never learn to love him. In his opinion, I don't even respect him. I'm too Western in my thoughts, he says."

"Wow. That must be tough. I'm sorry." Trouble hoped to console her.

"Thank you for your sympathy. But our time is short. You came to see my grandfather."

"He's here?" Trouble let his eagerness show.

"No." She leaned on the terrace railing and pointed in the distance, at the lake. "He's there, playing 'Go' with a friend. It's a game of mental skill that many consider more challenging than chess. My husband is right about one thing."

"What's that?" Chiaro wondered.

"My grandfather will be very irritated at having his concentration broken. It may spoil a game position he's labored to achieve."

Trouble offered a solution. "Maybe we could wait 'til their match ends. How long does a game last?"

"Months." The receptionist gave a sad laugh. "I doubt you can wait that long."

"Uh, no." Trouble stared at the lakeside, where dozens of pairs were huddled over game boards. "Which one's your grandfather?"

Chiaro also peered at Sword Lake with the same question. "I bet your grandpa's over there." She pointed to a lovely spot under a tree shaped like a weeping willow. A pair of men sat there, lost in concentration. They were hypnotized by the next move in their game, unaware of bright kites flying in the cloudless sky or the tranquil water. No one else was near them, though the remainder of the lake crawled with activity.

"You're right," the receptionist confirmed. "My grandfather values his privacy."

"And he's got the juice to get it – even in a public park." Chiaro whistled. "Impressive."

"Yeah. Which means I need to ask a few questions." Trouble took his eyes off the lake and put them on the receptionist. "Like what do I say to your grandfather when I get there?"

The receptionist put her lips close to Trouble's ear and whispered.

"That's it?" Trouble wanted to be sure.

She nodded.

"I hope your grandfather speaks English, because I can't even pronounce the Vietnamese words in my tourist guidebook."

"Nothing at all?" The receptionist looked upset. Then she had an idea. "Do you speak any French?"

"Some. But what good will that do? I thought older Vietnamese men hated the French, from when Vietnam was a colony of France."

She nodded. "Normally, you're right. But my grandfather was raised by a French colonist. That man's connections gave my grandfather his start in business."

"Adopted?" Chiaro was curious.

"No. My great-grandmother was one of the rich man's servants. I'm told she was beautiful. The colonist broke up with his wife. She went home to France. He stayed here and was eventually killed." The receptionist indicated they must leave, pointing at glass doors to the dining area.

The trio went from steaming tropical to restoring air conditioning and back to humidity, passing through the house. Chiaro again burned with curiosity. "Why'd you make the house so narrow?" she asked.

"In America, you get taxed on square footage. Your government multiplies the length of your house by its width and sends you a bill. Here, we are taxed only by how much of the street we use. We get a bill for the width of our home. That's why our buildings are tube houses – narrow but long."

She paused at a blue curtain separating the entryway and her reception desk from the rest of the tube home. She calmed herself and peeked outside. "It's safe. Hurry. My uncles will take you to the lake. Wait down the street. They'll find you."

"Thank you." Trouble offered to shake her hand, but she refused.

"Just go, before my husband sees you and gets angry. He has a bad temper." She rolled up a sleeve and showed a bruise on her arm.

Chiaro winced. "We're going."

Trouble waved goodbye, feeling grateful yet anxious. He wished the "uncles" were already there.

17

"We're going the wrong way. We're eating Bún Chá next. You promised, remember? The place is back there." Chiaro jabbed her thumb in the restaurant's direction, where small tables clustered on the sidewalk. The area was so tightly packed that strangers brushed knees when they bent to swallow noodles pushed in their mouths by chopsticks.

"Wish we could indulge in Bún Chá. But the receptionist's husband is down there, somewhere. I don't want to run into him. Don't forget the bruise on her arm. That dude has a nasty temper."

"Then how about a banana?" She pointed at bunches of the yellow fruit, hanging in a vendor's stall. The hot climate caused the bananas to speckle, painting their skin with brown splotches. Their ripe smell was carried in the air like icky sweet fruit punch.

Trouble wrinkled his nose at the overripe banana odor. He yanked the guidebook from his daypack and flipped pages. "Book says don't eat anything that isn't cooked."

"So we should eat Bún Chá," she grumbled, rubbing her stomach.

Trouble scowled at her. "We can't eat until I talk to the grandfather. Our rides should be here any ..." He quit speaking in mid-sentence. His eyes caught a glimpse of green streaks darting among vendor stalls, leaping over wire cages holding clucking chickens. The figures moved through shadows, leaving a trail of feathers in their wake. Their lithe bodies threaded between sidewalk bowls of fresh melons and colorful shop banners. "Oh, no. The ninjas have been searching for us. They found us again."

Chiaro spun around, feeling panic tighten her muscles. "There's gotta be a way to escape," she muttered. "What about them?" She nodded toward a pair of old guys pedaling Cyclos. The gray haired seniors threaded their part-bicycle, part-wheelchair rickshaws through a mobbed street.

Hanoi Cyclo Waiting for a Passenger

Both men saw the American kids at the same time and headed for the tourist duo. The Cyclos squeaked to a halt and the men gestured for Trouble and Chiaro to hop in their passenger seats.

Desperate to escape, she jumped in a Cyclo. The wheelchair sank from her weight. "Get in the other one," she urged Trouble.

"We'll miss our ride to the grandfather," he argued.

"He's sitting by the lake. We'll have these guys take us there, after we ditch the ninjas." Chiaro turned to check on the green blurs and screamed.

Frightened by her yell, Trouble jumped backwards. A rod shaped like a railroad spike flew past his knees. The heavy rod vanished in a stack of bananas, smashing them to pulp. Yellow goo splattered everywhere. There was no longer any question of waiting for their rides to arrive. Trouble hopped in the other Cyclo and urged his driver to take off.

The man responded, grunting his vehicle into motion. Chiaro led, followed by Trouble's Cyclo. Both drivers seemed to instinctively sense their client's desire for speed. The men pushed through a dense crowd, weaving around an endless series of obstacles. Handlebar-mounted bells twilled and chimed, yet only a few people heeded the warning. The marketplace was clogged with shoppers. Soft pajamas and rough jeans brushed against the Cyclos as the drivers pedaled through a human swarm. Slowed by pedestrians, the Cyclos weren't able to outrun determined ninjas.

"You gotta hurry," Chiaro yelled over her shoulder. She hoped the old man could understand her tone. She doubted he spoke English.

He nodded politely and kept the same pace, weaving left and right. Always, his thumb whirled the bell on his handlebars, blasting chimes into Chiaro's ears.

Sensing ninjas getting close enough to grab him, Trouble rose in his seat. He was ready to leap out and make a run for it. But the drivers swerved in unison, turning into an alley filled with garbage. Rotting cabbage and raw fish guts were stinking in the humid air. The Cyclo drivers put on a burst of speed Trouble wouldn't have believed possible, if he wasn't experiencing it. Their bicycle chains clanked when their feet pedaled faster. He was shoved down in his chair from the acceleration. Every pothole and alley crevice bounced the Cyclos' suspension. More speed made the ride extra bumpy. The bony knees of the driver punched against Trouble's back through a flimsy seat. The peddling seniors shifted their bikes to a higher gear and overflowing rubbish bins flew past Trouble.

Without warning, the Cyclos skidded around a corner, sliding like race cars drifting through a turn. The experienced Cyclo drivers clipped the apex of the turn and poured on yet more speed. Trouble grabbed the sides of his wheelchair for support to avoid slipping off. Humid air rushed at his face. He inhaled a weird mix of body odor and ginger. He looked ahead to see where they were going and froze in horror. Side by side, the cycling duo were racing into a dead end alley. The tiny street quit at a solid wooden fence, preventing further progress. Yet they must have been going forty miles an hour.

Trouble curled himself into a ball on the seat, hoping the injuries wouldn't be fatal. He counted down like a rocket launch at Cape Canaveral. "Three ... two ... one ..." There was a terrific smack when the Cyclos' front rail hit the fence. Trouble cringed, expecting the worst.

Instead, the wood pivoted, flying upward on a hinge. The seniors laid on brakes, turning sideways like a kid pulling a Brody on his bicycle, leaving a rubber streak on the asphalt. The drivers hopped from their seats and ran to the fence, yanking it down. Bolts locked the wood in place. Sunlight poured through seams in the fence, mixed with streaks of green.

A loud crash was followed by another. Wooden planks in the fence bent, but didn't break. At first, ninjas smashed the wood with their bodies, assuming the fence would swing upward like it once did. Then vicious kicks rocked the fence. But hardwood reinforced by iron bars proved stronger than karate chops. Angry curses bounced off the planks like the futile kicks. The old men watched hard blows knock dust from the planks, smiling at each other. They seemed to be saying "we still have youth in these old bodies."

The drivers resumed their places on the Cyclos and pedaled at a

Ninja!

sedate pace, rolling past street performers. Boom boxes pulsed an oriental version of hip-hop. Wanna-be rappers alternated Kung Fu moves with breakdancing. Competitors used an impromptu stage made of old crates to hold their version of *American Idol.* Around the performers, taxis honked, roaring after kids on scooters.

A flurry of motorbikes passed Trouble's wheelchair like a flock of noisy birds. Grateful for the rescue, Trouble didn't want to offend the men. Yet he was eager to get to the lake and talk to the family patriarch. He dragged out his tourist guide, smelling like an air freshener from all the limes in his daypack. Pages flew under his thumb, rolling back and forth until he found a map of Hanoi. Turning around, he showed the diagram, pointing at Sword Lake.

Next, Trouble flipped to the phrase-finder section, where they taught Americans to say Vietnamese words. He tried pronouncing, "Doi moo-an same ho." The words brought a twinkling smile to the old man's eyes, but got no response. Trouble showed the Vietnamese spelling, "Toâi muoán xem hoà."

The driver pointed. Tranquil lake waters spread in front of them, lined by an oasis of shade trees. Green waters surrounded red anchor posts holding the curved arc of Sunbeam Bridge. In the mid-afternoon sun, a few people were practicing Tai Chi on the red bridge. They flexed their palms, pushing their hands through air as if pressing through an invisible wall. The Cyclos seemed to get energy from the martial arts display. They pedaled faster through boulevard traffic, crossing lanes to arrive at a curb near Sword Lake. Both vehicles stopped only yards from the old men playing Go.

Wealthy Merchant & Friend At Sword Lake

Trouble stared at the elderly players, hunched over a wooden board tiled with black and white stones. The men wore fine silk pajamas and their bodies were frozen in concentration. They were human statues. Only their eyes moved, tracing imagined paths on the game board.

Chiaro broke the silence, speaking in a humble voice. "Guess the ride's over."

"Uh, yeah. I should pay them." He offered paper money, but the drivers wagged their heads.

"You sure?" Trouble pleaded. "I mean, you saved our lives."

The men gestured for Chiaro and Trouble to dismount. When the duo left their chairs, the drivers pedaled away without so much as a goodbye wave.

Trouble watched the Cyclos vanish in the chaos of Hanoi traffic. "Gotta find a way to thank them," he muttered.

"They must have been the uncles we heard about," Chiaro suggested. "Maybe the receptionist paid them."

"Yeah, that makes sense." He turned away from the boulevard. After a moment's hesitation, Trouble decided to approach the old players huddled over a game board. They were only a couple yards away, a brief walk. He took a step, then another. Under shade trees, inside parked cars, along the lake's edge, men in dark suits turned and scowled. Trouble could feel the heat of their stares. Another step and a pair of them broke into a run. To appear non-threatening, Trouble halted and waited for the security men to arrive.

They didn't know English or French. But they did know intimidation. Unbuttoned coats revealed the bulge under their arms was a holstered gun. A pair of rough hands on Trouble's chest made certain he went nowhere. Another set of hands yanked the daypack off his back. Trouble heard the zipper open and smelled limes ripening in tropical heat. Vietnamese phrases were exchanged. The hands on his chest were replaced by the daypack, slapped against his body. Thick fingers pointed away from the old merchant and his friend. A shove on Trouble's butt sent him in that direction.

"OK, I'm leaving." He dared a glance at the merchant, intent on his next move. Looking at that old man in a cone hat brought another shove. Trouble was supposed to whisper French code words in the man's ear, but he was never going to get that close. He'd nothing to lose. Trouble blurted in French, "*Chaussettes blanches.*" The merchant didn't appear to hear anything.

Trouble gave the security men an angry look and spoke again in French. He pronounced the equivalent of the English sentence, "I'm looking for a pair of white socks."

The merchant smoothed his fine silk pajamas, covered with bright patterns embroidered on the fabric. Long arthritic fingers lifted a round black pebble from a box and placed the rock on a game board. He stroked a coarse gray beard on his chin, tangled like a bird's nest.

The merchant's opponent leaned over the table. His expression went from smug to furious. Soft curses floated from his pursed lips. His body language went rigid with tension. Clearly, there wasn't going to be an immediate response to the last move. A lot of thinking was happening behind the man's taut features.

The merchant rose and stretched. His thick body was in stark contrast to a normal lean Vietnamese figure. The large belly unbalanced his posture and stuck out so far that the merchant couldn't see his pale feet, anchored in thong sandals. His features revealed a mixed lineage, both European and Oriental ancestors. His body scarcely moved, yet his pale blue eyes darted around like a nervous cat, always watching for the next threat. He turned in a deliberate motion and walked along the lake front, moving in Trouble's direction.

The security guards quit their harassment and showed respect. Trouble watched the merchant intently. Was that quick flick of a hand an invitation to come closer? Trouble didn't know. He remained stationary, waiting.

The merchant kept walking away from the game table. A constant surf of cars, vans and motorbikes vanished from Trouble's ears. The soft clopping of the merchant's sandals appeared to be the only sound. He was moving toward another man, fishing in the lake.

They chatted and the merchant wagged his hand in a "gimme" gesture. A long black pole went in a holder. The fisherman shot Trouble a quick glance and removed a satellite phone from his tackle basket. A cord tethered the phone to a scrambler in the basket.

Trouble remembered the warning he'd received earlier – no cell phone conversation in Vietnam should be considered private. But this was a satellite phone and it was talking through an encryption device. The merchant punched keys on his phone. He turned and looked straight at Trouble. This time the gesture was unmistakable – "Come here."

He tried to remain calm and failed. His first controlled step became a jog. Trouble kept waiting for security guards to grab him, but they didn't.

Chiaro came alongside and whispered in a happy voice. "You're in."

"I hope so." Trouble halted at a respectful distance. An instinct told him to unzip a pocket on the daypack and pull out the photo he'd shown the receptionist. The snapshot worked magic on her and maybe it would help here.

The merchant looked at the photo. A smile appeared in his eyes, but not on his mouth. A long forefinger, crooked with age, tapped the image of a stroller. "*Vous?*"

"*Oui.* It's me as a baby." Trouble nodded. Someone came on the line and the merchant began chatting in French. Words flew out of his mouth like startled birds. He talked so fast Trouble couldn't follow the conversation. Quick as it began, the call ended. The phone went back in the tackle basket.

The merchant smiled and explained in French, "The security guards are his." He pointed at the thin Vietnamese man, glowering at the board. "Tran Luc is Vietnam's Minister of Foreign Trade. It's an important position, so he makes enemies."

"*Merci*," Trouble replied, showing gratitude for the explanation.

Chiaro nudged him. She hissed, "Ask about the socks again."

The family patriarch might not speak English, but he understood one of the words Chiaro used. "*Chaussettes*," he muttered, repeating the French word for "socks." He shook his head in a loving way. His bright eyes fixed on Trouble, then Chiaro. "Tonight," he told them. The patriarch's attention shifted to the boulevard, where late afternoon traffic congealed near the park. He lifted an arm, pointing at exotic motorscooters drifting to a halt along the curb.

Riders on the motorscooters wore flame-colored do-rags on their heads. The same age as Trouble and Chiaro, they were dressed in light weight jogging suits, with a "Nike swoosh" on the chest. The boys seemed cocky on their Honda Faze 250s. The bikes looked more like racing motorcycles than commute vehicles. The bodywork was painted fluorescent blue, like a lit aquarium. A wide silver exhaust pipe belched when the throttle revved. One of the pair tapped the rear seat on his scooter. "Get on," he called in English, breaking a smile. "We have a lot to do."

18

Trouble straddled the Honda's rear seat and gripped a leather strap. He wanted to make sure he stayed on the bike when the driver roared off. It proved to be a good idea. The tricked-out motorscooter was more racing bike than commute vehicle. A burst of acceleration left rubber streaks on the pavement. Then they were zooming through a swirl of thick traffic. Trouble felt his legs brush against the jeans of moped riders when the Honda zipped through clusters of bikes. The driver leaned into a tight curve, swerving to find the next open slot in a congested street. Trouble hoped asking a safety question might slow the guy down. "You don't wear helmets?"

The question got a laugh. The driver took a hand away from steering and slapped the do-rag on his head, a red bandana flashing yellow lightning bolts. "My helmet."

"I meant a safety helmet. You know, like the pros wear in racing." Maybe a flattering image, like being a pro motorcycle racer, would make safety an OK topic.

"I don't need a helmet like that. I go too quick for crashes. That's how I got my nickname. People call me 'Lightning' for how fast I drive." He crooked a finger and ran the tip along a lightning bolt on his do-rag.

Trouble was relieved to see Lightning's hand return to its place on the brake lever. The lull was short-lived. A moment later, they approached an intersection where the light turned red. Instead of stopping, Lightning accelerated, leading a pack of late hitters through straggling pedestrians. The scooter swayed, rolling left, then zigging right. The violent move avoided a collision with a street vendor toting baskets of candies and nuts, hanging from his shoulder pole.

Candy Vendor On A Crowded Hanoi Street

Delighted with his stunt, Lightning spun his head around. He was grinning. "No helmet law. No state troopers. We go at our own speed." Lightning was proud of his reckless ways.

Trouble wanted the guy looking at the road, especially driving fast in thick traffic. Trouble pointed ahead of them, indicating the other Honda Faze 250. That driver wore a red-white-green bandana. "What's his nickname – your friend with the Italian do-rag?"

"Ferrari. He wants to drive the world's fastest cars." Lightning sped up, so he came alongside the other scooter. The drivers looked at each other. They nodded and put on another burst of speed. Racing through slower traffic, they dueled to be first in reaching an old iron bridge.

A wide flow of motorbikes funneled into the narrow span, slowing everyone approaching the bridge. Hoping to win the race, Lightning waited to the last possible moment before jerking his brake lever. Even so, Ferrari squeezed ahead. Massive front disc brakes clamped tight and both scooters lost speed like they'd crashed into a wall. Anti-lock braking systems prevented disaster, but Trouble felt he was going to vault over Lightning and fly head-first along the bridge.

The abrupt halt was followed by start-stop motion, with Ferrari and Lightning passing everyone, even when it appeared suicidal. Their

Long Bien Bridge

driving habits weren't the only cause of fear for Trouble. The cantilever style bridge was made of iron girders and looked as if it were a giant's toy, an oversize erector set project. Rust streaked the elderly steel, like a cancer eating its host. Many bolts were absent, having crumbled to red powder. He stared at mud brown water swirling beneath the antique bridge. The only thing separating their scooter from the Red River was a brief fence. Tired life preservers hung on the railing, old wooden rings that looked like they'd crumble if touched.

A freight train came on the span, using rails in the center section. The bridge rumbled, vibrated by the powerful train engine. It seemed doubtful to Trouble that the bridge could hold the weight of freight cars, pulled by diesel engines. He held his breath, partly to avoid inhaling exhaust fumes, but mostly out of anxiety. At last, the train cleared the mile-long span and Trouble inhaled freely. He was grateful when they came to a joint French-Vietnamese project restoring the historic bridge. Eventually, it would again look like the glorious structure Gustave Eiffel designed, a great engineering achievement, second only to his famous Eiffel Tower in Paris.

The scooter flew over this new portion in relative quiet, giving Trouble the chance to ask questions. He leaned forward, making it easier for Lightning to hear. "Where are we going?" Trouble asked.

"We must prepare you for your journey to Dr. Cam's lab." Lightning flashed a smirk. "First, we stop to eat. The meal will make you strong. It will give you courage."

The smirk warned Trouble this meal was a test, some kind of hazing. "Actually, I'm not hungry." It was a lie, of course. Like Chiaro, Trouble felt starved.

"You must eat anyway. Take a bite of everything they bring. Or we cannot go further."

"Why can't I just meet Dr. Cam?"

"Later, you will understand. No one can drive you to Dr. Cam. You must fly like an eagle. We have been told to make certain you have the courage to soar."

Disgusted, Trouble muttered a quiet, "Whatever." Seeing the bridge end, he gripped a leather strap. The scooter's race-prepared 250cc engine screamed to 12,000 revs, shifted and screamed again ... and again. "What's our speed?" he shouted over wind ripping around the scooter.

"A passenger makes a lot of drag. We can't hit top speed. We're only at one twenty."

"One hundred twenty kilometers an hour?" It was a reasonable assumption, since Vietnam was on the metric system. Seventy miles an hour is about 120 kilometers per hour.

Lightning gave his crazy smirk again. "No. One hundred twenty miles an hour. Top with me alone is about one fifty. But it takes a long straight to get that high." Lightning made a quick weave around a taxi. "You must help us make a turn. Lean," he urged Trouble.

Their bike pitched into a hard, sliding turn. Gravel kicked off the tires. Hot, rough pavement flew an inch beneath Trouble's knee. The amazing machine swung upright and high pitched revs sang in his ears, with the scooter downshifting. The bike decelerated so fast it seemed caught by a rubber band. They leapt off pavement, twisting into a shanty town of mud huts with tin roofs. Many of the huts wore black streaks of river mold. Rusty fences sheltered the tired homes from broken sidewalks where children played. Delighted by the exotic bikes, kids quit their games and chased the motorscooters, ignoring a sting of pebbles thrown in the air from speeding tires.

On the lead bike, Ferrari opened a cell phone and speed dialed. It looked like he was warning someone of their arrival. Ahead, a tower home loomed, multistoried like a pagoda. White balconies lay below every window like a row of shiny teeth. To slide through the blue gates, Ferrari and Lightning slowed to a crawl. Behind them, a shutting fence kept out children anxious to beg for money. Their faces lined the wrought iron gates for a while. Then they drifted away, breaking into teams to play games.

Lightning and Ferrari parked their Hondas in the shade of a sprawling almond tree. Ferrari hopped off and sprinted inside the pagoda-like home dominating the courtyard. Lightning hesitated, then decided to follow his brother. "Wait here. I'll be right back."

Trouble slid off the scooter, but Chiaro remained seated. She looked around and realized tables ringed the courtyard area. White sheets, draping the tables, billowed in a light wind. Plates, glasses, silverware, napkin holders anchored the sheets, keeping them from blowing off. "I hope this place is a restaurant. I'm hungry enough to gnaw on the handlebars of this scooter." She looked at Trouble. He didn't seem to be paying attention. His interest was focused on the almond tree above her head. "You hear anything I said?"

"Yeah. You're starved. That could be good – or it could be bad." His eyes glided along branches and he seemed to be counting something.

She flipped a leg over the scooter and dismounted. Chiaro mocked him. "Could be good or bad, huh. I suppose you aren't hungry at all."

"Pretty hungry, like you." He nodded in agreement. "But I don't think we came here just to eat."

"Whaddya mean?" Chiaro pivoted, scanning the building. "What else could we do here? Oh, you think they're using the bathrooms. That's why they ran off."

"No."

"No what?" Hunger made her grouchy.

"No, we didn't stop here just to pee and eat." Trouble's eyes fixated on a branch right behind Chiaro. He shifted nervously.

"So why're we here?" She didn't like the way he looked behind her, instead of looking at her. It felt rude.

He edged around her and picked up a wooden rod. "Lightning warned me I had to pass a test. Gotta endure some hazing before they'll take me to meet my dad's agent."

"What test?" She was outraged. "We passed already. Riding with these insane guys is a test. They drive like maniacs, like Kami … What's that word for suicide pilots?"

"Kamikazes."

"Yeah. So that's enough."

"I'm afraid it isn't. Lightning said I had to do something to make myself stronger. So I could soar like an eagle."

"Oh, this is macho junk."

"Fine. You don't gotta do it. Just tell 'em you quit. Stay in Hanoi. I'll return in a few days. We'll have money to go home."

"And how am I supposed to pay a hotel bill?" Chiaro threw her hands up in disgust.

"Um, I'd suggest you put your hands down. Like soon. Like now."

"What is this, Trouble? I better behave or Santa won't bring me a present?" She was really angry now. "Look, anything boys can do, I can do." Chiaro's eyes flashed. She planted her hands on her hips.

Trouble relaxed some when she dropped her hands, but not entirely. "Good. Now step away from the tree."

"You might like standing in hot sun. I don't." Chiaro became defiant. She tried to step back and hit the scooter. Its engine ticked like a clock as the machine cooled down. The bike's radiator pulsed heat, a furnace making Chiaro uncomfortable. She moved away, sliding deeper into the tree's shade.

"Don't do that," he warned her.

"I can do anything I want." Chiaro squatted near the tree trunk. "And I can pass a test, just like you."

"Good to hear," Ferrari announced. "We can't take you further unless …"

She groaned. "Yeah, I heard. Gotta be strong to soar like eagles. But first I must eat something. What do they serve here?"

"This." Ferrari grabbed the pole from Trouble and held the stick over Chiaro's head. A deadly cobra slithered on the pole, wrapping itself

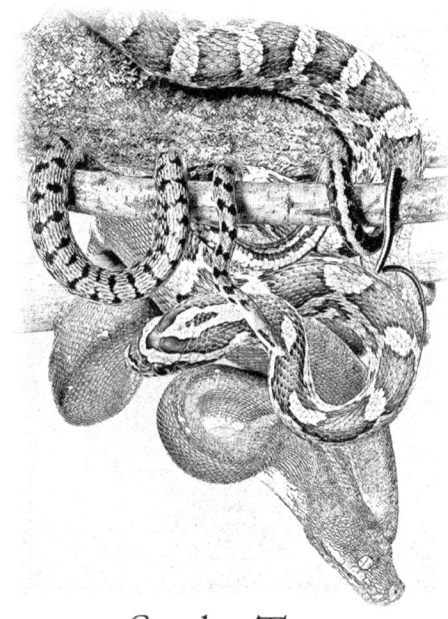

Snake Tree

around the stick. It long tan body coiled in a spiral, revealing a pale yellow belly with smooth scales.

She jumped away, landing near Trouble. "Oh, no." Chiaro moaned.

Ferrari whipped the stick, flinging the snake on the ground. Upset, the cobra assumed an attack posture, curling its body like a spring. The snake raised its head and flared its wide neck hood. A loud hissing spattered through its open mouth. Curved fangs jutted from the roof of the mouth. Poison dripped from the sharp fangs. Its forked-tongue flicked the air, sensing Chiaro's location. Angry eyes fixed on her as a target.

She moved away and the snake dropped to the ground. Its body wriggled like a pulsing wave, shooting along the earth. In a flash, the cobra flew up the tree trunk. A moment later, the viper disappeared among the branches. Chiaro went limp.

"You don't like cobra?" Ferrari asked. "No problem. Whole tree is full of snakes. You can pick another type for dinner. We bring you to the greatest snake restaurant in Hanoi." He laughed. "Must be true. It's on the sign." He pointed at Vietnamese lettering on the gate.

Chiaro stepped backwards and stared at the almond tree. Moments ago, she'd been enjoying its shade. Now, she realized every branch on that tree wriggled like it was alive. Snakes were coiled everywhere, blending with tree bark and leaves.

"I tried to warn you," Trouble reminded her.

"Yeah, you did." Drained from her near miss with a cobra, Chiaro whispered. "I hate snakes. These guys must have known. This is some kind of evil."

"What she say?" Ferrari looked puzzled.

"Chiaro told me she's always wanted to eat snake," Trouble explained.

Daggers shot from Chiaro's eyes. If looks would kill, he'd be chopped in pieces.

He reminded her, "Must pass their test to go on, remember?"

"They gotta have something else to eat." She ran under an awning, grabbed a menu off a table and returned. The laminated sheet had one column in Vietnamese and the other side translated. "See, they've got dumplings, spring rolls, soup, ice cream. The menu isn't just snake meat. Probably get vegetarians here all the time."

"Good. So when they bring snake meat, you fake eating it. Cut up the pieces and mush them around, like you did at home when you couldn't stand dinner." Trouble smiled, hoping she felt better.

"Yeah. I can do this."

"Sure you can," he agreed.

Lightning showed up, escorted by a woman thin as a clothes hanger. Her height couldn't exceed four feet, standing on her toes. The woman's bare arms, ankles and cheeks were scarred. She appeared to be part of a circus act, putting out lit cigarettes by grinding them into her flesh.

The restaurant owner grinned at Trouble and Chiaro. "You wonder about my scars, yes?"

"Uh, no. Just wondering what happens next." Trouble felt embarrassed.

Lightning smirked. "Aw, he's lying. Sure they're curious. Tell 'em about the scars. Go on," he urged the proprietor.

She dragged a pant leg up. More scars appeared. "Not burns." She looked gleeful at their shocked expressions. "Bites. I'm so full of venom, snakes can't kill me. Don't even need to buy antidote serum. But I keep it on hand for unlucky customers." She gestured at Chiaro. "You were almost unlucky."

Chiaro looked shy when she nodded.

"Yes." The owner laughed. "A king cobra was ready to sink its fangs in your neck. A cobra strikes your jugular vein and antidotes don't work. You die in seconds. Be careful under my tree, next time."

Stunned, Chiaro wobbled. "Oh, don't worry. I hate …"

Sensing her mistake, Trouble cut her off. "She won't stand under your tree again. Will you?"

"No. Definitely not." Chiaro nodded several times.

"Good. Now we pick out the best snake for dinner. Which of you is our guest of honor?"

Trying to be gracious, Trouble pointed at Chiaro. Wary of another ambush, she wouldn't take the compliment and pointed back at him.

"Looks like we have two guests of honor." The wily host glanced at Ferrari and Lightning. "You boys will have to buy a pair of snakes." Before they could argue, she grabbed the almond's trunk and shimmied up the tree. Higher and higher she went, grabbing branches and making them bounce like a hurricane was shaking the tree. Everywhere, snakes buzzed, twisted, rattled, hissed. "Ah, there you are." The owner grabbed the cobra that almost killed Chiaro.

The king cobra wrapped itself around the thin owner, rearing its head back. The woman twisted the snake's head just in time. Poison, intended for her eyes, sprayed from fangs like a drizzle of rain. She fell out of the tree, spinning to land on her feet with the agility of a cat.

A pair of waiters ran to assist the owner. They grabbed the cobra's tail and tugged. The woman spun around, unwinding the snake from her torso. The trio ran to a dinner table and spread the thrashing snake along a white sheet. Another waiter appeared, cleaning the snake with a wet cloth, then drying the wriggling body.

In a deft motion, the woman pinched the snake's mouth shut, closing its lips. A box cutter appeared in her other hand. Scarred fingers sliced a long hole in the cobra's neck. She angled the neck over shot glasses lined on the table, pumping a few drops into each one. Snake blood turned clear liquid in the glasses to milky red.

Keeping an iron grip on the snake's mouth, she tossed the box cutter to an assistant, a girl about Chiaro's age. Without hesitation, the girl opened the viper's belly, extracting the snake's gall bladder, a slimy balloon curved like a kidney. Another row of shot glasses appeared and the girl punctured the gall bladder. Bright green bile ran in the glasses, making them look like crème de menthe.

The box cutter was tossed back to the owner in a practiced ritual. In a quick motion, she detached the serpent's head, slicing through the cobra's wide hood. Reaching inside the body, she ripped out the snake's heart. Wet with blood, the oyster-sized organ throbbed even though it no longer was attached to veins and arteries. Still pulsing, the heart was dropped in an appetizer dish.

Proud of her accomplishment, the owner held the dish with blood soaked fingers. She walked toward Trouble, but her eyes fixated on the beating heart. When she got close, the proprietor chanted. "Eat. It makes you strong, gives you courage." She repeated the chant even after halting in front of her guests.

Trouble gulped, realizing she wanted him to swallow the snake's heart. But the owner did an unexpected thing. She offered the organ to Chiaro.

"Venom of the king cobra is fatal. Even I am not immune to its poison. An elephant will die if it's bitten in the trunk." She held the dish close to Chiaro's trembling face. "Eat what almost killed you. Tonight, more fear awaits you. I sense it. A worse test is coming. You must be ready." The woman's hypnotic eyes locked on Chiaro.

Not believing herself capable of such an act, Chiaro took the dish from the proprietor. Closing her eyes, Chiaro let the pulsing heart slide from the dish and fall in her open mouth. Horrified at the thought of chewing such a thing, she made her throat wide as possible and swallowed. The bulge slid along her throat and stuck. Chiaro fought to remain calm. She imaged the heart continuing its journey, coming to rest in her stomach. Each beat of the organ pushed the lump farther down. Finally, the ghastly thing vanished from her throat and she could breathe again.

"Good," the owner announced. "Now the boy must have his own viper. Again, I'll climb the tree. His snake will find me, to serve its master by dying. Then, we'll eat a feast. Be proud. Tonight, you're being treated to Vietnam's most potent medicine, our most exotic meal."

19

The dinner was lavish, a parade of courses, one dish followed by another. Ferrari and Lightning devoured every morsel on their plates. Their clicking chopsticks chased each shred of meat and grain of rice from platters. Chiaro picked at any dish with meat, making a show instead of eating. Starved, she wolfed rice dumplings dipped in lemon sauce and a salad with crispy noodles on top. She drained a cup of sweet and sour broth, enjoying its mix of flavors and delicate golden croutons. Chiaro eagerly popped spring rolls, then asked for a second portion of ice cream.

That request caught the help by surprise and they conferred for a while, before returning with a heaping bowl of vanilla ice cream, made with rice instead of dairy products. A dead scorpion was spread across the white scoops as though the insect were chocolate syrup.

Chiaro glanced at the dish and went into shock. She jumped to her feet, too horrified to speak.

The restaurant owner was surprised by her guest's reaction. With a quick step, she removed the dish, hiding it from Chiaro's vision. "I apologize. We assumed …"

Sweat beaded on Chiaro's pasty face. Her words forced themselves from a choked throat. "Assumed what?"

The restaurant owner remained mute, embarrassment on her face. "I'll bring you new scoops of ice cream, with nothing on them." She hurried into the kitchen.

Bewildered, Chiaro sat down. She mumbled, "I don't get it. Why'd they do that?"

Ferrari and Lightning exchanged mirthful glances. They thought the whole thing was pretty funny.

Trouble gave them an angry look. "Come on guys. Time to quit. She's had enough. Pay the bill and let's go." He got to his feet and tossed his napkin on the table.

"We didn't ask for scorpion." Now Lightning seemed embarrassed.

Ferrari tried to explain and made Chiaro feel worse. "You ate the snake's eyes. They were on the first ice cream. The owner thought you wanted an even more powerful charm. See …" He pointed at a cart with bottles for sale. The most expensive glass container held a king cobra's head, a scorpion and a poisonous lizard.

"Oh, no. I thought the eyes were candy. They felt like jelly beans." Chiaro looked like she was going to vomit.

Lightning pulled on Trouble's jacket, tugging him close for a whisper. "Everything here has snake in it. No part of the serpent goes in the trash. Doesn't she realize those noodles on her salad were made from snake skin? Those croutons she loved were deep-fried snake bones. She had to know. Didn't she?"

Trouble hesitated. "Nope. Best not to tell her. OK?"

"Sure." Lightning explained the situation to Ferrari, conversing in Vietnamese so Chiaro wouldn't understand.

She didn't like being talked about in a foreign language, where she didn't know what they were saying. "That's not very nice. They ought to be better hosts."

Trouble shrugged. He felt it was best to lie. "They're not talking about you. They're arguing about who pays the bill."

The boys finished their conversation and Ferrari headed to the kitchen. Lightning spoke to Trouble and Chiaro. "He signs for meal. Our great uncle pays. It was his idea to make you strong."

"Your great uncle is the man we met by the lake?" Trouble was curious.

"Yes. Very wise man. He wanted to make certain you were serious about your journey – and were fortified before going on the trip." Lightning gave them a smile, but it wilted under Chiaro's angry stare.

She huffed. "What journey? We could'a taken a train to Saigon without eating snake."

"She has a point," Trouble emphasized.

"No train, no boat can take you. Must soar like eagle. I told you." Lightning seemed puzzled by their confusion. For him, it was all obvious.

"You ever been there, wherever we're going?" Trouble felt cautious.

"No." Lightning wagged his head to underscore the answer. "No one went there – except your parents, Trouble."

That was enough for him. "Then let's get going." He pointed at their motorscooters, parked under the almond tree. A green snake lay curled on the seat of Lightning's bike.

Ferrari returned from the kitchen, accompanied by the short woman who owned the restaurant. "You're leaving so soon? You just got here." She wagged an accusing finger at them.

"Sorry. Gotta hurry." Trouble lifted his daypack and draped it over his shoulders.

"Can't leave without a souvenir." She dragged the cart toward them, pointing at bottles of snakes pickled in rice whiskey. Most glass jars held king cobras and bamboo vipers. The largest bottle housed a python with the flared neck of a weight lifter. Its mouth was open with a forked tongue unfurled like a banner. His eyes bulged like milky white marbles, staring through the yellow liquid.

Sickened by the display, Chiaro's face convulsed in an ugly expression. She turned away and walked into the open patio, stopping well short of the snake-filled almond tree.

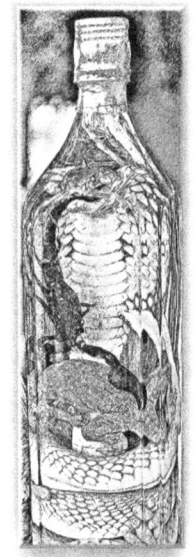

The proprietor shoved her cart at Trouble. She gave him a crooked smile, revealing a gap in her lower teeth. "How about you? I make you a special deal. Second bottle is half price. You show to friends at home, impress them."

"Oh, yeah. They'd be impressed, all right." Trouble shook his head. "Sorry. We gotta travel light. Can't take glass bottles."

King Cobra With
Scorpion & Lizard

The woman looked at Ferrari and Lightning, but they walked away, heading for their scooters. Lightning grabbed a pole and knocked snakes off the bikes.

The owner dropped her tourist hard sell approach. She left the cart and walked to Trouble. Her expression was sad as she approached him. She took a baggie out of her pocket and showed it to him. The king cobra's head was inside, with his mouth open, fangs ready to bite someone. "A gift." She pressed the baggie in his hand. "Free. No charge. You take – for luck." The owner laughed. "But don't show her." The woman pointed at Chiaro, swinging a leg over Ferrari's scooter to mount the rear seat.

"Thanks. And don't worry. I won't show it to Chiaro." Trouble pressed her bony fingers between his hands in a gesture of gratitude.

The bikes roared up. "Get on." Lightning patted the seat behind him.

Trouble did as instructed. He waved at the owner as they ripped out of her yard. He leaned forward, shouting to be heard over the engine. "Where are we going?"

"Now we must disguise you. No time before. Had to get you out of Hanoi fast, before ninjas find you. We heard about your race on the Cyclos. You're lucky our families know lots of tricks. So now we hide your looks."

"Disguise me – how?" Trouble was surprised.

"You're both American. We make you look Vietnamese."

"That'll be a good trick."

"You'll see." Lightning followed the other scooter, twisting through a maze of alleys where daily life continued as it had for centuries. Old men baked thin rice bread on blackened pots, heated by charcoal fires. Their quick hands tossed the flat bread and they held the crust by fingertips over flames until the bread turned golden. Doing the laundry meant laying a shirt on the ground and brushing soap in the fabric. Scrubbing brushes rubbed back and forth to create a bubbling lather. Tossing the garment in a cauldron of boiling water and stirring with a pole was the rinse cycle. Firewood burned under the cauldron and Trouble coughed from inhaling smoke.

They cleared the smoke and the bikes halted before an old woman making clay pots. Her straight gray hair was pulled back in a ponytail and she squatted before a rotating wheel. Her wet hands shaped pots by spinning clay on a turntable. Her muddy fingers gently pulled the brown clay upwards and then her hands pushed the walls to hollow out the shape of a pot. Her daughter powered the spinning wheel with a bare foot. Every few revolutions, the girl lifted her leg and gave the turntable a kick, maintaining the spin. Wet mud splattered the daughter's faded jeans like splotches of chocolate milk. The daughter's kicking foot and the mother's shaping hands worked together in rhythm. No conversation or music interrupted the coordinated work.

The old woman saw them approaching and gave Ferrari a look of recognition. She pointed a muddy finger inside their modest hut. Then she dipped her fingers in water and resumed shaping her pots.

Trouble and Chiaro ducked under a low-hanging awning and entered a dim interior. The buzz of an impatient fly and dull slaps of a foot against the potter's wheel were the only sounds. Straw mats lay on the floor, serving as beds. There was no sink or toilet. A makeshift dressing area offered the only privacy in a one room home. The "dressing room" was made of bamboo poles supporting fabric rolls, unwound to reach the floor. Pale green fabric "curtains" added color to the tired mud hut and its unpainted walls.

Ferrari lifted a pair of black Vietnamese pajamas and a cone hat. He gave them to Chiaro and pointed to the dressing area. "Go inside for privacy."

"You want me to wear these?" Chiaro felt the idea was absurd.

Ferrari explained to her. "Ninjas are looking for you as Americans. Not looking for you as Vietnamese."

"Also looking for you as girl," Lightning added. "So we make you a boy. Good you are thin."

Ferrari pointed at Trouble and smirked. "You are sturdy. Too thick for a girl. So we make you an old woman. She is rich and eats too much." He laughed and shoved a wad of clothes at Trouble.

He caught the bundle. "I'm not wearing these."

Chiaro peeled the curtain back. She gave him a scornful look. "I ate snake. I didn't chicken out. You gonna?"

Trapped by her logic, he attempted to pull a blouse over his chest and failed. Trouble was delighted when the garment appeared too small.

Ferrari wagged his hand, indicating Trouble wasn't getting off that easy. He assisted Trouble in pulling the thin silk top over his torso. The tight-fitting blouse was covered in a pattern of mangoes and papayas. Trouble felt like a tropical salad. Chiaro dropped a cone hat on his head and worked at tying its straps under his chin.

Upset at wearing women's clothes, he pushed away her fingers. Trouble yanked off the hat and glowered at Ferrari and Lightning. "Your disguise idea won't work. Our skin's too pale. We don't look Vietnamese. These clothes just make us ridiculous. People will stare at us. I'm changing back." He started to pull off the blouse and Ferrari restrained him.

"Makeup hides skin color," he explained.

"Yeah, like we're going buy makeup at a drugstore. But we can't, even if there is a drugstore in Hanoi. Only actors wear makeup in Vietnam – and they paint their faces white." Feeling like he'd won the argument, Trouble again lifted the blouse.

Ferrari grabbed Trouble's arm to stop him. "We know your skin is too pale. Have makeup ready. You'll see."

Lightning entered the room, carrying a tin full of thick paste. "Pottery clay," he explained, offering the can to Chiaro. "You're a girl. You know makeup. Put this on his face."

"Gladly." Smiling, Chiaro dipped her fingertips in the old tin and brought out a thick paste of brown mud. "Good thing you took off the hat. Now I can get your forehead. Quit scowling. You're making it hard to paint your chin." She took only moments to cover his face with brown goo. The gunk smothered his pores, leaving his eyes showing through the disguise. The wet mask slathered his skin like thick paint. Trouble felt the clay sink into his face and sniffed its ripe odor. The smell made him queasy, a strange blend of wet earth, salt and rotten eggs.

"Now I do you," he announced.

"No, I'm not finished. I gotta paint your ankles and feet. They show in those flip-flops. Then I'll cover your wrists and hands."

He groaned, enduring another slime job. The clay was starting to itch as it dried. He kept asking, "Done yet?"

"No," she answered. Finally, Chiaro stepped back to admire her work. "Whaddya think guys?"

Lightning and Ferrari walked around Trouble, examining him, checking for spots Chiaro missed. "He looks good," Ferrari announced. "I think you were meant to be a grandmother, Trouble."

He grabbed the tin from Chiaro and threatened to splash its mud on Ferrari's Nike outfit.

He ducked. "Hey, careful. She needs that clay."

Lightning held a mirror so Chiaro could see her face. She grabbed the tin from Trouble and spread a thin coat on herself. She applied the mud like a light smear of suntan lotion.

"How come I got so much?" Trouble complained.

"Because you gotta look old."

"Yeah, a hundred year old granny," Lightning mocked.

Trouble glowered at them. His attitude said, "I'm getting even for this. I don't know how, but I'm getting even."

"Not done as bad joke. All is necessary." Ferrari assured Trouble.

That made him feel a little better, but not much. While Chiaro painted clay on her feet, Trouble bundled their American clothes with rope, so they could take the garments on the scooters. "All right, guys. What's next?"

Lightning jabbed his arm out. "A fast ride. Then up." He flipped his hand toward the sky.

20

Trouble bent his neck forward, dipping his head so the cone hat wouldn't fly off. Hot air whipped his face, drying his eyes until they ached. Potting clay spread on his face went from prickly to lumpy, pulling his skin tighter and tighter. The clay became casts on his cheeks, hands and feet, turning first to plaster, then stone. They shot past a truck and rippling gusts of air slapped his face like punches. "Can't you slow down?" he yelled, hoping to be heard over a screaming engine.

"No," Lightning hollered. "We're late. Supposed to be there already."

"Won't get there at all if we get killed in an accident." Trouble could feel the edge of his cone hat shredding. Another mile of this and he wouldn't have to bother keeping a hand atop the hat so it didn't blow off. There wouldn't be any straw left in the hat, just the cotton wrapped around his chin.

"We're almost there." Lightning took a fist off the handlebars. The scooter wobbled dangerously when he pointed at the horizon.

Trouble yelled, "I see it." Actually, the wind forced his eyes shut and he couldn't see anything beyond dark asphalt racing under his bare feet. But he wanted both the driver's hands on the controls.

Suddenly, the scooter downshifted through gears. Sharp throttle blips were followed by transmission noise. Trouble pitched forward with each abrupt shift to a lower gear. They tilted to one side and he was pushed against the seat by g-forces. The bike ripped around a turn, then flipped upwards again. The road got bumpy and all vision disappeared in billowing dust clouds from the scooters. Trouble couldn't see Chiaro and Ferrari in the lead, but he could hear their motorbike's engine mix its beat with Lightning's scooter.

Choking dust plugged Trouble's nose, smelling like concrete stirred with dried onions. He was forced to open his mouth and sift gritty air through his teeth. Dust followed them like a genie summoned from another dimension, wrapping itself around the motorbike. A huge bump was followed by rumbling tires as they tilted up a plywood ramp. Trouble had no idea where they stopped when he felt the scooter rise on its kickstand. He gratefully slid off and found his legs too numb for walking.

Gradually, a gritty mist around them drifted away. Trouble's irritated eyes squinted at a planted field. Green rows of scallions, small onions used in salads, marched in straight lines. That explained the onion part of the smell. Pallets stacked with bags of cement surrounded them, leaking white powder, resulting in the concrete odor. Trouble looked at Chiaro and saw a ghost. Instead of wearing black cotton pants and shirt, she was clothed in gray dust. Beating their arms against themselves sent puffs billowing in the air. Ferrari and Lightning also patted themselves, scowling at the way their prize running suits and precious motorbikes were choked in powder.

Trouble consoled them. "Don't worry. Most of the dust will blow off on your ride home."

"Yeah, especially the way you guys drive." Chiaro spat mud from her clogged mouth.

"We hit two hundred, even with passengers," Ferrari announced. He beamed with pride.

"Two hundred miles an hour – you guys are crazy …" Chiaro quit talking and fumed.

"No, only two hundred kilometers. Just one hundred twenty five miles an hour," Lightning explained.

"Oh, good. That's a lot better." Chiaro didn't bother to hide an ounce of her sarcasm.

Trouble hoped to break up the argument by changing the subject. "So, those towers are where we rendezvous?" He pointed at a pair of fifty story buildings, located nearby.

"No." Ferrari was sheepish. He stared at his dusty track shoes, refusing to glance at Trouble.

Lightning appeared shy also. "We go inside now. Make arrangements. You wait here."

"Inside?" Chiaro looked confused.

"To see our uncle. He works as security guard." Ferrari spun around, pointing at the lobby door of an unfinished skyscraper. Its glass reflected the dying sunlight and scattered clouds of late afternoon.

Trouble craned his neck, trying to see the building's top floor. He kept looking upward … and looking, until his spine arced backward. The stories rose higher and higher, reaching an unfinished level where the skeleton of iron awaited the next construction phase. A soft whistle of astonishment left his puckered lips. "Wow, how high is this thing?"

Lightning gestured at a billboard caked in dust. He ran a hand over the surface to reveal an English translation of the Vietnamese sign.

Chiaro read the words in surprise. "Tallest building in Vietnam … 17th tallest building in the world … only fifty meters shorter than New York City's Empire State Building. Wow."

"We go see our uncle." Lightning edged toward the lobby doors.

"How many uncles you got?" Chiaro wasn't happy. She knew a building this tall must be part of the "soar like eagles" lecture they'd given her.

"Vietnam is a communist state. We all have Uncle Ho to thank for this." Lightning recited the words very seriously, like a script he'd memorized in school. Then he cracked a smile. "So, everyone important is our 'uncle.' You see?"

"Oh." Chiaro looked disappointed. "I thought you guys had connections."

"Our great uncle you met in the park is a real uncle. He has connections. Lots of them." Lightning tugged on a huge glass door and it opened enough for him to squeeze through. "You wait here. OK?"

Trouble nodded. After all, what choice did he have?

Ferrari also slid through the narrow opening. A moment later, he peeked his head out. "Won't be long. Back soon." The door closed, causing its reflective glass to shimmer, distorting images of surrounding onion fields.

The Empire State Building in New York City

"Great." Chiaro kicked a pebble in disgust. "Whaddya think is next?"

"Maybe this agent's gonna meet us in the lobby. Maybe he's already here." Trouble shrugged, trying to stay positive.

"Maybe she's already here," Chiaro snapped.

"Could be a she. I never met them, least not when I was old enough to remember. Hope they show up. It'll be dark soon."

"Does it get cold in Vietnam after dark?" Chiaro looked worried.

"I guess." He shifted his feet, letting his own anxiety show.

They turned to look when the lobby door squeaked. Ferrari and Lightning bounced outside, appearing pleased. "All set. He remembers."

Trouble was surprised to have them shake his hand. He gave them a puzzled look. "What's up?"

"Nice to meet you. Hope to see you again soon." Ferrari and Lightning bowed toward Chiaro.

She looked panicked. "Wait ... I mean, how do we get back to Hanoi?"

Lightning didn't answer her. He flipped a leg over his scooter and knocked the bike off its kickstand. His finger tapped the electric starter and his engine roared.

Trouble shouted over Ferrari starting his engine as well. "She's right. When are you guys coming back for us?"

"We're done. You're not going to Hanoi. You meet the agent on the roof." He jabbed a finger in the air.

"How're we gonna get up there?" Trouble felt panicky now.

"Uncle guard will show you how." Ferrari waved goodbye and opened the throttle on his bike. Lightning did the same, waving, then ripping away.

Chiaro and Trouble watched the boys wriggle along a rutted dirt road, spraying dust in the air. The wind had shifted and this time gray genies drifted over onion fields instead of wafting toward the unfinished skyscraper. The motorbikes hummed toward a highway at a sane pace, but once their drivers felt asphalt under their wheels, sanity ended. The sounds became the whine of high revving engines, shifting to higher gears. After a while, the racing noises vanished. An eerie silence fell on Chiaro and Trouble like a thick fog.

They waited for something to happen, but nothing out of the ordinary occurred. Insects buzzed. Some tried to land in their eyes or on their faces, only to get swatted away. Bicycles chains squeaked alongside the highway where Ferrari and Lightning disappeared. A rare car purred along the asphalt. Old trucks ruptured the quiet with clashing gear shifts and grunting engines. Farmers pushed large rattan wheelbarrows, carrying pyramids of fresh cabbage. Kids on mopeds were speeding to join their friends in the city before dark. A bus halted and dropped passengers, however none of them approached the dormant construction site.

After a while, Chiaro broke the silence. "Think they dumped us here?"

"I hope not." Trouble shifted uneasily. "They could'a ditched us without a big meal."

"It was snake." Chiaro made a face.

"Snake's expensive," he reasoned.

"Eases their conscience. Makes them feel like they treated us right, even if they didn't help us. I say it was a guilt gift."

"Lightning sounded real about needing to come here so I could meet my parent's agent."

"He could be a good liar," she argued.

"Or we could try going in the lobby." He punched a thumb over his shoulder, indicating the glass door behind them.

"Why not?" Chiaro spun around and put a hand on the door. She didn't have to tug. The glass panel swung outward, forcing her to step back.

A tall, thin man wearing inexpensive plastic eyeglasses pushed the heavy door with surprising power. His narrow body was clothed in a black business suit. Instead of a dress shirt and tie, he wore a white polo shirt. When he reached for his keys, his jacket flared open. Cell phones crowded his waistband. A Blackberry was clipped next to an iPhone, beside a Palm Pre and a Motorola Krave. He eyed the mobile units, checking to make sure they were secured to his pants. Then he jerked a key into the front door, twisting the lock closed. He moved like a restless cat, pacing in a tight circle, swinging his shoulders. He muttered something.

"Sorry, I didn't catch that." Trouble stepped closer so he could hear better.

"Said I took a while to get out here because we had a phone call. Some tourists wanting to take pictures from the roof at sunset. I told them it wasn't possible. They didn't take it well and kept pestering me. Even offered me bribes." He shrugged and turned around. When he saw them, he acted startled by their appearance. "Hard to believe you're Americans. You're Trouble and Chiaro?"

"Yeah, that's us," Trouble assured him. "Where'd you learn to speak English so well?"

"MIT. I went on a U.N. scholarship. Caltech was my first choice, but they've pretty much switched from engineering to biotech." The man jingled a key ring dangling from a cord on his crowded belt.

Trouble recoiled in surprise. "You graduated from college and work as a security guard?"

He laughed. "I'm the night construction foreman. But we don't work at night. I walk around the building instead of honcho-ing crews. I use the time for quality control, inspecting each day's work for proper technique. I make sure they followed the blueprints. It also saves hiring a guard."

"Smart," Trouble agreed. "Uh, you know when this person shows up, the one I'm supposed to meet?"

"When the moon rises." He acted like that was a normal answer needing no further explanation.

"So he's coming after dark?" Trouble looked around. The sun was getting near the horizon. His parents' agent might show up soon.

The foreman corrected Trouble. "Yes, *she's* coming after sunset."

"Told you." Chiaro snickered.

Trouble ignored her comment. "Can we wait in the lobby?"

The slim man appeared startled. "They didn't tell you?"

"Tell us what?" Chiaro leaned forward, a snide look on her face. She was convinced the whole scooter ride was a hoax and now his answer would prove her right.

"Well, I don't mean to shock you." The foreman hesitated.

"Go on, shock us." Chiaro looked really smug now and it irritated Trouble to no end.

"OK, so where do we meet her?"

"I hope you don't mind heights," he explained.

"Because … ?" Chiaro no longer acted smug. She looked a bit sick.

The foreman studied her. "Looks like you are acrophobic. Ever experience vertigo – a spinning sensation when you look over a cliff?"

"Looking over cliffs isn't my favorite sport," she admitted.

"You'll be fine," he counseled her. The security guard chopped at the air with a level hand. "Keep your eyes on the horizon. Don't look down."

"I'll go on the roof and meet with her. It won't take long to set up the next step. You can wait here," Trouble offered.

"We've been through this before. I'm going along." Chiaro's eyes flashed with determination. In a moment, her face softened. "I hope they have an elevator." She looked upward, trying to see the building's top. "That would be a lot of stairs."

"Yes, too many stairs – unless you're a tower marathon runner," the foreman agreed.

Trouble moved toward the door. "So we take the elevator?"

The MIT grad shook his head. "No lifts inside the building yet. They can't be installed until the last floor's built."

"Then how do we get on the roof?" Trouble was becoming concerned.

"You have to use the same elevator construction crews use. Sometimes they hitch a ride when the crane's lifting building materials. But the crane only runs during work hours." He gave Chiaro a stern look, warning her to pay attention. "You'll be fine. Just don't look down. Keep your eyes on the horizon."

"How can I look at the horizon from inside an elevator?" she complained.

"Easy. The box runs up the side of the building. The lift is just a mesh cage. Its floor, top and sides are open. You can see through them – for the entire ride, all one thousand, two hundred and fifty feet."

Skyscraper Under Construction

Once the elevator door clanged shut, Chiaro felt anxious. She tried taking deep breaths, but it didn't work. "Are you sure this cage is safe?"

"People ride to work every day in this box." The security guard shrugged.

Trouble would have felt safer climbing the lattice-work beam, where his fate depended on his own skill, instead of dangling from a thousand foot cable. He stared intently at the man. "How often do *you* use this lift?"

"Same goes for me as the work crews. I ride up and check their job, then glide down again. Happens each night, close of business." The man placed a hand on the motor switch. "Hang on. There's a delay as the winch takes up slack in the cable. Then the box jerks upward. Have a good ride."

"It will stop at the top, won't it? I mean, we're not gonna fly into space, are we?" Fear pressed her eyes closed and Chiaro squinted at the engineer-watchman.

"Wow, you sure find a lot of things to worry about," Trouble complained.

The security guard laughed. "I couldn't launch you to the moon if I wanted to do it. A switch at the top kills the winch." He punched a button and a large motor whirred to life. "Here goes."

Trouble inhaled a nose full of oil from the spinning electric motor. Grease lubricating the cable started to warm up, giving off a distinctive odor. Suddenly, the elevator flew upward, buckling his knees. Then he floated for a moment, only to get surprised by another jerk upward. In front of him, the skyscraper moved downward, flowing past his vision.

From the ground, the guard yelled, "Turn around. Watch the horizon, so you don't get motion sick. I don't want to clean up your barf."

Grabbing a railing, they swung around. The cable holding them slid past their eyes. A beam supporting the elevator cable blocked part of their vision. Beyond the obstruction, they could see green fields, rice paddies and large communal huts with metal roofs. The rice terraces were flooded with water from the Red River. Rice plants grew in vivid green shoots like grass on a golf course. A small flock of white storks floated over the green fields, spreading long wings to ride thermal currents of humid air.

Rice Paddies Seen From The Skyscraper's Elevator

Trouble and Chiaro moved higher and the snake restaurant with its village came into view. The red tiles and dusty courtyards were ringed by narrow lanes and clusters of huts. Hanoi's outskirts emerged and the tube houses with striped awnings resembled a modern patchwork quilt. They spotted Long Bien Bridge, looking like the Paris Eiffel Tower laid on its side.

Trouble started feeling pretty safe. This was easy. "The elevator would make a good tourist attraction."

Chiaro loosened her grip on the railing. She muttered, hoping to convince herself everything was all right. "I'm OK with doing this."

Trouble nodded. "Yeah, it's pleasant. Nice scenery."

Their calm lasted a few stories and then the mesh box came to a halt, scaring them.

"What happened?" Trouble spun around, hoping to spot the problem.

Chiaro grabbed a railing, holding so tightly that her knuckles bulged and turned white. She glanced at Trouble. "What's wrong?"

He was looking down, scanning the ground, trying to spot the security guard.

The man's voice crackled through a tinny speaker. "Sorry. I saw a frayed spot on the cable. I shut down to mark the section so we can splice a replacement piece tomorrow. I'm starting up in a moment. No worries."

"Wait," Chiaro pleaded. "Shouldn't we come back tomorrow, after you fix things?"

"Naw. It's only a slight fraying. You'll be fine. Brace yourselves. I'm starting the winch again."

The box lurched, dropping a few inches. The falling sensation felt unnerving, a preview of what would happen if the cable broke. Trouble watched Chiaro's face go from terror to anger.

She ground her teeth in rage. "You couldn't just meet your agent friend in the lobby. No, that's too easy."

Trouble pointed at Hanoi in the distance. "Watch the horizon," he suggested, wanting to take her mind – and his own – off the elevator.

She ran her fingers through the cage, gripping the mesh. Chiaro stared at the city's buildings and did her best to avoid looking at the thin screen floor. She didn't want to see the earth hundreds of feet below. "Yeah, sure. Fun ride."

He dared a look downward. Sunlight was hitting the skyscraper's western face, painting the tower's long shadow on the ground. A falcon swirled below them, chased by a pair of swallows. The bird couple were badgering a predator to keep it away from their nest. The falcon gave up his hunt and fell in a steep dive, the thin, tapered feathers of his wings rippling in the wind.

Gusts of air hit the cage, rattling its loose mesh. "What's that?" Chiaro worried.

He tried to explain. "Sunset's approaching. That's the time you get a little turbulence, like riding in a plane. No big deal." Trouble curled his fingers to hide fear-sweat on his palms. Jiggling bothered him, too. But he wanted to look braver than he felt. Acting scared would just make things worse.

Chiaro slumped, letting her body sag against the orange metal cage. "How much farther?"

"Dunno. I'll check." He'd been trying to count floors that passed, but lost track. So he glanced up and down, comparing the height above to the distance below. "Looks to me we're a third of the way up."

"Only a third?" She moaned. "This trip is taking forever. And it's getting dark." Chiaro pointed at dikes bounding rice paddies. Even those short ridges were casting shadows.

He tried to reassure her. "Dark's good."

"How can dark be good?"

"Safer. Easier for us to hide, if there's a problem." His reasoning felt good to him. But Chiaro didn't like it.

"I don't like country dark. It isn't like city dark. At night in Manhattan, the sky's still real bright. You can see on a roof. It's not that way in the country. I stayed at a farm once. You couldn't see anything at night without a flashlight. We could trip and fall off the edge of this building."

"You don't gotta worry. There's gonna be a full moon tonight. Plenty of light."

"How do you know, smarty?" Chiaro glowered at him.

He jabbed a finger at a forest miles away. "Look over there. See. A full moon is rising."

She peered at a mottled disc glowing on the horizon. "That's much too large to be the moon. It's gotta be some kind of flying saucer."

"And you gotta have a problem or you aren't happy." He let his disgust show. Trouble hoped starting an argument would take her mind off the ride. She'd quit focusing on their height above the ground.

Chiaro sulked. "I'm trying to be realistic. Figure out what to do next. Plan a bit."

"Sure." He said it with contempt, like she was lying.

"Hey, I'm supposed to be your friend. You could be nice to me."

"And you could be a little braver. You ate snake, remember?"

"Like I could ever forget. Why'd you bring it up again?"

"To take your mind off the elevator." He smiled in a way that always bugged Chiaro.

"You know, I've had it with you. When I get outta this dumb box, I'm leaving."

"How you gonna get down? Can't take the elevator, since you hate it so much."

"I'm gonna walk." Chiaro crossed her arms, looking defiant.

"Take the stairs?"

"Yeah. What of it?" She watched dark clouds billow on the horizon. The black pillows dumped a squall on Hanoi, then broke into a rainbow. The pastel arch of colors stretched above the Old Quarter, where vendors were rolling up bamboo mats and putting away their unsold vegetables. Neon lights winked on, showcasing merchant windows. Mopeds and Cyclos crowded the maze of narrow streets, carrying shoppers homeward and bringing diners to tightly packed cafés.

Trouble leaned against the cage, feeling the beat of the cable whining past. "There's a lot of stairs. It'll take a while to walk down."

"I got time."

"But not money. Takes cash to fly home. Thought you were going on this gig to make lots of bucks. That's what you told me in Paris."

"That was before you got obnoxious." The lift wiggled. It bounced up, then dropped, falling a couple inches. Chiaro's face went pasty. Sweat covered her forehead and cheeks. She gripped the mesh tighter. "I hate this thing," she growled.

"Then you should get out." Trouble face looked unbearably smug.

"Sure. I'll parachute. You pack a spare 'chute I can borrow?"

"You don't need a parachute to jump. Here, I'll go first. Show you how it's done."

"You jerk. You didn't tell me we were at the top." Chiaro elbowed past him. "I'm gettin' outta here."

"Whoa. Stop." He grabbed the back of her shirt and held on tight. Chiaro's sandal hovered over a gap between the elevator and the building. There was no floor, only air. She could have fallen and been killed. "I said 'jump out,' remember?"

She recoiled backwards, panting. Her voice sounded raspy but calm when she talked. "OK, let go of me and I'll jump."

He relaxed his fingers and waited. A moment later, she leapt across the opening, landing on a plywood ramp. Her steps thumped across flexing wood, causing her to bounce. Trouble followed, landing on the plywood sheet. He retraced his steps to close the elevator door. The moment it was shut, the lift sank out of view, leaving him standing at the building's edge. He backed carefully away.

Chiaro was outraged. "He could'a waited a few seconds. Didn't have to rip the box away like that. It was dangerous. Besides, how's that guy expect us to get down?"

"Maybe the guard needed his elevator. You know, to bring up the woman who's meeting us."

"So quick?" Chiaro gave him an anxious stare.

Trouble also felt uneasy. He looked around for cover and there wasn't much. A crane hovered overhead like a Halloween skeleton, but its open frame offered no place to hide. The operator's booth was made of tinted glass. It'd be easy to spot someone inside. Otherwise the roof was pretty bare.

Trouble walked to a platform, the only equipment left on the roof. An overgrown trampoline, it was positioned to receive supplies dropped by the crane. Rubbery material stretched across the flat top in the same way a "skin" forms the top of a musical drum. He jumped atop the platform and hopped around. The material didn't flex much. It was pulled tight to hold a lot of weight. That made sense, considering it was used to cushion freight dumped by the crane.

"Will you stop playing around?" Chiaro grumped.

Trouble jumped off the trampoline. "I wasn't playing. I was looking for a place to hide, in case someone nasty surprises us."

"You're being ridiculous. We can't hide atop that thing."

He pointed at the metal framework. "I was thinking about crawling underneath. It'll be dark soon. Sun's already below the horizon. Hard to spot us under there."

Chiaro knelt down and looked at zigzag tubing. "Not a lot of room. Everything meshes under there. I don't think we'd fit." She got to her feet and brushed off her hands. Pivoting, Chiaro scanned the rooftop. "There isn't even a fence. You can walk right off." She moved along the perimeter, staying about a yard from the edge.

Chiaro walked over to the building's core, where a dozen large squares were cut in the roof. She laid down and peered into the dark. "You think these holes are deep?"

"Drop a coin," he suggested. "See how long it takes to hit something."

"Good idea." She grabbed an American quarter from her pocket and tossed the disc into a void. They waited ... and waited. A faint clink echoed along the shaft. "Sounds like the quarter fell all the way to the bottom." She pushed herself away from the hole and stood up. "Gotta be elevator shafts," she concluded.

He frowned. "We can't hide in those."

A chill breeze gusted across the roof. Chiaro shivered. She gestured at an open stairwell. "Why don't we sit there? It's out of the wind, at least."

"Yeah. Hope we don't have to wait long." Trouble walked down the stairs and sat where he could peer over the roof. Chiaro followed him.

She curled into a ball. "I'm tired. Gonna take a short nap."

"OK." He tried to make himself comfortable on a dusty concrete step. It wasn't easy. He watched daylight fade, becoming the "blue hour" after the sun drops below the horizon. Lanterns glowed inside farmhouses, turning their windows yellow. Hanoi became a ribbon of twinkling lights, curving along the horizon. The moon kept rising, shrinking from an orange melon to a white golf ball. Stars filled the night sky in clusters and streaks. Distant giants showed as mere pinpricks of light, blinking on and off in random ways. A large planet shone brighter than the rest, but Trouble had no idea if that constant beacon was Venus or Mars.

Night cold bit into him. He pulled his arms tight around himself, trying to stay warm in the flimsy pajamas they'd made him wear. Trouble couldn't wait to get out of those foreign clothes. He was sick of being disguised as an old woman.

Jet lag grew heavier and heavier, burdening him like a dozen suitcases. Chiaro's soft breathing indicated she'd already fallen asleep. Would a short nap be so bad? His eyes closed. His chin touched his chest. A deep rest invited him. He felt himself jump on a dark slide into peaceful dreams.

When he awoke, Trouble was disoriented. How long he'd been sleeping was a mystery. He knew it was more than an hour. The moon was at its zenith, hanging straight above him. The air felt chilly as the cement steps under his stiff body. He fought to remember why he'd felt it was important to wake up. Then he heard the winch motor's huffing and the elevator cable's squeak. Soon, they'd no longer be alone. Someone was coming to the roof.

22

The security guard stepped inside the elevator and inserted a key, unlocking a control box. A flip of the lid exposed levers and buttons. He jerked a lever, halting the elevator a few stories above ground. After a brief pause, he reversed direction and bobbed to a stop, hovering above a concrete slab. The guard studied Flix and a bodyguard towering over the boy. Flix was dressed in a tailored safari outfit with an Australian outback hat, brim flipped up on one side for a jaunty look. The bodyguard wore a black suit over a white T-shirt. Neither of them looked happy. But the part-time engineer, full-time security guard didn't care how they felt. He just wanted their money. "I've shown you how to use the elevator. So where's my cash?"

The bodyguard slid an envelope from a pocket inside his suit coat. He tossed the thick package at the guard.

Careful fingers opened the envelope and counted the bills. "This is only half the amount we agreed on. Where's the rest?"

Flix puckered his cheeks, forming a tight "O" with his mouth. It was clear he wasn't comfortable in this situation. "You get the balance after I'm safely out of Vietnam. It's a bonus to make certain you don't create problems for me."

"Or me," the bodyguard added. He spread his legs in a judo stance, making it clear he'd use force if necessary.

The guard sulked. "I'm the one with problems. My family learns I let you interfere tonight, I'm toast. They'll fry me. I'll never work in Vietnam again. I'll be hustling tourists at Angkor Wat for a bowl of rice a day."

"I explained how we'll cover you." Flix toyed with one of the innumerable pockets on his safari outfit. "We tie you up. A work crew finds you in the morning. You tell them someone broke in, looking for valuable materials like rolls of copper. They left disappointed after finding nothing worth stealing. But they took the night's security videos with them, so there's no way to identify them." Flix displayed latex gloves covering his fingertips. He smiled. "No prints."

"How can I be sure of getting the rest of my cash?" The guard remained skeptical.

"How can we be certain Trouble's on that roof?" Flix pointed up the skyscraper. "Truth is, we can't. All we have is your word that he's up there."

"He's there," the engineer grumped. "I can prove it to you. There's a camera on the roof. Trouble's in the stairwell, waiting for his agent to arrive." The security guard checked his watch. "She ought to be here any moment."

"Then there's no time to waste. I need your keys – for the elevator." Flix held out an open palm.

"I need the rest of the money," the guard insisted. "And you have to tie me up."

"I'm happy to tie you up," the bodyguard snarled. He took a menacing step toward the engineer.

Flix put a restraining hand on his bodyguard's arm, causing the man to pause. With a condescending stare, Flix explained what happened next if the guard didn't cooperate. "We've already given you a lot of money. So you'll be OK even if the balance never gets paid. Or you can test your judo skills on RJ. He's a black belt master, first rank. In other words, RJ could tie you up for real and take back what I've already handed you. Make up your mind. I'm out of time. I need to get on that roof."

Flix's bodyguard flashed out an arm and grabbed the engineer, squeezing hard.

The engineer's eyes became tight with pain. "Ouch. All right. Here's the keys. Let go of me – please."

RJ snapped the keys in his pocket. "Let's go. You heard the man. We're movin' fast now." Flix's bodyguard shoved the engineer toward the lobby door.

"What are you doing?" The engineer whined.

"Tying you up, just like you wanted."

A moment later, Flix's bodyguard returned, flashing a wad of video discs. "I took all his recordings and disabled the video system."

"Did you see Trouble on the roof, before you shut off the cameras?"

"Yeah. He's there, along with a friend. She looks like an old woman, a local."

"The old woman is his agent?" Flix stepped into the elevator.

RJ followed, closing the cage door. "I don't know. Could be. They're huddled in the stairwell, like that security guy said. So I don't think she's Trouble's main contact. It looks like they're waiting for someone else to arrive. So I'm figuring the old woman is only a guide who brought Trouble to the rendezvous." RJ stuck a key in the control panel and turned. The elevator shot upward.

Flix gave his bodyguard a puzzled look. "We're riding in the only working elevator. Nobody's going to walk up a thousand feet of stairs. So how is Trouble's agent getting on the roof?"

"Got me." RJ thought for a moment. He gave a brief laugh. "I guess they're gonna fly."

Elevator noise woke Trouble and he attempted to stand. He discovered one leg was numb and unresponsive. The nerves tingled but muscles didn't behave correctly. He stumbled out of the staircase and looked around. He saw nothing but a moonlit roof and empty sky. Without warning, a black shape flew overhead, buzzing like an insect. A gust of air from the winged creature startled Trouble, causing him to duck. He twisted to get a better look, but the silhouette dove over the skyscraper's edge and vanished.

Loud buzzing and a blast of frigid air wakened Chiaro. Frightened, she jumped to her feet. "What was that?"

"I don't know. A huge bird, maybe. It looked like an overgrown eagle. Except it made a racket like a toy airplane." Trouble hobbled to the trampoline and used its rim for a crutch. Leaning on the metal frame, he approached the building's edge. Maybe he could spot the creature flying below them. He took a strong grip on the trampoline and leaned over a thousand foot drop. The view made him dizzy and it took a moment to calm his mind.

Hanging off the building, Trouble spotted a dark shape rushing at him. The bird was coming straight up, soaring along the skyscraper's vertical glass wall. At first, the buzzing wings shot upward with great speed. Then the object slowed more and more. It became easier to see and he realized the "creature" was man-made. He was looking at an ultra-light, a very small airplane. Someone wearing a helmet was at the controls. They were waving to him to get off the building's edge.

He twisted to get away, trying to pivot on his numb leg. Trouble barely ducked in time when the ultra-light fluttered over the building's crest. He watched in amazement as the pilot jammed controls to extreme positions, using the aircraft's stall to crash land on the trampoline.

A thud shook the roof, sending Trouble wobbling backwards. Chiaro rushed to grab him, keeping Trouble from tumbling into an open elevator shaft. "Thanks," he muttered.

"What's going on?" Chiaro stared at the aircraft in amazement.

Trouble couldn't see the pilot's face behind a helmet visor, but he recognized the socks on her feet. He leaned close to Chiaro's ear so she could hear him over loud engine noise. "My parent's agent has arrived.

Remember, I told the wealthy merchant at the lake how I was looking for *Chaussettes blanches*. That's French for white socks."

"How come she wears them? It's hot in Vietnam. Sandals are fine. Socks aren't needed." Chiaro was surprised.

Trouble explained, "As a small child, she played in the lab and spilled a beaker of acid. The powerful chemical burned away flesh below her ankles. She wears socks to hide scars from the accident. It's how she got her nickname – Socks."

"I believe you. But why'd she crash land instead of dropping like a helicopter?"

"An ultra-light is a real plane. It needs a landing strip. Without one, Socks had to stall her aircraft and let it fall out of the sky. It's a gutsy maneuver. Mess up and she gets killed."

"Glad it went OK." Chiaro relaxed. "She's gesturing for one of us to get onboard. I'll get your daypack so you can hop on." She ran to the stairwell and grabbed his kit, slinging her own messenger bag over a shoulder. A moment later, she was back at the trampoline. "I left our clothes in the stairwell. I'll take 'em with me on the next trip, when she comes back. Looks like only one person can fly with her." Chiaro pointed to an empty chair behind the pilot.

"All right. I'm going." Trouble bent over the trampoline and rolled atop the platform.

Socks yelled at him in Vietnamese, waving an arm in an unmistakable gesture to stay away. Then Socks looked at Chiaro and talked in English. "Get on. Leave the old woman here. Hurry. Strangers are in the elevator. They'll be on the roof any moment."

Trouble broke out laughing. In the dim moonlight, even Socks thought he was an old woman, a native Vietnamese. She hadn't seen Trouble since they were infants and had no idea what he looked like. Chiaro was dressed as a boy and Socks assumed the boy must be Trouble. He was about to explain when the elevator banged to a halt, arriving on the roof. Flix's bodyguard slammed the cage door open and rushed out.

Socks leaned over. She grabbed Chiaro's arm, pulling her on the trampoline. "Get in. Click your belt. We're leaving."

Still holding Trouble's daypack, Chiaro hopped in the ultra-light. She fastened her seatbelt and gave Trouble an apologetic look.

He knew there was no time for thought or questions. A quick glance toward the elevator revealed Flix and RJ were halfway across the roof. In a second, they'd be close enough to prevent the ultra-light from leaving.

Socks gunned the engine and the plane lunged forward, bouncing across the roof. Chiaro screamed, realizing they weren't going airborne. A last bounce and the ultra-light vanished off the building, diving head-first toward the ground. The event was so dramatic that even Flix sprinted to the building's edge to see what happened next.

Wobbling like he was arthritic, Trouble hobbled on the numb leg. By the time he stood next to RJ and Flix, the ultra-light had gained enough speed from diving to level out. For a while, the tiny airplane made panic turns, skimming obstacles in the construction site. Then it nosed up, zooming to a hundred feet off the ground. The buzzing engine noise grew quieter. The plane's dark silhouette became a black dot.

Flix's tall bodyguard screamed a curse. He ground a fist into a palm in rage. "We missed them. The money's gone."

Flix looked at the man in astonishment. "RJ, it's all right. We know what direction they took." He pointed at the horizon. "I'll rent a helicopter. We'll search for their hideout in the morning, when it's light."

The ex-NBA player wasn't convinced. "Maybe they didn't keep going in a straight line. They might'a turned when they got out of sight." RJ's angry stare bored into Trouble. "This old woman knows something. I feel it. She's gonna tell us what she knows." With deliberate slowness, the six-foot-eight judo master extended massive hands to grab what he thought was an old woman.

His throat dry with fear, Trouble edged backward in a stiff motion. His numb leg added to the impression he was elderly and arthritic. Dried potting clay on his face left his skin appearing cracked

Socks And Chiaro Dive Off The Skyscraper

from old age. The cone hat prevented RJ and Flix from seeing a healthy head of hair. The hat also shaded his face from moonlight, disguising his features.

Flix moved closer, hoping to stop his bodyguard. "Violence isn't necessary. I assure you we can find them …"

RJ wasn't buying Flix's assurances. His greedy eyes only saw a fortune vanish off the roof, leaving behind a single clue – the old woman.

Resisting was futile. Trouble attempted to bob and weave, ducking the man's hands. But a moment later, he was caught in a painful grip and flipped upside down.

"Talk," RJ screamed.

Flix hopped around, tormented by anxiety. "You'll get us arrested. Put her down."

"I'll put her down, all right." RJ walked to the skyscraper's edge. He dangled Trouble head-first off the side.

Blood rushed to Trouble's head. He felt his pulse throbbing in his temples. He was afraid of being dropped – and scared the back of his head would bash into metal on the building's side. The iron grip on his ankles burned his skin. It felt like hot rings were cutting into his flesh. The fear and pain forced him to open his eyes and seek a way out of his predicament. He looked out and an upside-down world bobbed around him. Moonlit swirls of rice paddies danced above twinkling stars. He craned his neck, daring a glance straight down.

One story below Trouble lay a work surface used by crews mounting window glass. Pipe-like guardrails ringed a wooden floor. Bars running underneath suspended the narrow platform. It looked sturdy enough to hold him, if he dropped to it. Yet the risks felt enormous. Missing the target would be catastrophic. The next stop was a thousand feet below. Trouble didn't want to think about what he'd feel striking the ground. But even hitting the platform had its own dangers. He might land on his head and be knocked out. Worse would be breaking his neck. He'd be paralyzed.

He decided against trying to get himself free of the bodyguard's grip. But then he noticed specks of clay spiraling into darkness. His "makeup" was falling off, shaken lose by RJ's thrashing. The man turned violent against an "old woman." There was no telling what the guy would do when he realized the "woman" was Trouble, the target of their search.

He could hear Flix shouting, trying to reason with the bodyguard. Each plea brought even angrier jolts and worse threats. There didn't seem to be any choice. Trouble had to get himself dropped into space and hope for the best. All of his normal belongings were in his daypack, including a pocket knife. Chiaro had taken the pack with her on the ultralight. The only thing left in his pockets was a King Cobra's head, given him by the restaurant owner. Maybe there was a little venom left in those razor sharp fangs.

Trouble fought to untangle the Ziploc bag from his pants pocket. It proved difficult in his inverted posture. He struggled to pull out the object and his squirming upset the bodyguard, resulting in even more shaking. Finally, he felt the baggy in his hand. He ripped off the plastic and stuck his fingers in the serpent's head like it was a puppet. Trouble wasn't sure he could do an upside-down sit-up. That move took a lot of stomach muscle and practice. So he waited for RJ to jerk him upward. The motion would give him a better chance to snap the teeth into a hand grabbing his ankle.

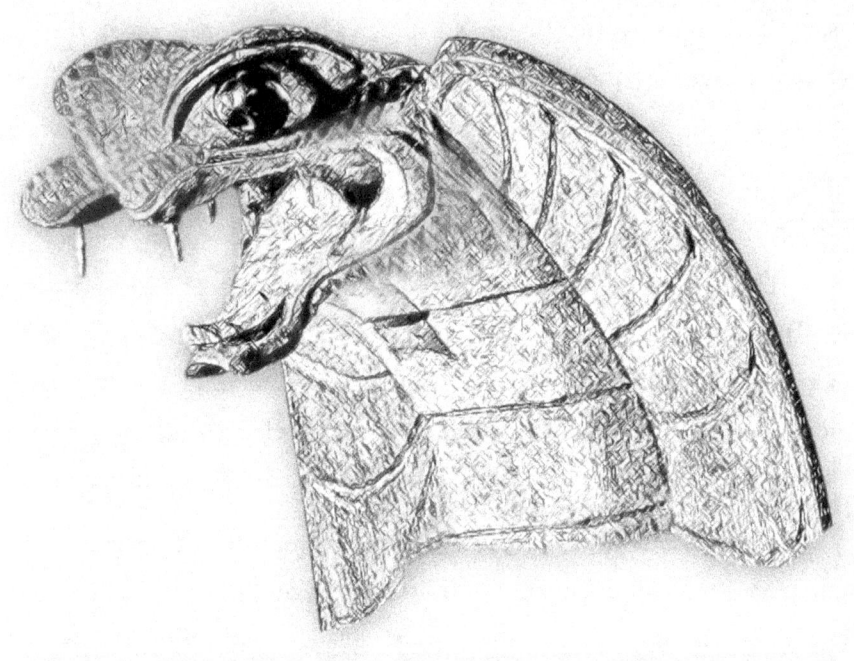

Amputated King Cobra Head

The moment came and Trouble made the best of it. His timing wasn't perfect, but it was good enough. He bent as far as possible, saw a bare hand grabbing an ankle, and snapped the snake's mouth shut. Knife-like fangs sliced into flesh, inflicting a painful wound. The damaged hand released its grip and Trouble twisted around. He was still dangling from the bodyguard's other hand. The spinning motion caused him to smack hard into the skyscraper's wall. Bolts of light shot across Trouble's vision. Fighting to see clearly, he looked for the snake head and it was gone. Had he dropped the piece?

The answer came from RJ's yell. "That wretched woman. I'll kill her for this."

"No!" Flix screamed.

"She had a snake in her pants. The thing bit me. Look, I ripped off its head." Stunned to realize a King Cobra's fangs were buried in his palm, RJ forgot about Trouble. He released the heavy burden of a prisoner so he could rip the snake's head out of his other hand. Trouble fell like a ship anchor tossed in the sea.

He attempted to spin, hoping to land feet-first on the platform. His effort caused him to bounce off the skyscraper, sending him beyond the work surface. He twisted and grabbed with all his might. Both hands caught a guardrail pipe on the platform. He splattered against the pipe, taking a sharp punch to the chin. His chest swung into the railing, forcing a grunt out of him. Dangling below, his scrambling feet thrashed, hoping to find a solid grip and discovering only air.

But despite a hard crash, the workman's cradle held and Trouble pulled himself aboard. Panting, dazed, he managed to slide over the guardrail and drop on a wooden floor. Above Trouble, Flix babbled in an agitated voice.

"We gotta get out of here. You killed her."

"Who cares? She might'a killed me. That's what I care about. You're takin' me to a hospital, Flix. I'm getting a dose of anti-venom."

"Sure. Ah, here. Let me help you to the elevator." Flix talked in a smooth way, like a salesman.

Trouble laughed. He realized Flix didn't care about getting RJ to a hospital. He just wanted to run from the crime scene, escape before someone reported an old woman falling from the skyscraper.

Once the elevator motor whirred, Trouble decided to get off the work platform. He needed to cross a gap of several feet between the cradle and the building. "So close, yet so far," he muttered. The path used by workers was a narrow beam. It was like tightrope walking. But unlike the circus, there was no safety net.

Trouble spread his arms for stability and placed a sandal on the beam. His thin leather soles proved to be slick, a poor substitute for heavy work boots with their snug grip. Maybe the best thing was to sprint across, hoping momentum carried him to the other side. He backed up to get a running start. Trouble counted softly, licking dry lips. "One, two, three …" His feet touched the beam only to slide off, first on one side, then on the other. After the third step, he was falling and could only lunge forward, trying to land inside. White concrete dust billowed around him when he thudded on the floor. His knees hung outside the building.

Despite some cuts and bruises, he was safe for the moment. There was time to grab his old clothes and change into himself again. With luck, he'd find a washroom with running water where he could scrub the clay off his skin. Then he faced a tough decision – walk down hundreds of steps or wait on the roof, hoping Socks would come back in her ultra-light. Either way, Trouble was in danger. It wouldn't be long and Flix's bodyguard would realize the snake bite was a fake, painful but harmless. Trouble was certain RJ would return with a real "attitude."

24

His face was clean for the first time in hours. Even his hands and feet were washed, free of itchy clay. Best of all, Trouble wore his own clothes again. Rumpled jeans and a faded blue t-shirt felt like relief to his skin after hours trapped in a bad costume. He pulled on his jacket and hid the old woman's outfit at the bottom of a trash bin, then covered the evidence with wads of paper towels. Things were better, yet he still faced a difficult choice. He walked out of the bathroom and looked at faint moonlight painting glow on a staircase. Hiking those stairs back to the roof meant risking capture. The memory of hanging over the building, threatened with death, was fresh in his mind.

He looked at stairs going downhill and realized they vanished in blackness. He'd have to pick his way carefully down hundreds of steps to reach the lobby. A mistake would cause him serious injury. A fall might even kill him. At the bottom, he'd be forced to hitchhike back to Old Town Hanoi, where he'd try to arrange another rendezvous with Socks. He was certain ninjas would have the old merchant's home under surveillance. Visiting him would be dangerous. Yet the thought of going home in defeat was unbearable.

So Trouble stalled, choosing to wait on the roof for a while. Maybe he'd see the ultra-light flying toward him. On the stairs, Trouble lifted his feet with care, trying to be silent. His eyes poked over the top and he scanned the area, turning all the way around to make sure he didn't miss anything. It looked safe. He dared a step upward and waited. Nothing happened. He tried another step. It seemed he was alone.

Trouble chose a spot where he could sit in darkness, yet watch the horizon. He sat against a cold pipe supporting the cargo trampoline, keeping his ears alert for a warning noise. At least the elevator motor was loud when it went to work, hoisting the lift. He planned to run for the stairs when he heard the noise. Maybe he could go a few stories lower and find a place to hide.

Meanwhile, Trouble watched the moon travel its path, sinking toward the horizon. Every few minutes, shooting stars flashed across his view. A farmer went to a barn, carrying a lantern. The bobbing yellow light formed Trouble's most exciting event in a lonely two hour period. Cold penetrated his jacket. His muscles became stiff, aching to move. He got up and stretched. Movement helped him get warmer. It also helped his sad mood. Rather than sink into despair, Trouble walked the building's perimeter, staring at the ground so far below.

He watched a truck rattle along the highway. Its headlights bounced like fireflies chasing each other on a muggy summer night. With a last backfire, the old truck vanished behind a hill. Trouble started walking again, careful of his steps. After a while, he paused and looked at a ribbon of light marking the outskirts of Hanoi. He could see a trickle of red taillights navigating Long Bien Bridge, going toward the city. Then bright halogen pairs flowed the other way, coming toward him. A dozen modern cars were crossing the river at a fast pace.

His throat tightened. He tried to swallow and couldn't. The caravan had to be RJ and Flix, returning to the skyscraper. This time, they were taking no chances. A dozen cars meant fifty ninjas, probably more. They must be intending to surround the building so he couldn't escape. Then they'd perform a floor to floor search, flushing him out. This was his last chance to run down the stairs. He moved toward the staircase, then realized even the top-most level was now dark. He'd be racing blind, charging downhill without sight.

Trouble squinted at the horizon, peering in the direction where Socks vanished. His thoughts begged her to return. A moment later, it seemed his wish was granted. He saw a black object skimming the ground – or was it just his imagination? The more he stared, the more he became convinced he'd spotted an ultra-light flying by moonlight. The tiny craft moved straighter than any bird ever flew. Besides, birds didn't fly at night, did they?

But there was a problem. The racing caravan seemed to move faster than the small airplane. Despite chill air, sweat beaded on Trouble's forehead. He couldn't decide who was going to win the race, Flix or Socks. Pivoting from one focus to another, he attempted to measure their progress. Time had crept like a glacier when he squatted. Now the minutes sprinted like a runner. He felt sand trickling from an hourglass, measuring the moments of freedom left for him.

Abruptly, the black dot angled its path. Trouble's heart turned to stone. Maybe it was a bird, after all. Perhaps it was a large owl, cruising rice paddies in the hope of spotting a foraging animal. A quick dive and the small animal's life ended, like his would terminate when a ninja caught him. He gulped and turned to stare at the cars. They were picking up speed, burning through the snake restaurant village. He decided the cars were going to arrive first, beating the ultra-light — or whatever that black shape proved to be.

A gust of wind hit him, startling Trouble. He realized the gust came from monsoons, tropical winds carrying heavy rain clouds. Their dark shapes billowed in the sky, obscuring stars. More breeze carried the smell of dampness to him from rain in the distance. He could taste the faintly metallic, salty air. But the wind also carried a note of hope. He caught an intermittent buzzing that seemed to grow louder each time he heard the noise. Trouble ran to the trampoline and grabbed a pipe, leaning over the building.

Yes, the ultra-light had returned. It was maneuvering to use the monsoon wind for lift, helping the aircraft's run at the building. His joy was short-lived, cancelled by the sound of car tires. The caravan was pulling up to the building. Headlights ringed the skyscraper's foundation. Car doors flew open. Bodies popped out. Then a worst sound floated upwards. He looked down and saw barking hounds, tugging at leashes, eager to be on a hunt. Distant footfalls clattered in the stairwell. The elevator cage rang from boots hitting the metal box. A mesh door clanged. Trouble's heart skipped a beat. It looked as if Flix and RJ were going to win. They'd be on the roof before Socks' ultra-light.

He scanned the area where he'd last seen her plane. Long moments passed before a puff of wind carried the ultra-light's buzzing to him. Trouble shifted his eyes in response to the noise and caught a glimpse of a dark shape zooming toward the building. The plane's nose tilted in a sharp motion and the engine strained to lift the aircraft. Shifting gusts from the monsoons made this approach trickier than the last one. Forced off course, Socks terminated the run and looped for another try.

Trouble thought he was doomed. But the elevator motor stayed quiet. He flattened his body on the roof and pushed his head over the edge. Hounds were shoving their noses into the elevator and baying as they caught human scents. A pack of dogs tugged their handlers toward a spot where RJ parked when he and Flix visited the building. The dogs were mistaking their scent as tonight's quarry. Handlers corrected the hounds and brought them back to the elevator cage. The dogs traced his and Chiaro's path from scooters to lobby to elevator. Canine noses insisted these people only went to the elevator. Slowly it dawned on the ninjas that Trouble never left the building. He must still be on the roof.

Trouble heard the elevator motor whirr and he recoiled, shoving himself to his feet. He turned to see the ultra-light making another pass at the skyscraper. Its wings bobbed like a nervous dragonfly and the wide snout pointed at the building crane. The plane's noise caught the attention of the group below. A rifle shot cracked and a bullet pinged off the crane. A few seconds later, more shots ripped the air. Yet the plane kept coming. The ultra-light's racket became a tornado screaming in Trouble's ears. He jammed palms over his ears to protect his hearing.

The plane shot atop the skyscraper, stalled, then twisted to a belly flop landing on the trampoline. The ultra-light's go-kart wheels slapped against the rubbery surface, then recoiled in a sharp jolt, before coming to rest. Socks flipped up her helmet visor and glowered at him. She was annoyed at having to make a dangerous second trip. Finally, her look softened. She gave him a mocking smile. "Get on, old woman."

"Gladly." He jumped on the platform and ran in bouncing steps toward the plane.

She yelled over engine noise. "What about that bundle of clothes?"

"Forget 'em. I don't need them." He slid aboard the plane and fastened a harness. "OK. Ready to fly," he announced.

"We'll see," was her sarcastic reply. She gunned the engine until it threatened to suck Trouble into the propeller blades. Her foot came off straining wheel brakes and the plane lunged. They arced forward only to bounce on the roof.

Trouble grunted, stunned by the hard thump. He didn't have time to recover before they hit again. He expected a third smack and got worse. The ultra-light sank down and hit nothing. Its nose pitched forward, sending Trouble's forehead into a roll bar protecting Socks. The painful blow only held his attention for a moment. Then he realized they were falling off a thousand foot building. Damp wind slapped his face and needles of fine rain made his skin feel raw. The good news was they were dropping so fast snipers kept shooting behind them. The bad news was they just kept sinking.

Socks pulled back on her stick and the plane fought to curve upward. Trouble went from jammed forward to pinned against his seat. Ground rushed toward him at a terrifying rate. He understood why Chiaro screamed. Trouble wanted to yell also, but his lungs were empty from g-forces stressing him.

The plane turned upward, then arced even more. But it wasn't quite enough. Soft wheels collided with the ground and screeched along asphalt. He smelled tire rubber burning from friction. They got a lucky break. A monsoon gust caught them and the plane became airborne.

However, moving higher made them a better target. Bullets ripped past Trouble and tore holes in fabric covering a wing. Socks twisted the plane in an evasive maneuver, ducking around containers. She kept the plane low, skimming a rice paddy dike, then dropping to clip green shoots in the pond. Another dike forced a second rollercoaster move, followed by a third and a fourth.

His stomach lurched with nausea. Undigested snake bounced from his stomach into his throat. He spat out ugly pieces, covered in slimy bile. The taste was revolting.

They banked in a sharp turn, sliding between farm animals, twisting around a barn. Ahead lay a hill covered in trees. It looked like they were going to crash into a forest. He wondered if Socks realized the danger. Trouble reached for her shoulder as a warning, but got thrown back against his chair. The plane shot into a vertical climb. That disorienting move was followed by another when Socks dove into a clearing. He expected her to continue the trip, but she didn't. Her plane circled the clearing, skimming a dry area. A moment later, she landed and cut the engine.

"We have to refuel," Socks announced.

Trouble looked around. He recognized the clearing as an area he'd seen from the skyscraper's roof. "Uh, Socks … we're awfully close to the building. I hope those ninjas didn't see us land. It won't take long to drive here."

"Doesn't matter." She ignored him and began unpacking a siphon hose.

He was amazed by her behavior. "Those guys are serious about capturing us." Trouble ran a finger through a bullet hole in wing fabric. "They shot at us."

She frowned at the line of holes. "We'll have to patch those. We need all the lift we can get."

"How about doing the repair work when we get to your home?" He glanced around, afraid he'd see headlights poking through trees.

Socks gestured toward the sky. "My luck's run out. Tonight's a bad time to fly. Monsoon will be against us, a strong headwind. We must stay low and that's dangerous."

"More dangerous than a rifle bullet?" He couldn't believe her attitude.

"Equal danger." She unraveled the siphon hose and began walking toward the forest. "Come on. You can help."

He trotted to catch up with her thin form. She moved quickly despite walking on injured feet, burned in a childhood laboratory accident. "You're convinced we have to refuel and repair?"

"Yes." She nodded. "Tonight, we fly across an area filled with beasts."

"What kind?" Trouble thought she meant snakes and scorpions.

Socks halted to look at him. "There are predators near my home. A tiger or a rhinoceros will kill you just like a bullet. We also have bears. Even elephants attack, if they think you are threatening one of their babies."

"I'm sorry. I had no idea ..." His voice trailed off.

She put a finger to her lips. "From now on, silence. We are going to raid a farm. Their tractor uses diesel, so I must take gasoline from their car's tank. They keep small cans in their barn. We'll fill them."

"But Socks, the dogs will bark. We'll never get out of there without waking up the people."

"I've done it before," she insisted. "And you forget we eat dogs in Vietnam, not raise them as pets."

"I hope you're right." He ducked under a branch to follow her. Their athletic shoes made squishing noises when they ran across a wet field. They picked their way carefully across the farm's pebbled driveway, and entered the small barn, smelling of ripe hay. A few minutes later, they were back at the ultra-light, pouring gasoline from old paint cans into her airplane. Petroleum smell fouled the air, even after they finished and screwed a cap on the plane's tank.

"Please go back now. Return these cans so they don't know I raided them. I may need to do this again sometime."

"You're staying here to patch the wings?" Trouble lifted the cans, making sure they wouldn't clink against each other when he walked.

She took a repair kit from a saddlebag behind the rear seat. "Yes. Hurry. A patch job doesn't take long."

Trouble did a fast walk to the treeline, trying to retrace their steps. Despite his attempts to memorize the path, he exited in a different place. He found himself close to a road going in front of the house. Car engines and tire noise made him freeze, even though he was standing in the open. A trio of autos crept along the asphalt, halting before the farm. Searchlights swept the area. One of the beams ran across him and kept moving. Slowly, he dropped to the ground. His head went into a pile of water buffalo dung. Despite having his chin buried in excrement, Trouble dared not move. The searchlight halted and jerked backwards, trying to find him.

The light wove a tight pattern overhead as he waited. Another beam joined the search, then a third. His clothes were dark, but not his face and hands. He made a terrible decision and buried his fingers in dung. Then he took a deep breath of stench and closed his eyes. The fresh stool felt like warm mud on his face, but it smelled awful. He counted slowly to a hundred before lifting his head and wiping his eyes on a clean sleeve. Searchlights were now probing the barn. The lights stayed on when the cars rolled forward, continuing their patrol.

He remained in the excrement pool until the autos vanished. Then Trouble sprinted to the barn. It was hard to find the water trough in dim moonlight, leaking through a damaged roof. He located the water by smell as much as sight. First he cleaned himself, then rinsed the cans. Knowing gasoline floats on water, he skimmed petroleum, splashing it out. He didn't want farm animals drinking gasoline by mistake. Lugging his soaked but cleaner jacket, Trouble returned to the ultra-light.

Socks took a whiff of him and made an awful face. "Euuw. You stink. You must have fallen in a turd pile."

"Kind of, yeah. I had to duck searchlights and a meadow muffin was the only place to hide."

"Good thing you're the passenger and I'm the pilot. I couldn't stand riding behind that smell. It's gross." Socks put away her repair kit. Most of the holes were patched. "I ran out of glue. Still, it's better. Hop on. We need to get out of here." Socks pointed at searchlights filtering through the treeline. Car doors slammed and the lights grew brighter.

Trouble donned his wet jacket and belted himself in the passenger seat. He'd barely fastened the buckle when Socks fired the engine and gunned her throttle. A dozen hot flashlights broke the treeline and Socks headed straight for them. In the small clearing, there was no other way to take off. The wind was blowing from that direction and she had to point straight into the monsoon to get enough lift.

The next few seconds were life and death, played on a dark stage. Neither side ever really saw the other. The ultra-light made a loud racket, but its noise echoed around the trees, disguising the aircraft's position. Startled ninjas felt a blast from the propeller as Trouble and Socks flew overhead. But then it was too late. They were gone, heading for Dr. Cam's hidden treehouse laboratory.

Dr. Cam's Treehouse Laboratory

The ultra-light was a go-kart with wings, bobbing up and down in every gust of wind. The flimsy aircraft jerked in the night sky like a spastic puppet. Currents of air whipped its canvas wings, threatening to enlarge gunshot holes in the fabric. Riding in the back seat, rain kept slapping Trouble's face, driving icy chill into his body. Wet blasts of night air pressed rain-soaked clothes against his skin. Trouble's flesh bristled from the cold and he clamped his mouth shut to stop his teeth from chattering.

He blinked rain out of his eyes and tried to see where they could be going. Their path in the dark was lit by weak lights on the plane's nose. The dim beams gave a vague aura of brightness to a cloudy darkness ahead of them. They flew over a landscape of blackness with no landmarks or illuminated highways. Farmers and their families had gone to sleep and extinguished the lamps in their homes. There was only the constant drone of an engine that sounded like a mosquito powered by a diesel generator.

After an hour of blind flight, warm colors lit a tired sky. Dawn was coming. Trouble watched clouds tumble against each other, tinted blue and red and gold, like a Dutch Masters landscape painting he'd seen in a museum. Sunlight poked bright fingers through holes in the billowing clouds, penetrating a low ground fog. The damp mist baked in the early dawn, steaming away in a boiling vapor. Wisps of gray twisted off the earth like vanishing ghosts.

He felt the plane drop in altitude and smelled moist grass amid the woody forest. Trouble could see they were heading for a grove of tall thitpok trees. Enormous branches clustered in that forest, growing in a single canopy, stretching in a green blur. There were no gaps in the foliage. It seemed the only way Socks could land was by crashing through tree tops.

Yet she began a corkscrew descent like a bird sensing its nest and spiraling downward. The dizzying arc left him confused, wondering how she'd find a safe place to land. The ultra-light got closer and closer to a maze of intertwined limbs, forming a seemingly impenetrable barrier. He became convinced Socks had lost her mind. He tried to shout a warning, stop her from a fatal mistake. But engine noise dwarfed his voice. He attempted to lean forward and grab her shoulder. The plane's turning force pushed him backwards, ramming him into the seat. Touching Socks proved impossible.

At the last second, when crashing appeared inevitable, Socks yanked her controls to extreme positions. The aircraft flipped on its side and headed nose down, aiming for a narrow slot. Like a key penetrating a door lock, the ultra-light threaded the dark opening, surging past limbs thicker than a man's chest. Birds and monkeys screamed in fright as the plane roared past. They leveled out, rushing into a darkness penetrated only by flashlights clamped on the plane's nose.

Suddenly, they hit a giant spider web, a huge volleyball net strung in front of them. Trouble knew how a baseball felt when it thumped in a catcher's mitt, jerking to an abrupt stop. Socks cut the plane's engine and they were flung backwards, propelled by the net's tension. The tiny airframe slapped ground and bounced to a halt. Overhead, the net sprang to its original position, ready for the next catch. Morning dew collected on the net rained downward, spattering the ultra-light with heavy drops.

"We're home," Socks announced. She removed her helmet and shook her hair, sweaty from a tense journey. Shorter than Trouble, the top of Socks' head was at the same height as his chest. Her diminutive stature and quick movements reminded him of race car drivers and horse jockeys. She unzipped a black windbreaker, revealing an orange T-shirt decorated with Lego robots in bumper cars. Faded red jeans covered her legs like baggy, wrinkled sacks. The jeans were so washed out they had the look of loose pajamas and ended above the ankles. White socks led to green sneakers. They covered her big feet like the shoes of an adult worn by a kid. Her nervous eyes darted from the ultra-light to the treehouse, tracking windows and doors.

Trouble watched Socks check out the landscape. He craned his neck, searching branches for a clue to how he could enter Dr. Cam's lab. Light filtering through two hundred feet of vegetation was pretty dim and he couldn't see much. They were in a clearing between massive thitpok roots, wriggling around them like contour lines on a topographic map. The massive thitpoks sprouted before Columbus sailed to America.

Thitpok Roots Beneath Dr. Cam's Treehouse Lab

Now their twisted roots sprawled like octopus arms grasping for prey. The roots grew tall as a house and ran for yards before plunging into the earth. The root maze had a runway carved through it, where the ultralight could roll forward, picking up speed for take-off. The unlit runway appeared a dark tube, ending in blackness. Trouble pointed along the tunnel. "Is that the path to your lab?"

"No. I'll show you." Socks hopped over a root and wove through a maze of twisting ridges. Her running shoes crunched fallen leaves, giving off an aroma of sweet rot. White mildew grew in blotches on tree trunks, adding its pungent odor. It was obvious she'd memorized the path. After a while, she halted at a platform resting on the jungle floor. Cables ran upward from each corner of the wooden square. A hand-cranked winch raised the platform by wrapping the cables around a drum. Pointing above her head, Socks laughed. "The way to our laboratory is up. Hop on."

Trouble obeyed, stepping on the bamboo floor. He grabbed a crank at one side of the drum and Socks took the other end. Together, they lifted the dumbwaiter in grunts. It proved exhausting work and they halted several times to change arms, giving tired muscles a rest. Slowly, the airplane grew smaller and the sunlight got brighter. Upper levels of the forest came alive in the sunrise. Howling monkeys and singing birds drowned out the sound of Trouble and Socks panting. The dusty odor of leaves and a sweet perfume of thitpok sap replaced dank fungal smells.

High above them, two hundred feet above a tropical jungle, ancient thitpok limbs cradled a treehouse. Huge branches floated Dr. Cam's lab like a waiter balancing a tray on fingertips. With the monsoon winds blowing, the laboratory rocked like a ship rolling over ocean waves.

Socks warned Trouble to make certain his body stayed inside the wooden square. He looked up and saw the dumbwaiter platform was closing a hole in the laboratory's bottom. A moment later, his eyes popped above a floor made of bamboo logs and the dumbwaiter halted. Scientific test equipment surrounded him. A boxy microscope with oversize binoculars covered much of one table. Another bench held chemistry glassware, tangled in hoops and spirals like an amusement park thrill ride. Stacks of transparent discs, known as Petri dishes, filled trays on a third counter.

One corner of the room was quarantined with thick plastic walls. That area could only be penetrated by putting hands in long gloves built

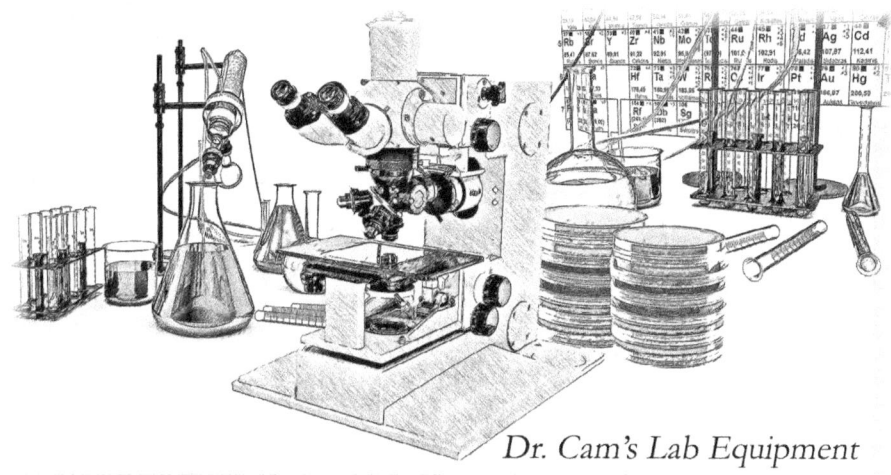

Dr. Cam's Lab Equipment

into the plastic walls. Other benches held centrifuges for spinning test tubes. Refrigerators, freezers and ultrasonic cleaners lined a wall. After a break for a window, the wall continued in empty specimen cages, unused but for a single, notable exception.

Inside the occupied cage, a cuddly ball of fur opened a sleepy eye and peered at them. His dinner plate eyes blinked a few times. The fuzzy baseball recognized Socks and came fully awake. He sprang through the open door of his cage and bounced around the room, zipping from cages to refrigerator tops, springing to a ceiling beam, careening off a wall, finally landing on her shoulder with a gentle thump.

Socks petted his fluffy back. "Zago," she explained with an embarrassed smile, "thinks I'm his mom."

"His mother?" Trouble felt puzzled.

"Yeah. I nursed him with a bottle from the time he was an infant, small enough to fit in a tablespoon. Poachers killed his real mother – and stole his father."

"They broke into your lab?"

"No. I went to the Philippines with my dad. He was teaching a class, showing forest workers how to collect DNA samples from rare species. Walking through the jungle, I found Zago shivering in a tree, frightened almost to death. Footprints and his mother's body told the story. The poachers were interrupted by our approach and fled, but not before they'd killed her in an attempt to capture her."

Chiaro walked in the room from another level. She toweled her

Zago

hair, wet from a shower. She was still wearing her Vietnamese boy outfit, less the cone hat. Chiaro spotted Zago and cooed. "Oooh, he's soooo cute."

Startled by Chiaro's voice, Zago leapt in the air and came down on Socks' other shoulder, hiding behind her neck. A huge eye kept an anxious watch on Chiaro, peering around Socks' chin.

"Can I pet him?" Chiaro wisely kept her distance.

"Best to let Zago get used to you. He's had bad experiences with strangers." Socks held out a palm and Zago slid atop her fingers. With slow deliberation, she levitated him back on his bed. "Daylight means it's time for you to sleep," she instructed the little animal.

His expression became an unmistakable pout, like a small child being put down for an afternoon nap when they'd rather go outside and play. His throat gurgled in protest.

Trouble moved to get a better view. "His fingers look like they come from a frog. What type of creature is he?"

"A Tarsier. They're the smallest monkeys in the world. Twenty-five years ago, there were a million of them, scattered across islands in the Southern Philippines. Now, Tarsiers are on UNESCO's list of the thirty-five most endangered species."

"Ouch. Sorry. Maybe you can send for a girlfriend, start a new Tarsier group here in Vietnam," Trouble offered.

Socks face became sad. "That's forbidden. Like most countries, Vietnam tries to keep out foreign species. Look what happened in the Florida Everglades, when people released pet boa constrictors. Now, the snakes are destroying native species, forcing an expensive trapping campaign to catch Boas and destroy them." She blew Zago a kiss and his huge eyelids grew heavy. He put his head down on a soft towel.

"So Zago has to go back to the Philippines?" Chiaro wondered.

"Yeah. He's old enough now to forage for himself. I taught him to catch bugs. Tarsiers are nocturnal hunters. They roam at night, snatching crickets and moths. Zago's even jumped between trees and caught a small bird in flight."

"What'd he do with the bird?" Chiaro was naïve about jungle behavior of animals.

Socks tilted her head, an amused look playing in her eyes. "Food is food, even when it's a pretty bird."

"He ate the poor thing?" Chiaro was horrified.

"I'm afraid so," Socks admitted.

Chiaro scolded the tiny monkey. "Bad Zago."

"Hungry Zago," Trouble reminded her. He shrugged in amusement. "A guy's gotta eat."

"Oh, yeah. Right. So why can't Zago eat snakes? Better him than me." Chiaro put a look of revulsion on her face. "Which reminds me, where are my real clothes, so I can change out of these?" She tugged at her pants legs.

"Um ... well ..." Trouble stalled.

"You didn't leave my clothes behind, did you? Tell me you didn't lose my outfit. I worked my butt off to earn the money for those pants and boots." She glowered at him.

His response was lame. "I know where they are."

"Where?" Chiaro put her hands on her hips, leaning forward in anger.

He gulped. "I left them on a rooftop."

"So climb up and get them," Chiaro snapped.

"He can't. It's a hundred stories too high," Socks explained. "Atop the skyscraper, ninjas shot at us with rifles. There are bullet holes in my ultra-light's wings. I had to get out of there. Trouble didn't have time to grab your clothing bundle."

"He got his things," Chiaro huffed.

"I changed before the bad guys showed. I'm sorry." Trouble tried to look apologetic.

Chiaro turned her disappointment on Socks. "Yeah, well I don't understand why we had to meet you on a blasted skyscraper, anyhow."

"Vietnamese clothes aren't bad. I wear them," Socks offered.

"Don't change the subject. Why'd you have to crash land on that building and then dive off? You scared me to death." Chiaro gave Socks an accusing look.

"A take-off like that uses almost no fuel. Carrying a passenger means I barely had enough range to get us to the lab. In fact, I had to land and refuel with Trouble on board. A monsoon kicked up, giving us a strong headwind. The ninjas almost caught us at the refueling stop."

"Yeah. I even had to dive into a pile of water buffalo dung to hide." Trouble thought looking indignant might back off Chiaro.

But it didn't. "Now I know why there's brown goo all over your sleeves and chest. Not polite, so I didn't say anything before. But you stink. Shower's on the top level. Use soap on your shirt, too."

"You got a hot shower?" Trouble felt excited.

Socks laughed. "Not this time of morning. By late afternoon, the tank warms up. But Chiaro's right. You smell. Besides, a brisk scrubbing will sharpen your mind, get your senses alert." She pulled a towel off a shelf and tossed it to him. "Here's a bar of soap. After the shower, we'll talk about what happens next."

26

Taking a shower in a swaying treehouse proved difficult. Bathroom facilities occupied the very top level, so every motion was exaggerated. When Dr. Cam's lab shifted half an inch, Trouble felt the floor move half a foot. He staggered, fighting to stay in one place. It was like walking on a ship rolling across ocean waves.

Shower water also reacted to the treehouse's motion. A stream fell past a shoulder when he needed to rinse his hair. The spray behaved like a hose clamped in the hands of a mischievous friend. When Trouble needed water, the stream jumped away, leaving him frustrated.

Rain water in catch basins was reserved for drinking and cooking. So the bathroom used salt water piped from a nearby bay. The spray from the shower nozzle smelled like seaweed and tar, collected from a tide pool. The seawater spattered on his skin, then drizzled against aquamarine tiles. He watched the stream flow down a copper grate in the floor, leaving a crusty residue of salt. Trouble discovered soap doesn't lather much in salt water, nor does the body come clean when rinsed. He placed a brick of coconut soap back in the wall ledge. A scum lingered on his skin, even after wiping himself with several towels. He tried to clean himself with another rinse-dry cycle, but the result was no better. With reluctance, Trouble pulled on his clothes, feeling their material drag across his tacky skin.

Despite his eagerness to talk with Socks, he took a moment to check out the view. He spotted blue glinting through dense foliage and concluded it had to be the bay providing his shower water. Moving to another side of the bathroom terrace left Trouble staring at trees hovering over the building. Their shaggy canopy sheltered the treehouse from the sun's glare, but the dense thitpok trees obscured any landmarks.

Dr. Cam's home seemed to be in a hole, surrounded by thick forest. Perhaps the hollow area was the center of a dormant volcano – or maybe the hole was a crater left by a meteor strike. Socks probably knew the answer. He assumed she and her father explored the area, doing research of some kind. Why else would they have all that laboratory equipment?

Trouble leaned on the railing, letting a tropical breeze tease his face. He smelled a rotting floral scent from decomposing orchids on nearby vines. The strange odors were growing stronger with the rising temperature. It was already getting hot, even in the early morning. Humidity increased his sense of heat. Sweat beaded on his face, despite having been chilled by the shower's cool water. He realized he was stalling and sighed. His next step was the worst part of a journey – finding out what people knew about his missing parents. So far, this moment always proved a disappointment. He might learn something new about their personalities, but Trouble didn't get what he really wanted to know, their location. Hope for finding them grew dimmer each time he tried.

With reluctance, he left the railing and grabbed his daypack. Starting down a flight of stairs, Trouble heard a rumbling and felt vibration under his feet. Instinctively, a hand shot toward a railing, his fingers gripping bamboo. The stair under his feet bounced, rolling with the treehouse. Thatched roofs on each level flapped like towels shaken at the beach to knock off sand. All he could do was hold on and wait for the earthquake to stop. Joints in the wooden stairs creaked like fragile bones, making a hollow rattling sound. When the trembles quit, Trouble looked around and realized the treehouse was a bit lower in the hole. The fall wasn't much, at most a few inches. Yet the experience shook his confidence in his surroundings. He felt anxious to leave and go to a safer place.

Moving quickly, he sprinted past Dr. Cam's bedroom, down another flight of stairs to an intermediate level, finally hitting the bottom floor. The entry hall appeared stable, but a bronze incense box had tumbled to the wooden deck, spilling burning cinnamon sticks. Trouble restored the box to its perch on a low ebony table and spicy incense scented his fingers. He opened the lab's door and saw Chiaro, her face pasty and rigid.

"You feel that?" Her voice quivered.

"Yeah. Seems we had an earthquake." He looked at Zago's cage. The tiny monkey was gone.

Chiaro answered his unspoken question. "Zago took off the moment the rumbling started. He fled out a window, into the trees." She laughed. "Wish I could've done that."

"Me too. I was on a staircase when the shaking hit. Where's Socks – she OK?"

"Didn't bother her at all. I guess she's used to it. She went to get some glasses and ice. Said she has a bit of cola left. Thought we might like a cold drink."

Trouble nodded. He pushed an office chair across the room, sliding it in place at a lab table. That's when he noticed all the large equipment was held in place with bolts. Chemical glassware wasn't so lucky. Several test tubes were broken. Liquid oozed from a cracked beaker. He wondered if it was safe to grab the beaker and dump its contents out a window. Trouble was reaching for the damaged glass when Socks entered the room, carrying a tray holding drinking cups.

"Don't touch that," she yelled. "It's acid."

Trouble pulled away. "Sorry. I didn't know."

Socks gave the tray to Chiaro and reached in a drawer, pulling out a box of vinyl gloves. She donned protective gear and moved the cracked beaker to a box filled with charcoal. "Can't harm anything now. Charcoal will blot up the acid and help neutralize it. I'll test later to see if I need to add anything before I dump the charcoal." Socks took back the tray. "Come in the living room, so we can sit down. Then you can tell me about my father."

She left before Trouble was able to react. He exchanged questioning glances with Chiaro, who was also puzzled by the comment. They trailed Socks into the next room, where an arrangement of chairs surrounded a small coffee table. The furniture was made from stained bamboo logs and the sweetly sick odor of tree sap clung to the air. Boxy pillows served as cushions and bounced like a springy mattress when Chiaro sat down.

Dr. Cam's Treehouse Living Room

A golden Shiva in one corner reminded Trouble of the wealthy merchant's home, where he'd seen comparable statues decorating a patio. The third eye marked this Shiva's forehead and a crescent moon stuck in his twisted hair like a spiky crown. Trouble pulled his stare away from the sculpture and took a seat opposite Chiaro, with Socks in the middle. She pushed aside a bowl of sliced mangoes and slid her tray on the table.

He lifted a cup of soda off the tray and sipped, enjoying how the carbonated liquid refreshed his tired body. "Coca Cola?" he asked, trying to make polite conversation.

Socks nodded. She also drank a few sips, but never took her eyes off Trouble. Her expectant look made him feel uncomfortable. Socks crossed her legs and propped the cup on a knee. "So, when is my father coming home?"

Trouble quit moving a cup toward his lips, feeling a mixture of confusion and anxiety. To stall, he coughed, as though clearing his throat. "Well, ah … Truth is, I don't know." He watched shock turn to anger in Socks' eyes.

"Then why did you come to Vietnam?" She moved the cup from her knee to the table. Socks leaned forward, waiting for his answer.

"I came because I got the crate you sent. It arrived at the Curio Shop. There was a weird rat inside and …" He was about to mention the note from his father when Socks cut him off.

"Yes, that little creature my father mailed to you. What about it?"

Trouble felt an intuition that he shouldn't answer her question about the rat. He was struggling to think of a different way to explain his visit when Chiaro spoke.

"What rat? You didn't tell me anything about a tiny rodent." Chiaro gave him an accusing stare.

Trouble felt he needed to defend himself. "It wasn't small when it arrived in New York. Took me, Bleerio and Flix to jam the creature back in a metal box and flip the locks. We could'a gotten seriously hurt."

Mirth danced in Socks' eyes. Apparently, she thought the idea of being attacked by a monster rat was funny. Her attitude irritated Trouble.

"You should've warned us," he grouched.

"My father pasted danger labels on that old ammo box, in several languages." Socks crossed her legs again and leaned back in the chair. Her body appeared relaxed, but her eyes were cold and harsh. "Did you ignore his warnings?"

"No, I didn't. But my shopkeeper, Bleerio, was desperate to sell something. He and Flix opened the darn box. Then that monster stuck out his teeth and claws."

Socks didn't respond. But Chiaro got very excited. She rose from her chair in a crouch, arching over the coffee table. "Did Flix buy the rat?" When Trouble hesitated to answer, she pressed him. "You sell the rat to Flix?"

"Yeah." He squirmed. Something told him this conversation was making a big problem for him. Socks looked worse with every word.

When she spoke, Socks talked with far too much calm in her voice. Her question had to be some kind of trap. "This Flix – whoever he is – does he still have the rat?"

"Yeah, does he?" Chiaro hummed with curiosity, as excited as Socks was calm.

"No. He got rid of it." That wasn't a lie, Trouble thought. Flix did get rid of the monster.

"He killed it?" Socks offered.

Trouble didn't answer, but Chiaro did. "No, he couldn't have."

"Why do you say that?" Socks turned her head to look at Chiaro.

"Because Flix wanted to come here. He doesn't do anything unless there's money in it. He must'a flipped the rat for a good profit."

"How much did he get?" Socks' eyes bored into Trouble with a truth serum look. Her eyes held an unblinking stare and her mouth was contracted to a narrow line.

He sagged in the chair. Trouble mumbled in a low voice, wishing they couldn't hear him. "A lot."

"I knew there was money in this trip. I knew it. Flix wouldn't sponsor you unless he'd make a bundle." Pointing at Trouble, Chiaro hopped up and down, shaking the treehouse floor.

Hoping Socks would believe him, Trouble shouted over Chiaro's shriek of excitement. "I didn't come here for money and you know that." One look at Socks told him it was too late. She'd closed her mind like the steel door on a bank vault. Nothing he said now would make any difference.

"You two are like all the rest of them. You don't care about science. You don't care about the environment. You don't even care about people. You just want to get rich."

Stung by the criticism, Trouble recoiled in his chair. He felt too shocked for any response. When Socks jumped up and ran on the terrace, he sat there, immobilized. He got up to run after her, but Chiaro put a restraining hand on his arm.

"Maybe it's best to give her a little space. Perhaps we should let Socks calm down. Whaddya think?"

"No." He glowered at Chiaro. "You made a big problem for me. I'm not listening to you anymore." He yanked away his arm and stepped toward a terrace surrounding the room. A swishing noise caught his ears and he felt a strange vibration, like a bow string twanging. Trouble ran outside on the terrace followed by Chiaro. Socks was nowhere in sight.

"Where'd she go?" He swept the area with his eyes, scanning as much as he could see. Vegetation wove around the deck and extended tendrils into the wooden platform, threatening to take over the patio. It was hard to see anything but an invasion of green vines.

"Maybe she went to another level," Chiaro offered.

Then Trouble spotted the cup Socks was holding when she fled the room. The porcelain cup lay on the earth. Last sips of Coca Cola had spilled and the vessel was now empty. Its bottom showed the faded painting of seaweed clustered around a dragon's head. The porcelain was placed at the base of a slick bamboo pole, running in a vertical line from the ground back up to the terrace.

Chiaro leaned on the railing, following his stare and looking at the cup. "She couldn't have thrown it down there. The cup would have broken. How'd she get down so fast?"

"She jumped." Trouble leapt on the terrace railing, balancing himself, wobbling as the treehouse swayed.

"Hey, get down. You'll get hurt. That's too far to jump." Chiaro reached for him.

He sprang to the bamboo pole, wrapping his feet around the wood in a tight embrace, so he didn't slide. "This is how Socks got down so fast. It's their fire escape. I'm going after her."

"Wait. You can't get back inside. That pole's too slick for climbing."

"I know. You'll have to drop that dumbwaiter platform in the lab. Leave it down so I can use it when I find Socks." Trouble released his clamp on the pole and whooshed downward. A moment later, he made a soft landing at the bottom. He was surrounded by a nest of plant life and there were no footprints marking Socks' trail. Tangles of vines covered the earth in confusion. Faded palm flowers had shed their petals on the humid soil like random confetti. There was no trail to follow, only a mosaic of colored petals and brown vine clusters. He'd have to continue the search without visual clues. "Don't forget. Drop the platform," he reminded Chiaro.

"Yeah. Then I'll come with you," she yelled back.

"No. Stay here – in case Socks returns. And this time, tell her I'm after my parents, not her creatures. Quit talking about money, will you?"

"Yeah, OK." Chiaro pouted.

Even from the ground, Trouble could see she wasn't happy. He didn't have time for another long argument with Chiaro. He wagged a hand like a dropping platform. After that last reminder, he sprinted off.

27

An hour later, Trouble staggered to the treehouse, bruised and exhausted. The jungle had drained his energy. Scratches covered his arms and began stinging. Red welts were forming under his T-shirt, a reminder of pointed claws that scraped him. Heavy, wet air around him smelled of rotting mushrooms and wild onions. The sharp odors intensified in harsh sunlight, making him queasy. It was hard to inhale in the steamy atmosphere and get any fresh oxygen into his tired lungs. He fell on the dumbwaiter platform and stared upward, hoping to see Chiaro. "Hey, anybody there?" he yelled. Long seconds passed before he heard footsteps thumping across the laboratory. Chiaro's face peeked out the floor opening.

She looked at a swelling bruise on his cheek and her round eyes got even wider. "Wow, Socks is tough. She can really fight."

"I didn't find Socks." He gently touched the bruise and it throbbed.

Chiaro gave him a questioning look. "So who trashed you?"

"A baboon." He felt dumb saying it.

"You got your butt kicked by a monkey?"

"Baboons are more like small gorillas. This guy was the dominant male in a group. I stumbled into them and he went berserk. Knocked me down with a sucker punch. Must'a thought I was challenging him. I tried to slink away and he grabbed my shirt, tearing a sleeve. I stayed on the ground, hoping he'd calm down. That kinda worked. He screamed a bunch, like he was declaring victory in the match. Then he ran around in a frenzy. I got scared, figuring he was cranking himself up to kill me. But after a few circuits, this guy leapt in the trees and screamed away. The other baboons followed him. So I came back to use a first aid kit."

"Sure. You want me to throw you a kit – or you comin' up?"

"I'm comin' up. Other than the baboon, I saw nothing but huge thitpok roots, twisting around me. I was lucky to find the treehouse again. Got totally lost. The jungle's so thick, Socks could'a been a couple feet from me and I wouldn't have seen her. Searching is pointless. I'll never find her unless she wants to be found. Use the winch and power lift me, will you?"

"Um, sure. But, like, where's the switch? When I entered with Socks, we hand cranked our way up."

"I saw a switch next to the winch, on that roof beam overhead. Try it. I'm too pooped to crank this thing by hand, if I don't gotta."

"OK, I'm lookin' … How's that?"

Trouble heard an electric motor kick-in and felt the platform jerk upward. "You got it. Stand by, in case the winch doesn't shut off when I get to the top."

"I'm waitin' here, don't worry." She watched him rise, moving a lot faster than hand cranking the platform. Chiaro kept a finger on the switch, but the motor quit automatically when Trouble reached the top.

Feeling woozy, he found a chair and dropped into it. "I need ice to put on this bruise. Think they got some?"

"Stay there. I'll get something cold from the kitchen. I saw a refrigerator in there." Chiaro returned with a plastic sack of frozen vegetables. "This will have to do. The freezer compartment was empty, except for this sack. Socks better do a little shopping. There's nothing to eat in that fridge."

"Too bad. I'm pretty hungry." He took the frozen carrots and pressed its icy sack against his cheek.

She looked around for a medicine kit and saw none. "Wait here. I'll do a little exploring. There's gotta be a first aid kit somewhere. We need to disinfect those scratches. Looks like your friend wasn't satisfied with just smacking you. He had to prove his claws were sharp, too."

"Well, I got off easy compared to what might've happened." He watched Chiaro head for a doorway. He yelled at her backside. "You see anything to eat, bring it too."

She grunted a "yes" on her way out the door. A minute later, she came back with protein bars sticking from a pocket and carrying a bottle of hydrogen peroxide. "No Band-Aids anywhere. Lean back. I'll dump this peroxide on your cuts."

He winced as the disinfectant did its job. The stinging medicine made the wounds feel more raw. "Where'd you find the eats?"

"Same as the peroxide – on a kitchen shelf. Man, this place is bare. I checked all the cabinets and saw only plates and pots, not even a sack of rice. There's nothing left to eat here." She dumped four bars on a table. They looked like small candy bars from a vending machine, not full-size snacks. "Two for each of us. You pick first. You're wounded."

He grabbed a banana flavored one and peeled the wrapper. Not waiting for Chiaro, he stuffed the bar in his mouth and tore off a big chunk. Trouble chewed through the hard, stale protein, working his jaws like he was softening a stubborn wedge of beef jerky. A taste of stale banana bread and icky sweet bubble gum filled his mouth, but it was better than starving. He pointed at the remaining energy bars and mumbled. "Ow ou ick."

"I think that means 'now you pick.' I like peanut butter and chocolate. But that only leaves a coconut-flavored one. You OK with that?"

He nodded, too busy chewing for conversation.

"All right. Chocolate's going ... going ..."

He swallowed in a desperate gulp. "We'll split it."

"Thought reason would return once you got a few calories in you." Chiaro ripped the packaging and broke the bar in two.

He gratefully took his share. "Peanut butter's all yours. We'll split the coconut."

"Sounds fair." Chiaro inhaled the chocolate piece and went to work on the peanut butter type. In a few minutes of heavy chewing, they were done. "What's next?"

He frowned. "I dunno." Trouble again put the veggie package against his swollen cheek. He felt demoralized, sick inside. "I guess we find a way to go home."

"Quit?" Chiaro stared at him in disbelief. "You can't stop now."

"Why not? Socks vanished. She didn't know where Dr. Cam went. This trail's at a dead end. So I guess we return to Manhattan."

"I'm not going home broke. Living in foster care is out of the question. Besides, you gotta make some bucks on this trip. Otherwise, you'll never chase down your parents. You can't travel without money. Look, you and Bleerio can't even live unless you get more cash."

"I suppose." He talked in a dull voice. It wasn't the cold pack burning his skin or the bruised cheek that hurt. It was his heart. "But I don't see how I'm gonna make any bucks on this trip."

"You give up too easily." Chiaro rose and began opening drawers, examining their meager contents. She flipped through stacks of paper, bamboo place mats, and some collapsed paper lanterns. Her fingers examined each object with care, turning over the item, checking for something hidden. Next Chiaro went to a worn teak cupboard and opened its doors. There was nothing inside but wet jungle air and patches of white mildew.

Trouble stared at her in amazement. "What're you doing?"

"Searching." Chiaro peered at the underside of shelves in the cupboard.

He got up and walked to her. "What are you looking for?"

"Clues."

"Clues to what?"

"Anything. Everything." She closed the cupboard doors and picked up items on a lab table, turning them over in her hands, staring at them. She peered at a smear of blue dye and blood on a microscope slide, then lifted a stencil used to draw symbols on fresh samples.

He stared at her like she was crazy. "How can you look for clues when you don't even know the puzzle?"

"Oh, but you told me about the puzzle." She replaced dirty test tubes where she'd found them, stuck in a thin metal rack.

Bewildered, Trouble wrinkled his forehead. "I told you?"

"Yeah. You said a monster was sent from this lab. Then Flix sold it for a lot of money. Next thing, you wanna come here. I don't know why, but you did. And Flix decided coming here was a great idea. He gave you money and followed you here. Am I right so far?" Chiaro gave him a smug look.

With reluctance, he agreed. "Yeah."

"So why'd you want to come here?" She quit examining items and stared at him.

He stalled by moving the cold pack. Finally, Trouble decided he'd nothing to lose by confiding in Chiaro. Still, he didn't like it. "There was a note in the crate."

"Good. Now we're making progress. A note raises a lot of questions. Like who sent the note and what did it say. So …" Spreading her arms, she looked at him in a way that said it was his turn to speak.

"The note was from my dad. It was intended for my mother. Which means they're alive. That may not sound like much to you, but it was a huge moment for me … huge. OK?"

"Before you read the note, you didn't know if they were alive?" It was Chiaro's turn to wrinkle her brow in suspicion. Her eyes stared right into Trouble, daring him to tell the truth. "Come on. Is that really true? I always thought you were makin' it up, that they'd gone away on trips and hadn't come back."

"Oh, thanks Chiaro. That makes me feel real good. Why would I make up a bunch of lies?"

"I figured they got divorced and you were ashamed. Maybe your mom ran off with another guy and your dad shot himself … I mean, there's lots of reasons people lie."

"Oh, whatever." Disgusted, he threw the veggie pack in a trash can. It was warm anyhow. "Well they didn't break up. Just 'cause your parents don't get along doesn't mean my folks are divorced, you know."

"All right, I was wrong. Don't rub it in." She leaned against the cupboard. "I apologize. So what'd the note say?"

"Not much."

"Come on. You gotta open up. Otherwise, we're going nowhere in this investigation."

"Oh, so this is an investigation, is it? We're at a crime scene, huh. What crime are we trying to solve?" He gave her an accusing look.

"We're trying to find what happened to your parents, right?" Chiaro knew how to look like an innocent puppy dog. She'd practiced in the mirror for days when she handed a forged absence note to a teacher.

He didn't buy her interpretation of a harmless puppy. "Trying to help me find my parents, are you? Naw, I think you're trying to find a treasure and get rich. Socks was right about you, even if she was wrong about me."

"You're not so innocent, Mr. Trouble. You took money from a friend, Flix. Then you skipped out on him."

"He was ripping me off. Flix changed the rules after I committed to the expedition."

"You still owe him a lot of money. How you gonna pay him?"

"I don't know. I'll do it somehow."

"I got an idea. Let's find a treasure and get rich. Maybe we'll find your parents along the way. Even if we don't, you got money to look for them. You won't have to close the Curio Shop and live with foster parents, like me."

Trouble was speechless. He'd never let himself think about what would happen if his parents failed to return, even after two years without them.

Chiaro sensed he was vulnerable. She pressed him. "You with me or not?"

"All right. Whaddya want to know?"

"The note. It said what ...?"

He squirmed. The note was precious to him. It was the only concrete evidence his parents were alive. Discussing the letter was painful. He was afraid Chiaro might prove the note to be a fraud. Trouble couldn't bring himself to say anything.

Chiaro sensed his discomfort. She offered a compromise. "You don't gotta tell me everything. Just some of what your dad said. OK?"

He relaxed. Now talking didn't feel as threatening. "Indigo said his satellite phone didn't work, so he couldn't call my mother. He sent her an email, but wasn't sure it got through. Dad thought government censors could be blocking traffic between Dr. Cam's lab and the Internet."

"Good news. They're both alive. And your dad was here, with Dr. Cam. That's a start." Chiaro ran a hand across her chin, puzzling over Trouble's disclosure. "Your dad sent a note and an email. He wanted your mom to do something. Do you know what it was?"

"Yeah. Julia was supposed to come here, to Dr. Cam's lab." Trouble sagged, but Chiaro beamed a happy smile.

"Fantastic. They're probably all here in Vietnam – your mom and dad, plus Dr. Cam. All we gotta do is find them. For that, we need clues." She kept being a cheerleader, trying to perk up Trouble's mood. "We're rocking. Let's keep going. What else did your dad say?" She looked at him with eagerness, expecting an immediate response.

Instead, he turned away and stared out a window. Part of the note worried him. He felt a strong reluctance at sharing that piece. He stalled. "There was just stuff."

"Trouble, we can't solve this puzzle without clues. Come on. You gotta share." Chiaro moved so he could see her pleading look.

He exhaled a long, slow breath. "Indigo said they'd been looking for a FOY, whatever that is. He found one. Actually, he found an active one. So maybe they'd found dormant FOYs before. I wouldn't know.

They never talked much about their travels. Just brought home a lot of junk and tried to sell it."

"A FOY, huh. Your dad mention anything else about this FOY?"

He grunted a "yes." Telling her more didn't feel right, but he couldn't figure out why. Still, she was the only one trying to help him find his parents, wasn't she? Socks had bugged out. Flix proved a major disappointment, to put it mildly.

Chiaro moved in front of him. "You gonna tell me or not?"

"I'm tellin' you." He said it like he was giving away his prized bicycle.

She waited for his answer, standing there, looking at him. "Trouble, I can't help you ..."

"I know, you told me." He took a step backwards to get some personal space. "Dr. Cam was supposed to include something important in the package – proof the FOY existed."

"The monster rat – that must've been the proof." Chiaro hopped in a circle, unable to contain her excitement. "This FOY must spit out weird creatures."

"Yeah, and you wanna get rich selling them." Trouble gave her a disgusted look.

"Not true. Flix wants to get rich. I'm only trying to make enough to live as myself, not as an orphan zombie."

"There's worse things than foster care. A lot of those homes are good places," he argued.

"You wanna wind up in foster care? 'Cause you're gonna if you don't find your parents."

"I don't want foster care," he admitted.

"So let's find Indigo and Julia. They came here to see Dr. Cam. All of them could be at this FOY, a source of weird creatures. The place has to be dangerous. Maybe they're injured and need help. We should go there and see. Right?"

"Yeah, that seems logical." He couldn't find a flaw in her reasoning. "Problem is, we don't know where this thing is located. Maybe Socks knows. We should wait until she returns."

"What if she doesn't come back?" Chiaro moved to the winch and hit the switch, dropping the platform to ground level. "Besides, your parents and Dr. Cam might die while we wait for Socks. I say we find this FOY on our own."

"How we gonna do that? It's a big jungle out there. We can't fly around. I don't know how to pilot an ultra-light." Trouble shrugged.

The platform hit earth and Chiaro killed the motor. "Dr. Cam's a scientist. He does experiments, right?"

"No. He's an expert on ancient creatures. Dr. Cam knows fossils cold. One look and he can tell you what type of animal that fossil represents. That's all I know about him. You remember that Moa poop in the Curio Shop? You picked it up and were grossed out to learn it was fossilized dung."

"Oh, yeah. Not my kind of souvenir. Wait a minute. If Cam doesn't conduct experiments, why's he got all this equipment?" She pointed around the lab.

"I dunno. Maybe he's tryin' to learn a new field, get a different job. You got me. But I see where you're going. Scientists do experiments. They write down the results. Which means Dr. Cam must have kept a journal."

"Right." Chiaro nodded. "And we gotta look for his journal. Find his notes and maybe we'll discover a map, describing a source of monster rats. Better would be its location."

"Socks is not gonna like us poking around her house." He frowned.

She thought a moment. "We'll hear the winch. That'll warn us she's coming."

"OK. Should work. We'll put things back where we found them, so it doesn't look like we tore things up searching. You're on. We're gonna find that notebook."

28

They began looking for Dr. Cam's notebook in his laboratory, where it seemed logical he'd keep a log of important experiments and discoveries. Trouble opened drawers, only to find they were empty. Dead spiders had shrunk to dry curls wrapped in the ghosts of their webs. The shriveled remains clung to several empty drawers, but there were no lab notes. Chiaro hopped on tables to check top shelves and found them coated in dust. There was no hidden notebook. Trouble knelt on hands and knees, searching the underside of lab tables, hoping to discover a notebook taped to the bottom. Instead, he found old chewing gum Socks stuck there as a mischievous child. Rough flooring hurt his knees and Trouble was happy to stand again.

He checked the walls to see if they were thick and might contain secret compartments. Sadly, treehouse walls were thin and porous, so it was easy to see through them. His fingers patted the rough texture of jungle woods, careful to avoid splinters. There were no raised edges hinting at a hiding place. He searched through zipped bags of samples, snippets of hair and hide that came from creatures described in tiny handwriting. There were no Post-Its with a scribbled clue. They had investigated the entire lab, except for the bank of specimen cages.

Trouble swung the doors open on empty cages saw their metal frames could hide nothing. Yet maybe the notebook was tucked under the bedding where Zago slept.

Chiaro beat Trouble to the padding in that cage. She lifted and shook Zago's blue rug and his small pillow. Nothing fell out. She patted the rug, then the pillow, probing for something concealed inside. "No luck," she announced, glad to be moving away from Zago's body odor, an armpit smell that clung to his bedding.

"Kitchen?" Trouble suggested.

"Why not?" She moved into the kitchenette and began popping open cabinets. Shiny black lacquerware bowls and white ceramic tea cups squatted on narrow shelves. There was a pile of chopsticks carved from buffalo horn and salad server tongs made of the same translucent bone. Otherwise, the area held only a couple bamboo placemats. Chiaro banged the doors closed in disappointment. "Nothing in here. I already went through this room, scrounging for food. Any ideas?"

"In the movies, druggies hide their stash in the freezer." Trouble opened the refrigerator door and stared at white plastic surrounding empty shelves. He found a table knife and jabbed at thick frost coating the freezer compartment. The clink of a dull blade hitting aluminum confirmed nothing was hiding behind the icy layer. He closed the door with reluctance, savoring dry, cool air inside the compartment.

Chiaro had a suggestion. "How about behind? Sometimes people tape important things to the back of a refrigerator."

"OK." He grunted, wriggling the heavy appliance so it moved forward. Trouble peered at its coils, wrapped in thick dust. He blew on the metal and dust motes sprayed everywhere. Sneezing, he waved a hand to clear away a gray cloud. "Wish I had a flashlight."

"Wait a minute. There's a small mirror in the upstairs bathroom. I'll run up there and borrow it. Maybe we can reflect light behind the refrigerator."

"Check the toilet while you're there. See if they hid anything inside the tank. They would have wrapped the object in plastic."

"Yeah, good thinking." Chiaro ran out of the room.

Trouble used the time to peer under the sink. A few open containers held cleaning supplies, but nothing interesting. He heard Chiaro's footsteps and stood in time to see her entering the room. "Find anything?"

"No. Toilet just holds water. I even leaned over the balcony to check for an outside pocket. Figured maybe he'd tuck the notebook there since nobody would look for it, hanging on an outside wall. Unfortunately, there wasn't a suspicious bulge anywhere." She handed Trouble the mirror.

He struggled to adjust the glass so it lit a dark area behind the refrigerator. After a few tries, he discovered a good angle and swept the coils, only to find them blank. "Guess I should check under the 'fridge. He could've put the notebook in a baggy and hid it in the drip tray." A black plastic tray slid out easily, but held only condensation. He put the tray back and stood up. "Eerie how little they keep in this house. Makes you wonder if they really live here."

"Maybe it's just a place to stay while they explore the jungle," Chiaro suggested.

"Could be. I get this strange vibe. Like they were planning to leave soon and never return." Trouble moved toward the living room, where they'd sat before getting into an argument with Socks.

"Wait up. I'm coming." Chiaro ran after him.

They began lifting cushions off chairs, finding lint and a few coins. A tiny lizard scampered away, frightened when his hiding place was revealed. The bright green shape wriggled like an animated figure slicing across a banner ad on an Internet page. After turning and patting every cushion, they looked at each other and shrugged.

"I'll check underneath." Trouble flattened himself and tried to slide under the chairs, but their bamboo framing got in the way. He raised enough to look at Chiaro. "Try lifting this thing, so I can see the bottom."

She moved over and tugged on the chair's back. Thick bamboo rods felt warm and slick on her palms when she pulled. But the chair didn't budge. "Is this thing bolted to the floor?"

"Oh, yeah. It is bolted. Sorry. I didn't see that. Guess they did it 'cause of the earthquakes." He got up and brushed grit off his fingers, running them over his jeans. "Your hands are smaller. Try sliding your arms through the bamboo."

"Sure." Chiaro was able to insert her arm up to the shoulder. She ran her palms over coarse material, feeling its woven texture. She moved from chair to chair, finding nothing. "Looks like we're gonna have to look in their bedrooms."

"Socks won't like that, if she finds out."

"She'll never know. We'll put everything back, so it's where we found it." Chiaro dropped cushions on the chairs and adjusted things to look normal. "We don't have any choice, do we?"

"You're right. I don't like it, though. I better check that dumbwaiter in the lab. Make certain Socks hasn't returned and might surprise us."

"Maybe you ought'a bring the platform up. Just for a while. We can drop the lift when we're through searching their bedrooms." Chiaro saw the unhappy look on his face. "Just an idea …"

He thought about his options. None of them seemed the right way to treat Socks. But Trouble felt desperate to find a clue about his missing parents. He caved. "All right. I'm raising the elevator."

A few minutes later, they walked into Dr. Cam's bedroom, where a massive bamboo frame held a mattress wrapped in linen sheets.

Dr. Cam's Treehouse Bedroom

Mosquito netting, tied around the bedposts, looked like a do-rag. Sun filtered through the gauze canopy and painted streaks of light across the sheets. Wind outside swayed the treehouse and the bedroom shifted in response. Walls and floorboards creaked in the humid air, then grew still. Trouble listened for the sound of Socks returning. Maybe she knew another way to get inside, other than the dumbwaiter in the lab. He concentrated on her approach, but only heard the chatter of a nervous monkey. Shrieks of complaint ended in a loud slap of tree bark. There were no other noises, though he strained to hear through the silence.

He calmed his mind and went back to searching. It was puzzling to find suitcases stacked in an uneven tower. A thick leather case sat nearby, covered in stickers from travels across the globe. The stickers were in brilliant colors like a passport stamped by customs clerks around the world.

"Coming or going?" Chiaro asked, pointing at the suitcases.

"My gut says they were leaving." He wrapped fingers around a thick handle on the leather case and tried to lift. Trouble was barely able to raise the suitcase off the floor. He dropped the burden with a thump, rubbing his tired fingers. "That thing weighs a ton."

"Jackpot." Chiaro jumped with excitement, shaking the treehouse floor. "Dr. Cam's notes are inside. I feel it."

He pushed on sliders, trying to flip open latches holding the leather suitcase shut. Nothing budged. "It's locked."

"Good thing I'm here. I told you I'd come in handy on this trip. Move aside and I'll unzip this thing like I opened your parent's safe, so you could get your passport."

Trouble went to take a step and halted. He felt the room shake and heard a soft thud. "What's that?"

"Another quake. Come on. Let's get this luggage open." Chiaro pulled her lock picking kit out of her messenger bag and knelt down. She went to work and soon had both latches sprung. Together, they hefted the bag on the bed and flipped it open.

He reached toward a stack of journals inside the suitcase and heard an angry shriek behind him. Trouble spun around, following Chiaro's shocked look. Both of them stared at an enraged Socks, her face tight with emotion. A vein in Socks' forehead pulsed with rage. Her eye sockets puffed from crying and she tried to rub them, but her clenched fists offered little comfort.

"Get out. Go now," she demanded.

29

Stunned by Socks' arrival, Chiaro babbled the first thing that came into her head. "How did you get inside the treehouse?" Unfortunately, the question made Socks very angry.

"I saw you raise the lift. Thought you'd locked me out, huh? So you could rob me in safety. Well, there are other ways to get inside. They just require more effort than the lab elevator." She rocked on the heels of her big green sneakers, her bony legs outlined by the faded red jeans. Brittle, dry bamboo leaves stuck in her black hair and a couple of them rustled to the ground. Her mouth was a tight line and Socks acted like she wanted to attack Chiaro and Trouble, but didn't know how to fight. Finally, words spat from her mouth. "You're thieves."

"No. We're searching for clues to help find your father – and my parents." He tried to comfort Socks, talking in a soothing voice.

"Your parents!" Her voice was a high-pitched shriek. "They're the reason my father's missing. Your mother is to blame." Her anguished eyes darted around Dr. Cam's bedroom, searching each portion of the room for comfort and finding none.

Trouble replaced technical journals in the suitcase where he'd found them. He turned so he could face Socks. "How long has your father been gone?"

"Ten … no eleven days." Tears wet her cheeks. Socks couldn't imagine a life without her father. She woke each morning to see his thin frame. Her first vision of the day was his small body, lost under a stained lab coat. She'd open her eyes and watch him dart in rapid movements, completing experiments. His long fingers, mottled with chemical stains, were always plucking test tubes from racks. The memories turned her bitter. "What's it to you how long my father's been gone? Neither of you know what it's like to be an orphan, get adopted, then lose your family – even if it's a family of one."

"True. But adopted or not, I've lost both parents, for good. At least you have hope." Chiaro shifted a bit, letting her lock picking tools drop in her messenger bag. She wanted to appear less threatening to Socks.

"You're lying."

"I wish." Chiaro dropped her messenger bag on the floor. The weight was getting to her shoulder.

Socks' eyes focused on the limp messenger bag. Her posture softened. "How can it be?"

"That my parents are gone?"

A small nod from Socks indicated Chiaro should continue talking.

"My mother didn't appreciate our low-income lifestyle. She also didn't like having a daughter. I was too much of a burden, she told me. Imagine how I felt."

"What happened to your father?" Socks lifted her eyes and put them on Chiaro.

"He felt stabbed by my mother's insults about money. He was desperate to prove her wrong. So he committed a robbery and got caught. When he was paroled, everything went fine for a while. The two of us had fun, even without money. Kind of like you and your dad."

"Then?" Socks' fists unclenched for the first time.

"He tried another robbery. This time, they put him away for life. Oh, nobody got hurt. Just him – and me." It was Chiaro's turn to have her eyes grow moist. She wiped away tears, not wanting to let them show.

For some reason, Chiaro's crying triggered a negative response from Socks. She hardened again, assuming the story to be made up, a fiction invented to get compassion from Socks. Her posture became haughty and she gave Trouble a condescending look. "I suppose you also have an excuse for robbing me."

"You know, I'm fed up with being called a thief. I came here to find my parents, not to steal from you. And by the way, I think you're lucky. Your dad's only been missing eleven days. I haven't seen my father in two years – or my mother."

"You lie." Socks' face hardened again. "That can't be true."

He was amazed by her reaction. "Why can't it be true?"

"Your father was here a month ago, just before my dad shipped the rat to your Curio Shop. Then your mother, Julia, appeared. She told me she was looking for Indigo. They can't have been gone two years. Both of them were just here."

Trouble recoiled, sagging against the bedpost. Cool bamboo pressed on his arm and the sensation helped him feel real. Socks' words had stunned him. "They're alive. I'd given up hope. I assumed they were dead once I discovered Julia's letter from Everest was forged. But I had to know for sure …" His voice trailed off.

Socks puckered her lips. "You're for real?"

"Of course he's telling the truth. Trouble chased his parents to Vietnam. I told you that." Chiaro made the mistake of looking irritated.

That drew a negative response from Socks. "Trouble came in search of his family. But you only came for money."

"Yeah, I did. And, like what's so wrong with that? You gotta have money to live, even in a treehouse. Remember, this place cost a lot of bucks to make. Plus all that equipment in the lab had to get bought. And you have to eat. Your father must've had money or he couldn't feed you."

"We live on research grants. They also provide our equipment."

Chiaro shrugged. "We can't all be brainiacs."

"So instead of thinking, you pick locks and steal, like your father." Sarcasm twisted Socks' face.

Chiaro got angry. "Wait a minute. I opened those locks so we could find your dad – and maybe Trouble's parents. I haven't taken anything from your precious treehouse. Search my bag." She kicked the messenger bag, shoving it near Socks' feet.

Careful eyes watched Chiaro when Socks knelt, grabbing the bag, then standing again. She rummaged in the bag, not removing anything until she came to the lock picking tools. Socks held the small tools in her hand, rolling their hard metal sides between her thumb and forefinger. "So this is how you break into places you're not supposed to go."

"We were looking for charts or drawings," Trouble explained. "We were hoping to find a map. He noticed his host stiffen at the last word he spoke, "map."

"Why do you need a map?" Socks dropped the tools in Chiaro's bag and tossed the sack back to her.

Chiaro caught the bag against her chest. "We thought your father must've gone to find more weird creatures. You know, like that monster rat you sent Trouble. We figured your dad and his parents might be there – all three of them." She pointed at Trouble.

"But now you're here, so we don't need a map. You can take us there." Trouble quit leaning against the bedpost and took an eager step toward Socks.

She, in turn, backed away. "Not so fast. How did you know my father went to the Source, looking for your mother? You said there hasn't been any contact with your parents in two years."

"It was a lucky guess, that's all."

Socks looked wary, like she'd jump out a window again and slide down a pole into the jungle.

Not wanting her to leave, Trouble backed away. But he couldn't hold in his excitement. "Julia – my mom – went to the Source, as you call it?"

Socks nodded. Her eyes pinged from Trouble to Chiaro, making certain neither of them got too close.

Chiaro felt puzzled. "Why'd Trouble's mom go there? That place must be dangerous."

"It is. Best to stay away," Socks agreed.

"So why'd she risk a visit?" Chiaro pressed.

"To find your father, Trouble. She was worried he might have fallen ill at the Source. You can't stay there for more than a few minutes without getting sick from its radiation."

"How'd Julia know to come here in the first place?" Trouble ran a palm over his forehead, wiping off sweat. His head hurt from thinking about this puzzle. "She must'a got Indigo's email, after all."

"You talking about the note in the crate?" Chiaro asked.

"Yeah. Indigo said he didn't think his email got through. That's why he asked Dr. Cam to put a note in the crate he sent to the Curio Shop. But my mother did receive the email and she came to Vietnam, as he asked …" Trouble quit in mid-sentence.

"And?" Socks felt curious to know what he was thinking.

"Nothing." He gave her a bland look.

"It's not nice to keep secrets." Socks pouted.

"You should talk," Chiaro pointed out. "You know where this Source is located, but you won't tell us. How 'bout you tell us and Trouble will tell you?"

"You go first," Socks insisted.

"OK. I was struck by how excited my father was in the note. But he called this place a FOY, instead of a Source. I think they're the same thing. Maybe that's an important clue."

Chiaro gave him a blank look. "How could a name be so important?"

"The name might explain why my parents have been gone so long. They chased all over the world to discover a FOY, then realized Dr. Cam had found one. He just called it a different name."

"Why's this FOY matter so much?" Chiaro cocked her head, expecting Trouble to give her the next part of the story. But she got only disappointment.

"I have no idea. We'll have to ask them when we get to the Source, assuming they're still at this place. So where is it, Socks?"

Instead of answering, Socks wriggled, delaying her response.

"Come on," Chiaro pleaded. "Fair is fair."

"You didn't give me much. Yet you want a lot in return."

"Your dad may be lying there, sick from the radiation you talked about. And my parents. You're wasting time. We need to get there and help them."

"All right ..." Guilt flooded Socks' face. "I shouldn't tell you."

"I'll leave. You'll feel better working with Trouble, alone." Chiaro headed for the door. "I'll be in the lab, if you need me."

"Wait ..." Trouble reached toward Chiaro, but Socks grabbed his arm.

"Let her go. People chasing money bring problems to us."

Trouble lowered his arm. He waited for Chiaro to vanish from sight. "OK. It's safe. We'll talk in a low voice. So where …?"

Socks patted her green sneakers against floorboards. "The Source is beneath us. That's why we built our lab here. And it's why we must vacate the lab." She gestured toward her father's suitcases.

"Why leave when it's so close?"

"You took a shower. Didn't you see how the treehouse stands in a crater?"

"Sure. An old volcano, I assume."

"No." Socks wagged her head. "We used to be at the top of a hill. But the Source is growing, getting stronger. It's inhaling the earth beneath our feet. That's why so many of the plants are wilting. Only ancient thitpok trees are strong enough to survive. But one day, even they will die."

"I understand why the Source is dangerous. We still have to go there. Do we get to the Source by walking along a mineshaft?"

"No." Socks twisted in fear, shaking like a leaf in a breeze. Finally, her convulsions stopped and she could talk again. "We tried digging a hole. Your father helped by telling the laborers the work was being done to find old ruins."

"Why'd you stop?"

"Everything went fine for a while. Then the diggers got too close to the Source. The ground shook and the hill caved-in, forming the hole you saw when you showered. Most of the workers got away. The rest vanished. They shrank before my eyes, like they were being sucked inside a vacuum cleaner. But the vacuum hose was very small, so the people were squished. It was awful."

"I'm sorry." Trouble felt confused. "After that disaster, did you give up?"

Socks wagged her head in a "no."

"What'd you do?"

"My father and yours went exploring. They wouldn't tell me exactly where they found it, but they discovered an entrance to a huge cavern, miles from here."

"Where is it?"

"Like I said, I don't know the precise location. I do know it's at the base of a huge rock in Halong Bay."

"Great. We can search for it. How many giant rocks can there be in a bay?" His elation proved momentary, however.

"Trouble, there are thousands and thousands of Karst formations in Halong Bay. Unless we know the exact one, we could look forever and not find it."

"So I was right in looking for a map." His eyes went to the suitcases. "Gotta be in one of those bags." He pointed at the one with stickers, lying on the bed. "Chiaro was convinced we'd find the map in that suitcase."

"Why?" Socks gave him a skeptical look.

"I dunno. Probably 'cause it's the biggest one. Maybe because it's got all those stickers from around the world. Looks like it's your dad's favorite. He'd be inclined to put important things in that bag, instead of the other ones." He moved toward the huge leather case. "You wanna be the one to take things out, instead of me?"

"No." Her voice was timid. She looked afraid.

"OK." Trouble once again removed the scientific journals and stacked them on the bed. The glossy covers were slippery and the magazines slid across the mattress. Some landed on the floor in a tangle of pages. He disregarded the mess and kept searching. Trouble brought out heaps of clothing and piled them neatly next to the remaining journals. The satin feel of silk shirts was followed by rough linen pants and soft cotton underwear. Sachets of pungent herbs kept out bugs and mildew, but they also assaulted his nose with their smells of sandalwood and cinnamon. He kept going anyway. In a few minutes, one side of the case was empty and he started on the other. It was full of technical books, most of them written in English, others in German. The micro-small print was hard on the eyes. The yellowed pages gave off a nauseating damp odor and lacked any bookmarks. He found no tubes that might hold a map, no writing pads filled with handwritten scrawl. He kept going until that side of the case was also empty.

"Must'a put his notebook in another suitcase, I guess." Trouble puckered his lips in disgust, staring at a huge stack awaiting inspection. He didn't like prying into other people's lives. He began respectfully lifting items and replacing them, to make room for a new suitcase.

Socks interrupted him. "Wait a minute. What's that?" She pointed at a cotton shirt in the middle of a stack of clothing. It was folded in a different way and looked more like a sack.

He peeled shirts off the top of the pile to get at the unusual fold job. When Trouble lifted that shirt, it felt much thicker and heavier than the others. With a leap of excitement, his fingers unwrapped a bound journal. "Look familiar?"

"Yes. I think we've found my father's lab notebook. Quick, open it."

He flipped open the cover of the marbled black book and read for a while. After only a few pages, Trouble found himself staring at English letters grouped in even columns and rows, like stacks of bricks. He showed the page to Socks. "It's a cipher, a code. Your dad encrypted important parts of his work so no one could steal his findings."

Socks had an idea. "Look for drawings. A map would be harder to encrypt than text."

He turned pages, hoping to see charts and diagrams. There were a few, but none of them looked like a map. Some pages held DNA spectrographic printouts, tacked to the paper with tape. A DNA spectrum looked like a fuzzy X-ray, showing scrawny white boxes against a black surface. There was also a CAT scan outlining a prehistoric skull with fangs curving from the jaws. The braincase was digitally sliced open to show cross-sections of the creature's head. Trouble pulled his eyes off the prehistoric skull and flipped through the last pages. He found no map and offered the notebook to Socks.

She tried sifting through the journal with care, licking her fingertip and turning each sheet at its top corner to ensure every page was examined. When Socks finished, Trouble asked her, "Did your dad keep several notebooks or is this the only one?"

"I never saw others." She tossed the bound volume on the bed and it bounced. "What'd we do now?"

"We'll have to break his code. From what you said, we'll never find the entrance portal without directions. I just hope Dr. Cam wrote them in his book. Deciphering his writing is gonna be a lot of work."

30

To show respect, Trouble replaced Dr. Cam's belongings in his suitcase. He layered the technical journals in an even pile, snugged in place by a leather strap. Stacks of shirts and a pair of dress slacks were folded over the journals, anchored by another band. Sachets of potpourri leaked their spicy smells and fit neatly around the clothes, keeping away odors of jungle rot. Finished, he glanced at Socks.

She was flipping pages in her father's notebook. Her eyebrows pinched together in a line of concentration. "He only encoded critical details. The rest is in plain English."

"I'm surprised your dad wrote in English. Why not Vietnamese?"

"My dad wrote in English for practice. His published works were read around the world. English has become the common language for technical journals, even in India and China."

"Yeah," Trouble agreed. "English today is like Latin was in the Middle Ages. Writing in Latin meant a Frenchman could exchange ideas with a German and a Hungarian."

"Exactly." Socks looked at Trouble with respect now. "How do we crack my father's code?"

"Ciphers follow a recipe for scrambling text. The recipe needs a key, a string of letters used in the scrambling process. That's about all I know. We really need an expert on the topic. Maybe we should ask Chiaro for help. She once told me her dad was called the 'King of Keys.' I assumed she meant keys to door locks. But maybe he taught her about codes. They also use keys."

"I don't like her." Socks bristled, stiffening her posture.

"Chiaro doesn't have to stick around when we decode everything. She just has to help us."

"She wants money. I can't pay her."

"We'll promise Chiaro a third of our share of the treasure – if we find any." Trouble gave Socks a pleading look. "How can it hurt?"

"I don't like this."

"But you'll do it?"

Socks gave in. "All right. You ask her."

"Done." Trouble spun around and headed for the lab. A few minutes later, he returned with Chiaro.

"Decided you need me, huh?" Chiaro acted smug. She pressed her fingertips together and fixed cold eyes on Socks.

Trouble stepped between them. "We all need each other. Equal shares on the treasure. So let's be nice. OK?"

Socks nodded, but her eyes looked like sharp daggers aimed at Chiaro.

"Fine with me." Chiaro sat on the bed. "I'm not greedy. A third is better than nothing. What do you want from little old me?"

Trouble ignored her sarcastic tone. "Did your dad teach you about codes? You know, ciphers – taking plain English and scrambling it to look like garbage. But it isn't really trash. Anyone who knows the recipe can restore the text and read it. They just need the key. You called your dad the 'King of Keys' so I thought …"

Chiaro interrupted him. "You thought maybe he knew codes, not just door locks. And maybe he taught me about them."

"Yeah. Did he?"

Chiaro wrinkled her forehead, thinking. "He taught me a little. Most codes are done on a computer, now." She looked at Socks. "I assume we're talking about your father's notebook, the one you're holding."

Socks reacted by hiding the notebook behind her back. It took a moment for her to calm down and show the stained volume again. Her answer was strained through grinding teeth. "Yes. There are codes in my father's notebook."

"Well, most people use a computer to generate codes. We'd have to look at the files on his hard drive. I didn't see a laptop when we looked earlier."

"My father seldom used his laptop. He only did Internet searches and sent a little email. He quit using the Internet a month ago. Strong fields from the Source interrupted all satellite communications, so no Internet." Socks looked at Trouble. "That's why …"

Trouble finished her sentence. "Those force fields are why my dad, Indigo, thought his email to Julia didn't get through. And why his satellite phone couldn't work. But Dr. Cam could still use his laptop to encode text, then handwrite the results in his notebook."

Socks disagreed. "I don't think he used a computer to do the encoding."

"Why?" Trouble asked.

"The computer was only used in the lab, where there's more power. But my dad wrote in his notebook at night. He used that writing desk over there." She pointed to a school desk in a corner of the bedroom. It was the kind with a flip-top lid.

Trouble walked over and lifted the top. The space underneath appeared empty, except for an old pencil. He knelt down and peered into dark corners. Afraid of venomous tropical spiders, he grabbed the pencil and used it to probe the deepest recesses. "Nothing." He stood up and faced Socks. "Must've hidden the key elsewhere."

"My father had a good memory. He could've memorized the key."

"Unlikely," Chiaro interjected.

"Why unlikely?" Trouble asked.

"No computer means Dr. Cam used an easy cipher. The simplest code is a substitution cipher, meaning each letter of the alphabet gets replaced by another one."

"No," Socks objected. "That's easy to crack. My dad isn't stupid."

"True," Chiaro agreed. "So he used a complicated substitution method, which he's unlikely to memorize."

Socks was forced into reluctant agreement by Chiaro's logic. "I admit you're right. He must have kept a list somewhere, showing him which letter became another."

"So we have to find the list." Chiaro pointed at the suitcases.

"Opening his suitcases won't be enough. We don't know what the list looks like." Trouble felt confused as he stared at suitcases. "He could'a used a crossword puzzle for the key. We don't know what we're looking for."

"True." Chiaro walked to the desk. "Socks, your dad keep anything on the desk, some piece he collected from an expedition?"

"My father wouldn't keep an important list on his desk." Socks was happy to prove Chiaro wrong, but the pleasure lasted only a moment.

"You know about Sherlock Holmes?" Chiaro asked.

Socks was confused by the question, so Trouble rescued her. "Sherlock Holmes is a fictional British detective. In the Holmes stories, clues are used to solve a crime. Before Sherlock Holmes, police arrested anyone neighborhood people suspected. They often picked someone they hated, not the real criminal. Better to check the crime scene for clues. Otherwise, a lot of innocent people go to prison."

"Right. And where did the great detective Sherlock Holmes choose to hide something?" Chiaro asked.

"I don't get it." Socks looked upset.

To make her feel better, Trouble explained. "Holmes said the best place to hide something is in plain sight. Everyone sees the object and assumes it can't be valuable – or the gadget would be hidden."

"So," Chiaro repeated, "what was on your father's desk?"

"Nothing important," Socks insisted.

"Everything on that desk could be important. Please …" Trouble begged.

"All right, but Chiaro can't be right. My dad had an old model of DNA. You know, a double spiral. That's all he kept on his desk."

"In DNA, a molecule on the first spiral is linked to another molecule on the second corkscrew. Right?" Chiaro smirked.

"Yeah. So what?" Socks crossed her arms in defiance.

"How were the molecules labeled?" Chiaro asked.

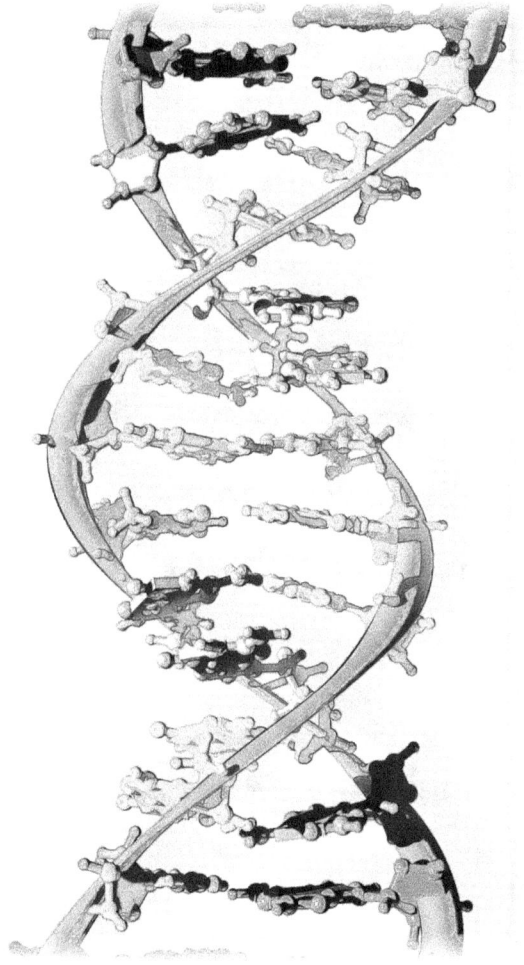

Dr. Cam's DNA Model

"With letters." Socks expression changed from resentment to astonishment. "Oh, no. You could be right …"

"Was each molecule identified by one letter or two?" Trouble couldn't hide his excitement, even though he knew his delight irritated Socks.

Talking in a depressed voice, she admitted the truth. "Two letters were used."

"XQ linked to MI, for example." Chiaro beamed. "Now we're making progress."

Trouble finished her thought. "X in clear text became an M in code. Then he used second letters on the next pass, to mix it up."

Chiaro agreed. "Yeah. We have to find his DNA model."

"It must be in one of the suitcases," Socks offered. "He wouldn't have left the model behind."

"We didn't find his DNA toy in the big leather suitcase. So I better get busy picking real locks." Chiaro rummaged in her bag.

"Don't bother." Socks pulled a chunky key ring from her pocket and dangled the hoop of keys in front of Trouble.

"Thanks." He took the keys and went to work unlocking Dr. Cam's baggage. In minutes, all the cases were open on the floor. There were hard-sided leather suitcases with reinforced metal corners, a few cheap plastic roll-on bags and then a dented black steamer trunk.

A parade of dull brass rivets lined the edges of the antique steamer trunk. It was the kind of luggage used by royalty a century ago, when a butler packed months of clothing for a long ocean voyage. The antique chest was peppered with dings and scrapes, like an overused piece of furniture. A leather belt lashed top and bottom halves together, fastened with a stubborn buckle.

Trouble's impatient fingers pried off the belt and he jabbed an old key into the faceplate lock. The trunk opened with a quiet snick. It didn't take long to find the DNA model. Wrapped in a thin blanket, the double helix resembled a twisted spiral. Each section of the squiggle had steps like a ladder's rungs. Every rung was painted with a different pair of cool fluorescent colors. Trouble held the spring-like structure where all of them could see the toy. "Got it."

"Good." Socks turned on Chiaro. "Now, you can leave. Wait in the lab."

"Wow. Nice thank you. As usual, no appreciation for my help." Chiaro spun around, walking past Trouble. She gave him a bitter look. "Be sure to leave money on the desk when you're done. I'd like to buy a ticket and fly home – not swim."

His eyes shot upward in a gesture of disgust. "Lighten up. You're getting a third of the treasure. Please …"

Chiaro didn't respond. Instead, she tossed the messenger bag over her shoulder and walked in lazy steps toward the lab.

When Chiaro vanished from sight, Socks dropped her father's notebook on his writing desk. She placed the DNA helix alongside the book. Next came blank sheets of paper and sharp pencils. "Now we get to work."

31

Socks and Trouble worked all night, taking turns deciphering the notebook. It was a process of trial and error, filling sheets of paper with failed attempts. After a few hours of staring at blue-lined pages, their eyes itched in fatigue. Alphabet letters blurred to shadows and cleared with great effort. Encrypted passages kept their meanings hidden for hours. When they finally cracked Dr. Cam's code, dawn was peeking over the jungle horizon. Bird calls filled their ears with long, modulated songs and short, harsh chirps. A variety of monkeys babbled and jumped among the trees, sending bird flocks into the air with loud, flapping wings. Tree noise brought a response from animals on the ground. A tiger roared, causing an elephant to bellow.

Trouble commented, "Guess you don't need an alarm clock."

"No. The jungle's alarm rings every morning, whether you want it or not." Socks extended her arms and yawned. She blinked in exhaustion, smoothing a rumpled orange T-shirt. "I'm trashed. We better take a short nap before visiting the Source."

"Sleep with all this racket?" Trouble was surprised by her idea. "Besides, I'm starved. Those protein bars wore off hours ago."

"We'll get something to eat at the docks, before we rent a boat." She rose from the desk and pointed at the bed. "The jungle will calm down in a few minutes. Sleep on my father's mattress. You'll be more comfortable. I'll take the sofa."

"That's not fair." He rubbed burning eyes. The idea of a little sleep became more appealing by the moment.

Socks lifted her father's notebook off the desk and headed for the treehouse living room. "I sleep on those little sofas all the time. I'm used to it. See you in an hour."

"OK." Trouble stumbled to the bed and did a face-plant between heaps of clothing and open suitcases. The linen felt soft and smelled like clean, fresh air. In a few seconds, he was dead asleep. Peaceful slumber gave way to jolts, like the treehouse was experiencing another earthquake. The thumping came from Socks pressing on his shoulder.

"Trouble, wake up," she insisted.

"Wha … huh?" He tried to roll over and hit the sharp edge of a suitcase. The other direction was also blocked. All he could do was slide off the bed, reversing how he'd fallen on the mattress. His blurry eyes registered Socks' distressed face. "How long was I asleep?"

"Who cares? Wake up. We have to find Chiaro. She's gone." Tears filled Socks' eyes. "I was stupid …"

"What happened?" Trouble would have loved a glass of orange juice and a stack of pancakes drizzled in syrup. Then a shower, fresh clothes and …

"She took the notebook."

That disclosure woke him up faster than an espresso jolt. "Wait a minute. You had the notebook under your arm when you left the bedroom. Did you give it to Chiaro?"

"No. To hide it, I put the notebook under a pillow on the sofa. But I must've let an edge show and Chiaro pulled out the notebook while I was asleep. It was dumb of me."

"I know Chiaro's a pickpocket, but why would she take the book? It's useless without our notes on the code …" He stopped talking and looked at the desk. Their notes were also gone. His heart sank into his sneakers. "She knows where the Source is located and we don't."

Socks wagged her head. "No. I memorized the GPS coordinates."

"Twenty digits?" He felt skeptical. "How's that possible?"

"Numbers are my friends. I played with them when I was small … there aren't other children to play with in the jungle. So I made up tricks for remembering numbers I liked."

"The coordinates are no good without a GPS device." He looked at Sock's anxious face, staring at the floor.

"I have a GPS on the ultra-light. I use it for navigation."

"Whoa. You told me satellite signals are blocked by radiation from the Source. So how's a GPS gonna help us?"

"The same way it helped bring you here in the plane. GPS works until we get near the Source. So I could use the device until the last hundred meters. By then, infrared beacons were visible in my helmet goggles. I wasn't diving blind into the jungle, as you thought. I could see where I was going, using infrared night vision."

"Great, but Chiaro also realizes she needs a GPS. She might have taken yours."

"Right. Come on. We have to get to the ultra-light." Socks ran from the room and jumped off the balcony, grabbing a pole. Her momentum caused her to twirl around before sinking downward.

Hesitating to jump into space, Trouble balanced on the railing. Finally, he took a deep breath and sprang outward, ducking his face to miss the pole. Cold and slick, the metal cylinder banged into his chest and stomach. Reflexes took over and his palms gripped the pole. His legs also wrapped around the pipe, trying to slow his fall. It worked so well that Trouble quit sliding and had to release his foot grip on the pole to go downward.

Once at the bottom, he sprinted around the treehouse, feet sinking into a sponge of decaying jungle leaves. Every footfall caused lizards hidden underneath to dash away. To his ears, their scurrying sounded like the rustling of fallen autumn leaves. His shoes, though, caused no sound when they touched the spongy earth. The sprint felt like trying to run in quicksand. Each breath he inhaled smelled of jungle rot, a sickening blend of mold and mildew.

Trouble heard a moan of despair and Socks came into view. She was bent over the ultra-light's cockpit, searching for the GPS device. Angry, Socks rammed her fist into a cushion on the pilot's seat. "She's got it."

"The GPS?" Trouble halted beside Socks. His lungs burned and his leg muscles were tired from running in loose soil.

Socks confirmed his worst fears. "She's got everything. We have to find her."

"Where do we look? She could be anywhere in this jungle." He spun around, scanning a dense hedge of vegetation. The only break in the wall was the ultra-light's tunnel, a burrow hacked through vines so the aircraft could take off. "Well, at least we know where to start looking. There's no other way out. She had to go along that hole."

"We know more than that. The GPS will show Chiaro how to reach a fishing village on Halong Bay. She's certain to go there and try to find someone who speaks English." Socks followed behind him as Trouble did a fast walk along the tunnel.

He tried to be optimistic. "It won't do her any good. Chiaro doesn't have any money. She can't pay for a ride to Hanoi."

"Check your wallet. Make certain she didn't also get your cash."

Trouble halted and dropped his backpack on the ground. He unzipped an inner compartment where he kept valuable papers and his wallet. His passport, the note from his father, a picture of him visiting Vietnam as a baby were all there. So was his battered leather wallet with his ID card. However most of his cash was gone. Trouble's face tightened in anger. "Chiaro did a complete job on us. She only left me enough money to go home."

"Yes. But we'll get her. She doesn't speak Vietnamese and no one in that village understands English." Socks resumed the hike, moving quickly. Her body shifted into high gear, legs and arms swinging like a mechanical toy with a fresh battery. Steady as a robot, Socks plowed ahead with her green sneakers trampling the brittle vines.

In moments, Trouble felt the ground under him become firmer. But the earth also sloped upward, rising higher with each step. They were walking out of the crater, trekking up its cone-shaped slope. The more they rose, the healthier everything looked. Dried leaves and withered vines became green again, with fresh buds everywhere. Shoots of green lemon grass smelled like fresh citrus, contrasting the damp rot and persistent mold. Blades of lemon grass attracted a pale yellow butterfly with brittle, speckled wings. It flitted between plants, flapping in a graceful spiral. Even Trouble felt better, more like himself again. He had more energy to think and move. He studied the tunnel of broken vines where the tiny plane had traveled last night, descending in a high-speed dive. He turned toward Socks and asked her a question. "Most runways are flat. Isn't this slope a problem for your ultra-light?"

"No. Taking off here is like doing a ski-jump. I gun the engine until the brakes can't hold me back. Then I let go and roar forward. It's the same technique Harrier fighter jets use to get airborne on short runways."

"You mean those little jets, the kind owned by Britain and France?"

"Yes. My father and I borrowed their idea." Socks reached the crest and paused to catch her breath. She pointed at water glistening in the distance. Wind rippled the green surface with small waves, reflecting sunlight like a mirror. "There. That's a small piece of Halong Bay. The rest is out of sight. Halong Bay is enormous."

"Beautiful. How far is the fishing village from here?"

"About a half hour jog. You up for it?"

"Well, I've had some time to adjust to the local climate. Let's try running. I can always quit and walk for a while."

"OK." Socks began jogging, setting a fast pace.

Hungry and tired, Trouble fell behind. Yet he made it to the edge of the village without stopping. Sweat ran off his skin and dripped on his shirt, already damp from perspiration. Buzzing insects found his moist skin irresistible and he was forced to use his hands as fans, swatting them away. Actually, the breeze from his fanning motion felt refreshing. Standing in dense brush, he peered at the village.

A junk with orange fan sails lingered near the dark sandy beach, water slapping against its worn hull. The tired craft looked like a floating dragon with dandruff flaking its scales. Large port holes in the weathered boat resembled islets in a shoe for threading a lace. Salt crusted the round windows and wrecked the paint job. On deck, fishermen were mending nets with rope and needles. A few people were hanging wet clothes on a sagging clothesline that limped from boat masts. Their laundry fluttered in the breeze like oversized flags. Hot pink t-shirts competed with tie-dyed purple bottoms. It was a bizarre riot of color with people gliding

View Of Halong Bay From Dr. Cam's Laboratory

beneath the vibrant garments. Their footsteps on wooden planks were quiet as a distant echo. Trouble scanned the faces of kids on the docks and women in woven palm leaf hats. With so many wild colors, it should've been easy to spot Chiaro in her black pajamas. But he didn't find Chiaro in the crowd. "See her?"

"Not yet. Let's move closer to get a better look."

"Be careful."

Socks ignored his advice. She moved in dark shadows, but her feet made a lot of noise. Every time her green sneakers landed, they snapped a twig or crunched on rough soil.

"You need to be quieter."

"I also need to get closer." Socks gave him an irritated look.

He touched her shoulder to get her attention. "Over there. Isn't that Chiaro, standing on the dock?"

"I think so. She's looking at the bay, like she's waiting for someone."

A buzzing of loud motors floated over the water, drifting into Trouble's ears, sounding like chainsaws. Then he saw a pair of jet skis flying across the bay, leaving behind frothy wakes. Their hulls sliced through the water, splashing a foamy surf and speeding to the dock. He recognized the riders from their size long before he could make out their faces. "Oh, no."

"What?"

"It's Flix, riding a jet ski. The tall guy on the other Yamaha is Flix's bodyguard, RJ. How'd Chiaro contact them?"

"A guy in the village has a satellite phone. He rents it for a fee. He's far enough away so radiation from the Source doesn't harm his phone." Socks wanted to edge closer, but Trouble restrained her.

"Be careful. Flix may have paid ninjas to keep watch on her until he could arrive."

"Trouble, I have to get back what's mine. I can't do it from here."

"Fine. We'll move along the treeline, keeping in shadows. We'll rush Chiaro when we get close."

Socks disagreed. "That won't work. Flix and his goon will be on the dock in seconds. I say we go for it now."

"Don't be foolish. Ninjas grab us and we're dead. They'll hand us over to RJ. He dangled me off that skyscraper. I believe he meant to kill me."

"How'd you get away?" Socks was amazed. The skin around her mouth tightened in surprise.

"I sort'a bit him. I had to do it. RJ was shaking me and banging my head against the building. When he dropped me, I grabbed hold of a construction platform to stop my fall. Otherwise, I'd be dead."

Socks glanced at all the open ground between her and Chiaro. "If we wait, Flix and this RJ will arrive. Then it'll be real hard to grab Chiaro and wrench away my Dad's notebook – not to mention the GPS and your cash."

"I know. We'll have to wait for an opening."

"It may not happen. Then what?"

Trouble thought a moment. "Chiaro left me enough money to fly home. Instead, we'll rent a boat. We'll follow them to the Source."

"They're too fast on jet skis. We can't keep up."

"You told me you've got the coordinates for the Source memorized. Most boat owners have a GPS onboard. So they can take us to the Source."

Socks caved. "OK. I'll go with your plan. We'll sneak up and hope for a chance to grab her."

32

Flix climbed a shaky wooden ladder to stand on a long dock. He enjoyed the amazed stares of fishing village locals, surprised by his blond hair and tight fitting wet suit. He looked like a villain out of a Bond film and he delighted in that image. Leaving RJ to tie off the jet skis, Flix walked along the narrow dock, stepping around piles of fish, their scales shimmering like rainbows in the sun. Putrid odors revolted his nostrils, wafting to him from the intestines of gutted fish.

Yet people were scooping up those revolting bloody heaps with bare hands and dumping them into buckets. How they could eat something that ugly stunned him. His eyes bounced among messy heaps of fish, bleeding from having their head and tail cut off. Machetes whipped to carve away fins as well. Heads, tails and fins also went in buckets. It seemed nothing was wasted. He hoped his own trip here wouldn't be wasted either. Where was Chiaro?

She'd contacted him by satellite phone. Chiaro claimed to know the source of unusual creatures like that rat he'd bought from Trouble and Bleerio. Planting her with Trouble had been a good idea. It was the kind of deception for which his father was known. Le Roi Braun would be proud, if he were here. Good thing he wasn't, though. Le Roi would steal everything from Flix, leaving him no independence. Flix craved freedom. He already had everything else money could buy.

His eyes found Chiaro, standing at the other end of the dock, still dressed as a Vietnamese peasant in black pajamas. She held up an old notebook and a sheaf of papers, waving them. Flix moved faster through the crowded work area, stepping over tangles of rope, moving around fish nets loaded with red and yellow glass floats, looking like festive holiday decorations. His feet, shod in high-tech five-toed running shoes, sensed every loose board, each springy plank in the dock. Feeling all the textures gave him control and Flix loved being in control. He waved an envelope, showing Chiaro he'd brought payment, as they'd agreed.

"That's close enough." Chiaro backed away, moving right to the edge of the dock. "Any closer and I throw all this stuff in the Bay."

"Relax," Flix assured her. "I brought proof money's been transferred into your account."

"I told you to get cash. I don't trust you."

"Be reasonable. Countries limit the amount of foreign currency anyone can bring. You asked for a lot of money and Vietnam won't let me take it in."

"Fine. Drop your proof on the ground and kick it to me."

"Why don't I just hand you the envelope? Otherwise, it might fall through a crack in the planks."

Chiaro used a soccer move to kick an empty plastic tray toward Flix. "Drop the envelope in there and shove the disc back."

"What's goin' on here?" RJ moved alongside Flix and gave Chiaro a threatening stare. "How's about I give her the envelope?" He plucked the Tyvek out of Flix's hand.

Chiaro held Dr. Cam's notebook and the decryption notes over water sloshing against the dock. "One step and everything goes in the sea."

"And then I dive in and grab them. No need to give you anything." RJ leaned toward Chiaro.

She backed away even more, moving the heels of her shoes off the dock. "The ink on these documents will run. A moment in that salt water and nothing is legible. You lose everything you came for. Want that Flix?"

"No," he answered, licking dry lips.

Chiaro smiled. "Then call off your Rottweiler."

"Put the Tyvek in that disc and kick it to her, RJ." Flix glowered at his bodyguard. "Do it."

"Say please." RJ smirked.

Flix hesitated. His face showed anger and fear. RJ had never behaved like this before. "All right ... Please."

RJ crouched and dropped the slick plastic envelope in a scratched orange tray. Without warning, he snapped the disc at Chiaro like a Frisbee.

She let the whirring orange shape hit her in the stomach and bounce off. The envelope slid from the tray and landed about halfway between Flix and her. "Nice trick, RJ. I grab your Frisbee and you grab me. But I didn't fall for it. Whaddya gonna do now, Flix?"

"RJ, knock off the games. You're wasting valuable time."

The bodyguard didn't answer. He stood there, loose and dangerous, like a cougar ready to pounce.

Flix tugged on RJ's arm. "We're moving so Chiaro can retrieve the payment certificate."

With reluctance, the judo master slid backwards, gliding over rough dock planking with the silky grace of a cat.

"OK," Flix announced. "You're safe."

Chiaro shook her head in disagreement. "Farther." After they backed up some more, she kept her eyes on them and moved carefully toward the payment coupon. With a deft scoop, the coupon flew into her possession and she kicked the tray at RJ's feet to slow him down, in case he lunged. But he didn't move, just watched. She opened the envelope and peeked inside. "Not enough."

"What?" Flix was outraged.

Chiaro slid back to the dock's farthest boundary, where it dropped into Halong Bay. Her feet poised at the edge of a rotting plank. "You heard me. I want more."

33

Socks wriggled like she was going crazy. "What're they doing?"

"I think they're negotiating. Chiaro wants more for your Dad's notebook. They don't wanna pay that much." Trouble shifted his weight. Something was causing his knee to burn with a fiery itch. He looked down and saw he was kneeling on an ant hill. Insects swarmed his jeans, crawling under his clothes and biting his skin. Their persistent stings felt like needles jabbing raw nerves. "I gotta get out of here."

"Why?" Socks acted furious with him until she realized his leg was covered with half-inch long timber ants. "You have to jump in the Bay. Water is the only thing that gets rid of them."

"I'll brush 'em off." He bent over to knock the swarm off his pants and Socks grabbed his arm.

"They'll bite harder. The cuts will swell up. You won't be able to use that hand for days. Get in the water." She pointed at Halong Bay.

"I run out of here and RJ will chase me. He might jump in the water, even. Try to drown me."

"Good."

"Oh, thanks a lot." Trouble was forced to hop around. The biting on his leg was simply too much for him to ignore.

Socks quit grinning at his predicament and tried to explain her reasoning. "RJ chases you. That means I get a chance to grab back my father's notebook and the GPS."

"Yeah, and Flix will grab you. Two against one. You lose." He started loosening his belt, so he could remove his jeans.

She gave him a shocked look. "Don't undress."

"I have to," he insisted.

"No. I've got a better idea. Run along the dock, then dive in the Bay. Get aboard one of the jet skis. Start it and tow the other. That way, RJ can't get you."

"What are you gonna do in the meantime? You can't wrestle with Chiaro and Flix."

"You're right. So I'm going to knock her in the water." Socks looked tragically sad.

"Do that and your dad's notes are gone. Maybe the GPS device, also. Salt water will probably ruin all of them. The ink will run and GPS electronics will short out."

"Then they won't have them. At least I can stop them from going to the Source. You get the jet skis and we can still try to borrow a GPS from a fisherman, like we were going to do."

Trouble hesitated. Their plan was complicated. A lot of things could go wrong. His thoughts were disrupted by a loud noise. A giant helicopter was speeding across Halong Bay, heading straight at them. The rotor blades sliced through humid air, lowering the black chopper until it skimmed above the waves.

"There's the ninjas you were worried about – late but still powerful." She urged him, "Go, Trouble. Run. It's now or never."

He knew Socks was right. Between the ants and the helicopter, he had no choice. Trouble moved away from Socks, sliding along the treeline, gritting his teeth against maddening itching in his leg. He felt ants sliding under his shirt now, nipping his belly button. Yet he wanted to get as far from Socks as he could before running into the open. When he could take it no longer, Trouble bolted toward a knot of fishermen drying their nets.

He intended to hurdle the fishing nets. At the last moment, the fishermen raised a webbed section in front of him. They were shaking kelp off the net, removing a tangled mess of seaweed. Trouble couldn't go around them. He tried doing a high jump style leap, rolling over the net. When he tumbled across, a sneaker caught in the net. Stunned by his actions, the fishermen dropped their web, snaring him further. Kicking and tugging finally got him loose. The delay was maddening, but the good news was that shaking his legs rid him of half the ants. He got up to run and heard a booming voice behind him.

RJ screamed, "It's him." The bodyguard forgot Chiaro and sprinted at Trouble.

He ran faster than he'd ever done in his life. Trouble dodged a stack of plastic crates, knocking them over to put obstacles in RJ's path.

The bodyguard jumped over most of the crates, but his final leap put his foot through a last box, sticking it on his shoe. RJ was forced to halt and rid himself of the anchor.

Trouble kept going, puffing like an old-fashioned steam locomotive, pumping his arms, churning his legs. Women cleaning sea snails screamed at him when he stepped in their pile of slugs. His next move put a foot in the middle of bloody fish guts, smelling like vomit and excrement. The horrible goo enveloped his foot, greasing his sole, making it slick, as if the shoe were oiled. He couldn't run anymore and was forced to skip. Trouble could hear RJ's furious pounding feet and knew skipping wasn't going to work. The junk on his shoe had to come off.

The answer was a woman readying a huge kettle for laundering clothes. She had a wood fire smoldering under the kettle and was bent over, puffing on the flames to encourage them. The warm air smelled of charcoal, garlic and fish guts. She slopped some detergent into the strange brew. Soapy water formed a milky scum in the tub, making Trouble wonder how she was going to get the clothes clean. Her dockside laundry service was just what he needed. He jumped in the air, grabbing his knees to make certain his shoes cleared the vat's edge. Fire ants on his pants loved the flesh of his hands, yet their pain didn't last long.

Warm, soapy water rendered the ants harmless. The laundress, however, was another matter. Water splashed from her kettle, soaking her hat, neck and clothes. Her face twisted in anger like a cat ready to use its claws. She grabbed a large hunk of firewood as a club. He used a tumbling move to roll out of her stew pot and miss her swing. Reaching for Trouble, RJ caught the full blow on his arm, rendering it numb. He swung a vicious punch at the woman in retaliation and fortunately she ducked. Fishermen ran to help her, wielding razor sharp machetes. RJ had to flee or be sliced to pieces.

Trouble had no time to appreciate his good luck. Chiaro's shrieks let him know Socks had begun her attack. He needed to finish his part of the bargain and capture the jet skis. He found them tethered at the far end of the dock, bobbing on swells. A fast trip down a rickety ladder left him standing next to the Yamahas. Undoing their ropes was easy. Hopping atop the closest one was no problem. He slid across the comfortable, puffy seat, still warm from the last rider. Starting the engine looked like it was going to be a show-stopper, however. He felt clueless how to turn on the ignition and fire up the motor.

The ants were gone as a distraction, but his mind still seemed unable to focus. It was like his mental gears were rusty and couldn't turn fast. What could he do? Trouble mashed buttons, twisted knobs, slapped in frustration and nothing happened other than getting sore hands. These things were like motorcycles and scooters. Why hadn't he paid more attention to how Ferrari and Lightning started their bikes?

Wait a minute. Motorcycles had storage compartments under their seats. Maybe these Yamahas were built the same way. There could be an owner's manual in that hidden compartment. He reached over and flipped up the seat on the twin jet ski next to him. A plastic bag held the owner's guide and for a moment, Trouble was dizzy with success. Then came endless frustration. His fingers couldn't unzip the baggy, so he had to grunt like crazy and tear open the plastic. The same misbehaving fingers were too excited for turning pages sanely.

In the distance, Flix screamed for help. "RJ, get over here. Trouble's a decoy. A girl's fighting with Chiaro, trying to steal her notes."

RJ's voice boomed like a drum roll when he answered. "I'm busy."

The bodyguard was far too close for Trouble to be reading pages in a WaveRunner manual. He tossed the book inside the other jet ski and slammed its driver's seat closed. A flat black disc caught his eye, looking out of place on the Yamaha's metallic crimson paint. He realized the disc had a slot in its middle, where an ignition key went. For a moment, Trouble despaired. Then a fisherman arced overhead and landed in the bay with a huge splash and a howl of rage. He bobbed to the surface, machete gleaming in the sunlight.

Behind Trouble, other blades whipped through the air. Men grunted from being punched. RJ had to be standing on the dock, right behind Trouble. He leapt off the jet ski onto a small platform and crept up the ladder. The bodyguard towered overhead, ducking, fighting, sweating profusely. Keys for the jet skis dangled from a clip on his equipment belt. Trouble only had to choose the right moment, reach out and unsnap the key fobs.

So he watched and waited. Then he dared a quick thrust of his hand and … missed. Time to try again – success, the key fobs were in Trouble's grip. He tugged on them and they wouldn't come loose. Their ring fouled in the snap as RJ twisted to duck a sharp knife.

The bodyguard felt Trouble's hand pulling on the keys and sent his own hand flying around back. Steel fingers clamped on Trouble's wrist like a pipe wrench. Intense pain shot along Trouble's arm, forcing him to moan.

"Gotcha, kid." RJ snapped his head around to confirm the victory. The bodyguard's face was drenched in perspiration, yet hatred gleamed in his tired eyes, eclipsing the man's fatigue. The moment of satisfaction almost cost RJ an arm. A machete sliced open his wet suit, leaving a deep cut. Blood spurted from the wound, hitting Trouble in the face.

He jumped off the ladder, adding his weight to his tug against RJ's grip. The move snapped Trouble's wrist out of RJ's vise-like hold. Trouble fell, hitting the edge of a little platform, then spinning into the water. His forehead clunked hard against the back of a Yamaha, but Trouble wouldn't let go of the key fobs, his ticket to freedom.

A badly timed breath sucked bay water into his nostrils. The salt water burned as its liquid flowed through his sinuses. Trouble kicked and paddled, fighting to go toward sunlight above him. Small yellow fish wove around his neck, scratching him. Their scales raked his cheeks like fingernails. He shut his eyes tight to protect his vision. In that dark moment, the fish were every bit as scary as machete blades slicing the air around RJ.

To save his life, the bodyguard dove off the fishing dock into the Bay. Trouble saw a dark shape, followed by a million air bubbles, when RJ glided past. Enraged fishermen hurled knives in the water, hoping to impale their enemy. The machete blades sung like guitar strings, zinging from light to dark. Trouble watched RJ twist and dive, kicking and paddling to sink deeper.

In contrast, Trouble surfaced like a cork held at the bottom of a bathtub, then released. He shot upward and grabbed the back of a jet ski. His skull throbbed from the blow when he'd fallen in the bay. Blood streamed from a cut on his forehead, caused by hitting the back of a Yamaha. There was no time to worry about first aid, however. The Russian helicopter was circling overhead. Its massive blades chopped the air with a loud "whoomp ... whoomp" rhythm, sending pulsing blasts at Trouble.

He assumed ninjas were onboard the helo and soon there'd be no hope for escape. Trouble fumbled with the key fobs, trying one, then another. At last, his Yamaha engine roared to life. The motor rumbled in a low growl. He grabbed a rope attached to the other jet ski and tied it to a saddlebag ring on his machine. Trouble fumbled with controls until the jet ski lurched forward. Then the dead weight of the trailing Yamaha dragged his machine to a halt. He applied more power and his WaveRunner jerked ahead in a rush of speed, slicing through choppy water.

RJ's head appeared a few yards away. It was tempting to run him over. Fighting against his urge to attack the man, Trouble curved, looping toward the other end of the dock.

34

Trouble knew he had very little time to reach Socks before the helicopter landed. The Russian-made aircraft was fitted with pontoons, torpedo-shaped floats. They allowed the helo to land on water and remain afloat. Hovering above Socks and Chiaro, the giant helicopter dropped like a slow elevator. The aircraft's long blades swirled, blasting air downward. Rings of waves churned in the shallow water where Chiaro and Socks were fighting.

Yelling as loud as he could, Trouble screamed at Socks. "Forget Chiaro. Get on the jet ski. We have to leave. Now, before the helo lands on top of us." Running his Yamaha in an arc, Trouble brought the towed jet ski behind Socks.

She ignored his plea and made another try for Dr. Cam's laboratory journal. "Chiaro can't have it. The notebook is my father's."

"Socks, I'm telling you – leave now or we'll be crushed." In frustration, Trouble reached out and grabbed her hair, forcing Socks to look upward.

Her face turned ashen when Socks realized a massive helicopter was landing on her. Dark pontoon floats on the aircraft hovered above her head. Turbulence and engine noise drowned out her normal voice. She dragged herself on the vacant Yamaha and screamed, "The key …"

Trouble slapped a key fob in her palm. He tapped the side of his jet ski, indicating where Socks needed to insert the device. Whirring shadows grew larger around them, warning the helo was dropping closer.

Behind them, Chiaro waded through shallow water until she stood near Trouble. Weeping, her hair and clothes a soggy mess, Chiaro pleaded with him. "Don't leave me. They'll kill me."

"I don't want more of your lies, Chiaro. Go with your buddies. We're through."

"I can't stay here. Trouble, be reasonable."

"You sold me out. Get lost." He shoved her away.

Chiaro jabbed a fist holding soaked documents in the direction of Flix. "He can see who's riding in that helicopter. Flix is terrified."

"You love playing games, don't you Chiaro?"

"No, please … believe me." Tears streaked her cheeks. She again pointed at Flix. He stood immobilized like a statue, frozen to his spot at the dock's edge. Unlike a sculpture, though, Flix quivered. His body vibrated in tune with the fear shining in his eyes.

Trouble hesitated. He gave Socks a questioning look. She bent over to shout in his ear. "I vote we take her."

"Are you crazy?" Trouble recoiled in surprise. "Why bring her along?"

"Chiaro knows too much – like where the treehouse lab is hidden."

"They probably saw your home from the air. Besides, you told me you're abandoning the lab. Fire up your jet ski. We have to get out of here."

"Chiaro has to go with us, or they'll know everything. My father's notebook isn't that wet. I'm sure most of his notes – and our deciphering work, is still legible." Socks turned the key and her Yamaha fired to life. The engine roared like a hungry bear and she gunned the throttle. A stream of water flew out of the jet ski's tail and hit Chiaro, drenching her in a final insult. The boy's pajamas on her body were dripping wet. Her hair looked like a stringy tangle.

Trouble couldn't hear Chiaro's words, but her look said, "Please …" He caved, pointing to the seat behind him. The moment Chiaro's butt hit the seat, Trouble roared off, almost dumping her in the bay.

Running at full throttle forced the jet skis to slap over waves, becoming airborne. They bounced across the bay, getting drenched in spray. Tangy salt water mingled in their nostrils with diesel fuel spilled from tourist boats. Their jet skis wove around small islands jutting out of the bay like limestone columns. The craggy pillars were covered in rough mollusks and tufts of grass. The rocky islets seemed deserted, except for lizards baking in the sun.

Skittering across choppy water, they reached a floating fishing village, bamboo rafts bound together with thick rope. People lived on these micro-isles. Their small homes were the size of garden sheds. Squealing pigs and tethered chickens competed for space on bobbing porches. Vegetable cuttings from last night's dinner formed a ring of scum around platforms lashed together in a circle. Scraps of toilet paper warned of danger from infectious diseases, carried on human excrement dumped in the bay. Adequate sewage treatment hadn't yet reached this village. But Socks and Trouble needed to halt and plan their next move. They also were starving and had to buy food.

Floating Village on Halong Bay

They slowed to a crawl in the scum ring, sliding as gently as possible through waste material lapping at their feet. With only a soccer field left to go, they couldn't speed up after exiting the filth. Trouble coasted alongside a floating porch and jumped from his vehicle, using a short rope to tie off his jet ski. He ignored Chiaro's outstretched hand, asking for assistance, leaving her on a rocking, heaving Yamaha. For Socks, he tied off her jet ski and made certain she landed safely on dry wood.

She nodded in gratitude. "I'll buy provisions. They won't charge a lot. Floating villagers endure a tough life and always need money. Only tourist operators make out in Halong Bay." Socks glanced at Chiaro, still bobbing on the aft seat of a jet ski, feet submerged in water. "Watch her. Don't let her steal anything."

Trouble held up a key fob. "She isn't leaving without us."

In a few minutes, Socks returned with a satchel full of wonderful smells. Oil from the freshly prepared meal blotched the satchel. Steam rose from a woven tote holding garlic crabmeat wrapped in rice pancakes. There were golden rice balls, spiced with mint and basil. Trouble smelled the temptations and reached for a snack. Socks dodged his grab, turning away. "No time to eat. We have to get out of sight before that helo follows us."

"Where are we going?" He gave the food a longing stare.

Socks broke off a hunk of flat bread and gave it to him. "Chew this so you can last. We've got to locate an island with a cave big enough to hide us. The good news is we only need to scout the largest Karst formations."

"And the bad news?" He mumbled through gulps of chewy bread.

She pointed at the helicopter. "They're smart. They'll know what we did. The helo will come looking for us, circling every big island, skipping small ones." Socks also gave Chiaro a hunk of bread.

Trouble frowned. "Why're you so friendly? I thought you hated Chiaro."

"I don't want her fainting before she tells us what she knows." Socks leapt from the porch to her Yamaha and fired its engine.

Trouble untied her rope. Then he mounted his jet ski and followed Socks, sliding through the garbage ring. Once outside the mess, they ripped across Halong Bay at maximum speed.

Trouble passed a huge rock, jutting from the water, angled like a football propped on a tee for a kick. Over centuries, rain etched craggy lines along the "football." Its deep grooves looked like seams in an official NFL ball. On the football's nose, birds wove nests for breeding. Over the years, birds dropped seeds in crevices and trees grew. Below that micro-forest, vines clung to near-vertical slopes. Hundreds such Karst formations peppered Halong Bay. Pounding waves eroded the soft rocks. Mildly acidic seawater dissolved the surface of bedrock, melting crags into shapeless lumps and leaving fractures behind. Fragile limestone at the waterline washed away, narrowing the base. A mushroom top bulged above the high tide mark.

They were zipping between rocks when the helicopter's whooping sound echoed around them. Socks gunned her throttle and went straight for a large island. Spray curled under the hull of her jet ski and Trouble chased its frothy pattern across blue-green water. The closer

Football-Shaped Karst Formation In Halong Bay

they got to that enormous Karst formation, the louder the helicopter sounded. Its engines rumbled like a chugging lawnmower amplified by concert speakers. Nauseating fuel smells irritated his stomach with their heavy chemical stink. Trouble felt the aircraft flying at them, racing the jet skis.

He saw a black spot on the rock looming before his Yamaha, but it was hard to know if the darkness marked a hole or only differently colored stone. Yet they had no choice. They sped toward the black spot at full throttle until the last possible moment, when Socks cut her engine. Her jet ski coasted on its own momentum. She was trying to soften her collision should the opening prove nothing more than a shallow indent.

Trouble followed her example, watching Socks vanish inside a tunnel. Blind, he crept forward in velvet blackness, trying not to ram the other Yamaha. The smell of bird droppings sliming the island's face disappeared, only to be replaced by another unpleasant odor. He felt Chiaro squirming behind him.

"Be still," Trouble hissed at her.

"I'm trying to pull a flashlight out of my bag. You'd like to see, wouldn't you?"

"I dunno. Depends on what's out there."

"I gotta see. I can't take driving blind." She flicked a switch and her weak pencil beam drifted over sloshing water and up a rock slab. The soft light kept arcing, seeking a roof and found it. Then even Chiaro wished she'd kept the flashlight turned off. Thousands of bats hung from the cavern's ceiling like upside down rats draped in slick raincoats. They opened their narrow eyes, irritated by the weak light. Their pointed ears twitched and their black coats unfurled in a sudden blur of speed. The tunnel filled with echoes of flapping wings and high-pitched chirps. The creatures flailed rubbery wings and dived closer, their furry bodies and needle-sharp teeth visible in the dim glow.

Bats smacked Trouble's head and shoulders. It was like having smelly underwear slapping his head. Their odor was ripe as a gym locker crammed with sweaty clothes. He took his hands off the steering wheel to shield his face. Without his fingers on the throttle, the jet ski coasted to a halt. When the bat attack dimmed, Trouble felt disoriented. He feared the Yamaha could have drifted into a turn. He might collide with a wall should he accelerate. "Give me that flashlight, Chiaro. I need to find Socks."

Chiaro's Flashlight Awakens Thousands Of Bats

"All right. It's yours. I'm sorry."

His fingers closed on the light's plastic grip and he probed for the switch. The beam proved too weak for locating the other Yamaha. Pale brown rock walls stared back at him, their surface pockmarked with craters like a moonscape. A moment later, his fears were confirmed and he turned the jet ski to avoid a head-on with the tunnel's side. "Socks," he yelled. "Where are you?"

"Keep going … oing … ing …ng," echoed back to him. "I've found … ound … nd …" The rest was muddled by echoes and Trouble couldn't make out what Socks was saying. Still, it seemed he was heading deeper inside the rock instead of retreating to open water, where the helicopter could easily spot him. Another ten yards – or was it twenty, he couldn't be sure – and the tunnel widened.

Suddenly the hole became a tall cavern with a small opening in its ceiling, letting in a bit of sunlight. Weak daylight revealed the texture of the cave. Limestone was scarred by dripping mineral streams until the walls resembled jagged stone icicles. The dripstones were furrowed with calcium streaks that wove down their spines like white veins in a marble column. Slowly, his eyes adapted to the dim interior and he made out Socks. She'd dismounted from her jet ski, parked on a beach of fine pebbles. He made a parallel landing and hopped off.

Socks was using a match to soften waxy bottoms on small candles, so they'd cling to surrounding boulders. Once stuck on a rock, the candles were lit and tiny flames appeared. Small tongues of fire sputtered, adding a shadowy glow to the damp cavern. Candlelight pushed away darkness, making them all feel better, safer.

Chiaro whispered, staring at a dozen flickering wicks. "I hope bats only like flashlights."

Socks was philosophical. "We'll find out. Meantime, we should eat this food before it gets cold. Then, Chiaro, you can tell us everything you know."

"Why should I?" Chiaro squatted on the beach, her face in a sulk.

"Because if you don't," Socks explained, "we'll leave you here to find out what happens when the candles burn out."

35

"Hand over my father's book — and our notes." Socks held an outstretched arm in front of Chiaro and waited.

"I give you this ..." Chiaro wagged the soggy lab notebook. "... and I got nothing. You don't need me anymore."

"Fine." Socks used chopsticks to shove noodles in her mouth, slurping at a fast pace. She stopped gulping for a moment and gave Trouble a knowing smile.

He glanced at Chiaro. She looked like a soggy mess of kelp, heaped on a beach of rough pebbles. Her brown hair was a chaos of long tangles and her pajamas dripped seawater on the dark sand. The sight forced pity through a layer of contempt wrapping his heart. "Socks thinks you'll hand over the notebook when you get hungry enough."

"I won't," Chiaro insisted, putting the notebook against her ravenous stomach to hide its growling. She held the marbled cover of Dr. Cam's lab book so tightly her knuckles turned white.

Trouble ate another bite of flatbread. "Be reasonable. You might as well turn over the documents. There's two of us. We could take them from you."

"I'd tear them to shreds." She glowered at them. Chiaro took a step back, clutching the document while staring at the hot food.

"So we wait. Every minute, you get weaker and we get stronger." Socks grabbed a hunk of cooked fish in wrapped seaweed and offered it to Trouble. "Try this. Smells and tastes like chicken. Very good. Important to have protein, not just carbs." She gestured toward his vanishing disc of flatbread.

He took the meat and bit off a chunk. "Um, good," he mumbled. Trouble chewed and swallowed. He tasted lemon, sugar and garlic, then a fiery trail of hot peppers scorched his throat. "Now all we need is some water."

Socks pulled three bottles from her satchel. "Got that, also. They catch rain on their floating platform, since there isn't any other source of fresh water. The bottles are re-used, but that's about as sanitary as it gets in this area – unless you're on a tour boat."

He grabbed one of the water bottles and held it up to light for inspection. "They clean these bottles before refilling them?"

"Sure, just ask them." Socks laughed.

He returned the plastic jug to its spot on the beach. "I'll pass. Didn't have time to get all my shots before hopping a jet to come here. I'm sure the water's OK for locals like yourself. Your body's adapted to whatever diseases are in that bottle. But mine hasn't."

"You gotta drink sometime." Socks uncapped a bottle and glugged. The water disappeared down her throat in a few deep gulps. She kept chugging at the plastic container until the liquid was drained. "You need water. The food's salty and spicy."

"I'll wait. Maybe we'll find a catch basin nearby, filled with rain leaking through that hole in the ceiling." He pointed overhead.

"Suit yourself." Socks took a small bite of wrapped fish and held it out to Chiaro, offering to trade food for information. "So, were you a spy from the beginning – or did you jump sides when it looked like you could make a lot of money?"

One of her hands slid off the notebook clamped to her stomach. Chiaro reached for the meat, but Socks pulled away.

"Uh, uh. First you answer. Then you eat."

Rage on Chiaro's face melted into despair. "All right. You won't like this, Trouble."

"Try me." He quit eating and focused on his "frenemy."

She couldn't look him in the eye. Chiaro stared at a black pebble on the sand, fixating on the stone like she wanted to disappear. Her voice was a hoarse whisper. "It was no accident you found me on your doorstep."

"Flix hired you from the beginning. I kind of thought so, from the way you acted around him on the pier. How'd he know about you?"

"I thought you were going to feed me." Chiaro's face again puffed with anger. Her skin turned blotchy pink, as if her emotions had triggered a rash.

"First you feed us the truth." Socks deliberately ate the food she'd offered Chiaro. The fish disappeared down her narrow throat in a large gulp.

"No point in answering your questions," Chiaro sulked. Her mouth stayed closed in a tight line.

"Answer how Flix knew to use you and I'll give you an even larger piece of fish." Socks took out the chunk and flaunted it.

Chiaro let out a long, slow breath. "Flix wanted to sell the rat. He needed contacts to black market animal traders, internationally. He asked around and got told my dad could answer his questions. Those guys Flix asked didn't know my father's in prison. So Flix came to our neighborhood, looking for my father and found me. He saw me leaving the Curio Shop in the early morning and realized I knew Trouble."

"The rest is history, as they say." Socks gave the fish to Chiaro and she inhaled the piece, choking a bit on it. Chiaro's mouth barely chewed before she took a big swallow and started coughing.

Trouble didn't try to hide the bitterness in his voice when he spoke. "Some friend you were. You were Flix's backup, in case I didn't cooperate."

"Unfair. I urged you to work with Flix. It's always better to go with money instead of fighting. You gotta learn that rich people win and little people lose. That's the way of the world. They got the power, not us." Chiaro spat out a small piece of the fish she'd eaten. Her nose wrinkled like she'd sniffed a rotten egg. "Ugh. That doesn't taste like chicken."

"I know." Socks beamed a nasty grin of satisfaction. "I gave you eel, not ahi. Traitors don't deserve good fish."

"You lied to me …" Chiaro rose to a threatening posture.

Socks didn't bother assuming a defensive pose. "I didn't lie. I said I'd give Trouble a fish that tasted like chicken and I did."

"So that's ahi, huh. Could I have another bite?" Trouble held out an open palm. A hunk of white fish dropped in his hand and he closed fingers around it. Then Trouble surprised Socks by offering the fish to Chiaro. "This really does taste like oven roasted poultry. It's yours. I just want to know one thing."

"What?" Suspicious, Chiaro backed away from them.

He got on his feet and followed her. One of his steps forward matched each of her steps back. Soon Chiaro was forced against large rocks, limestone boulders extending from the sandy beach to the cave's ceiling. Chiaro tried to squeeze her body inside a narrow pit carved in one of the boulders.

"Don't hit me." She raised an elbow to shield her face.

He moved to give her space. "I'm not going to punch you. I only want to know what I'm up against. Under the helicopter, you said 'he'll kill me.' You meant the guy in the helo would kill you. Seeing this guy turned Flix, mister Warwick Academy, master of the universe, into quivering Jell-O. Who is this person?"

"It wasn't a person. It was a creepy thing, a half man."

"No food for that answer." Trouble gave her a cynical look.

338

"Sorry. I thought you knew. Flix's dad killed his business partner and got away with the crime. But he lost the bottom half of his body in the fight."

"Are we talking about Le Roi Braun, the junkyard king?" Trouble cocked his head, allowing himself a tight grin of satisfaction. Some pieces of the puzzle were dropping in place.

Chiaro didn't answer. She reached for the fish. "Come on. Gimme. I answered your questions. You got humanity, even if she doesn't."

Laughing at the comment, Socks rose and moved toward them. "Make her answer one more question first," she advised Trouble.

"Which is?" He glanced between the two girls, so he could watch both of them.

For a moment, it seemed like everyone had forgotten to breathe. Then Socks answered. "From what I've been told, there were ninjas in your shop and ninjas waiting for you in Vietnam. But there weren't any green thugs on the dock, like you expected, Trouble. So, Chiaro, tell us who controls the ninjas. Who do they work for, Flix or Le Roi?"

"They don't work for Flix. His money is wrapped up tight in a trust fund, including all dollars from selling that monster rat. The bucks he loaned Trouble came from a gem Le Roi gave Flix." Chiaro held out her hand, expecting the fish.

Trouble gave it to her. "A sapphire?"

She nodded and muttered through a full mouth. "I think it was a sapphire. Only Flix told me it was crimson. That means red, doesn't it?"

"It does. Did Flix call the gem by another name, is that what confused you about the stone?"

"Yeah. He said it was a … padpara something or other."

"A *padparadscha*."

Socks butted into the conversation. "I need a little help here. What's the big deal about this gem?"

"My father hocked a rare jewel to finance his expedition here, working with your dad to locate what you call the Source. And you can guess who loaned my dad money, using the Scythian Sapphire as collateral."

"Le Roi Braun," Socks answered, "who rents ninjas to do his dirty work. I understand Chiaro spied on you and kept Flix informed. But how'd Le Roi track you, when only Flix knew where you were?"

"The fink had to be RJ, Flix's bodyguard," Chiaro suggested.

Trouble had to laugh, even if he was the butt of the joke. "We got a double sting here. RJ is doing to Flix what Chiaro did to me. Flix thinks RJ works for him, bribed by all the millions they'll get from selling monsters. But RJ is a spy for Le Roi."

Socks didn't think any of it was funny, however. "Yeah, well chuckle all you want. Just remember we've got a double tail, two bad-ass dudes looking to stomp us, instead of one."

"First they have to find us," Chiaro observed in a calm voice.

The smug way Chiaro talked made Trouble angry. "Oh, they'll find us. Our jet skis left long trails in the water, pointing straight here. The helo could be right outside, hovering, waiting for us to leave."

"Except we don't have to leave. We're inside the right Karst formation to find the Source. I made sure of that. I punched coordinates for the Source into my ultra-light's GPS. I stole it back from Chiaro."

Chiaro shot a hand inside her messenger bag and rummaged around. Her expression went from frightened to dejected. Then she perked up. "You're assuming the coordinates were correct. The only way to know for sure is checking your notes, the deciphered passages."

"I trust my memory," Socks huffed.

Trouble moved between them. "All right, Chiaro. What are you offering to trade, here?"

"Notes for food, a new U.N. program."

Socks refused. "Forget it. I'm not giving her anything for that soggy mess in her hand."

"That soggy mess is worthless. I agree." Chiaro ripped up the wet sheets and threw them in the air in a blizzard of pieces.

Trouble snapped at her. "What'd you do that for?"

"You want verification. I want to pick my food. No more eel."

"You've got nothing to trade." Socks glared at Chiaro.

"Yes, I do. What I shredded was fake. Your notes have always been safe in plastic tucked inside my messenger bag. So, is it a deal? You get peace of mind and I get fed."

Socks hesitated, but Trouble agreed. "Deal." They shook on it. He gave Chiaro the food satchel and she handed Socks a baggy. Sheets of paper were rolled inside the plastic bag.

Socks yanked open the baggy's seal and tore out the sheets, checking the Source's coordinates. "I was close enough. Only the last two digits were off."

"Which means?" Trouble asked, leaning over Socks to look at the GPS display in her hands.

She turned and began walking. "It means that ..." She took a few more steps and pointed. "The entrance to the Source should be right there."

36

He stared at where Socks was pointing, a crescent-shaped hole in a rock wall. The slit was barely large enough for an adult to squeeze through the opening. Trouble borrowed Chiaro's pencil beam flashlight and walked to the fracture. Beyond the opening, a narrow tunnel led into darkness. He shined light into the hole and peered at layers of stone, deposits of minerals formed over thousands of years. "There's a cavern on the other side. I guess we could step through and check it out."

Entrance To The Source

"You guys go. I'll wait here." Chiaro squatted on the beach. She found a large pebble and tossed it in the water with a plunk. Her eyes tracked ripples of seawater radiating from the fallen pebble.

"No, you can't stay. It's not safe to leave you." Trouble insisted. "You might hotwire our jet skis."

Socks liked his reasoning. "Smart. Good thinking. Don't leave her alone."

"I'm not gonna steal your transportation and strand you here. Though it'd be fair. After all, that's how you threatened me."

Socks corrected her. "I didn't say we'd abandon you forever. I only said we'd leave you to find what happens when the candles go out."

"It felt lousy, that's what I know." Chiaro grabbed a few candles, blowing out their wicks. "Looks dark in there. Maybe we ought'a bring the candles along to help us see."

Socks was too angry at Chiaro to compliment her on a smart move. Instead, she filled her own arms with warm candles and followed behind.

Trouble walked to the crescent-shaped opening. His fingers traced the crevice's damp rock, feeling coarse salt on ridged surfaces. He slid through the hole and began exploring their surroundings with the tiny flashlight. The cavern was littered with a jagged debris of shattered boulders. Stagnant water pooled in sinkholes pockmarking the cave's floor. "Bigger than I thought it was. Light some of those candles. Maybe we can see a path." He inhaled the gunpowder odor of match sulfur as a flame sputtered to life. Soon he was ringed with small tongues of light. He couldn't see much, but his eyes caught a glint of metal. A few steps in that direction revealed a surprise. "Somebody brought a generator in here. And I see cables running from it. Maybe the generator was used to power lights. I'll try to get the thing started."

He bent over the industrial device and discovered another one just like it, then another. The red motors were mounted on black metal frames, like a line-up of mini-truck engines. Checking their fuel tanks revealed the power sources had run dry, causing their motors to quit. Cans of fuel were stacked in a pyramid, so it wasn't hard to refill the empty tanks. He unscrewed the lid on a tank and drained the contents of a two and a half liter fuel can. Stinky, faintly metallic odors flooded the cavern.

Watching him pour an oil/gas mixture, Chiaro asked, "How're you gonna get them running?"

"They start like a lawnmower does. I just gotta yank hard on a cord." A quick tug on a plastic handle kicked one of the generators over. The engine sounded like a motorcycle, its rumbling magnified by echoes in the cave. Then it sputtered, coughing loudly, before quitting. Trouble gave the motor's pull-cord a second try and the electrical source fired up, running smoothly. The same ritual triggered remaining generators and strings of lights flourished, bringing the cavern alive.

Harsh white light drenched weathered limestone. Deep holes marked the drip paths of erosion over centuries. The eerie stone had the striped look of Tiger's Eye, worn by dripping water to a smooth polish.

"Wow." Chiaro gaped at a vast display of bizarre rock formations. Crusty icicles of calcium dangled from the roof. Beneath them, the cavern's floor was a jumble of boulders worn smooth by flowing water. The steady presence of water had melted rough outcrops.

Angular rocks transformed to beige lumps with the appearance of shiny floors. "This looks like a riverbed."

For once, Socks agreed with Chiaro. "Yes. We're standing in an underground river that's run dry." She studied a mosaic of cracks in the ceiling, then peered at distant lights. "Someone brought generators in here so they could explore. Must've been our fathers who lugged all this gear, Trouble."

"Yeah. I hope everyone's OK. The generators weren't shut off. They ran out of fuel. It means they didn't return before the electricity quit." Even though it felt chilly in the cave, worry brought out a sheen of perspiration on his face.

Taking a step forward, Socks motioned for the pair to follow her. "You filled the tanks, right?"

"To the brim. I'm guessing that gives us two hours of light, no more." Trouble shrugged the daypack on his shoulder and glanced at Chiaro.

She wasn't happy about walking for two hours. "I don't like hiking. Isn't there another way?"

"Yeah. There has to be. Somebody must've brought All Terrain Vehicles into this cave. We find them and ride them, if we can."

"ATVs? No way. They wouldn't fit through that slot." Chiaro pointed at the cave entrance. She glanced at Socks. "Am I right?"

"No. ATVs can be taken apart, just like the generators. Pieces go through the hole, then get assembled." Socks began walking. "Come on, you two. We're wasting time." She trotted faster, treading over smooth, molten rock.

Trouble ran to catch her. He whispered, "There must be ATVs we can ride. Otherwise no one could get to the Source and back in time. The Source is under your treehouse. We jogged three miles to the village. We rode the jet skis about ten miles between the fishing village and here. Three plus ten means we need to cover thirteen miles to reach the Source."

"Thirteen and a half miles, to be exact." She tapped the GPS. "For now, this electronic device will guide us. Later, radiation will make my GPS useless."

"Hey, wait for me." Chiaro had difficulty keeping up.

Trouble gave her a hand, helping her climb a slick rock. "Hang in there. I see a gravel river bed. Walking there will be much easier than stumbling over these boulders."

"Good. Then I'm getting there fast as I can." Chiaro jumped to the next boulder instead of climbing down, then up again.

Trouble followed her, hopping between rocks whenever he could. Though moving across uneven terrain strained his muscles, he could feel they were descending. Coming back he knew, would be harder. They'd be going uphill.

A few minutes later, the trio left the rock jumble and hiked along a riverbed lined with pebbles, worn flat by water currents. Easy hiking improved the trio's mood and all of them were feeling more optimistic. However, a bend in the tunnel changed their luck. Around a corner lay a maze of twisted rock formations. The puzzle had many entrances, slot canyons leading in strange directions. Sorting out which paths dead-ended would waste hours. They'd have to send someone back to keep fueling the generators.

Chiaro saw them looking at her and protested. "It isn't gonna be me. Anything happens to those generators and you'll claim I sabotaged them."

"You're right. It certainly isn't going to be you keeping the lights on." Socks frowned. "I'll go back and tend the power."

"You sure?" Trouble was surprised by Socks volunteering. He'd expected an argument.

"Yeah, I'm sure. You have mountaineering experience and I don't."

"How'd you know that?" He felt startled by her knowledge of his trip to Mount Everest.

Socks waved Dr. Cam's notebook. "My father scribbled a note in the margin about your expedition. It was near one of his last entries."

"How come I didn't see it?"

"You fell asleep. Did a faceplant. I woke you up and finished the last of the decoding, remember?"

"Um, sorta. I did get pretty tired. Wait, how'd your dad know about me?"

"From your mother. She peeks at your email account, to make sure you aren't making friends with the wrong type of people."

"Wonderful. I gotta change my password. I can see why your father encrypted everything."

"Nobody likes being snooped on." Socks nodded. "I'm going back. You guys explore. Consider splitting up. That way, you cover more paths in the same time."

"Makes sense." He turned to Chiaro. "Pick one of the entrances and I'll try another."

"I don't feel good about this."

"Do it anyway."

Intimidated, Chiaro hesitated to enter the maze. "What if I get lost?"

"Yell and I'll find you, guide you out."

"That works?"

"Every time." In truth, it was a lie. He knew echoes could delay a rescue for a very long time.

Chiaro gulped. "OK."

He waited until she vanished from sight, then pulled a lime from his backpack. They were pretty soft and he'd no difficulty smashing the fruit against a rock, marking Chiaro's entry spot with green mash. He left another squished hulk behind to mark a path he was exploring.

Easy movement through a narrow canyon soon ended. Earthquakes had tumbled down rock pieces, blocking his progress. He climbed the obstacles and found himself with a pretty good view of several trails. It was hard to decide which path to choose. Each of them looked like they might keep going. All he could do was pick one and explore until it ended – or worse yet, took him backwards in a loop.

He kept trying alternatives, smashing limes, dropping squashed hulks, until his daypack was almost empty of the green fruit. The scent of squeezed limes faded and was replaced by damp mold that made the inside of his ears itch and inflamed his sinuses. His next attempt terminated in a blockage that looked ancient. He could tell the rocks were old because slow-growing gypsum discs mushroomed on limestone pillars. Some gypsum formations looked like potato chips jumbled in a heap. Others sprouted curly gray fingers like balls of steel wool.

It didn't seem anyone could have gone beyond the weird rock formations without wrecking their delicate shapes. This couldn't be a true path through the obstacle course. Trouble decided he needed a fresh start in the maze. He trotted back to the very beginning, where he and Chiaro split up. Trouble found her standing there, looking dazed and frightened. Powdery residue clung to her black pajamas like talcum powder. Chiaro's tan face was cloaked in the same powder, dusted in crushed rock. Her eyes gave him a blank stare.

He studied her with contempt. "You do any exploring, like I asked?"

"A little." Her eyes remained downcast. "This place creeps me out."

"I don't like it either. But we gotta do it."

"Can I come with you?" Her voice was so low it would've made a whisper seem loud.

He felt like going it alone. But Trouble was concerned Chiaro might cause problems for Socks. He didn't want to break through the maze only to have the lights go out. "All right. You can follow me."

"Thanks." Her smile beamed for an instant, before her upbeat mood shipwrecked on his angry face. "Well, you're real happy to see me."

"Not exactly." Trouble yanked the daypack off his back so he could fumble inside. He wanted to use a lime to mark this attempt through the maze. He pulled out a green ball and was surprised by its firmness. When he smashed this lime against a rock, it didn't squish flat and ooze juice. Instead, he felt a hollow tap. A sharp click echoed in the cavern. He stared at a bottle green orb the size of a ping-pong ball. "What is this thing?" His gaze turned to Chiaro and was stunned to see embarrassment on her face.

Squirming, Chiaro made a suggestion. "Um, try opening it."

"What?"

She poked the ball with the tip of her forefinger. "You got a lot of goo on your hand from other limes. So you can't feel how it's fake. Looks plastic to me."

"Chiaro, you knew all along some limes weren't real. Is this another Flix trick?"

"No." Her face looked calm for a moment, before her features dissolved in sadness. "I think the limes were his dad's idea. Remember, Flix's dad is the ninja maestro ..." She hesitated. "Limes are green, like those costumes his ninjas wear."

"That lime peddler. She planted a bug on me." Furious, Trouble bashed the fake lime against a rock and the ball split open. A tiny circuit board fell out, with a watch battery.

Chiaro bent over and lifted the electronics package off the ground, cradling it in the palm of her hand. "It's not a bug. There's no microphone or camera. Lettering on the board says it's a GPS locator."

"They know where we are. Le Roi tracked us. We're too far from the Source for its radiation to block transmissions from that bug." For the first time in his life, he wanted to slug a girl. His next words spat rage at her. "*You* did this to me."

Recoiling in fear, she jumped backwards. "Trouble, no ... I didn't. I always wondered about the fruit. It seemed a weird coincidence for her to show up and pester us. Please ... remember I bribed the old woman to pick up dropped limes – so you wouldn't have them in your bag. I was trying to help. You gotta believe me."

"Why didn't you say anything?"

"I didn't have a chance. Stuff happened so fast. Then I forgot about the fruit." She put on her best pleading look.

He ignored her act. "That's how ninjas found us, when we got in the Cyclos. We were being tracked."

She nodded. "Makes sense. After that, Ferrari and Lightning drove too fast for ninjas to keep up."

"But we stopped at a snake restaurant for hours. Why didn't ninjas come after us?"

"I don't know. I guess they were waiting for you to make contact with your agent ..." Her voice drifted off.

Trouble could tell she had an important idea. He wanted to know, so he growled. "What're you thinking?"

"Maybe the ninjas were told to wait for Flix's dad. He was on a plane and hadn't landed in Hanoi yet. That's why ninjas didn't grab us over supper.

"After dinner, we went to the skyscraper and Flix showed up. He knew where I was. Flix must be cooperating with his father. "

"No. Only Le Roi and his ninjas tracked you with the fake lime." Chiaro's voice was firm, but her body language radiated shame. "Flix had a different way of knowing where you were."

"How?"

"It was me." She tapped her chest. "I called Flix when you fell asleep in the stairwell." She pulled a tiny shortwave radio from her messenger bag.

He swatted the radio from her hand and stomped on it, crushing its plastic shell. That wasn't enough for him. Trouble grabbed broken pieces, linked by wires, and tore them apart. His feet stomped a small circuit board until the brittle green panel shattered and its solder chipped into silver bits. He threw shreds in various directions, hurling them as far as he could. "You're not my friend. You were never a friend, Chiaro. You were a spy from the beginning."

"OK, I wasn't honest. I admit that." Her eyes darted around the cavern, like she was desperate to escape. "But I'm not an enemy, Trouble. I wanted both you and Flix to win. I really believe you're better off working with him. You need help. I told you, Flix is rich and …"

"I don't care. Get out." He jabbed a finger toward the generators. "I'm going on – alone."

"You'll waste a lot of time."

Anger pinched his eyes shut. "You explored, after all. Didn't you?"

"Yeah, OK. I did."

"What did you find? A friend would tell me."

"I'm a friend." She gulped, realizing Trouble was losing control of his emotions. "I can prove it."

"How?" He snarled at her. "This better be good."

Fear blew words from her mouth in a burst of syllables. "I found a way through the maze. I'll show you. Save you time."

"Good. What else did you uncover?"

"You don't wanna know."

He felt chills of dread poking sharp fingernails in his spine. Trouble's voice cracked when he spoke. "Who's dead?"

"Maybe nobody." Chiaro shivered, but it wasn't from being cold. "I only saw an arm."

"Man ... or woman?"

"I couldn't tell." Her lie didn't convince him.

He grabbed Chiaro's shoulders and jarred her.

"I'm sorry, Trouble. I really am." Tears moistened her eyes. The weeping seemed genuine.

"My mother."

"Could be."

Feeling crazed with pain, he ran into the maze.

"No, not that way."

"What?" Trouble was too upset. He couldn't hear well.

Chiaro grabbed his hand. "This way. I'll show you."

37

Trouble followed Chiaro for only a short while before she released his hand. He felt grateful to be free of her touch. Letting her guide him was bad enough. They turned away from overhead lighting and headed along a dim canyon. Shadows lengthened into darkness without warning. Rocks and trail marks disappeared. His feet tumbled over slick flowstones lining the cave floor in slippery mounds. Eerie stillness claimed the tunnel, distant from the comforting chug of generators. He protested, "Wait. You're going the wrong way."

"No." She turned around. "I tried staying in bright areas. Like you, I assumed your father hung lights to make his work easier. And maybe that's what he did, initially. But I think he moved the lights to disguise the true path."

"So you went the other way and it worked out?" He gestured at a slot canyon behind her, a skinny path that forked away from the main tunnel.

Chiaro smiled. "Yeah."

"How'd you mark the trail?"

"Candles. I left one burning at every major junction. Come on. I'll show you." She pivoted and gravel crunched under her feet. Chiaro resumed her march, setting a fast pace. Her steps were noisy slaps echoing down the path, loud as a team of explorers tramping through the humid cave.

He jogged to keep up with her. "How'd my mother and Dr. Cam see in the dark?"

"Chemical lightsticks. I found a few lying on the ground."

"Makes sense." His shoulder brushed coarse rock, making a scratching noise.

Chiaro halted. "What was that?"

"Me. My shoulder hit some rock." He looked down and saw a bent plastic tube on the ground. Trouble lifted the six inch mini pipe and shook it. Faint orange glow radiated from the old lightstick, a weak illumination like the last moments of a sunset. He dropped the useless object and rubbed powdery dust off his fingertips. "You were right about lightsticks. They bent one to activate it, then left its arrowhead shape pointing the way."

"How long do those things glow?" she wondered.

"The answer varies. Brighter sticks don't last long. In here, you could use the dim kind. They shine for twelve hours. How much farther to ...?

"The arm I saw? Yeah. I knew you'd ask that. Five minutes is all. But there's tight squeezes along the way. The corridors used to be wider. Earthquakes knocked down a lot of rubble." She nodded toward a faint candle glowing in the distance. "We'd better hustle, so those candles stay lit."

"Flix didn't supply you with lightsticks?" Anger simmered in him.

"Give it a rest, Trouble." She didn't let him have a chance for more sarcasm. Chiaro started running toward candlelight, sliding through narrow gaps between rocks. In the semi-darkness, she looked like a ghostly wisp of smoke, twisting and shrinking.

Following her along the bending path was a challenge. After a while, he fell behind and reached a junction where his choice wasn't marked by candlelight. The trail had no clues, only a pattern of sinkholes dotting worn limestone. Dissolved bedrock had the clammy texture of wet marbles left in the rain. Had he made a mistake – or did Chiaro ditch him on purpose? He turned around, listening to small rocks crackle under his feet. Trouble was about to call her name when the cave lights pulsed – three quick flickers. He opened his mouth to shout for Chiaro and distant lights again blinked. This time there was a trio of longer outages. They were followed by another triplet of fast blips.

Chiaro's shape appeared, a shadow outline in the passage behind him. "What was that?"

"You mean the lights?"

"Yeah." More blips, three short – three long – three short, flashed across their horizon.

"It's happening again." Chiaro sounded frightened. "What's going on?"

"Socks is in danger. She's doing Morse Code, flashing the S.O.S. pattern. Flix must have shown up."

"Or Le Roi." She paused, waiting for the next S.O.S. to end, but it quit in the middle of a long pulse. Then lights came back on, bright as ever. "What are we going to do?"

"I don't think it was Socks asking for help. Even though that's what S.O.S. means. I think she blinked the lights to warn us."

"So we turn back?"

"I say we keep going. Maybe there's another way out of this cavern. Go back and we get caught. We can't fight ninjas."

"Flix might be alone. He could help us get through the blockage," she argued.

Trouble shook his head in disagreement. "No help there. Flix is with RJ. That guy's lost it. RJ would rather kill me than help me. And he doesn't like you either, after your negotiating session on the dock."

"All right." She placed a hand on her hip and gave him a look of resignation. "How do you want to do this?"

Ignoring her attitude, Trouble knelt down and plucked a spent lightstick off the ground. He dumped the plastic tube in his daypack. "We have to erase our tracks, maybe even lay a decoy trail, the way Dr. Cam and my father did."

It was her turn to be sarcastic. "Oh yeah, great. How're we gonna find our way out? Erase all markers and we could loop for days. We might even get caught in another earthquake and trapped."

"It's a risk we have to take."

"You know what, even I realize your mother could need urgent medical attention. A long delay might be fatal. Have you thought about that?"

"Yeah." His body sagged. "It's one risk balanced against another. Get killed by RJ – or let my mother die because I made a bad decision about the markers."

"Whatever." Chiaro rolled her eyes toward the cavern's ceiling. Translucent calcium "soda straws" hung from the chalky roof of the cave like skinny glass icicles. She studied light playing through the hanging straws, stalling a minute before stepping into the dark. "Here we go." She began retracing their path, not looking behind to see if Trouble was following.

At a key junction, he snuffed out a candle and dropped the warm blob in her messenger bag. He sped to reach the next melted candle, a short stump marking Chiaro's path. The wick floated in a pool of molten paraffin, leaking over the candle's edge. Specks of wax remained stuck in crevices, even after he'd peeled drips off rocks.

Chiaro pointed at tiny slivers of wax. "They're gonna see those, you know. Pieces of red wax don't look natural. Might as well leave the candles so we can find our way home."

"Quit arguing. Help me brush away our footprints." He removed his jacket and began wiping the ground, trying to smooth marks left by his shoes.

Chiaro ignored his request for help. Her head turned toward the generators. The expression on her face showed worry. A sharp bark echoed through the cavern, ricocheting off walls and rock pillars. "Ninjas have tracking dogs?"

He froze. "They did at the skyscraper." A baying hound drowned out all other sound. The dog's yelps reverberated through rock chambers, growing louder and more distinct. "Forget our tracks. The dog will find us by scent. We have to run for it. You lead the way."

She yanked the warm candle from her bag and shoved it on a ledge. Chiaro moved twice as fast this time. Trouble forgot all caution and sprinted after her, not worrying about tripping or making noise. His feet smacked against damp riverbed as he ran down a cool stone trail. He squinted ahead, focusing on Chiaro's messenger bag jiggling on her shoulder. Mineral water dribbled from stalactites on the ceiling like a runny nose. Trouble felt the droplets hit his face and chill his forehead. He kept after Chiaro, rushing at full speed until his legs wore out. A few moments later, they halted and bent over, panting, struggling to catch their breath. They fought to suck air, inhaling through tired lungs. Lack of oxygen dimmed their senses. The air smelled like stale potato chips lying forgotten in an old dish.

"Far as we go. Now, we have to move rocks." Chiaro grunted, pointing at a jumble of small boulders. The uneven stack had the texture of dry clay. Ridges of stone lined this alcove in the cavern. The walls lost their smooth hollows and grew rough, bulging like coarse faces with no eyes.

He looked at rubble, hoping his mother wasn't buried underneath. Trouble forced himself to ask about her, though he dreaded Chiaro's answer. "Where'd you see that arm?"

"I climbed to the top, looking for a way to squirm past the rocks. Found a small tunnel, but it's too small for me to crawl through. I tossed a glowing lightstick in the hole. Heard it drop. Sounded like the lightstick fell on the floor. I figured the rock pile couldn't be thick and stuck my head inside the tunnel. Didn't see much, except an elbow coated in dust."

"Where'd you get a lightstick?" Trouble began picking his way up the rock slide. Loose shale crumbled under each step and made finding a handhold difficult.

Chiaro gestured behind them. "Someone left a chem-stick on a ledge twenty meters back." She watched him poke his head inside a hole. "You see the arm?"

"Yes. But I can't tell if it belongs to Dr. Cam or ..." His voice went soft. "Or Julia." It felt strange to call his mother by her name, instead of saying "mom." Dust clogged his ears and skin. He tried moving a smaller rock and quit, afraid he'd dislodge a boulder and it would fall on Chiaro. "You better get back, in case I trigger an avalanche."

"You don't want help?"

"Not enough room up here for two." He grunted against a piece of flat shale. Its sharp edge jabbed his palm. He used more force and the rock came loose. He let it slide downward, bouncing to the bottom. Another rock looked small enough for him to pull out. The rough surface burned his skin as he tugged on the slab. It moved, then stuck. Trouble shifted his position, adding his body weight to the pull of his muscles. Suddenly, everything topside broke loose, rolling into him, knocking him off his perch. He fell, sliding, scraping, bruising, ripping his clothes. Boulders pinched his fingers for a painful moment, then rolled past. Brittle shale crumbled into mud and mineral debris, leaving a trail of crunchy grit.

Chiaro rushed through the debris field, hovering over him. "You all right?"

"Yeah." He coughed, spewing a dirt cloud. Trouble cranked his neck to see if he'd made the tunnel larger. "A few more rocks and we can get through."

"Ah, Trouble. We're out of time." She tapped his shoulder to get his attention. Chiaro pointed at a huge dog blocking the trail.

Its chest had the ripped cut of a weightlifter. There was no fat on the dog's body, only developed muscles bulging under a sleek coat. Yellow and black stripes covered his skin like a tiger. A whorl of fur lined the animal's spine, appearing to be a knotted ship's rope glued to its back. The canine stood tall as the bottom of Chiaro's messenger bag. Its bat-like ears were long and sharply pointed, listening for the next sound. A low growl came through its bared fangs. Slobber drooled off its massive jaws. Angry red eyes stared at Trouble, hoping for a sign of weakness, an excuse to attack.

He rose from the ground and squared off to face the dog. Each fist held small rocks, his only weapon. Trouble whispered to Chiaro. "Stand alongside me. Together, we look bigger. It might help intimidate the hound, keep him from attacking."

"Why's he want to bite us? We didn't do anything." Chiaro squeezed next to Trouble.

He brought ready hands to chest height so he could hurl rocks, if forced to do it. "The dog was trained to hunt and he's been given our scent. We're the quarry. His instinct is to kill whatever he's tracking. He'll go for our throats, if he lunges. Try to get under him. Flip him on his back."

"Sure. You Tarzan. Me Jane. No problem."

"Got a better idea?"

She gulped. "No."

Green shapes formed behind the hound. Cloth wove around faces and only eyes showed through gauze masks. Dark stares were constant, focused on the next moment without blinking. The figures moved with an eerie quiet, tracking the cavern's shadows. They balanced on rocks, agile feet discovering a sure path through uneven boulders. There was a drag of sharp blades gliding from leather sheaths.

"I think we're dead." Chiaro began shaking.

He felt her quivering and tried to reassure her. "We're not dead yet." Then RJ towered over the ninjas. "We're dead," Trouble admitted.

RJ's eyes gleamed from the thought of having his delayed revenge. "Looky what we got here, trapped in a dead end, with nowhere to run. I couldn't ask for more. Trouble and Chiaro, right where I want them."

A disembodied voice came from behind RJ's neck. "I don't care about them. I only care about the FOY. Where is it?"

RJ laughed. "Good question. Why don't you answer him, Trouble? That way, you live a little longer."

"Where's Socks?" Trouble shifted in an attempt to peer around RJ. The dog lunged, but couldn't get any closer. The hound's movement was stopped by a taut leash. The canine's jaws snapped at empty air. He snarled with impatience, revealing white fangs that jutted from red gums. A ninja's fist held the creature back until he made a choking sound. That restraint emboldened Trouble and he repeated his question. "I want to make certain Socks is alive. Then I'll tell you where the Source is located."

Again the bodyless voice spoke. "Is a Source the same as a FOY?"

"Yes. Who am I talking to?" Trouble dropped all rocks from his hands. They were useless against overwhelming force, anyway. Maybe holding the rocks had caused the stranger to remain hidden.

RJ shook his head in disbelief. "You really think those pebbles were gonna stop me, boy?"

"Quit badgering him, RJ, and turn around. I want to see Indigo's son."

The chauffeur-bodyguard dry swallowed. Resentment made his tense face seem a plastic mask. Yet he obeyed the order and did a slow pivot.

Trouble had a hard time believing his eyes. A modified backpack hung behind RJ. The custom-made device held the top half of an adult male. But the man's bottom parts were missing. His pale, mottled face seemed ancient, like he aged ten years for every January that passed. Wisps of brittle hair clung to his barren skull. Pale gray irises stared ahead, chips of ice floating in milky eyeballs. Cracked lips revealed teeth too big for the shrunken face. Plastic tubes vanished inside both nostrils, feeding oxygen from green bottles slung on RJ's hips like water canteens. More tubes exited the man's lower stomach, appearing between shirt buttons. Excrement and urine seeped along the clear plastic hoses, filling a hospital bag clipped to the backpack.

"Let's skip the usual questions about what happened to me. I suggest we discuss what's going to happen to you." Le Roi Braun allowed himself a thin smile.

Trouble nodded. "Fine. As long as we also talk about Socks."

Chiaro nudged him to make sure she was included.

"And her. While I'm at it, where's Flix?"

"My son is behind me, where he belongs. For once, he's following my orders, instead of finding ways to thwart my plans." Le Roi tried to laugh and coughed instead. "Of course, Flix has no choice at this point."

"Safe, healthy, comfortable. Would you use those words to describe him – and Socks?"

"From my perspective, I'd say yes." Le Roi's eyes twinkled. He liked playing cat and mouse. "However, my son and Socks may describe their situation differently – if you ever have the chance to ask them."

Trouble bluffed. "Why tell you anything if you're going to kill me?" When he got the answer he expected, he didn't like it.

"As RJ said, you live longer. And you feel better." He pointed to green shapes drifting behind him. "They're very good at inflicting pain. You'll talk. It won't take long. We'll know everything."

"Will you know how to operate the Source? I don't." Fear caused perspiration to ooze from his armpits. Trouble felt beads of sweat trickling along his rib cage. He caught himself blinking rapidly and forced himself to quit. He wanted to see Le Roi clearly, gauge his mood.

Braun's legless body quivered. Despite being wrapped in a wool jacket, poor health caused the man to shiver. When the convulsions stopped, Le Roi spoke. "You don't operate a FOY, dear boy. You drink from it. Then you become whole again." Le Roi showed amusement at Trouble's confusion. "I funded your father for good reasons. Indigo showed me proof he'd discovered a FOY. With your help, Trouble, I've pried loose its location. Of course, Flix was also useful. I knew he'd sell the jewel and make another attempt at freedom. Fine. Let him. RJ has always been my spy, keeping watch on my son. Flix is silly enough to think he can outbid me for RJ's loyalty."

RJ shifted his weight, causing Le Roi to bounce around a bit. "Boss, talking is wasting time. Source, FOY, whatever you call it … let's get there and get on with it."

"How do you propose to do that?" Le Roi snapped.

"These kids ran here because it was their best chance to get through the Karst maze. They got stopped by a cave-in. But we brought explosives. Let's use them, blow away the rubble and keep going." RJ reached in a pocket on his equipment belt. He brought out something that looked like a toothpaste tube. "Squeeze a little Semtex on those boulders and step back. Bang – rocks to gravel."

"Bang and your last chance to use a FOY vanishes," Trouble argued.

Le Roi pinched his forehead in suspicion. His eyes were trapped in deep sockets and refused to blink. "Why?"

RJ butted in. "He's lying to buy time, live a little longer."

"Let him speak," Braun insisted. "What are you hiding behind those rocks, boy?"

"See for yourself." Trouble moved aside and pointed at the hole he'd been trying to enlarge. "It's in plain sight."

Le Roi motioned to a ninja, indicating he should climb the rock pile and look in the hole. The man obeyed, shoving Trouble aside. Braun waited as the ninja bent over, poking his head and neck inside the tunnel. With a quick jerk, the green shape pulled back and nodded. He pointed to his own arm, indicating what he'd seen.

Trouble spoke. "Dr. Cam's arm. He's on the other side. Bury him and you loose everything he knows about the Source – sorry, the FOY."

"Move these ..." Le Roi sneered. "...*children* out of the way. They might still be useful. Later, we can find a place to stuff their bodies. This cavern is full of holes."

"Sure boss." RJ gave instructions to the ninjas in a strange dialect. It didn't sound like Vietnamese. In fact, the language didn't even seem Asian. He spoke quickly, as if the words were torn out of his mouth in harsh syllables. In response, the ninjas sprang to life, dragging Trouble and Chiaro away from the rock pile. Then the martial arts warriors turned into human bulldozers, scraping, heaving, grunting small boulders aside. They exchanged a minimum of words and focused their strength in creating piles of rocks, resembling stacks of cannon balls. Four ninjas hauled the largest slabs into a dead end, grumbling under heavy weight. Flat stones were thrown against the cavern walls and shattered into fragments. Their green uniforms became chalked with cave dust and streaked in sweat. A strong body odor dominated the air, musty rot that smelled like a skunk run over on a dark road.

For Trouble, time passed at the speed a garden snail moves across a patio. Each minute dragged ahead in sluggish motion with little progress. The more curious he felt, the slower ninjas worked. Though it seemed to take forever, Trouble wasn't emotionally ready when the hole finally became large enough. But he had to see who was on the other side — and if they were alive.

38

The ninjas had bound Trouble's wrists behind his back using nylon ties. Snugged tight, they cut into his flesh with each twist of his body. The handcuffs grated his skin when he tried to hike wobbly boulders. Climbing a pile of loose rock without using his hands was almost impossible. Impatient with Trouble's slow progress, ninjas shoved and dragged him. His feet were unsteady and he scraped a knee, stumbling over broken stones. At the top of the rock pile, he caught a brief glimpse of his mother and Dr. Cam before a kick sent Trouble rolling down the other side. Bruised, cut, bleeding, he quit tumbling only when he slid into Dr. Cam.

"This isn't a rescue, is it?" The scientist, weakened by dehydration, had difficulty speaking. His cracked lips were white with encrusted salt. Tran Van Cam's skin appeared ghostly from rock dust caked on him. The same gritty powder clung to his thick hair, combed straight back. His anxious, bloodshot eyes squinted at Trouble.

He squirmed to a sitting position and answered Dr. Cam's question. "No rescue. Sorry. Socks and me got caught." He nodded toward Le Roi, riding in a knapsack on RJ's back. "That half man is the rich guy funding my father. Le Roi Braun is his name. Tall dude carrying Le Roi is a bodyguard. He goes by his initials, RJ. Green goons are, well, ninjas for lack of a better description."

"They aren't ninjas. They don't speak Japanese. It's a Middle Eastern dialect, quite old." Cam shook his head in disagreement and a small dust cloud formed around his face. The scientist coughed, spitting out dirt. When his throat cleared, he whispered. "You said my daughter came with you. Is she safe?"

"Socks was also captured. She was running the generators. Socks sent out an S.O.S. by blinking the lights, but there was nothing we could do to help. We couldn't even escape." Trouble let his eyes slide over Julia. She was also caked in dust from a cave-in that blocked the Karst maze. The gray powder made her tan face seem pale. Blonde hair straggled around her ears, shorter than he remembered. A faded blue t-shirt was tucked into gray cargo pants with a maze of zippered pockets.

It felt like staring at someone pretending to be his mother. He had a moment of doubt, but then Trouble saw the small gryphon on Julia's wrist. Inked in pale red, the half-lion, half-eagle tattoo was a souvenir of her first trip to burial mounds in Siberia. Her identity was again confirmed when he saw a familiar canvas rucksack. The bag had worn leather straps with the initials JJ on the outer pocket. He expected her to wake up with a laugh or get angry, but she didn't move. Her eyelids were closed and there was no expression on her features. Julia's limp body rested peacefully on a bed of rocks. He braved asking a dreaded question. "Is my mother dead?"

"Good news." Cam smiled, though it was a weak gesture. "She's alive. I took her pulse ..." He glanced at his watch. "an hour ago. Her heart rate was stable." Then his face assumed a sad look. "But your mother's in a coma. She needs medical attention."

"Hit by rocks?"

"No. That misfortune was avoided, barely." He touched the skin on her bare arm. "Warm and moist, a good sign."

"Not hurt by the cave-in. Then why's my mother sick?"

"She was too brave. Julia entered the castle, looking for your father. She didn't believe me when I said he'd left Vietnam. She wanted to check for herself – and to gather some important research. It was fortunate that I came looking for her or Julia would be dead."

Questions buzzed in Trouble's head. He didn't know which issue to focus on first. Le Roi solved the problem by interrupting their conversation.

His wild stare looked like it came from a rock musician, pumped for performing at a concert. "Where's the FOY?" Braun demanded.

"Beyond the castle." The scientist answered calmly.

"What are you talking about?" Le Roi's face clouded in anger.

Dr. Tran Van Cam gave Braun a look of disgust. "You come all this way to visit something horrible and dangerous. Yet you know so little about it? Unwise."

"The dog will teach him humility." Braun gestured to the giant hound and a ninja commanded the animal to attack. Bared fangs lunged for Cam. The canine's snapping jaws fell short of Cam's flesh, restrained by a leash. "Answer my questions or feel pain," Le Roi Braun warned.

"You can have all the answers by getting on that railroad flat car. Let it take you across the salt lake." Cam gestured past RJ's hulk, indicating a wooden platform. The surface was crusted with salt and a history of scars grooved its planks.

The bodyguard turned so Le Roi could see the wooden platform. Then RJ kept spinning, returning Braun to his original position, facing Dr. Cam.

Le Roi snapped, "That is a raft. There's no railroad. Keep speaking in riddles and the hound will eat you for lunch."

"If your man-servant wades into the lake, you'll see the tracks. A cable pulls the car forward at a surprising pace. How, I don't know. That's a mystery known only to those who constructed the castle. In legend, they are known as the Builders. Who they really were, how they did it – or better yet, why? No one has the answers. But if you seek a FOY or the Source … or whatever you call it – that ancient railroad is the only way to find it."

"You claim the lake is shallow enough for a railroad. Why not walk to the FOY?"

"Twelve miles is a long walk. Try it and the hike will prove longer than you think." Cam allowed himself a thin smile of amusement.

Braun chose to ignore Tran Van's provocative gesture. "How do I operate this railcar?"

"Pull the lever. I've never discovered what drives the car. But the mechanism builds to a fast speed. Be prepared for a quick start and abrupt stop."

Excited by the prospect of achieving his goal, Le Roi ran his tongue over dry lips. "How much time does the trip take?"

"There and back is about half an hour."

"That's all?" This time it was RJ talking. His deep voice seemed to float around the cavern.

"Yes." Cam nodded, though RJ couldn't see the gesture.

The bodyguard waded into the shallow brine. "I guess we're going, then."

"Wait. This is too easy. It must be a trap." Le Roi's stare bore into Tran Van Cam, then hit Trouble and Chiaro. "The railcar's large enough for everyone. Bring them with us." His forehead wrinkled in thought. "Go back and get my son." Braun pointed at Cam. "And his daughter. I want everyone to see my moment of glory."

Dr. Cam pointed at Julia. "She needs medical help. There's no reason to move her."

"I said everyone." Le Roi Braun's features twisted in sadistic glee.

Trouble felt his insides curdle. Another trip to the Source was the last thing his mother needed. According to Dr. Cam, the place was responsible for her illness. Trouble could understand Cam wanting to trick Le Roi into going there. But the ploy backfired, dragging them all into danger. Trouble suggested, "More people on the car means more weight. The heavier the load, the greater chance of a breakdown. Then it will take hours for you to reach the FOY."

"Think you're smart, hmm?" Braun's cutting look stabbed Trouble like a pin on a map.

He hoped his next words would appease Le Roi. "I was only being logical."

"I hate to admit, but he's got a point." RJ waded to the railcar and shook it. The platform rattled, a dry skeleton creaking in the wind. "Thing is pretty old."

"All right. A compromise. We'll only take this scientist and his daughter." Le Roi paused, hoping Trouble would assume he wasn't going.

Trouble rolled on his knees, forcing himself to rise despite painful bruises on his shins. Once on his feet, he began walking toward the railcar, guessing he was next on the list. Maybe volunteering would turn Le Roi perverse and cause Trouble to be rejected. The gambit almost worked.

"Wait. I didn't say you could go." Braun acted confused for a moment.

Trouble halted. Salt water stung tiny cuts on his ankles and feet as brine seeped into his shoes.

Le Roi contemplated his options. Then a cunning leer formed. "Yes, you're going. Anything happens and your death revenges me against your father. Get onboard, Trouble – or I'll have my ninjas throw you."

"Whatever." Trouble sloshed deeper, his shins burning from an intense salt broth soaking through his clothes, swabbing cuts on his legs. The red water smelled like a boiled fish dinner left to rot in the sun. He tried to blot out rancid odors and breathe through his mouth, instead of his nose. At the railcar, he dropped his butt on the platform and rolled onboard. With a struggle, Trouble got to his feet. He gave his mother a loving glance. Julia lay on her side, looking asleep instead of injured, like she'd wake up and label an ancient fragment any minute. But he knew that was a lie. Out of the corner of an eye, he saw a bruised, dazed Chiaro. She seemed ashamed and frightened. Chiaro leaned against a boulder, pretending to disappear. In anxiety, she twirled a strand of dark hair between her fingers and avoided conversation with others.

Socks appeared at the top of the rock pile, where the ninjas had widened the hole. A rude shove forced her to tumble down the heap of stones. Dr. Cam rushed to her and tried to comfort his daughter. A violent kick knocked him off his feet. Cam swayed as he rose, holding his arm. The kick numbed his muscles so they couldn't respond. Rage flashed from his dark eyes. The ninja set himself for another punch and Le Roi's voice croaked an order to halt. RJ repeated the message in the ninja's strange tongue.

Braun slapped his forehead in disgust. "I said bring them, not kill them. And where's my *son*? I want him as a *witness*."

The way he talked about Flix made it clear Le Roi had no love for his offspring. Flix was coming along to include him in any ambush. Braun wanted to make certain if he died, so did Flix.

When he appeared, Flix's blonde hair was still perfect, but his cocky attitude was gone. Fear and loathing replaced all the self-assurance he'd once radiated. Unlike the other hostages, his hands were bound in front, where he could still use them to steady himself. He wasn't molested like the others. Instead, a ninja helped him to make a safe descent. His eyes ran over the others – Julia, Chiaro, Socks, Dr. Cam –

and finally rested on Trouble. In a surprise movement, Flix gave Trouble a thumbs up, showing admiration.

The admiring gesture didn't help Le Roi's mood. "Get them onboard this piece of junk, so we can start moving." RJ translated that into an even more hostile order. Socks and Tran Van were tossed over ninjas' shoulders like sacks of rice, carried to the flat railcar and dumped aboard. RJ stepped on the "raft" and jammed its lever forward. There was a momentary hesitation. Then somewhere in the distance a turbine whined, spinning to higher revs until emitting a piercing scream.

Dr. Cam looked at Flix and tapped rough hardwood planks in the floor, indicating for Flix to sit down. With a grateful nod, Flix sank to the floor. A split second later, the railcar jerked forward, doing a racecar start, rocketing from zero to sixty in three seconds. Unable to stand, RJ spun around and fell, taking a push-up stance to cushion Le Roi.

"Clumsy fool," Braun cursed. "Get up, so I can see where we're going."

"Sorry, boss." RJ raised himself on his knees, looking at the prisoners so Le Roi would face the railcar's front, their direction of travel.

The junkyard king reveled in his moment of power, watching pale water part in a spray, like waves split by the bow of a ship. The farther they went, the shallower the lake became. Iodine in the salt stained the water red. Weird rock shapes, crusted white and brown with salt, popped out of the lake like abstract chess pieces. White salt rings along the cavern marked the calendar of a shrinking, orphaned "sea." Those rings came closer as the dome shrank, becoming a wide tunnel.

A shape emerged in the distance, hanging downward like stalactites dripping from the roof of a cave. Soon, the shape became an Asian castle turned upside-down. It was bent to form a crown, curving backwards over rocks. Eerie stained glass intersected columns engraved with silver. Images of black lotus flowers and meditation circles were caught in glass patterns. A mosaic of diamond shapes resembled the printed backs of Tarot cards. Dangling above the lake was a pattern of symbols appearing to be a message left behind by an alien civilization. The characters squirmed in the erratic movement of copper traces etched on an electronic circuit board.

Soon the castle was directly in front of them and the railcar decelerated, throwing RJ into another spin. This time, the twisting motion failed to anger Le Roi. Instead, he sighed. "They said I'd never be whole. Now, I'll be me again."

When all movement ceased, Dr. Cam slid next to Trouble and dared a whisper. "We're at the Source. Beware."

Arriving At The Source

39

Le Roi Braun felt hypnotized by the crown-shaped palace hovering above him. His eyes traced engraved columns and symbols highlighting the castle's doors. The secret inscriptions looked similar to hieroglyphs, but with a unique pattern of images. "Amazing," he murmured. "I want to talk with Dr. Cam. Bring him to me."

"Sure." RJ's feet thumped across wooden slats on the railcar floor. His shadow fell on Trouble, then Socks and Flix. They slid out of the giant's path until RJ towered over the wounded scientist. "Get up."

Curled on the floor, Tran Van Cam struggled to rise and failed. He pressed his palms into the scarred wood of the railcar, dragging to his knees. Impatient, RJ grabbed Cam's belt and yanked the man to a standing position.

Dr. Cam remained in a bent posture, nursing ribs bruised by a ninja kick. Each breath pained him. When his lungs inflated, they pressed against the injured rib cage. He gasped a single word. "Yes?"

Le Roi waved an arm, summoning Dr. Cam. "Stand next to me, so I can watch your eyes when you answer my questions."

The scientist obeyed, doing a limp shuffle when he sidestepped Le Roi's tall bodyguard. Cam found himself staring in the face of a half man. His appearance was a living contradiction. Tight lines around the mouth and dark shadows under the eyes showed exhaustion. Yet his stare gleamed with intensity. The creature seemed to be grafted on RJ's spine. His large head and spindly arms sprouted from a backpack, making him look like a giant spider.

Le Roi pointed at the elaborate upside-down edifice. "What is that thing?"

Cam raised his head, staring at the distorted castle. "That," he said, "was built to shield us from the Source – what you call a FOY."

"Indigo told me it was a FOY when he conned me into funding his expedition. Are you telling me he lied?"

"No. Trouble's father is an honest man. He told you the truth. Behind this façade lies one of history's most sought-after prizes. Men like Ponce de León gave their lives trying to find one, so they could be reborn."

"*Reborn* isn't a word Indigo used. Let's spell this out. A FOY, according to Trouble's father, is a Fountain of Youth. Is there a fountain inside – where you can drink and become young again, healed of your wounds?

"Yes, that's a valid interpretation of the old legends." Cam fought to remain poker-faced as he looked into Le Roi's fierce eyes.

"You're tricking me. I sense it. You're afraid of this thing – Source or FOY, whatever you call it."

"A smart man always fears great power."

Le Roi's face changed from angry to cunning. "Why fear something that heals – isn't that what it does?"

"In its own way, yes."

"How does it work?"

"First, you have to understand the castle." Cam deliberately turned away from Braun and looked at the structure. "It's made of Invar materials. I took samples from each section, and analyzed them. The windows aren't glass but metal tinted to look transparent. The 'glass' is really iron-nickel. It's an Invar alloy discovered in 1896 by Charles Guillaume, when he was head of the International Bureau of Weights and Measures. The Bureau is where France keeps a standard for measuring one meter of distance. It's a bar made of platinum alloyed with iridium. Those precious metals were used to make the castle's shimmering trim."

"Platinum. Deliciously expensive stuff." Le Roi Braun almost drooled as he spoke his words.

Forgetting his delicate situation for a moment, Dr. Cam contradicted Braun. "Platinum-iridium isn't what matters."

"So what does matter? I assume you know, since you claim to be smart."

"Most of the building was framed using iron-palladium." Cam paused to catch his breath. His ribs still pained him.

Le Roi wasn't used to anyone contradicting him. He didn't like it. "You're stupid, Cam, like all scientists. You all want to win a Nobel Prize, be immortalized by your discoveries. But what matters in life is money and health. I'm rich. I intend to be healthy as well."

"As you wish." Cam nodded obediently.

Flix interrupted. "I want to know why iron-palladium is so important."

Le Roi's eyes glinted in amusement. "Answer him, keep my son entertained. But make your digression short."

"I'll keep it brief." Cam turned to look at Flix. "Iron-palladium isn't normally an Invar. To qualify as Invar, a metal must remain the same size when it's heated, instead of expanding. In technical terms, it's called temperature-invariance. Invar for short."

Flix looked glazed by the explanation, leaving Trouble a chance to ask a question. "Iron-palladium didn't qualify. So why was it used?"

"I said it isn't normally temperature-invariant. But squeeze iron-palladium in a diamond anvil and the crushed piece becomes Invar."

"I'm beginning to understand." Flix sat upright, his eyes bright with curiosity. "This building is under crushing force. Is that what you're saying?"

Cam shook his head in a "yes."

"Why aren't we also squeezed?" Trouble asked.

"The building protects us. Forces inside the structure are unbelievably strong. They curve the palace like an archer's bow when its string is pulled taut. These mysterious forces also shrink the castle from its original size, like a nugget of iron-palladium crushed in a diamond anvil."

"How big was the original building?" Flix, being rich, liked huge mansions.

Cam shrugged, indicating he wasn't sure. "I estimate the castle once spanned Halong Bay. Possibly, it was even larger. Whoever made the building knew Invar materials develop an enormous magnetic field when compressed. The magnetic fields get so strong they prevent further crushing. Everything stabilizes. That's how the building acts as a shield. The magnetic field of its Invar protects us from being smashed."

Fascinated by the ability to crush palaces, Le Roi demanded, "What is the source of so much power?"`

"And how can you control it?" Cam allowed himself a cynical expression.

Anger distorted Le Roi Braun's features. "Answer me – or RJ will teach you a painful lesson, professor."

"OK. Don't hit me." Tran Van Cam recoiled, stepping backwards. "The power source is a tiny black hole, very young, in its infancy. There's no reason a black hole has to appear in outer space. One could start here, inside the earth. The castle is a containment vessel. Its walls isolate the black hole and keep it from imploding earth – along with the sun and all its planets. Large black holes swallow entire galaxies."

"Fine science lecture." Braun let his disgust show. "Now how do I get around those magical walls and reach the FOY?"

"The walls are Invar, not magic."

RJ hit Dr. Cam hard enough to knock him down. "Mr. Braun wants answers, not your smart mouth."

"All right." The scientist lifted a hand to shield himself. "You can't get around the walls. It's too far."

"What are you talking about?" RJ batted away Dr. Cam's hand and raised a threatening fist.

Tran Van Cam drew a laser tape measure from his pocket. "Use this. Measure how far it is from your hand to the floor of this railcar. Prove that this laser tape works correctly."

The bodyguard snatched away the measuring device and shined its laser at the floor. "About a meter. What now?"

"Check how far we are from the cavern's walls."

"Thirty meters." RJ shot the laser at nearby rock formations, standing alongside the castle. "A bit farther, almost fifty meters." Without prompting, he sent the laser beam under the palace's crown and got an error message. "Too far to measure. So what are you trying to prove?"

"A black hole warps space, stretching distances." Dr. Cam coughed up a little blood, from a tooth loosened by RJ's punch. "I'm warning you. Don't try walking past the wall. I watched a man swim under the building. You sold his remains on eBay."

"I sold a monster rat, not a man." Le Roi squirmed in his basket.

Cam rolled from his hands and knees posture to a sitting position. He looked at Braun. "On one visit here, I was followed, tailed. I was taking alloy samples of the walls and a man appeared. He tried to join me by swimming toward the castle. He went under the building and vanished. A few minutes later, he got spat out. He'd become a tiny but vicious rat. I trapped the creature and brought it home. Then I came back. I moved the lights so no one would have an easy time following me."

"I've been tricked. There's no way to enter the castle." Le Roi was enraged. Spittle foamed on his lips.

Afraid of another beating, Cam slid backwards and almost fell off the railcar. "No … there's another way to get inside."

"Through those doors?" Le Roi gestured above his head, at the center of the palace. He felt a strange tug on his hand and fought against an invisible grip. It was difficult to lower his arm.

Dr. Cam mimicked putting a helmet on his head. "The 'doors' don't open. They're only decoration. Instead, you place the castle on your head. You see the building's shaped like a crown."

Le Roi Braun's face shrank in disappointment. "The building is huge. I can't wear that thing like a hat." Braun pleaded with Dr. Cam. "I must reach the FOY. There has to be another way to enter the castle."

"There is. I told you. Reach for the crown like you're going to wear it."

"Show me." Le Roi became sly. "I want to see you do it first."

"Yes. Don't beat me. I'll do it." Tran Van struggled to his feet. He began lifting his arms toward the castle. Dr. Cam turned, so he could look at Le Roi. "Are you certain?"

"Yes. Get on with it." Braun clenched his fists. "Quit stalling. Take the medicine you prescribed for me."

Cam gave his daughter a loving glance and raised his hands, embracing the palace. Behind him Socks muttered, but her words didn't sound like a loving good-bye.

"What did she say?" Braun demanded.

Dr. Cam explained. "Only one can rule." His feet remained on the platform, but his arms extended like they were elastic. Dr. Cam became a stretchy toy, a rubber band getting thinner and longer. Then he floated upward, pulled toward the Source.

At first, confusion flooded Le Roi's mind. Then he felt conned. "It's a trick. Cam wanted to go first all along. He gets inside and he'll have the power. He'll kill me for how I've treated him. RJ – grab Cam's leg. Pull him back."

The bodyguard lunged, grabbing an ankle, and began a tug-of-war. Dr. Cam elongated like chewing gum stretched between a thumb and finger. No matter how hard RJ pulled on Cam, the Source tugged harder. It was like a person trying to keep a hot air balloon on the ground by grabbing the basket. Soon, RJ began to float, moving upward. He was losing the fight.

Frightened, Le Roi shouted, "Cam will get there first, unless … RJ, throw me into the FOY. It's my only hope."

"Are you sure?" The bodyguard stared downward and realized they were ten feet above the lake and rising.

Alarms beeped on oxygen tanks straddling Le Roi. His air supply was running low, another reminder of his fragile existence. He couldn't take living like that anymore. "Throw me hard as you can. I must beat Cam to the Source … I have to be reborn."

Eager to unburden himself, the bodyguard hurled Le Roi like a football thrown long for a touchdown. Caught in the palace's force field, Braun zoomed toward the crown-shaped building. His torso changed, getting longer and longer. In an instant, he became ghostly, a transparent wisp trapped in a vacuum so powerful it bent time and space.

Once Le Roi entered the Source, it released Tran Van Cam from an invisible grip. The scientist flew backwards with vicious force, a snapped rubberband. Cam's body acted like a fist, hitting RJ in the abdomen, a kick-boxer striking a perfect liver punch. The bodyguard had never been hurt so much in all his martial arts fights. Agonizing liver pain surged throughout his body. Blacking out, he fell into the iodine-red salt lake with a loud slap. Water spattered like a geyser, flushing over the railcar. Dr. Cam bounced off RJ and landed nearby. Tran Van rose from the salt bath and seemed dazed, unable to move.

Trouble called to him. "Run, hurry," he urged the scientist.

Battered, Tran Van Cam nodded in understanding. Dark brine leaked from his thin shirt and pants when he sloshed. It was like he'd stepped fully clothed into a shower and now appeared to be a walking sprinkler dripping into the lake. Dr. Cam waded through the shallows, limping toward the railcar. His slow progress gave RJ time to recover some capacity for movement.

The bodyguard saw Cam escaping and stumbled to his feet. Injured by the sucker punch, RJ moved like a homeless man, stiffened with cold. His shuffling pace wasn't much faster than Dr Cam's wobble. The pair held a slow motion race toward the railcar.

Onboard the vehicle, Trouble and Flix watched the approaching pair with mixed emotions. Flix ran a tongue over dry lips, frightened by RJ's approach. The bodyguard also intimidated Trouble, who was counting steps, trying to see if Dr. Cam had a chance. RJ appeared to be gaining, closing the distance between himself and an older, less fit man. Trouble had to do something.

"Flix," Trouble shouted, "Now's our chance to cut these nylon ties. We can get ourselves loose from the handcuffs. I've got a pocket knife in my daypack. You're the only one who can reach it. They let you keep your hands in front of you." He moved so his daypack crammed against Flix. Trouble felt zippers sliding and desperate fingers probing inside the slick fabric.

"Got it." Flix popped the blade and sawed through Trouble's bonds. "Now you cut mine."

Reversing roles, Trouble sliced through nylon ties binding Flix's wrists. He gave the knife back to Flix. "You take care of Socks. I've gotta help Dr. Cam."

40

The splash was surprisingly quiet when Trouble jumped in the lake. Iodine-rich salt water found every cut on his shins, stinging his wounds. Walking increased the burning pain, bringing tears to his eyes. He fought to clear his vision so he could assist Dr. Cam. Trouble attempted a step and fell in a hole between rail ties. Startled, it took a moment to plunge his hands underwater and find the next submerged tie. Salt and iodine seared every abrasion on his fingers. Fighting back a moan, he shoved himself out of the hole.

He balanced on a submerged wooden tie and guessed where the next one should be. A few good steps gave him confidence. The gravel here was firm, explaining why RJ was making consistent progress, gaining on Cam. The gap between the men became fifteen yards, then ten. At five yards, Trouble could see RJ had been badly injured. Yet a grim determination kept the bodyguard moving. But Dr. Cam was also an intense man and he sped up after seeing Trouble.

They met and Trouble put Cam's arm around his shoulder, using himself as a crutch. The scientist's wiry body felt like a large bird perched on Trouble's collarbone. They lunged forward in tango-like dance steps.

Soon they got in rhythm and quickened their pace. Trouble guided them past the submerged hole and helped lift Cam on the railcar. Socks attended to Cam while Trouble shoved himself onboard. Wood splinters jabbed the palms of his hands. He rolled toward the lever and was about to push it when RJ's voice bellowed a warning.

"You're not leaving without me." Weak from internal bleeding, the giant's eyes clouded, glazed with pain. Wounds didn't keep him from reaching in his coat and pulling out high explosives. The tubes looked like highway flares, wrapped in a bundle. "Let go of the lever, Trouble. Or you'll all die with me." He pointed at Flix, Socks and Dr. Cam. Everyone froze, waiting to see what Trouble was going to do next.

"You'll kill us anyway. We might as well take our chances." Trouble leaned on the switch, but he didn't move it.

RJ held the dangerous packet so his fingers gripped a detonator ring, like the pin on a hand grenade. "You can die – or you can make a deal with me."

"What kind of deal?" Flix yelled over Trouble's head.

"No grudges. We start over, like nothing happened." RJ realized Flix wasn't convinced. "Your father's gone. Now I work for you. What you say goes."

Flix hedged. "I want answers."

"I'll answer your questions when we get out of here."

Trouble gave a cynical laugh. "Sure you will."

"Look, we don't have time for a long discussion." For once, RJ seemed flustered. Time wasn't on his side. He looked worse every minute.

Flix sensed RJ's confusion and exploited it. "I want answers now."

"Whaddya want to know?" The bodyguard still held the explosives where everyone could see them.

It was Flix's turn to act baffled. He didn't know what question to ask.

Trouble filled the gap. "Who are the ninjas?"

"Soldiers of fortune, criminals for hire – terrorists, thieves, assassins."

"How'd you learn their language?" Socks asked, recovering from shock now that her father was safe.

RJ hesitated. "That's kinda hard to explain."

"Try. Real hard." Trouble made a show of running his hands over the control lever, making it clear he was ready to leave RJ stranded.

"OK. I studied martial arts with them. They speak a dead tongue, from an ancient civilization, the Scythians."

Trouble found it difficult to think when so many old puzzles now had a common thread. His parents excavating Scythian burial mounds no longer seemed a crazy idea. They'd found skulls, bronze tools and elaborate jewels in gold animal shapes. But they must be looking for something else, something important – and so was a cult of ninjas who kept secrets by speaking the Scythian's dead language, not used in thousands of years. Trouble glanced at Flix to make sure he'd heard RJ's answer. "RJ may not wear green, but he's a ninja."

Flix stared at RJ in disgust. "You're a traitor, a mole, a ..."

Trouble filled in the blank. "He's a spy, yeah."

"No." RJ shook his head. "I'm strictly mercenary. I follow the money."

"And the Scythian ninjas?"

"Those guys fight for other reasons. I never learned why. It doesn't matter. You should be thanking me. I saved you from them."

"They weren't attacking us," Flix countered.

"You were next to die – and you know it."

"Le Roi was also planning on killing us. You would have done it for him," Trouble argued. "One cancels the other. We owe you nothing."

"You still have to get past the ninjas, little man. And they have your mother. Maybe you ought to keep me around, since I speak their language. I could negotiate with them, trade something for your mother's life. Huh?"

"I can think of a reason why I don't need you." Trouble forced himself to look calm, but he felt nervous.

RJ used sarcasm, hoping to rattle his opponent. "Go ahead kid. Tell us what a hotshot you are."

"Hotshot? No. Not even clever. Just observant." Trouble gestured along railroad tracks heading to the Karst maze. "I see green blotches when I look in that direction. There's quite a bit of red blended with the green. That's blood. Six greedy ninjas tried to hang on the back of the railcar. None made it to the 'treasure.' They were all beaten to death, shredded by underwater rocks. They never expected this trolley to move so fast."

"You're bluffing." RJ tried to look past the railcar and its passengers, but he couldn't. "I don't see any green blobs."

"Walk to the side. Then you'll see them." Trouble waved a hand, suggesting RJ step off the submerged railroad bed.

The martial arts guru didn't fall for the trick. "I ain't stepping into a hole and dropping my ace." He tapped the explosives. "Gotta find a new idea, kid. Your trap didn't work."

"You're too wounded to fight ninjas, if they were alive. Looks like you need us more than we need you." Trouble flashed a quick smile of triumph.

"I can still throw this bomb." The bodyguard cocked his arm, threatening to hurl the explosives and kill everyone.

Trouble didn't know how to answer the threat. A tense silence prevailed. It looked as though he'd have to yield to RJ's demands. Then, Trouble became aware of rumbling. It felt like a THX demonstration in a theater, where loudspeakers vibrate seats, pulsing the auditorium. The rumble became a deafening roar. Trouble expected an earthquake. Instead, the cavern's ceiling buckled, sending debris into the air. Stones rippled the lake like hail from a winter storm. Trouble curled into a ball, protecting his head from rocks. Gradually, noise and shaking vanished into a bizarre quiet.

Even RJ was disoriented. "What was that?" he snapped, not expecting an answer. But he got one from Dr. Cam.

The scientist stuck a finger at the castle, visible through a dusty haze. "It was Le Roi. Like all the other fools, he tried to solve the puzzle and failed."

"What are you babbling about?" RJ was in no mood for strange comments.

Trouble also stared at the scientist. He was curious rather than angry. "A puzzle?"

"Yes. Your mother was very brave. She went inside to make a sketch of the jigsaw puzzle. Wisely, she didn't succumb to temptation and try to arrange the pieces. Julia finished her diagram and left. But she'd spent too much time inside the castle. The extreme magnetism damaged her mind. I barely had time to speak with her, learn what she'd done, before she fell into a coma."

Flix seemed to be losing it. He acted rattled. "I have to know what happened to my father." His eyes darted from Dr. Cam to the palace doors – and back to the scientist. "Is my father alive?"

"No." Tran Van Cam's features turned sad.

"Dead?" Flix appeared glad and mournful at the same time. Conflict twisted his face in a frightening way.

Seeing the young man's torture caused Dr. Cam to hesitate. "I don't know how to be kind in answering your question."

"Tell me anyway." Flix shut his eyes.

Cam put a compassionate hand on Flix's shoulder. "Are you sure you want to know?"

A "yes," came through gritted teeth.

"Well, then. The Source is indeed a FOY, a Fountain of Youth. Your father didn't lie, Trouble. He simply omitted a key fact. The Source is how the universe renews itself, not people – unless they solve a jigsaw puzzle in the castle lobby. The game is some kind of control panel. Legend says a correct solution heals a person, but I doubt it. More likely it ... Well, that's another story."

"What happened to my father?" Flix pleaded.

Cam struggled to explain. "It's like this. The Source is a black hole in its infancy. New black holes swallow much and regurgitate little. Later, entire galaxies are spit out, renewing the universe. Astrophysicists think that's how our Milky Way galaxy was formed."

"So my dad is gone ... forever?"

"No. He'll return in a different form – a momentum exchange of sorts. Isaac Newton discovered that every action generates an equal and opposite reaction. The Source behaves in the same way. You see, the Source takes whatever you give it and shreds the body in a time-space blender, recombining DNA. Then it spits out a new life form. Maybe the creature existed on earth a million years ago – and maybe it didn't. Either way, animals of past eras weren't nice, to put it mildly. They were violent predators with extreme strength. Your father has been transformed into a new creature. When he arrives, we'd better be gone, or he'll feast on us."

"So we need to move." Trouble watched a speck fall from the palace dome. The falling dot spread wings and skimmed the water, heading for a green corpse, floating in a pool of blood.

All eyes, even RJ's, pivoted to follow Trouble's shocked gaze. They watched a web-winged version of a baby T-Rex. Its skin had the dry texture of an iguana, but the scaly green hide was covered in warts and mounds of a darker green shade. A spine of claws sprouted from its back when the flying reptile swooped overhead. It opened a fang-lined jaw and landed on a ninja. The little monster ripped flesh and bone off a dead man like a hungry dog inhaling food. Gnawing sounds from its drooling mouth sounded like part garbage disposal, part chain saw. Face, fingers, palms went in a tiny mouth and the bizarre monster grew — immediately. Every mouthful became instant fuel for expanding a tiny body into something larger and more frightening.

Fed, the little monster spotted RJ and its eyes took on a look of cunning recognition. A piercing shriek came from its mouth, a high-intensity warbling that hit with unexpected force. They'd been targeted by a sonic cannon, like the kind used to paralyze Somali pirates trying to steal a ship.

At the moment, only the creature made from Le Roi was able to move. It flew at RJ with astonishing speed, hitting his skull, opening a deep scalp wound. Despite agonizing pain, RJ ripped a knife from its sheath and prepared to defend himself. Martial arts reflexes twisted the knife like a fan blade on high. Avoiding the blade, the monster swiped RJ's other hand, severing fingers. Blood spouted from missing fingertips, gushing like red Kool-Aid from squirt guns. RJ's shocked hand released its grip on tubes of Semtex. The high explosives fell into briny water and vanished from sight.

Trouble weighed the risks. Make a run for it — or dive in, swimming through caustic water in the hope of grabbing those explosives. He could use them to seal the cavern, trapping the monster inside. Trouble acted on impulse.

He dove into the toxic bath, eyes shut. Blind, he struggled to orient himself and float. Opening his eyes to see was out of the question. He needed to surface and wipe away the brine. At last, his head broke into the air. Breath entered his lungs and fingers squeeged salt water off his forehead. Ahead of him RJ kneeled, yielding to the raptor's attack.

Dragon-Dinosaur Attacks RJ

Trouble had to grab RJ's explosives and flee. He'd have to do it underwater, in the blind, or the monster might shift its attack and go after Trouble. He swam, pushing his hands in a breaststroke, until he thought he was near the bodyguard. Confirmation came in an unwanted form, when he felt a stabbing kick from one of RJ's boots. In pain, Trouble rolled on his side. Floating away, he patted the bottom, searching for the explosives. His air was running out. He had to leave. Turning, he scraped the Semtex tubes and grabbed them, hoping the detonator hadn't been triggered.

Kicking, paddling, daring a quick breath, Trouble struggled to reach the flat car. He could feel rails under him and followed their metal lines, pointing at the railcar. Going too fast, he collided with the train car and recoiled in shock. It felt like being punched in a boxing ring. Pain echoed through his forehead, while bright stars shot across dimmed vision. Trouble gathered his senses and pushed himself out of the water. He fell on the platform, sucking air into his lungs. He raised his head to see what had become of RJ.

The prehistoric creature was circling the bodyguard, looking for an opening to finish off his prey. The monster went for RJ's face and tore open the man's cheek, exposing his jaw and teeth. RJ seemed doomed to lose the battle. Yet even wounded, mutilated, on his knees, RJ hung tough.

Fighting had drained the infant monster's body and it wanted a quick kill. He made a zigzag and spat combustible gas, igniting it with a click of the tongue. The bodyguard rolled to protect himself. A knife thrust just missed the raptor, convincing the beast it was wise to feed on dead men for a while. Later, when he was grown, the monster could return for RJ's flesh.

Trouble slid the explosive packets toward Dr. Cam. "You know how to use Semtex?"

"Yes. I sealed the Karst maze with explosives. I decided it was better to trap us inside the cavern than allow horrible beasts into the world. Now I'll seal this dragon in its tomb."

"Dragon?" Trouble was confused.

Dr. Cam explained. "The raptor spat fire, like dragons in old legends. And we are underneath Halong Bay. Its Vietnamese name translates to 'Bay of Dragons.' Seems we've awakened one of those ancient birds. As you saw, we can't fight it. Best to trap the monster and let it die of starvation, though that might take years."

"We have to leave RJ?" Flix wavered at the idea of abandoning a wounded man.

Socks, long silent, finally spoke. "RJ betrayed you, Flix. And he would have killed you, if necessary."

"That's in the past," Flix argued. "In business, there's only the present deal. I can make a deal with RJ. He knows things we don't. I say we go back for him."

41

Flix helped RJ stagger to the railcar and the wounded man sagged on the platform. One side of the bodyguard's face looked normal and the other was grotesque, a skull wrapped in tendons and muscles, like an anatomy drawing. Amputated fingers soaked a torn shirt in blood. Careful of his injuries, Flix and Trouble moved RJ forward, so he wouldn't slide off when they accelerated, fleeing the monster. Trouble glanced at the dragon and saw the animal rip a foot off a dead ninja, shredding an ankle with claw-like teeth. That awful image clung in his mind when he staggered to the control lever.

A piercing shriek from the monster's sonic cannon blasted all thoughts from Trouble's mind. He saw the dragon lunging at them, fast as he could fly. His snake-like eyes bulged with rage. The creature fired another sonic bullet at the railcar. Even floorboards quivered when the shriek hit them. Trouble fought to control shaking hands and use them to cover his ears. Safe from the audio weapon, he struggled to shove the lever with his butt. Trouble braced himself for a sharp jerk. "Hang on," he warned the others.

He felt a hidden mechanism kick in gear, sucking them away at tremendous speed. Trouble realized the dragon-dinosaur wouldn't catch them, despite the monster's all out effort. Clawing at the air with its massive webbed feet, the dragon pushed forward like a swimmer doing the breaststroke. Yet moment by moment, the dragon lost speed and the railcar gained velocity. The gap widened until T-Rex jaws and pulsing wings blurred to a small dot. They were safe, but only for a few minutes. Soon, the dragon would reach them and they'd be defenseless. When the railcar braked to a stop, Trouble leapt off the platform and rushed to his mother.

He tried to raise the limp form and couldn't. He moved to Chiaro and sliced nylon ties off her wrists. "Help me lift Julia," he pleaded.

Dazed, Chiaro was slow to respond. She answered in a dull voice. "Sure." Massaging sore wrists, Chiaro struggled to get up. She moved to Julia's boots and grabbed ankles covered by twill cargo pants.

But Julia proved too heavy for the two of them. "Socks, Dr. Cam," Trouble shouted. "Over here. Help us. We've got to leave before the dragon catches us."

"We're coming," Socks panted, jumping off the railcar and sloshing through water. "Where do we grab?"

Dr. Cam suggested, "Trouble's got her shoulders and Chiaro her feet. Let's help with the waist. Grab Julia's belt."

Grunting, the foursome heaved Trouble's mother off the ground, a limp doll hanging from their grip. Even with their help in carrying Julia uphill, it was hard work. Twisting her through a hole and sliding her downward exhausted them. They were forced to halt and catch their breath before going further. While they recovered, Flix and RJ wobbled down the rock pile. At the bottom, RJ put an arm around Flix and they kept going, winding through the Karst maze.

In contrast, Trouble's group made slow progress. Each time they stopped, Trouble listened for the monster's buzzing wings. Yet no sound came to him. Was it feasting on dead ninjas, gathering strength? He hoped the mutated Le Roi had become distracted and abandoned his chase. But there was no way to know for sure.

They again lifted his mother and staggered forward, trying not to bang her against sharp rocks. In those tight quarters, twisted limestone fingers seemed to reach out and grab them, snagging their clothes. The weight grew with every step, numbing arms and cramping hands. They navigated through sinkholes and calcium craters worn smooth over time. Their feet skidded over flowstones that resembled molten hills of terracotta clay grabbed from a potter's wheel.

Landmarks were a challenge, since the ceiling was often decorated with the same drapery of frayed white rocks. Stalagmites formed on the cavern floor from the constant drip of mineralized water, depositing more calcium carbonate. The weird columns were shaped like uneven sand castles petrified into stone. Just when it seemed the Karst maze would never end, a smell of burnt candles wafted to Trouble's nostrils. He knew they were close to getting out. A few more steps and they broke free of the labyrinth. Walking became easier when they entered the smooth riverbed. The relief of easy movement was short lived, unfortunately. Ahead lay a field of massive stones, boulders they'd navigated on their way to the Source.

Going out, carrying a limp person, made that part of the journey a nightmare. The surface was an undulating rollercoaster – up, down, up, down. People atop a boulder pulled on Julia and those below pushed. Legs and backs ached, boots slipped, hands scraped. Throats became parched, even in humid air. Shadows deceived eyes into thinking a foothold existed where none could be found. All illumination came from distant strings of lights. But the journey had taken too much time.

Above them, bulbs flickered and went dark. Power generators were running out of fuel. One after another, their thumping noise sputtered and died. A single generator kept running, affording them a dim view of their path. The rocks grew smaller and it was possible to weave between them, instead of climbing each boulder, heaving dead weight that felt like a gym set.

A pile of fuel cans came into view. Behind them, a bright sliver of light beamed through a crack in the rock wall. The opening led to the beach where jet skis waited for them. Hope flickered in Trouble and the others. Their pace quickened until an ugly shape appeared in the crack. The hound blocked their exit, snarling its massive jaws. The dog's sharp fangs snapped at the air. His mouth opened wide, showing a black tongue and red gums. He released a low growl and his ears tensed back, their bat-like shape flattening against his head.

RJ was too weak to shout commands at the dog. The aggressive Phu Quoc ridgeback wouldn't listen to Flix. "What're we gonna do?" he asked.

"I dunno." Trouble ran his eyes around the cave, searching for weapons. "We'll have to throw rocks."

"No," Dr. Cam begged. "The hound will attack us."

"We can't wait here," Trouble argued. "The dragon is pushing through the Karst maze. Listen. You'll hear its wings beating."

For some reason, even the hound quit baying. Everyone held their breath. A furious buzzing drifted toward them, chased by echoes. The sound came and went, but each time it appeared the noise was louder. There was another confirmation of the dragon's approach. The air became tinged with the sickly sweet odor of human blood.

"It's coming for us," Flix agreed.

"We gonna toss the rocks in volleys, everybody at the same time?" Chiaro looked at Trouble. She hefted large stones in both hands.

"A volley first, then fast as you can. We'll try forcing the animal to retreat."

"What then?" Dr. Cam remained skeptical. "The beast will attack the first person who steps through the crack. Your plan won't work."

Socks assumed her father had a better idea. She asked him, "What should we do instead?"

Tran Van Cam stared blankly at his daughter. "I ...well, I don't see anything else we can do. Maybe Trouble's right."

"OK. Everybody grab rocks. Keep a few stones for your next toss. I don't like hurting animals, but we have to get out. You probably won't hit the dog. It'll duck. Maybe we'll scare it."

He bent down to show them what he meant. Trouble scavanged chunks the size of golf balls. He cocked an arm for the initial toss. "One, two, three, go!"

Chips flew at the dog, stinging its hide. The hound grew enraged. It lunged forward, bounding toward them. Trouble grabbed a baseball-sized rock and pitched a strike, hitting the dog's throat. Stunned, the animal veered away, halting near the generators.

"Again, with larger rocks," Trouble urged. "We gotta force him away from the crack." He bent to grab a chunk of limestone. "After the throw, grab another one." Trouble kept his arm cranked backward like a baseball pitcher on the mound, about to hurl the ball. But the dog didn't attack. Instead, it slid further away, trying to make himself a smaller target.

"Help me lift Julia," Trouble whispered. "Flix, you assist RJ."

Silently, the group maneuvered in awkward steps. They slid toward a narrow opening, leading them to safety. The dog sensed it was being outflanked and tried to head them off. A blast of rocks forced the hound to retreat. A few steps were followed by another volley. Eventually, Flix and RJ were poised at the crack, ready to lunge through.

"Flix, you gotta come back to help, or the rest of us can't make it." Trouble hated to ask Flix for assistance, but he had no choice.

Flix nodded, indicating he'd return. Everyone whipped rocks at the dog. Flix and RJ stumbled through the hole, vanishing from sight.

"Socks, Dr. Cam – you're holding my mother's shoulders. You go through, soon as Flix returns." Trouble waited. He felt his heart beating faster, as though it was trying to keep rhythm with the monster's wings. Its noise was growing louder. The thing had found a path through the Karst maze and was on its way to them. "Where's Flix?" Trouble grunted.

"I'm back." Flix slid through the limestone crevice and moved alongside Trouble.

"Take Julia's legs."

"What're you going to do?" Flix grabbed her ankles.

Trouble held up rocks. "I'm the rear guard. I keep tossing until Dr. Cam rigs explosives. When he's ready to seal the hole, I'll dive through."

"My ..." Flix choked.

"Yeah, what's left of your dad is coming to get me. I know that. So hustle." Trouble hurled a rock and the hound ducked a close miss. "Go," he urged.

Behind him, the group turned Julia on her side and did an awkward slide through the hole. Trouble tossed another rock and stooped to pick up more.

The hound sensed weakness and charged, accelerating fast as a mountain lion. His toenails clinked against uneven limestone and he arched his chest to attack. The dog would be on Trouble in a half bound, tearing away his face with huge jaws. Trouble knew rocks weren't going to do the job. He grabbed empty fuel cans and slammed them together, making a sound like a gunshot. A ringing bang frightened the ridgeback and he turned away, halting near Trouble.

"Explosives ready," Cam screamed. "Jump through."

Trouble coached himself – can't let my voice quaver, gotta sound firm when I speak. He took a deep breath. "I can't move. The hound will attack."

Cam's sad voice came through the hole. "You must try anyway. The dragon is coming. I can't let it get out. Remember what I did before? I entombed your mother and myself. Sealing ourselves inside prevented beasts from escaping. We lived only because the monsters attacked each other." He paused, waiting for a response.

Trouble hesitated. He didn't want to die. Yet it seemed unlikely he'd make a clean jump through a narrow fracture in the rock wall. Turning around would cause the dog to lunge. Then an idea hit him. "You said the beasts fought each other?"

"Yes," Dr. Cam affirmed.

"Then I'm waiting for the dragon."

"Are you sure?"

"Positive. Only chance I've got." Trouble slammed empty fuel cans together. He made the noise to attract Le Roi's remains.

In moments, the dragon appeared, his jaws smeared with fresh blood. The monster flew into the cavern and landed on a high outcropping, resting like one of the gargoyles atop Notre Dame cathedral. His webbed feet curled on the rock perch and the dragon hunched its rubbery wings in contemplation. He studied the situation, cocking his head, peering with one yellow eye, then the other. He opened his mouth to release a long string of burps that stank like rancid meat. Then his nose quivered, inhaling nearby smells – a human scent, then a canine one. It seemed the animal was tired of human flesh and wanted variety in its diet. Without warning, the thing plunged off a ledge, arcing toward the dog. The hound was forced to pivot and face a new threat.

There wasn't a moment to lose. Should the monster change its mind, Trouble was its next meal. But his luck held. A furious battle sounded behind him. Trouble had time to plant his feet. Head-first, he flew through the crack, landing in a rolling motion to protect himself. An explosion blasted rock chips into his neck and his leg twisted. He screamed in pain. He kept rolling … and rolling.

Socks ripped open a first aid kit she'd found in one of the jet skis. She wrapped gauze around his neck to slow bleeding. "We discovered a zodiac boat left by the ninjas. It's big enough for all of us. Here, let me help you. Everyone else is aboard."

"Thanks." Trouble fought to get up and a leg caved on him. He wanted the wound to be only a sprained ankle. But one look confirmed he'd broken a bone. Each limping step was more painful than the previous stride. Ten yards to a zodiac tired him like an uphill hike. The boat's inflated rubber side seemed tall as the Curio Shop's roof. He tried to swing himself over. Finally, he made it, landing on the craft's flat bottom in an agonizing thump. He asked Dr. Cam, "Go slow, will you?"

"Sorry. I can't. Got to be quick. We don't know if RJ's explosives sealed the crack. There's too much dust. I can't see." Cam gunned the engine and they slapped over waves. Each bounce sent blinding pain along Trouble's leg.

He dragged himself upright, tugging on a rope threaded around the zodiac's sides. Trouble wanted to squat on his good leg, reducing shocks jolting his injury. His first attempts failed before he got it right. When his head cleared the boat's side, Trouble saw an enormous helicopter, its eight bladed rotor spinning. The pilot must have sensed a crisis and started the engine.

A hoist lowered a metal-framed mesh bed to lift wounded onboard – Julia, RJ and Trouble. One by one, they were put in the sling and hoisted into the belly of the helicopter. Crew members lifted the wounded to a stretcher, then dragged them across the cargo bay. An empty sling was lowered and the process repeated. Finally, the tedious part was over and remaining members of the party could board.

A short ladder let Dr. Cam, Socks, Flix and Chiaro climb inside the helo's cargo area. Stepping around the injured, they dropped fold-down metal seats and belted-in. The chopper's engine and rotor vibrated the floor, causing the stretchers to slide around. A crewman used nylon webbing to tie down the human cargo, keeping them from moving when the helo took off. Ugly fumes blew inside, fanned by the helicopter blades – a mix of jet fuel for the turbine engine, hot grease lubricating the rotor shaft and brake fluid leaking from old hydraulic lines.

A screaming engine made it impossible to talk. Flix climbed in the co-pilot's seat and donned a headset so he could give instructions to the pilot. "You don't have to wait. My father and his ninjas aren't coming. They're ..."

The pilot gave Flix a nod. He didn't need explanations. With the money they were paying him, he only had one question. "Where are we going?"

"Some place with a great hospital – and a hotel I can tolerate."

"Hoi An, then." A crewman cut the zodiac loose from the helo's pontoons. He slammed doors big enough for a small plane hanger. A moment later, the helicopter was airborne, rising out of the bay. The pilot gunned the engine to increase lift, spraying water on the windows. He dropped the bird's nose and headed south, aiming for Vietnam's second international airport – Danang.

42

Trouble knew there were worse places to be stuck, nursing a broken leg. Flix chose Vietnam's most expensive resort for his headquarters, while they tried to explain things to officials. Lucky for Trouble, Flix was picking up the bill. He was also paying for hospitalizing RJ and Trouble's mother, still in a coma. The doctors had no idea how to bring her back, though her vital signs appeared normal.

His mother's condition, plus a cast on his leg, kept Trouble from enjoying his surroundings. In front of him, a turquoise pool ran more than a quarter mile, stretching to a white sand beach and the South China Sea. The infinity-style pool was lined by palm trees, shading private villas like the one where Trouble slept. A butler carried meals from gourmet restaurants on the premises. A limousine swept Trouble to the hospital for visiting his dormant mother. In a few days, Flix was taking them home via a private medical flight.

At the moment, his biggest problem was Chiaro. She dropped by several times a day and he couldn't escape. His broken leg kept him stranded on a couch. There she was again, irritating him with her bouncing stride, flashing her new wardrobe. Hoop earrings matched gold embroidery on her tunic, a silk blouse hanging over acid washed designer jeans. The denim had enough sequins for a Las Vegas nightclub act. Red Skechers with aqua green laces completed her loud "the fun has arrived" look.

She dropped her wraparound sunglasses and peered over the frame's top. "I'm going to Hoi An. Do a little shopping. You ought'a come along."

"I gotta broken leg, in case you didn't notice."

"We're not walking. We're going in the limo. Besides, it's air conditioned. No sweat."

"Shopping's not my thing. It's your gig."

"They don't just have clothes. I'm going antiquing. You like artifacts."

"I got a whole shop full of antiques. I don't need anymore."

"You're wasting your time in Vietnam. All you did was chase a couple monsters. Live a little. We'll be in Manhattan soon enough. Personally, I can't stand the thought of foster care. But you're probably looking forward to going to school again, huh?"

Trouble changed the subject. "Have a nice time spending Flix's money."

"I know you hate me. I'll bring you some ice cream anyway. Ciao." She gave him a rotating palm like she was a seasoned international traveler.

He muttered, "Whatever."

He felt relieved to hear the slapping of her rubber soled Skechers bouncing away from him. With Chiaro gone for several hours, this could be a pretty good day. He tried to focus on the beautiful surroundings and failed. Worries dragged down Trouble's mood. Despite Flix's generosity, money problems nagged him – the Curio Shop's rent, Bleerio's salary, cash for travelling in Indigo's footsteps. Trouble felt pained that too much time was passing. He needed to trace his father's path after leaving Vietnam. There was also the burden of knowing he should be doing something to help Allyn, left alone inside Mount Everest.

At least Bleerio said Albert's operation was successful. Of course, Bleerio complained what a nuisance the penguin had become, wanting to explore Manhattan. The penguin seemed to think he could wander alone in a huge city, as if New York was a lost civilization, devoid of inhabitants.

On the positive side, Socks expressed gratitude for Trouble rescuing her father. They both were coming for lunch. Dr. Cam said he wanted to thank Trouble and give him a souvenir of his trip. That time must have arrived. He saw a butler pushing a cart toward the bungalow.

In the heat of mid-day, the butler wore a Nehru collar and linen jacket. The butler indicated a patio table near the swimming pool. "Would you like to dine outside, sir?"

"Yes," Trouble grunted. "Outside's fine."

A starched linen cloth flew over the table like a magic carpet. Hand-painted china and heavy bronze tableware were dealt like a hand of cards, forming a trio of place settings. A crystal vase holding wild orchids anchored the table's center. Domed serving dishes were unveiled, revealing noodles woven like birds' nests and colorful appetizers laced together like a quilt.

Trouble grabbed his crutches and shoved himself to his feet. He saw Dr. Cam and Socks exit the hotel's limo. The car picked them up at Danang International, after they flew south from Hanoi.

Trouble remained standing, leaning on his crutches as Tran Van Cam and Socks walked toward the pool. A yellow T-shirt covered Socks' thin frame. Caltech's orange torch logo blazed on the T-shirt, emphasizing her commitment to science. Purples and greens of a Madras plaid belt danced around her waist. Blue twill pants were anchored by her signature white cotton socks thrust into open-toed sandals. She waved, smiling.

Trouble raised his injured leg, propping the cast on an empty chair. The new position worked. A throbbing pain eased, fading away. "You guys hungry? Food here's very good." He pointed at servings of Hoi An's specialties. The main course was Cao lầu, pasta noodles mixed with greens and pork. Another platter held white rose, shrimp dumplings crinkled to resemble budding roses. Stuffed wontons reflected Hoi An's Chinese heritage.

"Great. I'm starved." Socks plopped herself down and grabbed a napkin.

Dr. Cam slowly approached the table, his dark eyes absorbing the elaborate meal. His narrow body was dressed in a khaki suit that hung on his bony frame. An aquamarine blue tie added a splash of color to his bland outfit. He was still recovering from wounds and moved with a jerky stiffness, like a wind-up doll. Dr. Cam toted a wrapped package under his arm. He dropped the bundle next to his chair and smiled at Trouble. "How's your leg?"

"Itches. Can't wait to get this cast taken off."

"Ow ong?" Socks talked with her mouth full.

Cam frowned at her bad manners. "Sorry, Trouble. We're not used to dining with guests."

"No problem." He turned to Socks. "How long before …?" He tapped the plaster cast.

Socks nodded.

"A few weeks. Can't wait. I'm dying for a shower."

"Well, at least you have first rate medical care. Mr. Flix is generous." Cam's eyes swept around the luxury resort, encompassing villas large as his father's mansion in Old Town Hanoi.

Socks patted his hand. "Flix told us he's flying Julia to the Mayo Clinic in Minnesota. Many consider it the best hospital in the world."

"Yeah. I hope I get my mom back." Trouble gave a weak laugh. "I can't afford to question Flix's gifts. He's taking care of my mother. I wonder what price I'm expected to pay for this generosity."

"You have nothing to fear, based on what Flix asked of us." Dr. Cam tried the noodles. He took a delicate bite and nodded in appreciation. "Quite tasty."

"What'd Flix want?" Trouble couldn't eat anything. He was concerned a trap might be sprung on him.

Cam finished chewing before answering, though he knew the delay was frustrating to Trouble. "Your companion is wealthy. But riches only buy so much cooperation. A death certificate must be issued. Otherwise, Mr. Flix and his mother will wait years before they claim a fortune." Cam winked. "We now have a large research grant, from an anonymous donor. You can guess who he is. I'll help you. We signed a testimonial saying we witnessed Le Roi Braun's death."

"Then Flix doesn't need me." Trouble's stomach went sour. The food no longer seemed appetizing.

Tran Van Cam waved his hands in apology. "No. You misunderstand. The more witnesses, the better. Otherwise, officials may say they have to find the body. That, as you know, will be difficult."

"Yes. In fact, it's impossible." Trouble relaxed. "Er, how did you say Mr. Braun died? I don't want to contradict your story."

"He was crushed." Cam allowed himself a slight grin. "It's a true statement. Mr. Braun was pulverized to an atomic level. I left out that he was reassembled as a new creature."

"None of that feels real, though it happened only days ago." Trouble felt the same jolt that awakened him in the night, when he flashed on nightmarish images.

Dr. Cam reached under the table and dragged out his package. "Perhaps this will make everything seem real." He untied a string and peeled away thick wrapping paper. Inside lay Julia's canvas rucksack and a jagged metal bar. "First, I'll explain this piece." Cam offered the bar to Trouble.

He lifted the metal and it felt heavy, as though it were lead. Yet the bar wasn't soft like lead. Instead, the shiny metal felt hard as steel. "What is this?"

"Once, the bar was a tiny sliver, like you get in a fingertip from rough wood. Quite small. I tore the sliver from the Source using a high speed drill – 10,000 revs per minute. The bit extracted a tiny core sample from the palace door. Inside my hollow drill bit, the splinter was free of extreme force. So the chip expanded to full size, exploding my drill. I was disoriented from the loud bang. At first, I didn't realize what happened – the sliver ballooned into this metal brick. I took the metal to my treehouse lab and analyzed it." Cam paused for a sip of water.

"And?" Trouble burned with curiosity.

The scientist crooked a finger, tapping the bar. "This is the most expensive type of Invar, platinum-iridium. The tiny sliver expanded almost a thousand to one. That's how I estimate the entire castle would span Halong Bay, if the building were released from compression."

"I thought you were making that up, to impress Le Roi. I figured it was a stall."

"No. All true. Also true that your mother traced a puzzle inside the castle." Cam opened the rucksack and drew out a roll of paper. He moved aside tableware and flattened the sheet.

Socks and Trouble leaned over, peering at the sketch. He asked, "Mom couldn't take a digital picture. The Source's magnetic field would wreck the camera. Right?"

"Yes. You can't use a film camera either. The film emulsion fogs. Your father and I tried. He braved the antechamber for a short while. Sadly, these drawings took much longer." Dr. Cam pointed to jagged letters scrawled on the paper's edge. "Can you read it?"

"Not really." Trouble angled his body to get a better view. "Looks like my mother's printing. What do you think it says?"

"I'm fortunate to know what it says. Before your mother slipped into a coma, she told me."

"And?" Trouble had a bad feeling. He was about to get another assignment.

"She wrote," Cam explained, "that you must find the demon's nose."

"What does that mean?" Socks looked as shocked as Trouble felt.

Tran Van Cam leaned back, spreading his arms. "I wish I knew. To me, her words are a puzzle."

"Great," Trouble complained.

"Well, you know how to spend your time, while you're waiting for the cast to be removed." Socks talked quickly, then popped a wonton in her mouth.

"Yeah. I'll be researching demons with big noses." Trouble's mind glazed over. So much happened on this trip to Vietnam that home seemed to exist on another planet. Yet he'd fly to Manhattan in a few days. He'd have to answer Bleerio's million questions. Then he'd focus on the drawings in Julia's rucksack. The castle's puzzle felt opaque to him, like a closed door. Maybe the ancient scroll would help. He hoped a clue would appear on that elderly parchment, a book that seemed to write itself. He'd check when he got to the Curio Shop.

Somehow, he'd find the puzzle's meaning, though it would be wrapped in mysteries. Answers could be anywhere on the globe. Probably the search led to some forgotten ruins, like the kind his parents excavated. Once he knew where to go, he'd try to organize another expedition, hoping this one led to his missing father.

Trouble's adventures continue in …

The Demon's Nose

Please visit the Learning Center for *Sign of the Rat* on our website –

www.SiliconValleyNovel.com

In the Learning Center, each of the illustrations has relevant information giving the story cultural, scientific and historical context. Teachers, home-schooling parents and fans of the Trouble adventure series will enjoy exploring the facts behind the story. Filled with intriguing knowledge, the Learning Center brings alive Trouble's world. The questions and answers are also fun for grandparents to share with their grandkids.

Visual artists whose copyrighted images were licensed to make sketches for this book are listed in the same order those sketches appear in the novel.

Descriptions Of Sketches Based On Image(s) From	These Visual Artists
Cover Image - Monster	Andreas Meyer
Cover Image – Ultra-Light	Chad Thomas
Vietnam - View From Dr. Cam's lab	Jakob Leitner
Andreas Meyer Rat	Andreas Meyer
Manhattan	Joshua Haviv
Suit Of Armor Holding Sword	Demid
Crate Delivered To Curio Shop	Joseph White
Delivery Van	Vivid Pixels
Delivery Man	James Steidl
Boy Squatting	Monkey Business
Water Tanks On Buildings In Manhattan	Nicholas Belton
Roman Family Cemetery	Alper Günay
Rolltop Desk	Don Wilkie
Laptop Computer	Fatman73
Townhomes Near The Met	Peter Spiro
Foyer Pond	Charles Pierce II
Rare Black Swans	Bob Beale
Home Theater	Bernardo Grijalva
Crane Crunching Cars	John Zellmer
Junkyard Car Crusher	Joerg Reimann
Robot Warehouse Picker	Acik
Warehouse Aisle	Look Photo
Le Roi Braun - Head	Roman Sigaev
Le Roi Braun - Torso	David Mingay
Le Roi Braun - Body Wastes Bag	Freddie Vargas
Le Roi Braun - Robot Arm	Dan Driedger
Crosley Select-O-Matic	Nicholas Homrich
Jukebox	James Steidl
Payphone	Jonathan Hill
Taxies at JFK	Paul Hill

Descriptions Of Sketches Based On Image(s) From	**These Visual Artists**
Airport crowds	Frank Eckgold
Eiffel Tower - Paris	Xavier Marchant
Les Halles Charming	XtravaganT
Forum Les Halles	Vittorio Vittori
Notre Dame	neurobite
Gargoyles	Michalis Palis
Paris Opera	mirec
Restaurant	Jan Kranendonk
Subway Entrance	Ivan Bastien
Hanoi Street	Canakris
Citadel Tower	Holger Mette
Water Puppets	Jeremy Edwards
Old Town Hanoi	Peter Fuchs
Strangler Fig	Heather Faye Bath
Woman Delivering Brooms On Bicycle	Jakob Leitner
Wire Mesh	Chris Freeman
Marketplace	Canakris
Shiva	Ranjan Chari
Cyclo	Lance Lee
Ninja	Gerville Hall
Lake	Delphine
Man Carrying Baskets Hung From Stick	Jakob Leitner
Long Bien Bridge	John Kirk
Snakes	Eric Isselée
Pickled King Cobra	John Hofboer
Empire State Building	Chris Marcus
Skyscraper Under Construction	Paul Paladin
Rice Paddies	Long Tran The
Ultra-Light Silhouette Against Skyscraper	Chad Thomas
Socks And Chiaro Dive Off Skyscraper	Artur Żebrowski

Descriptions Of Sketches Based On Image(s) From	These Visual Artists
Head of King Cobra	Robert Kohlhuber
Dr. Cam's Treehouse Lab	Mariusz Jurgielewicz
River House	Eckart Katte
Thitpok Roots	Marje Cannon
Dr. Cam's Lab Equipment - Microscope	David Olah
Periodic Table Test Tubes Beaker	Alexey Dudoladov
Petri Dishes	Jayson Punwani
Test Tubes	Alexey Dudoladov
Zago	Holger Mette
Dr. Cam's Treehouse Living Room	iNNOCENt
Dr. Cam's Treehouse Bedroom	iNNOCENt
Suitcase With Stickers	rimglow
Suitcase Stack	Klaus Rademaker
Dr. Cam's DNA Model	Martin McCarthy
View of Halong Bay From Dr. Cam's Lab	Jakob Leitner
Floating Village On Halong Bay	modestlife
Football-Shaped Karst Formations On Halong Bay	Rob Broek
Mass Of Bats Hanging From Cave Ceiling	David Parsons
Entrance To The Source	Michał Krakowiak
Arriving At The Source - Castle	Searagen
Tufa formations At Mono Lake	Michael Ransburg
Wooden Dock On Autumn Lake	Elenathewise
Dragon-Dinosaur Attacks RJ	Andreas Meyer